CHIRAL MAD

3

AN ANTHOLOGY OF PSYCHOLOGICAL HORROR
BY WRITTEN BACKWARDS

Edited by Michael Bailey

WWW.NETTIRW.COM

Also by Written Backwards

ANTHOLOGIES

Pellucid Lunacy
Chiral Mad
Chiral Mad 2
Qualia Nous
The Library of the Dead
You, Human
Adam's Ladder

ALLEYON

At the Lazy K by Gene O'Neill
Liars, Fakers, and the Dead Who Eat Them by Scott Edelman
Artifacts by Darren Speegle
Other Music by Marc Levinthal

COLLECTIONS

Bones Are Made to Be Broken by Paul Michael Anderson
Yes Trespassing by Erik T. Johnson

The Cal Wild Chronicles by Gene O'Neill:
The Confessions of St. Zach
The Burden of Indigo
The Near Future
The Far Future

CHIRAL MAD

3

FICTION

01. THE POETRY OF LIFE • RICHARD CHIZMAR — 15

02. THE LAST RUNG ON THE LADDER • STEPHEN KING — 21

03. A RIFT IN REFLECTION • HAL BODNER — 41

04. WINDOWS, MIRRORS, DOORS • JASON V BROCK — 57

05. PRAYER • MORT CASTLE — 71

06. THE AGONIZING GUILT OF RELIEF (LAST DAYS OF A READY-MADE VICTIM) • PAUL MICHAEL ANDERSON — 89

07. THE BLACK CROW OF BODDINSTRAßE • EMILY B. CATANEO — 119

08. A FLASH OF RED • ERINN L. KEMPER — 131

09. RED RUNNER VS. THE SURGEON, ISSUE 18 • JESSICA MAY LIN — 141

10. THE DEAD COLLECTION • MERCEDES M. YARDLEY — 159

11. WATCH ME • MEGHAN ARCURI — 169

12. THE BIGGER BEDROOM • JOSH MALERMAN — 177

13. THAT PERILOUS STUFF • SCOTT EDELMAN — 203

14. KNOW YOUR CODE • RAMSEY CAMPBELL — 235

15. 3-DOT PEOPLE • GENE O'NEILL — 257

16. SILVER THREAD, HAMMER RING • GARY A. BRAUNBECK — 277

17. THE OFFERING ON THE HILL • RICHARD THOMAS — 315

18. THOSE WHO WATCH FROM ON HIGH • ERIC J. GUIGNARD — 337

19. BLOOD DUST • MAX BOOTH III — 359

20. THE WHIPPING GIRLS • DAMIEN ANGELICA WALTERS — 371

21. SECONDS • JACK KETCHUM — 387

POETRY

01. FAIR • P. GARDNER GOLDSMITH   19

02. FAIL-SAFE • JONATHAN BALOG   39

03. FOLIE À DEUX • SYDNEY LEIGH   55

04. REFLECTING ON REFLECTIONS • BRUCE BOSTON   69

05. MIRROR IMAGE • MARGE SIMON   87

06. BLACK RIVER #1 • ELIZABETH MASSIE   117

07. PRESCIENCE • ROSE BLACKTHORN   129

08. THE SPEED OF SOUND • CIARÁN PARKES   139

09. WELCOME HOME, DARLING • STEPHANIE M. WYTOVICH   157

10. WHISPER #1 (A WARNING) • ERIK T. JOHNSON   167

11. WHISPER #2 (A PROPHECY) • ERIK T. JOHNSON   127

12. PUT ME TO DREAM • STEPHANIE M. WYTOVICH   201

13. RECOGNIZING TREES • CIARÁN PARKES   233

14. ARBITRATION • ROSE BLACKTHORN   255

15. BLACK RIVER #2 • ELIZABETH MASSIE   275

16. REFLECTIONS THROUGH THE RAVEN'S EYE • MARGE SIMON   311

17. BEYOND SYMMETRY • BRUCE BOSTON   335

18. FOLIE À PLUSIEURS • SYDNEY LEIGH   357

19. INSOMNIA IN REVERSE • JONATHAN BALOG   369

20. PROMISE • P. GARDNER GOLDSMITH   385

OBSERVATIONS ON HORROR BURNOUT

CHUCK PALAHNIUK

IT'S NO SURPRISE that horror appeals to a younger audience. Older people forget how it feels to lack agency in life. To be controlled by circumstances beyond our control. The young are arbitrarily thrown together with peers who might be budding psychopaths, junior murderers in the making, and this mix of strangers is expected to coalesce around the goal of getting an education. Let's not pretend. The education system too often becomes a predator-versus-prey situation. The sadist stalks, testing potential victims until he or she targets someone to attack.

Stephen King gets it right. For most teens, being beaten or raped isn't their greatest fear. In many ways, hands-off bullying is worse than physical violence. In books like *Carrie* and *Christine*, and stories like *The Body* we see King's protagonists publically humiliated. All human beings want dignity, and older ones have many means to attain it: money, education, skills, associations, social position, talent, wit. But the only advantage most young people possess is their vitality. Their youth and attractiveness. Once a villain strips away their public dignity, they have nothing on which to fall back.

To be beaten, physically beaten, and survive grants the victim a measure of public respect. Plus a more realistic expectation of legal recourse. But to be humiliated is a living death. More often leading to an actual death by suicide than a murderous, vengeful lashing out.

Conditions improve after high school, but then the young person is faced with the fear that vitality is dwindling and must be quickly replaced by a new advantage. College or military service offers a new structure with potential skills and connections, but the fear lingers. How will you fare in the outside world? Once the structure of school is complete, will you find a career? Success? A mate? Older people forget that young people live with this terror.

My personal formula for a successful plot is to show the reader his or her worst-case scenario. Show a character subjected to it, and show that character survive. In my books *Fight Club* and *Choke*, it's public humiliation, because for young readers that trumps any monster.

Studies done by the United States military conclude that what women fear most is physical pain. What men fear most is humiliation, public ridicule, loss of social status.

Max Brooks tells me that *World War Z* hit such a cultural nerve because his generation has been subjected to media hype about a new apocalypse every few months for their entire lives. From Swine Flu to Bird Flu, Ebola, AIDS, Y2K, climate change, and 2012. With the zombie, Max's generation has one unified metaphor to carry all its doomsday anxiety. Effective or not. George Romero told me that zombie culture isn't the goldmine it appears to be. At the time, only the film *Zombieland* had been profitable. So maybe even the zombie is losing steam.

Other friends, friends who teach on the high school and college levels, say horror is dying out as a genre because of psychotropic medication. Their students are so anti-depressed and mood-equalized that nothing ruffles their feathers. Should a zombie invasion occur, these well-medicated kids won't bat an eye.

To me, the best horror has always centered around a topic the current culture couldn't openly discuss. It's said the vampire represented venereal disease or the emigration of Jews from Eastern Europe. The Frankenstein monster stood for the Industrial Revolution or the fact that medical science was able to save so many mutilated soldiers in World War I, and civilians on the street were forced to see living, breathing evidence of the horrors of war. *The Boys from Brazil* stood for our fear that Fascism was still incubating, somewhere. *Burnt Offerings* was about how we're enslaved and destroyed trying to maintain our property and possessions. No really good horror story is about what it appears to be about.

That said, our culture seems to hide nothing these days. Every topic is fair game. If the monster was the mediator, we don't seem to need one.

My personal, crackpot, half-baked theory is that the vampire and the zombie serve the same function for current audiences. They both represent the homosexual. For heterosexual women, the vampire is the well-groomed, cultured consort who will never make sexual demands of them. For heterosexual men, the zombie is the menacing, infectious "other" who wants nothing more than to infect/recruit and consume them.

Whatever the case, horror stories serve as an inoculation. A small dose of a larger contagion, meant to prevent us from ever contracting a full-blown case. Maybe older people no longer need their booster shots. They've already seen friends die, and family members. They've weathered school systems and careers. It could be that the next monster will be a metaphor for mammoth student loan debt. Or the collapse of the real estate market—wasn't that the first season of *American Horror Story*: a family trapped in a dream home they couldn't sell as it slowly isolated and destroyed them?

Horror stories are a buffer between us and our real fears. Who knows? Maybe future generations will laugh over the global warming message of *The Day After Tomorrow* the way we laugh over the nuclear and chemical hysteria of the giant desert *Tarantula* and *The Incredible Shrinking Man*.

For me ghost stories seldom count as horror. Yes, sometimes they present an unresolved crime which must be set right. Too often they simply demonstrate life after death, ultimately comforting us. Seldom do they really scare me.

For a writer, the greatest achievement is to create the next great monster. For that is to foresee the future. To be the truest truth teller.

Whatever that next great monster will be, I miss being scared by the make-believe.

THE POETRY OF LIFE

RICHARD CHIZMAR

I'M FORTY-EIGHT YEARS OLD and have been a music teacher for twenty-seven of those years, and I still believe there is no sweeter sound in this world than the sound of a child's laughter.

Sometimes, when I hear it, I stop and listen and almost wish I could somehow bottle it up to save for later. This might happen when I am teaching a class or shopping for groceries or walking past one of the two playgrounds that bookend the neighborhood in which I live. I'll pretend to find a reason to stop—my shoelace is untied or perhaps I need to check the price on a particular can of soup—and I'll stand there and close my eyes and just drink it in. That beautiful melody.

Regrettably, I've never had any children of my own. Never married. Never found that kind of love.

I came close once. A long time ago when I was attending university. But it wasn't to be.

I say regrettably, but only because of my deep affection for children. I have never once complained or second guessed my lot in life, not even during those infrequent long sleepless nights that sometimes come to me when I have no choice but to lay there and stare at the dark ceiling and fight my troubling thoughts.

People often worry about me, that I am secretly sad or lonely or depressed. No shortage of pity for the spinster. But they needn't be concerned.

I have my books and my television and my students. An older

sister in Florida who emails me jokes and cute videos of kittens. A four-year-old Border Collie named Ginger. No cats, yet.

And then there is Shirley, my best friend and next door neighbor.

Shirley is a beautiful black woman. Sixty. Widowed. Mother of two adult boys who live out of state and rarely visit. We take turns at each other's houses several times per week. Playing cards and watching our shows. Sometimes we cook or share Chinese delivery. And while she will never warm my bed on a cold winter night, she warms my heart in a different way. I love her very much.

Shirley is also a kind woman and always smiles when I talk about how hearing a child's laughter fills my heart, how it fuels me. She is the one who first started calling it the poetry of life. We were sitting on the front porch one summer evening, drinking lemonade and doing crossword puzzles, and I fell in love with those words the moment she said them.

The poetry of life.

It was the perfect description of not only the sound itself, but also how I felt when I heard a child's laughter.

It was *poetry*. It was *life*.

I even started using it in my classes. I invented a lesson plan where each student would think about what constituted the poetry of life for them and then they would write down those thoughts. Then I would help each student turn those thoughts into a song.

Of course, many of the boys wrote about basketball or football or video games. And, of course, many of the girls wrote about their best friends or Taylor Swift or Justin Bieber. They were ten years old, after all.

But there were also some surprises.

Some *poetry*.

One little girl wrote about sunrises and how they reminded her of the little sister she had lost a year earlier to cancer.

Another girl wrote about flowers and how they helped her forget all the sadness and ugliness in the world.

Yet another wrote about spider webs and how if she stared at them long enough they looked like maps to her, maps to imaginary worlds.

And then there was my favorite: the little boy who wrote about thunderstorms and how they sounded like music inside his head, how they filled his heart to the point of bursting.

The poetry of life.

But I will never hear another song now.

Not after the message I received on my phone an hour ago.

Not after what the school board has decided.

I'd tried to call Shirley right away. Shirley had a way of calming me when my mind went dark and troubled. I called her twenty-two times, but she wasn't answering.

So I'd gone to the playground next. Thinking that if I could just hear that sweet sound one more time it might bring me peace and guidance.

But it hadn't worked.

The poetry was gone.

I'd felt *nothing*.

This not only confused me, it terrified me.

And for the first time in my life, I felt truly alone.

I have time to think all this as I pull into a parking spot and turn off my car and listen to the ticking of the cooling engine.

I have time to think all this as I walk across the parking lot and into the school.

I have to walk slow.

The guns are heavy.

FAIR

P. GARDNER GOLDSMITH

In the forest I see you once again
Whispering, listening, with sunlight in your eyes

It's a joy
To see you smiling once again
Temporarily, but sometimes rules will bend

It's a joy
To see you standing there

Stark white
Hair flowing in the air

It's a joy
To watch you waiting there

Smile so peaceful
Slicing through the air

In the window I see you now and then
Blissful, catalogical, the list begins again

Then the memory comes back to me my friend
Terminating but impossible to end

It's a joy
To see you standing there

Eyes white
Staring though the air

It's a joy
To know you're waiting there

On the threshold
Beckoning, so fair.

THE LAST RUNG ON THE LADDER

STEPHEN KING

I GOT KATRINA'S LETTER yesterday, less than a week after my father and I got back from Los Angeles. It was addressed to Wilmington, Delaware, and I'd moved twice since then. People move around so much now, and it's funny how those crossed-off addresses and change-of-address stickers can look like accusations. Her letter was rumpled and smudged, one of the corners dog-eared from handling. I read what was in it and the next thing I knew I was standing in the living room with the phone in my hand, getting ready to call Dad. I put the phone down with something like horror. He was an old man, and he'd had two heart attacks. Was I going to call and tell him about Katrina's letter so soon after we'd been in L.A.? To do that might very well have killed him.

So I didn't call. And I had no one I could tell...a thing like that letter, it's too personal to tell anyone except a wife or a very close friend. I haven't made many close friends in the last few years, and my wife Helen and I divorced in 1971. What we exchange now are Christmas cards. How are you? How's the job? Have a happy New Year.

I've been awake all night with it, with Katrina's letter. She could have put it on a postcard. There was only a single sentence below the "Dear Larry." But a sentence can mean enough. It can do enough.

I remembered my dad on the plane, his face seeming old and wasted in the harsh sunlight at 18,000 feet as we went west from New York. We had just passed over Omaha, according to the pilot,

21

and Dad said, "It's a lot further away than it looks, Larry." There was a heavy sadness in his voice that made me uncomfortable because I couldn't understand it. I understood it better after getting Katrina's letter.

We grew up eighty miles west of Omaha in a town called Hemingford Home—my dad, my mom, my sister Katrina, and me. I was two years older than Katrina, whom everyone called Kitty. She was a beautiful child and a beautiful woman—even at eight, the year of the incident in the barn, you could see that her corn-silk hair was never going to darken and that those eyes would always be a dark, Scandinavian blue. A look in those eyes and a man would be gone.

I guess you'd say we grew up hicks. My dad had three hundred acres of flat, rich land, and he grew feed corn and raised cattle. Everybody just called it "the home place." In those days all the roads were dirt except Interstate 80 and Nebraska Route 96, and a trip to town was something you waited three days for.

Nowadays I'm one of the best independent corporation lawyers in America, so they tell me—and I'd have to admit for the sake of honesty that I think they're right. A president of a large company once introduced me to his board of directors as his hired gun. I wear expensive suits and my shoeleather is the best. I've got three assistants on full-time pay, and I can call in another dozen if I need them. But in those days I walked up a dirt road to a one-room school with books tied in a belt over my shoulder, and Katrina walked with me. Sometimes, in the spring, we went barefoot. That was in the days before you couldn't get served in a diner or shop in a market unless you were wearing shoes.

Later on, my mother died—Katrina and I were in high school up at Columbia City then—and two years after that my dad lost the place and went to work selling tractors. It was the end of the family, although that didn't seem so bad then. Dad got along in his work, bought himself a dealership, and got tapped for a management position about nine years ago. I got a football scholarship to the

University of Nebraska and managed to learn something besides how to run the ball out of a slot-right formation.

And Katrina? But it's her I want to tell you about.

It happened, the barn thing, one Saturday in early November. To tell you the truth I can't pin down the actual year, but Ike was still President. Mom was at a bake fair in Columbia City, and Dad had gone over to our nearest neighbor's (and that was seven miles away) to help the man fix a hay rake. There was supposed to be a hired man on the place, but he had never showed up that day, and my dad fired him not a month later.

Dad left me a list of chores to do (and there were some for Kitty, too) and told us not to get to playing until they were all done. But that wasn't long. It was November, and by that time of year the make-or-break time had gone past. We'd made it again that year. We wouldn't always.

I remember that day very clearly. The sky was overcast and while it wasn't cold, you could feel it *wanting* to be cold, wanting to get down to the business of frost and freeze, snow and sleet. The fields were stripped. The animals were sluggish and morose. There seemed to be funny little drafts in the house that had never been there before.

On a day like that, the only really nice place to be was the barn. It was warm, filled with a pleasant mixed aroma of hay and fur and dung, and with the mysterious chuckling, cooing sounds of the barn swallows high up in the third loft. If you cricked your neck up, you could see the white November light coming through the chinks in the roof and try to spell your name. It was a game that really only seemed agreeable on overcast autumn days.

There was a ladder nailed to a crossbeam high up in the third loft, a ladder that went straight down to the main barn floor. We were forbidden to climb on it because it was old and shaky. Dad had promised Mom a thousand times that he would pull it down and put up a stronger one, but something else always seemed to come up when there was time ... helping a neighbor with his hayrake, for instance. And the hired man was just not working out.

If you climbed up that rickety ladder—there were exactly forty-three rungs, Kitty and I had counted them enough to know—you ended up on a beam that was seventy feet above the straw-littered barn floor. And then if you edged out along the beam about twelve feet, your knees jittering, your ankle joints creaking, your mouth dry and tasting like a used fuse, you stood over the haymow. And then you could jump off the beam and fall seventy feet straight down, with a horrible hilarious dying swoop, into a huge soft bed of lush hay. It has a sweet smell, hay does, and you'd come to rest in that smell of reborn summer with your stomach left behind you way up there in the middle of the air, and you'd feel... well, like Lazarus must have felt. You had taken the fall and lived to tell the tale.

It was a forbidden sport, all right. If we had been caught, my mother would have shrieked blue murder and my father would have laid on the strap, even at our advanced ages. Because of the ladder, and because if you happened to lose your balance and topple from the beam before you had edged out over the loose fathoms of hay, you would fall to utter destruction on the hard planking of the barn floor.

But the temptation was just too great. When the cats are away... well, you know how that one goes.

That day started like all the others, a delicious feeling of dread mixed with anticipation. We stood at the foot of the ladder, looking at each other. Kitty's color was high, her eyes darker and more sparkling than ever.

"Dare you," I said.

Promptly from Kitty: "Dares go first."

Promptly from me: "Girls go before boys."

"Not if it's dangerous," she said, casting her eyes down demurely, as if everybody didn't know she was the second-biggest tomboy in Hemingford. But that was how she was about it. She would go, but she wouldn't go first.

"Okay," I said. "Here I go."

I was ten that year, and thin as Scratch-the-demon, about ninety pounds. Kitty was eight, and twenty pounds lighter. The ladder had always held us before, we thought it would always hold us again, which is a philosophy that gets men and nations in trouble time after time.

I could feel it that day, beginning to shimmy around a little bit in the dusty barn air as I climbed higher and higher. As always, about halfway up, I entertained a vision of what would happen to me if it suddenly let go and gave up the ghost. But I kept going until I was able to clap my hands around the beam and boost myself up and look down.

Kitty's face, turned up to watch me, was a small white oval. In her faded checked shirt and blue denims, she looked like a doll. Above me still higher, in the dusty reaches of the eaves, the swallows cooed mellowly.

Again, by rote:

"Hi, down there!" I called, my voice floating down to her on motes of chaff.

"Hi, up there!"

I stood up. Swayed back and forth a little. As always, there seemed suddenly to be strange currents in the air that had not existed down below. I could hear my own heartbeat as I began to inch along with my arms held out for balance. Once, a swallow had swooped close by my head during this part of the adventure, and in drawing back I had almost lost my balance. I lived in fear of the same thing happening again.

But not this time. At last I stood above the safety of the hay. Now looking down was not so much frightening as sensual. There was a moment of anticipation. Then I stepped off into space, holding my nose for effect, and as it always did, the sudden grip of gravity, yanking me down brutally, making me plummet, made me feel like yelling: *Oh, I'm sorry, I made a mistake, let me back up!*

Then I hit the hay, shot into it like a projectile, its sweet and dusty smell billowing up around me, still going down, as if into heavy water, coming slowly to rest buried in the stuff. As always, I

could feel a sneeze building up in my nose. And hear a frightened field mouse or two fleeing for a more serene section of the haymow. And feel, in that curious way, that I had been reborn. I remember Kitty telling me once that after diving into the hay she felt fresh and new, like a baby. I shrugged it off at the time—sort of knowing what she meant, sort of not knowing—but since I got her letter I think about that, too.

I climbed out of the hay, sort of swimming through it, until I could climb out onto the barn floor. I had hay down my pants and down the back of my shirt. It was on my sneakers and sticking to my elbows. Hayseeds in my hair? You bet.

She was halfway up the ladder by then, her gold pigtails bouncing against her shoulder blades, climbing through a dusty shaft of light. On other days that light might have been as bright as her hair, but on this day her pigtails had no competition—they were easily the most colorful thing up there.

I remember thinking that I didn't like the way the ladder was swaying back and forth. It seemed like it had never been so loosey-goosey.

Then she was on the beam, high above me—now I was the small one, my face was the small white upturned oval as her voice floated down on errant chaff stirred up by my leap:

"Hi, down there!"

"Hi, up there!"

She edged along the beam, and my heart loosened a little in my chest when I judged she was over the safety of the hay. It always did, although she was always more graceful than I was . . . and more athletic, if that doesn't sound like too strange a thing to say about your kid sister.

She stood, poising on the toes of her old low-topped Keds, hands out in front of her. And then she swanned. Talk about things you can't forget, things you can't describe. Well, I can describe it . . . in a way. But not in a way that will make you understand how beautiful that was, how perfect, one of the few things in my life that seem utterly real, utterly true. No, I can't tell you like that. I don't have the skill with either my pen or my tongue.

For a moment she seemed to hang in the air, as if borne up by one of those mysterious updrafts that only existed in the third loft, a bright swallow with golden plumage such as Nebraska has never seen since. She was Kitty, my sister, her arms swept behind her and her back arched, and how I loved her for that beat of time!

Then she came down and plowed into the hay and out of sight. An explosion of chaff and giggles rose out of the hole she made. I'd forgotten about how rickety the ladder had looked with her on it, and by the time she was out, I was halfway up again.

I tried to swan myself, but the fear grabbed me the way it always did, and my swan turned into a cannonball. I think I never believed the hay was there the way Kitty believed it.

How long did the game go on? Hard to tell. But I looked up some ten or twelve dives later and saw the light had changed. Our mom and dad were due back and we were all covered with chaff … as good as a signed confession. We agreed on one more turn each.

Going up first, I felt the ladder moving beneath me and I could hear—very faintly—the whining rasp of old nails loosening up in the wood. And for the first time I was really, actively scared. I think if I'd been closer to the bottom I would have gone down and that would have been the end of it, but the beam was closer and seemed safer. Three rungs from the top the whine of pulling nails grew louder and I was suddenly cold with terror, with the certainty that I had pushed it too far.

Then I had the splintery beam in my hands, taking my weight off the ladder, and there was a cold, unpleasant sweat matting the twigs of hay to my forehead. The fun of the game was gone.

I hurried out over the hay and dropped off. Even the pleasurable part of the drop was gone. Coming down, I imagined how I'd feel if that was solid barn planking coming up to meet me instead of the yielding give of the hay.

I came out to the middle of the barn to see Kitty hurrying up the ladder. I called: "Hey, come down! It's not safe!"

"It'll hold me!" she called back confidently. "I'm lighter than you!"

"Kitty—"

But that never got finished. Because that was when the ladder let go.

It went with a rotted, splintering crack. I cried out and Kitty screamed. She was about where I had been when I'd become convinced I'd pressed my luck too far.

The rung she was standing on gave way, and then both sides of the ladder split. For a moment the ladder below her, which had broken entirely free, looked like a ponderous insect—a praying mantis or a ladderbug—which had just decided to walk off.

Then it toppled, hitting the barn floor with a flat clap that raised dust and caused the cows to moo worriedly. One of them kicked at its stall door.

Kitty uttered a high, piercing scream.

"*Larry! Larry! Help me!*"

I knew what had to be done, I saw right away. I was terribly afraid, but not quite scared out of my wits. She was better than sixty feet above me, her blue-jeaned legs kicking wildly at the blank air, then barn swallows cooing above her. I was scared, all right. And you know, I still can't watch a circus aerial act, not even on TV. It makes my stomach feel weak.

But I knew what had to be done.

"Kitty!" I bawled up at her. "Just hold still! Hold *still!*"

She obeyed me instantly. Her legs stopped kicking and she hung straight down, her small hands clutching the last rung on the ragged end of the ladder like an acrobat whose trapeze has stopped.

I ran to the haymow, clutched up a double handful of the stuff, ran back, and dropped it. I went back again. And again. And again. I really don't remember it after that, except the hay got up my nose and I started sneezing and couldn't stop. I ran back and forth,

building a haystack where the foot of the ladder had been. It was a very small haystack. Looking at it, then looking at her hanging so far above it, you might have thought of one of those cartoons where the guy jumps three hundred feet into a water glass.

Back and forth. Back and forth.

"Larry, I can't hold on much longer!" Her voice was high and despairing.

"Kitty, you've got to! You've got to hold on!"

Back and forth. Hay down my shirt. Back and forth. The haystack was as high as my chin now, but the haymow we had been diving into was twenty-five feet deep. I thought that if she only broke her legs it would be getting off cheap. And I knew if she missed the hay altogether, she would be killed. Back and forth.

"Larry! The rung! It's letting go!"

I could hear the steady, rasping cry of the rung pulling free under her weight. Her legs began to kick again in panic, but if she was thrashing like that, she would surely miss the hay.

"No!" I yelled. "No! Stop that! Just let go! Let go, Kitty!" Because it was too late for me to get any more hay. Too late for anything except blind hope.

She let go and dropped the second I told her to. She came straight down like a knife. It seemed to me that she dropped forever, her gold pigtails standing straight up from her head, her eyes shut, her face as pale as china. She didn't scream. Her hands were locked in front of her lips, as if she was praying.

And she struck the hay right in the center. She went down out of sight in it—hay flew up all around as if a shell had struck—and I heard the thump of her body hitting the boards. The sound, a loud thud, sent a deadly chill into me. It had been too loud, much too loud. But I had to see.

Starting to cry, I pounced on the haystack and pulled it apart, flinging the straw behind me in great handfuls. A blue-jeaned leg came to light, then a plaid shirt...and then Kitty's face. It was deadly pale and her eyes were shut. She was dead, I knew it as I looked at her. The world went gray for me, November gray. The only things in it with any color were her pigtails, bright gold.

And then the deep blue of her irises as she opened her eyes.

"Kitty?" My voice was hoarse, husky, unbelieving. My throat was coated with hay chaff. "Kitty?"

"Larry?" she asked, bewildered. "Am I alive?"

I picked her out of the hay and hugged her and she put her arms around my neck and hugged me back.

"You're alive," I said. "You're alive, you're alive."

She had broken her left ankle and that was all. When Dr. Pedersen, the GP from Columbia City, came out to the barn with my father and me, he looked up into the shadows for a long time. The last rung on the ladder still hung there, aslant, from one nail.

He looked, as I said, for a long time. "A miracle," he said to my father, and then kicked disdainfully at the hay I'd put down. He went out to his dusty DeSoto and drove away.

My father's hand came down on my shoulder. "We're going to the woodshed, Larry," he said in a very calm voice. "I believe you know what's going to happen there."

"Yes, sir," I whispered.

"Every time I whack you, Larry, I want you to thank God your sister is still alive."

"Yes, sir."

Then we went. He whacked me plenty of times, so many times I ate standing up for a week and with a cushion on my chair for two weeks after that. And every time he whacked me with his big red callused hand, I thanked God.

In a loud, loud voice. By the last two or three whacks, I was pretty sure He was hearing me.

They let me in to see her just before bedtime. There was a catbird outside her window, I remember that. Her foot, all wrapped up, was propped on a board.

She looked at me so long and so lovingly that I was uncomfortable. Then she said, "Hay. You put down hay."

"Course I did," I blurted. "What else would I do? Once the ladder broke there was no way to get up there."

"I didn't know what you were doing," she said.

"You must have! I was right under you, for cripe's sake!"

"I didn't dare look down," she said. "I was too scared. I had my eyes shut the whole time."

I stared at her, thunderstruck.

"You didn't know? Didn't know what I was doing?"

She shook her head.

"And when I told you to let go you ... you just *did it?*"

She nodded.

"Kitty, how could you do that?"

She looked at me with those deep blue eyes. "I knew you must have been doing something to fix it," she said. "You're my big brother. I knew you'd take care of me."

"Oh, Kitty, you don't know how close it was."

I had put my hands over my face. She sat up and took them away. She kissed my cheek. "No," she said. "But I knew you were down there. Gee, am I sleepy. I'll see you tomorrow, Larry. I'm going to have a cast, Dr. Pedersen says."

She had the cast on for a little less than a month, and all her classmates signed it—she even got me to sign it. And when it came off, that was the end of the barn incident. My father replaced the ladder up to the third loft with a new strong one, but I never climbed up to the beam and jumped off into the haymow again. So far as I know, Kitty didn't either.

It was the end, but somehow not the end. Somehow it never ended until nine days ago, when Kitty jumped from the top story of an insurance building in Los Angeles. I have the clipping from *The L.A. Times* in my wallet. I guess I'll always carry it, not in the good way you carry snapshots of people you want to remember or theater tickets from a really good show or part of the program from a World

34

Series game. I carry that clipping the way you carry something heavy, because carrying it is your work. The headline reads: CALL GIRL SWAN-DIVES TO HER DEATH.

We grew up. That's all I know, other than facts that don't mean anything. She was going to go to business college in Omaha, but in the summer after she graduated from high school, she won a beauty contest and married one of the judges. It sounds like a dirty joke, doesn't it? My Kitty.

While I was in law school she got divorced and wrote me a long letter, ten pages or more, telling me how it had been, how messy it had been, how it might have been better if she could have had a child. She asked me if I could come. But losing a week in law school is like losing a term in liberal-arts undergraduate. Those guys are greyhounds. If you lose sight of the little mechanical rabbit, it's gone forever.

She moved to L.A. and got married again. When that one broke up I was out of law school. There was another letter, a shorter one, more bitter. She was never going to get stuck on *that* merry-go-round, she told me. It was a fix job. The only way you could catch the brass ring was to tumble off the horse and crack your skull. If that was what the price of a free ride was, who wanted it? PS, Can you come, Larry? It's been a while.

I wrote back and told her I'd love to come, but I couldn't. I had landed a job in a high-pressure firm, low guy on the totem pole, all the work and none of the credit. If I was going to make it up to the next step, it would have to be that year. That was *my* long letter, and it was all about my career.

I answered all of her letters. But I could never really believe that it was really Kitty who was writing them, you know, no more than I could really believe that the hay was really there...until it broke my fall at the bottom of the drop and saved my life. I couldn't believe that my sister and the beaten woman who signed "Kitty" in a circle at the bottom of the letters were really the same person. My sister was a girl with pigtails, still without breasts.

She was the one who stopped writing. I'd get Christmas cards, birthday cards, and my wife would reciprocate. Then we got divorced and I moved and just forgot. The next Christmas and the birthday after, the cards came through the forwarding address. The first one. And I kept thinking: Gee, I've got to write Kitty and tell her that I've moved. But I never did.

But as I've told you, those are facts that don't mean anything. The only things that matter are that we grew up and she swanned from that insurance building, and that Kitty was the one who always believed the hay would be there. Kitty was the one who had said, "I knew you must be doing something to fix it." Those things matter. And Kitty's letter.

People move around so much now, and it's funny how those crossed-off addresses and change-of-address stickers can look like accusations. She'd printed her return address in the upper left corner of the envelope, the place she'd been staying at until she jumped. A very nice apartment building on Van Nuys. Dad and I went there to pick up her things. The landlady was nice. She had liked Kitty.

The letter was postmarked two weeks before she died. It would have gotten to me a long time before, if not for the forwarding addresses. She must have gotten tired of waiting.

> *Dear Larry,*
>
> *I've been thinking about it a lot lately ... and what I've decided is that it would have been better for me if that last rung had broken before you could put the hay down.*
>
> *Your,*
> *Kitty*

Yes, I guess she must have gotten tired of waiting. I'd rather believe that than think of her deciding I must have forgotten.

I wouldn't want her to think that, because that one sentence was maybe the only thing that would have brought me on the run.

But not even that is the reason sleep comes so hard now. When I close my eyes and start to drift off, I see her coming down from the third loft, her eyes wide and dark blue, her body arched, her arms swept up behind her.

She was the only one who always knew the hay would be there.

FAIL-SAFE

JONATHAN BALOG

At 33,000 feet, a star falls with no brakes
Look up, and watch a single spark
Descend toward a billion identical points
See, distance is an equalizer
From far enough away, everything looks the same

At 25,000 feet, epiphany kicks in,
Bringing neurons to a boil
Lateral thought hides under a wing
And coping mechanisms fire into the dark
From here, hindsight is something we've outgrown

At 9,000 feet, the city is fit with brass shoes
Movements are weighed by a dreamlike slowness
As distance becomes anathema
Becomes the worst enemy we've ever had
As if someone had thrown time itself into the quicksand

At 2,000 feet, equations collapse
Consciousness is dragged kicking and screaming
Toward whatever passes for a center these days
And the future clears its schedule to make way
For a calm that rushes over everything

A RIFT IN REFLECTION

HAL BODNER

DEATH WAS NOT nearly the frightening experience that Phillip feared it would be. No devils awakened him into the hereafter with prodding pitchforks intent on avenging his sins. He found no purgatory, nor any other form of Stygian psychoanalysis to help him work through his unresolved corporeal issues. No beings of purity awaited to clothe him in white robes so that his voice could join in singing praises to a Heavenly Father in which he never really believed.

Contrariwise, death was a languid and easy existence, a simple state of being. It triggered the fond memory of a lazy picnic he and David had shared many years ago. Pleasantly stuffed on runny cheese, pâté spread on crusty bread and a veritable harvest of fresh berries, the two of them had quaffed just enough Riesling to be lightly tipsy. Some hour or two after the bottle was finished, they sprawled in the afterglow while the late afternoon sun slowly dried their sweat slicked bodies, limbs intertwined, half asleep and content.

If pressed, Phillip would say he was contented in death—quite a different experience from what he'd known before he crossed over. Life had often been a trial. If he accurately interpreted the behavior of the still-living who sometimes visited the graveyard, these new generations were quite open about who they chose to love. But in Phillip's day, clandestine assignations were required and an unceasing aura of oppressiveness was the norm. One's job, one's family, one's home, even one's liberty was constantly at stake, not to mention the possibility of being badly beaten merely if you carelessly took the wrong route home from a bar and were attacked for no other reason than that you were wearing the wrong clothing.

David had been younger, less reserved, more willing to take risks. He was always an inveterate marcher, an eager protestor, an industrious gatherer of signatures on petitions, even before the Plague Years. He often did things that Phillip tried, but failed, to understand. But even David knew the wisdom of caution, of not flaunting what he was when he was in dangerous surroundings.

Death changed all that. There was no longer any need for such fusses. The pervasive, smothering fears were gone. The politicking was moot for such as he and David, best left to those who still breathed and cared about those things. No longer did he wake each morning, his chest tight with anxiety until he had searched every millimeter of his body, breath held in anticipation of spying a dreaded purple spot or obsessively measuring a mole he'd had for years to see if it had grown bigger. No more did he explosively thrash in the bedclothes, jolted into terrified wakefulness by a dream that David was gone, only to waken fully to the mechanical hiss of air from the guestroom and the oppressive knowledge that the nightmare had already arrived.

The not knowing had been the worst. The horrific six months of vomit and shit and sweat and stink had been horrible, populated as they were with nurses swathed head-to-toe in surgical masks and gowns and rubber gloves like neurotic mummies. Yes, those times had been bad, worse than bad. But at least, death offered a finite end. It was the times that came before which had everyone in an agony of pins and needles while they waited.

Until someone developed a test, an atmosphere of furtiveness pervaded as if by not drawing attention, one could somehow avoid the consequences of a becoming a target. Yet, unbeknownst to so many, the Mark of Caine had already figuratively been painted on their foreheads. Perhaps selfishly, Phillip breathed a little easier after that. But for David, a biomedical Sword of Damocles loomed, poised to sever so very many young lives.

By the time a course of treatment was finally announced it was too late for David. Not that it would have mattered. The early regimens failed, as did the next, and the ones after that. Toward the end of his own much longer life, long after his old friends who had survived the first wave had grown numb to tragedy, or perhaps just complacent, Phillip heard murmurings of "manageability" and "preventative" therapies, and even more vague promises of vaccines on the horizon.

But by that time, thirty-odd years had flown and Phillip was tired. Not just physically; the unceasing mental stress had taken its toll as well. When his time came, he welcomed it and he received an unexpected gift that he had never dared hope to experience again. In death, Phillip once again could be carefree.

There were limitations, of course. The Universe was not without its rules, no matter how arbitrary. When he arrived, he'd pestered the others for a reason, an answer to the question - why? Why were they limited to such a narrow radius of existence, a perfect circle with a radius of exactly twenty-three feet, four and three-quarter inches from the center of each burial plot? Outside of that perimeter, while they could still see the Living, the Dead were blind to other Dead.

It made for small communities and, since most of the Dead no longer cherished the major prejudices and anxieties of the Living, there was little conflict between them. What gripes they shared were petty ones. Though most of the older Dead had lapsed into restive slumber, some of them lay where a large number of cremains were interred. Inevitably, the cemetery echoed with querulous complaints about people's rest being disturbed each time a funeral party showed up bearing urns containing the ashes of new arrivals. Others, whose plots were located in full burial areas, bemoaned the lack of variety. They hardly could have been happy being stuck with the same thirty or so companions throughout eternity.

Every day, Phillip took a few moments to appreciate how lucky he was to have given in to David's pestering. Back then, two unrelated men generally did *not* purchase cemetery plots together. While the attempt to do so was not entirely unheard of, it was distinctly queer—in both senses of the word. Had they tried, it was likely that the cemetery would have rejected them entirely. David urged him to take the chance but Phillip was never comfortable with the idea.

In the end, they compromised. They purchased a pair of plots which, while they were not side-by-side, they deemed to be close enough. They arranged two headstones of identical design as well, seeking to surreptitiously mimic the physical togetherness that they feared the cemetery staff might have denied them had they tried to establish it more overtly.

Life had never been easy for the two men, though Phillip had more difficulty adjusting than his younger partner. At first, they lived with mandatory secrecy and the fear of discovery; they lived knowing that a small slip up could yield violent repercussions. Later, they lived ostracized and rejected by family and friends. They continued to live in hiding so that they could maintain a roof over their heads and put food on the table. They lived with caution, unwilling to compliment neighbors on what fine, handsome sons they had for fear of it being taken the wrong way, averting their eyes when taking in sports events lest their expressions be accurately interpreted as containing admiration for more than the mere skill of the athletes. In the end, of course, they lived as lepers, diseased pariahs. And once David was gone, Phillip lived in loneliness, managing to eke out a drudgery of existence for another few decades before the pain at last subsided.

Perhaps in some cosmic penance for all the obstacles Life had thrown into their paths, Fate smiled upon them in death. By sheerest luck, Phillip and David's plots were located exactly forty six feet and nine inches away from each other.

Forty-six feet and nine inches.

With a full half inch margin to spare.

Joy was his over-riding emotion now, but it was a gentle thing, not the frenetic hullabaloo of mortal jubilation. When his spirit

44

first rose from the grave and he realized where and what he was, he made a beeline toward David's plot. Those few moments along the way while he crossed those twenty-some feet were sheer agony, half convinced as he was that his new state of being was unique or, if not, that David's ghost was long gone.

"David?" He called out hesitantly when he reached the end of his invisible tether and could go no further. "It's Phillip. I'm here sweetheart. I'm here at last."

A short eternity seemed to pass until a beloved form took shape, no longer ravaged by cancer and wasted away, restored to the seeming vigor of his youth. It was the man he had first known, first loved, unseen except in his dearest dreams for more than thirty years, returned to him at last.

Phillip was not unaware of some of the other specters around them, most going about their own business but some few watching curiously. Though he felt a faint pang of unease, a discomfort at any blatant impropriety, in his initial excitement at seeing David again, he flung his arms around his lover, for once unable to muster concern about what strangers might think. Though neither of them could truly feel the embrace, it was enough. Finally, they shared a moment, however brief, of quiet bliss.

A quartet of mature women stood watching, two of them were able to see the entire reunion, a third was restricted to observing Phillip alone. The last could see nothing.

"Look at that." Mrs. Briskin, who was buried under the rose bush gently prodded Mrs. Susskind, who had a plot right up against the lake, with her elbow. "Young love," she said with affection.

"Love?" Mrs. Susskind's eyebrows rose. "The fegalehs?"

"Goldie!" Mrs. Briskin chastised her friend. "Such language! It's a new world out there."

The other woman shrugged. "If you say so, Minnie. If you ask me, after Goldwater lost, the whole country went kaput." She snorted with a kind of amused disgust, a sound that was unique to Jewish widows of a certain age.

"What's going on?" Esther Futterman whined. "I'm out of range."

She tugged at Ruth Meinster's sleeve.

"Don't ask me," Ruth replied. "As far as I can see, he's hugging air."

Minnie Briskin ignored them in favor of continuing her argument with Goldie Susskind.

"You're telling me, if your Harry wasn't buried in Florida, you wouldn't get a little excited?"

"If my Harry ever looked like *that*," Mrs. Susskind pointed to David's youthful muscular figure and, incidentally, scored the winning conversational point, "... My whole life would have been excited."

"Live and let live," Ruth advised her friends, without realizing the irony. "Just live and let live."

The first pair of old biddies wandered off, followed by Mrs. Futterman complaining to Ruth Meister in their wake. The other ghosts steered clear of David and Phillip as well, respecting their privacy for now. Reunions were not uncommon, but they were few and far between. As this part of the cemetery slowly filled and ran out of room for new interments, they would eventually cease altogether. The current occupants knew this and, consequently, they cherished the novelty of these increasingly rare meetings while keeping their distance so as not to spoil their new neighbors' moments of discovery. There would be plenty of time later to gossip over the details.

"You look ..." Phillip breathed, amazed at David's restoration.

"As do you, Phil," he replied. "Not a day over forty."

"Seventy-three," Phillip snorted, a little embarrassed by the compliment.

"None of that matters now."

The two men soon settled into a routine. Between their graves, roughly equidistant, there was a small marble funerary bench. For hours on end, the two men perched upon it, talking, holding hands and reminiscing. Amongst the other spirits, it was soon acknowledged as David and Phillip's special meeting spot, and they largely refrained from intruding upon the lovers' privacy.

"Wasn't there ever anyone else?" David asked one day.

"After you?" Phillip sat up. He'd been reclining with his head in David's lap while his lover stroked his hair. "Or before?"

"Ah! So there *were* others!" David smiled mischievously. His eyes crinkled up in that winning way he had. David had always had an elfin cast to his smile, slightly devilish yet inviting at the same time. The expression had instantly captured Phillip's heart the moment he'd first seen the younger man sitting in the first row of his graduate class at university. How he had ached to see it again!

Playfully, Phillip punched him in the arm.

"Tricks. On occasion. You wouldn't know about this, obviously, but as one gets older, one sometimes has to pay."

"Really?" David's eyes grew round with affected shock and he pressed his fingers to the center of his chest like an old spinster. "How sordid!"

Phillip chuckled. "It was only a few times. Never satisfying. As years went on..." He shrugged. "The need grew less. After all..." He lay his head back in David's lap and reached up to stroke his lover's cheek. "I spent thirteen years with the best. How could anyone follow your act?"

"I'm sorry," David said, serious now.

"For what?" Phillip abandoned his efforts to recapture the quiet intimacy they'd shared all morning, and sat up fully. Apparently, David had something important on his mind.

"For leaving you so soon," he all but whispered.

"As if it was your fault?" Phillip clasped both of David's hands and looked into his eyes. "As if it was any of our faults."

They sat for a while, hand in hand like that, simply enjoying their nearness to each other.

"Life," Phillip said after a long silence, "was not always fair."

David looked at him, questioning, but said nothing.

"You missed the worst of it, thank goodness. And toward the end—of my days, not yours—things were changing, altering with frightening speed."

"For the better, I hope."

Phillip shrugged. "I suppose. After you were taken from me, I didn't pay a lot of attention. We needn't concern ourselves with that any more. We're together now. It almost makes me believe in God."

"A slut and an atheist!" David kidded.

"I couldn't bear it without you," Phillip told him, seriously. "Not again."

"Maybe," David said and leaned his head on Phillip's shoulder, "this is our reward. So much was taken from us. A half inch of respite was the least the universe could repay us. We were owed."

Months passed and soon, a few years had gone. In that time, the two lovers had the luxury of connecting as few mortals do, spending hours conversing. Sometimes the matters they discussed were profound, at other times they concerned themselves with trivial things. And while it was inevitable that they would, each limited by his own restricted territory, come to know the spirits of their respective neighbors, they spent the vast majority of their time together, loving each other as best they could.

Yet their existence did not continue entirely uninterrupted; there was ever the occasional incident or event.

Ruth Meinster's daughter-in-law joined them and the two women did not get along. Phillip amused David, who was out of range, with stories of their squabbling, most of which centered around the antics of Dr. Seth Meinster, Ruth's son. Uproar resulted when the good doctor showed up to pay his respects to his late wife with his new bride in tow. A bottle-blond Italian Catholic, she briefly united mother and daughter-in-law in their outrage until the intensity of their emotion faded into mere grumbling discontentment.

A teenaged girl was with them briefly, perhaps nine months in all. A welcome companion to young Brian, a lonely lad who had died in a mid-century car crash, she was the only other young person buried within Phillip and David's shared range. Brian doted on her; at last someone had arrived with whom he had something in common, even though their living days were separated by almost fifty years. When she was exhumed for reasons that no one knew, and the grave was left permanently empty, Brian was desolate. But within a week or so, he was once again his stand-offish self, lurking in moody isolation, rarely moving more than a yard away from where his bronze nameplate was slowly being obscured by weeds.

That was the thing, David told Phillip. The Dead seemed unable to maintain strong emotion for long. Passions could be roused, but they faded quickly. Once again, the two men were confronted with how blessed they were. Their love was deep but unassuming, tender but not exciting, stalwart but not forceful. In death, the two men relaxed into caring for each other again as a matter of course, placidly and without turmoil or angst. Perhaps Death was grateful for the lack of drama and, in return, granted them the peace they felt they had earned.

They were finally content. Life could throw them no more curve balls. No longer did they care what anyone thought. If the act of sex was an impossibility, more casual intimacy was not; in the simplicity of tender caresses and soft whispers, the raucousness of an orgasm seemed less vital and not as necessary in comparison.

Of course, there were times when merely being together by itself grew tedious. When that happened, they gossiped like sorority girls, swapping anecdotes of those of the cemetery's denizens that the other could not see. The area immediately surrounding Phillip's headstone consisted of perhaps thirty graves and a small mausoleum. David's stone was adjacent to a section of smaller plots where cremains were interred, gleaning him closer to fifty spirits with whom he could interact if he chose. There was enough fodder so that trading quips at the expense of their neighbors' various machinations and squabbles became an amusing way to forestall boredom when it threatened.

For some time, Fate was kind to them, perhaps almost long enough to equal the balance of the lifetime together that they had been denied. But as the weathered inscription above the door to Tyler McInniny's mausoleum should have reminded them: NOTHING LASTS FOREVER.

None of the ghosts felt the earthquake physically, of course. Yet some found themselves caught up in the drama of the event and echoed the cries of alarm of the Living. For most though, watching the violent upheaval was nothing more than a welcome and entertaining novelty.

All across the cemetery the terrain shifted and warped. The more mature and stately trees fought the undulations, shedding weaker limbs in a shower of leaves and shards of bark while their less venerable companions merely swayed to weather the violence. A miniature tidal wave crashed against the embankment surrounding the lake; the water undermined the roots and, before it toppled, great swathes of earth crumbled and washed away.

The shaking was so bad that, when it ceased, some of the grave markers no longer precisely matched the identities of the deceased who had originally been buried beneath them. Less obviously, below the sod handfuls of earth invaded spaces previously occupied by naught but stale pockets of air and desiccated bones. Aged moisture-rotted coffins splintered, and the remains within them were jostled to and fro. Even the concrete burial vaults were not immune. Unable to withstand the rocking, some cracked and flung shards of stone to the surface to lie with jagged edges poking above the grass.

Eventually the landscape settled and everyone's excitement diminished. Though the rearrangement of boundaries was a nice change for many, all too soon the less welcome effects of the cataclysm began to make themselves known.

Mrs. Susskind was gone, vanished entirely when her grave was washed into the lake and her casket sank out of range. The McInniny crypt was reduced to rubble. And Phillip mourned to see that the bench he and David shared was damaged beyond repair.

The marble uprights had cracked and one side of the slab had fallen and leaned crazily a-kilter, clearly unsafe for any mortal being to sit upon.

It was a sad, pathetic sight, made more so when Phillip realized that the little bench had come to hold a deep significance for him. It was here that he and David had first been reunited and it had become a symbol of their togetherness. Though the caretakers would undoubtedly replace it, he would be sorry to see it go and, no matter what they erected in its stead, he would always hold the memory of the original in his heart.

It took a while for Phillip to become aware of the gravamen of the change. Some of the others, of course, realized immediately but hesitated to point it out to him. After the earthquake subsided, Phillip sat on the bench, waiting long into evening. His concern, when David failed to arrive, was mild. It had happened before. Every so often, one or the other of them had drifted off into his own mental fog for a while, unaware of the passage of time; the Dead are not so fixated upon the measuring of hours and minutes and seconds as are the Living. For them to fail to meet was uncommon, but not unknown.

Days passed and, sometime within that span, Phillip allowed the knowledge to sink in. At one point, Minnie Briskin braved an approach and offered to ferry messages back and forth but Phillip didn't respond. It was as if he had moved beyond all of their boundaries, as if he could neither hear nor see even the closest of his fellow specters.

"It makes no sense," he thought, bitterly. "Some people are taken in their prime. Others of us are forced to linger beyond anything we thought we could endure. It's all so senseless. Senseless and … arbitrary."

Another flash of resentment overtook him but he impatiently repressed it.

True, their life together had been all too brief. In death, they had been given a second chance. If both were fated to be equally as brief, so be it. David would never truly leave him, nor would he leave David.

Even now, he imagined him standing just a few inches away with his hand stretched out. Phillip rose from the shattered remains of the bench and dared a few steps toward David's grave until he came up short. He pressed his hand against the invisible wall that he must needs accept though he could not understand it.

He stood there for a very long time. Was there a matching pressure from the other side of the barrier? Was there the slightest bit of warmth against his palm? Did he hear, almost imperceptibly, a sigh of grief that matched his own?

He rested his cheek against the spot. And waited...

FOLIE À DEUX (THE MADNESS OF TWO)

SYDNEY LEIGH

Under a thin veil of harvest light,
your hand goes cold in mine

Your skin becomes that of the moon itself—
I touch your cratered face,

hear the faint echo
of a heart let loose inside your chest.

There is a weightlessness here
with which we are unfamiliar.

We search for water that isn't there
for life in a place where we are

alone.

SYDNEY LEIGH

This lunar love
will not last—

it is an insincere
and fabricated

as the Sea of Vapors
in which we dissolve.

For days we wander,
waiting for the eclipse—

for others
to see

what we are.

WINDOWS, MIRRORS, DOORS

JASON V BROCK

I

THE APOCALYPSE arrived on a Tuesday. At least for Marion.

However, this was not some 9/11-type catastrophe, or the collapse of civilization due to a global pandemic. No, she had learned *real* apocalypses were always personal. *They always involved a cast of characters, too. Sometimes just one, but frequently extras ... though never more than required.* The circumstances—the inciting events, the setting, and so on—just served as a backdrop for the emotional and psychic dramaturgy which encapsulated that most human and elusive of all cosmic principles: *the moment.* Additionally, and ironically, said moment is different for everyone, even those who come to share it due to accidents of fate.

For Marion, it was the death of her identical twin sister on a stark, bitterly cold Tuesday morning. The cast had included her, Annette, the doctors and nurses; the last act took place in the hospice, and the catalyst had been her sister's cancer, which set those final performances into motion—piecemeal scenes that would eventually devolve into a protracted and painful melodrama saddled with a poorly scripted, wholly unsatisfactory finale.

Who writes *these things?* Marion sometimes wondered, and with more than a touch of sarcasm.

Another thing she came to understand after Annette's loss was that these private apocalypses were not always quick; in many situations, they were slow—in her case the leisurely unraveling of the threads of a life over the span of more than thirty years. Yes, *death* can be quick, binary—one moment living, the next not. Nevertheless, the end of all things for the individuals who survive such trauma—the demise of a loved one; a disaster, manmade or natural—often takes much longer to resolve … frequently months or years, if ever.

Slow and steady. But the race is never won, she reflected.

Of course, Marion had not come to these conclusions through any sudden epiphany; it was experienced as a gradual dawning … more precisely an *erosion.* An implacable, sinister loss of color in the day-to-day machinations of existence as the bubble of her daily life shrank in influence and experience. It would all perhaps end horribly, as is the way with reality, but for a long time she tried to concern herself chiefly with the possibility of new beginnings, with the mystery of a fresh, if unwelcome, start—spinning the anguish and pain into a different worldview she had not previously considered. After a time, this faux optimism subsided, and she eventually realized that the *finality* is what truly mattered. *That was where the lesson was to be found,* she mused. Endings only become apparent in retrospect; in the *moment*, the events as they are happening seem as impermanent as any others that precede them, or those that inevitably follow. Only with hindsight does the true gravity of the delineation between the world *before* and the world *after* become comprehensible.

In the final analysis, the grind and joy of anyone's life comes down to a few bullet points, she decided, *at most a couple of paragraphs highlighting a few key moments:*

- Birth—*shared with Annette …*
- Education—*first in public school, then through scholarships to some excellent colleges to feed the fire for performance …*
- Career—*traveling the world as an actor of stage, TV, and film …*

- Marriage—*to Nick, the alcoholic New Yorker, ending after just a year; then, in 1985, to my Southern gentleman, Eric, with his troubled, gifted son, Patrick…*
- Children—*dear, sweet Patrick, who went to Australia as a young man before finally leaving us for good…*
- Loss—*of my beloved Eric to an aneurysm; my parents to old age; Annette to cancer; my career to depression and anxiety; of friends through attrition; of youth and vitality …*
- Death—*the great unknown for anyone, and, unlike birth, without the comfort of my lovely twin…*

In her more cynical moods, Marion questioned why it all mattered. *Live long enough and everyone loses* everything: *friends, family, health, perhaps their mind … eventually even life itself.* Just as some creatures thrive in shadow, shunning the light, avoiding the attention of others, so do others prosper at the margins of society, at the interface *between* the darkness and light. At one time, she had been one such creature of the sun … after Annette's passing, she found her world increasingly pulled into the waiting blackness. A piece of her died that day, and the hole that was created had continued to spread throughout her being ever so gradually. She struggled to stay at the interface as best she could; it was not easy, as she grew older, as the losses compounded, as the light receded. She coped as best she could, but sometimes it was like awakening from a coma into a completely unlit room: it was difficult to make sense out of what had become of her life in such a context.

Left to her own devices, she passively observed the world as its pace quickened and her enthusiasm waned; it frequently left her feeling like an insect, a kind of drone. *Drones understood—either through cognizance or intuition—their place, their role in society.* Insect societies were brutal, efficient hierarchies, she understood, but they were not rooted in vendetta or spite; the caste was established at birth, and was impervious to negotiation. The individual supplicated to the group hive mind, the collective enterprise of survival. In many ways,

Marion admired this simple, methodical approach to life; it required no insight, no conscious thought, and did not reward devious or Machiavellian behavior. No individual was more important than any other and all members were independent of the social constraints and expectations of some egomaniacal leader or the vanity of a clique. Yet, even a drone had *purpose*. Increasingly, Marion felt no such impulse; it was as though she were being controlled by an outside force, or had become an imposter within her own body, manipulated from without by an alien consciousness which influenced her actions, and—ever more—her *reactions*, like some master puppeteer, an irony she found by turns bemusing and disconcerting. She was an actor, and actors *were*, in some ways, simply puppets, vessels, *tabulae rasae*, for the roles they inhabit. While this was true enough, she was beginning to feel less like a vessel and more like the literal text—as though she had no meaning unless imbued by some external proxy speaking the words aloud. When she looked in the mirror in the mornings, she recognized herself less and less, and worried that one day the last speck of her self-conception would simply vanish as she mundanely cleaned her face—as though her physical being might melt away into the spiral of the emptying sink, taking her humanity and soul along with it.

Wash those troubles right down the drain …

As a result of this erosion and dissociation, Marion had reduced her activities. Though she was still attractive—her shoulder-length black hair streaked with dramatic white highlights, her skin was taut, youthful, her figure still tight for a woman in her late sixties due to walking the stairs of her apartment building almost daily—she felt no need to engage others, merely observe them. Her building, where she and her second husband Eric had moved as her career bloomed in the early 1990s, was now her haven, her cocoon. She watched everything, taking silent delight in her surreptitious voyeurism, and spent more and more time in the comforting nostalgia afforded by the apartment, with its trove of old books, her awards and photo albums, Eric's collection of miniature cars, and even Patrick's former bedroom, which carried a certain enigmatic charm, and remained essentially as he left it before he departed in his late twenties.

Maybe one day I'll see him again . . . I hope so. God I miss him.

She recalled reading an article once that passing through doorways was tied to forgetting what one was doing in the moment; that the scene change from room to room had a way of mentally resetting one's actions and purpose on an unconscious level; as though the doors of perception *actually changed* when moving through a portal such as an entryway, even a window. In some ways, the idea comforted her, yet, in others, it was disquieting, as though she was doomed to wander from place to place and lose the context of why she had, or what the purpose of the change really was. To that end, occasionally, a maternal tug compelled her to go inside Patrick's old room, relax on the bed, and contemplate the lively assortment of his antique marionettes suspended from the ceiling, the brightly painted automatons seated in lifelike tableaux, the wistful hand-carved little manikins resting on the bookshelves and windowsill. As a child, Patrick had been deeply involved in magic and puppetry. His Asperger's syndrome had limited his interaction with friends at school, but not his interior world. He built several old-style animated dolls that could move and walk, and had developed into quite a ventriloquist. As she regarded the dusty remnants of someone else's life in Patrick's room, Marion wondered if there was a certain trade-off to being extraordinary at something—whether an amazing facility with words, exceptional acting talent, visionary artistic ability, or making animated puppets—in that one must *lose* something at some point: a loved one, a limb, a sense, one's purpose. She had experienced much over the years, most of it good, but it appeared to be front-loaded, and now she was paying the dues she managed to forego in her youth. Not that she cared anymore, but this certainly seemed to be the case. For example, the

paparazzi no longer noticed if she came or went, and she doubted any of the younger ones even knew she had twice been nominated for an Academy Award, or had a brief fling with Jack Nicolson in the debauched heydays of the late '70s, when she lived in LA.

This has become another world, she noted, regarding the sad effigies. *And not my world.* Now, she felt as though she had become a sort of female version of the Minotaur: Huddled in the center of the old brownstone, the twisting, voracious labyrinth of the City reaching ever farther away from her daily experience or care. The immediate mazes of her mind, her apartment, and her neighborhood had reduced her domain to a few blocks, some great performances captured on celluloid and in her memory, a couple of girlfriends, and the other occupants of her building...the erstwhile art dealer couple who vanished after a shadowy trip to Prague; Mr. Trinity, the musician who remained aloof and strange, practicing his horn seemingly day and night for all these many years; others came and went like ghostly spectators in a T. S. Eliot poem. For a long time, this was her life.

Until tonight.

II

Marion twists the phone cord with her fingers, slumping into the loveseat. In the background, Sinatra gently croons from the record player; the window is open and, seven stories below, the City rumbles outside like a giant cat. Night has fallen, and the afterglow of sunset bleeds eerily red against the horizon. In the distance, an autumnal thunderstorm is gathering power.

"That's what the doctor said, Marti."

Tears roll down her cheeks as she listens to the voice on the end of the line. Marion leans forward and retrieves her wine glass, lifting the ruby liquid to her lips and taking a few swallows. Swirling the contents to inhale the bouquet before placing it back on the table, she sighs deeply.

"That's right. Dr. Williams said it might be why I've been more tired the past few months. Also why I wake up standing in the hallway sometimes, or screaming," she pauses in thought. "The emotional lability part explains the laughing fit I had at the funeral for Pete."

She listens again, rubbing her cheeks with her sleeve. Pulling a tissue from the box on the table, she dabs at her light blue eyes.

"I don't know…He said this new medication can sometimes slow down the progression. The doctor also explained it might help control the night terrors and the waking hallucinations, like when I thought that guy was following me around reading my thoughts a few weeks ago." She pauses once more. "No guarantees, of course."

More minutes pass as she listens. She takes another sip of wine. Thunder shakes the building. "Listen, I better get off the phone. It's starting to storm here. I don't want to get electrocuted. Thank you so much, Marti. And thank you for getting me to go to the doctor …I feel like it can be dealt with. We'll see. Yes—let's plan on dinner Friday. Okay. Love you, too. 'Bye."

She places the handset into the cradle, staring at the telephone. A bright flash sears, followed in a few seconds by a deep roll of thunder. Darkness has taken over, the light pollution of the City a shifting pink mix of sodium lamps, headlights, and sheets of rain. The pattering downpour is soothing to her, the smell refreshing, clean. She closes her eyes, comforted by the soothing white noise of the rainstorm merging with the street sounds underneath. Sinatra morosely catalogs the years as she drifts off to sleep.

A bolt of intense lightning awakens her. The room is coal dark, and she cannot see anything. Even the light pollution is gone: *Oh, no…A blackout.* She hates blackouts. Marion glances at her watch, squinting to see as her eyes adjust to the gloom: *9:48. Been out about an hour…* She stretches, rising to get the flashlight in the pantry.

Stumbling to the kitchen, she trips on a chair in the den, stubbing her toe. She rummages in the junk drawer in the pantry and finds the light. The beam is weak, yellow. She shakes the torch and it gets a little brighter, but not much. *It'll do for now,* she decides. As she pans the beam around the apartment, the furnishings appear different, similar, but different. *Older, perhaps.*

"Trick of the shadows, that's all…"

Marion walks to the bathroom, her bladder full. Sitting on the commode, she turns out the light, not wanting to waste the battery. She had neglected to get fresh ones at the store yesterday. She will remedy that tomorrow.

She goes to her bedroom, hoping to find another flashlight. The lightning slashes again, the intensity of the storm increasing. It is raining even harder now, a deluge. The air is thin, musty, and very cold. In the beam of the light, she can see her breath. She shivers and her skin prickles from the chill. In the bedroom, she sees that the furniture is again arranged differently than she remembered. It looks strange; the bedclothes are unrecognizable. She stumbles again and crashes to the floor, hitting her forehead on the post of the bed.

"Christ!"

Marion brings her hand up to her head, and feels a small gash there. It is bleeding, but not heavily. She stands and goes over to the vanity, where she has some first aid items in one of the drawers. Finally, she locates the Band-Aids and iodine. Looking into the mirror, she screams.

In the mirror, she sees her silhouette, but it is not her. The reflection looks like her, but has no cut on the forehead. It has the same attire, but the movements are off, as though they are delayed, which she knows is impossible.

"Marion?" The image in the mirror is speaking, but Marion is not. Her head feels light. Another bolt flashes a bluish cast over the macabre scene. In the mirror, Marion can see that the room is the same, but there is another person behind her: She spins around, holding the flashlight in front of her like a weapon. There is a figure standing there. *Looming.* It is a man who appears to be in his late forties attired in a dark suit, slim and clean-shaven; his face is vaguely familiar, as though she has met him before, yet too perfect, waxen.

"Good evening, Mother," he says. His voice is reedy, halting. "It's me, Patrick."

Marion shrieks again, bringing her hand to her face. "How-*how did you get in here?*" She tries to control the timbre of her voice, fails.

The man's head deliberately tilts to the side as he stares at her, his milky eyes unblinking in the wan glow of the flashlight.

Behind her: "The same way I did, Marion," her sister's voice coos from the mirror. "Through your dreams. Your fears."

Marion quickly turns to face the mirror again. The reflection looks exactly like her, but it is moving independently. In the background, Patrick is still standing with his head cocked to the side, like a puppy trying to sort out where a sound is coming from. He shuffles a few steps forward, stiff, slow, then stops.

She holds the reflection's gaze, looking directly into its eyes. "Why are you here? Why is Patrick home? *What is happening?*"

The mirror image laughs quietly, shaking her head. Patrick moves forward once more and stops.

"Don't you want us here?" the likeness asks from the other side of the looking glass.

Marion does not know what to say. She tries to string words together in her mind, but they are jumbled, her thoughts foreign, baroque. She swings the light up into the mirror: The beam does not reflect back, but passes through the image's body and travels to a point of infinity on the horizon line on the opposite side of the glass. She swallows in incomprehension.

"I-I must be dreaming now," Marion says at last. The image responds a few milliseconds later, mimicking the mouth movements, but actually replying: "No. You're not dreaming now. We are here with you, on this night. We have not abandoned you, Marion, we just had to move on … it was never personal. We just couldn't stay anymore. You deserve the truth."

In the mirror, Patrick moves forward again, and Marion now hears the whine of his internal gears and machinery. The wind blusters against the building as the rain continues. Another lightning flash reveals a few more details of his face: The gaps on either side of his chin where the jaw is configured to articulate when he speaks, the blank, featureless glass eyes that roll in the hollows of the automaton's head. He pauses once more, now just inches from Marion.

"We are here to comfort you in this time of great need, Mother. Father will be here soon."

Marion closes her eyes, feeling faint. Her heart skips as a crack of thunder fills the space. Lightning flashes through her eyelids, momentarily reddening the scene, as she yields.

III

When she is found a few days later, Marion will be on the living room loveseat in a state of relaxation with her eyes closed. She will have a flashlight in her hand, and she will have a cut on her forehead; the blood will be dry.

The building supervisor will be the one to find her, as he has been watching her movements for days, ever since she came to his unit and explained that her son and sister will be visiting soon, and she wants to introduce them. The supervisor will have found the conversation disturbing, as he remembered when the son died—while visiting family in Australia some years prior—and that her sister, Annette, never returned to the unit they shared after she went to hospice. As far as he understood it, Annette had passed away after a tough battle with cervical cancer. In fact, Marion told him the news herself.

When the Medical Examiner arrives, she will inspect the premises, and find no signs of foul play, just a well-conditioned older woman in repose. Nothing suspicious will be in the apartment. Going room by room, the M.E.'s team will photograph the scene, and will note that one of the bedrooms has many dummies and puppets decorating it. One particularly impressive figure will be in the woman's bedroom, facing a large vanity with a shattered mirror; its eye sockets will be empty.

Upon further inspection at the morgue, the M.E. will discover that the woman has clinical Lewy Body Dementia, and that her eyes, strangely, are milky white—as though they never had pupils or irises. Her body will be cremated; no one will claim the ashes. The case will then be closed, and the apartment emptied.

Her obituary will sum up Marion's life in two neat paragraphs.

REFLECTING ON REFLECTIONS

BRUCE BOSTON

Mirrors facing mirrors
cast reflections
upon reflections,

fast as the speed of light,
duplicating reality
down a tunnel to infinity

until even the world's
most powerful telescopes
peering down that tunnel

can distinguish nothing
more than the fuzzy pinprick
of a telescope looking back.

PRAYER

MORT CASTLE

THE MAN FLOATS to seeming awareness, though dazed, then descends once more into unconsciousness. His dry lips sometimes make a tiny *peh-peh* noise, like something you'd hear in the woods late at night without recognizing the source.

Then he says quite plainly, "Tylenol."

> They surround you with comfort. Angels.
>
> No, those who will help you die.
>
> *Are you in pain?*
>
> *Should I get you something?*
>
> *Do you need something, Mr. Jablonski? Hank?*
>
> It's all right. You think you've said that but you can't be sure. You open your eyes.
>
> The priest is here. Nice guy. You've spoken with him. Filipino, hardly any accent.
>
> He's here to give you Last Rites.
>
> He's here for your confession.

April 16, 2015

Unit 17

Hospice of the Comforter

The airy sunlight suffuses the room.

The Christ on the crucifix above the bed seems at peace.

Hank. That's what he asked to be called when the Comforter took him in. Hank, Henry Jablonski.

A good man, a good Catholic.

Hank Jablonski had sense, knew that he would most likely be alone for this—transition—and so he planned wisely and the money saved by years of frugality would take care of his earthly ending and what was left over would go to the church.

The chaplain of the Comforter, Father Witmer Tortosa, seated at the bedside, has talked with Father Kelso at St. Joseph the Worker, and knows the regard Hank's parish priest has for this dying man. Hank was working class, bought a house on the GI Bill, married young: Laura, his high school sweetheart. Maybe the last generation to do all right without a college degree: Sold janitorial supplies and washroom cleaning services. Lost his wife to cancer when their only child was eight.

Mary was the daughter's name.

Sad about Mary, tragic, but Hank accepted the will of God.

Hank Jablonski had faith.

Hank's eyes are closed, his face placid, but his lips move.

Father Witmer Tortosa leans in closer. Hank's breath is sweet, like flowers.

"Mr. . . . Hank?" Though he does not call Hank "my son"—the 33-year-old Father Witmer was ordained only two years ago—he feels the eternal connection of Holy Mother Church, that blessed assurance, that he and this man share.

They believe.

In an age of unbelief and disbelief and disdain of belief, they believe.

They believe in the Father and the Son and the Holy Spirit.

They believe in salvation.

They believe in prayer.

Yes, Father Witmer has sometimes doubted his own personal abilities, sometimes questioned not what God has asked of him, never that, but his own adequacy when he has been summoned to do what a priest must, to ease the fears of the dying, to help them leave this world in a state of grace so that they might dwell forever with the Lord.

Father Witmer does not doubt: *Blessed be the name of the Lord.*

"Hank?" Father Witmer touches Hank Jablonski's shoulder, not expecting an answer, lucidity.

"Father Witmer." Hank's voice is quiet but does not seem weak or even for that matter old.

"I am here," Father Witmer says.

"There were four Marys," Hank says. "I don't believe that was coincidence. I didn't understand it then and do not fully understand it now. My daughter was Mary. There were other Marys …"

6:30 AM
Wednesday September 29, 1982
Elk Grove Village, Illinois

She wakes with a scratchy throat and a sniffily nose. She does not want to stay home from school. She likes school.

Her mom talks sense. She needed to stay home today, really, so she can nip this in the bud and besides, she doesn't want to infect others.

You're not being a friend when you share your viruses, her father says. Stay in your pajamas, kiddo, watch some *Love Boat* reruns. Drink lots of OJ. Take a Tylenol.

And she reluctantly says okay and next thing you know, there's a heavy thump and her father finds her unconscious on the bathroom floor.

The paramedics are damned good. If there had been a way to save her, they'd have saved her.

She is pronounced dead at Alexian Brothers Medical Center in Elk Grove Village. She was 12 years old.

Her name was Mary.

April 16, 2015
Unit 17
Hospice of the Comforter

"Your daughter? I do not understand."

Is that a ticking laugh or a faint precursor of the death gurgle? It is not a sound that Father Witmer has ever before heard. Its unfamiliarity disturbs him like a subtle threat.

"No, you do not understand."

> Eight people dead.
> Eight people dead.
> How many times during how many sleepless nights did you tell yourself you were not responsible. You had to say it aloud sometimes, like a prayer, like saying the Rosary:
> I did not kill them.
> I did not kill them.
> But the one, that one...
> Evil. He was truly evil.
> But even so, I did not kill him.
> I did not.
> God killed him.

Father Witmer says. "The dead people."

Hank has been whispering: *Marys and dead people and terrible nights without sleep. A God Who killed...*

The word most clearly enunciated: Evil.

Father Witmer senses this is not the incoherent muttering of a man giving up the ghost. Father Witmer cannot stop himself from thinking he is on the verge of learning something dreadful and important.

Like working a toothache that you probe to greater pain with the tip of your tongue, Father Witmer urges, "Tell me."

Ꮬ ∞ ᏸ

Mary Jablonski grew up motherless and step-motherless.

You see, things were different back then. I lost my Laura, lost her when I loved her so much. That was it. I knew there would never be another woman for me.

Mary had the nuns at St. Joseph's, and they were good to her, they were very kind and patient, and across the street, we had the Lawsons and the Radeckis, and they had lots of kids, lots of girls, and she was with them all the time. Right after school, she'd go right over to Toni and Louise Radecki's house and be there until I got home from work, and if I was going to be late, I'd call and Mrs. Radecki would feed her. Oh, we lived in the suburbs and people were laughing even back then about how the suburbs are dull and how everyone in each ticky-tacky house was really all alone, but that's not how it was: we had neighborhoods with good people and it was okay.

Mary never gave me one bit of trouble. Never. I'm being truthful, not just because I loved her and was so proud of her and not just because I lost her. I remember, she wanted a hamster when she was in third grade. The deal was, it would be *her* hamster and she had to take care of it. So she got the hamster—she called it Snorky, like that TV show, *The Banana Splits*—and she took care of it. I never had to do a thing, not even remind her. And when Snorky died, we talked about it, I remember, and then we buried her hamster. She never wanted another pet, not even a fish.

The closest Catholic high school was 22 miles away. It was the other direction from my territory so taking her and picking her up, well, it just wouldn't have been practical …

Okay, tell the truth, I couldn't really afford it.

Lots of Catholic kids went to the public high school, Arlington Heights. It was fine. She liked it. She got good grades. She didn't do drugs or alcohol.

Seventeen, she wants to date and I talk with Mrs. Radecki about it and we set up rules and all. I meet the guys she dates, and they're okay high school guys, a couple with hair longer than I care for, but it's okay, they're nice enough, and really, there was never anything serious going on, not then.

And I felt God was watching over her, my Mary.

I don't understand the ways of God. We see through a glass darkly, but there will be a time when we will understand. I've talked a lot about this with Father Brennan and then Father Kelso when he replaced Father Brennan.

We know God is there and watches over us...

I believe that.

So Mary graduates and takes courses at Moser Secretarial School in Chicago, she rides in on the train, and no surprise, she graduates with honors and gets a good job at Sears. She's living at home, saving money, thinking about buying a clean used Pacer—yeah, people bought Pacers back then, funny looking cars—and then she meets him.

I liked him. I liked the way he smiled, like he wasn't too full of himself, and I liked his handshake, because it didn't say he had anything to prove, and I liked the way he treated Mary, always the gentleman.

I liked him.

I *liked* him.

He told me, after they'd been dating for a while, that way back when the boat got to the USA, great grandpa realized if you want to succeed in this country, it's better for your name not to have too many "Cs" or "Zs" or end in an "i" or an "o."

That's how Kwiatkowski became Kwiat.

That was his name: John Kwiat.

"So many," Hank says.

His eyes open. He looks at the priest and Father Witmer can feel himself being seen.

"Can you tell me why so many had to die, Father?"

ଔ ∞ ஐ

Noon
Wednesday September 29, 1982

The second person to be killed was Adam Janus. He was 27 years old, had a civil service job, the PO, but stayed home that day. Not feeling well. The sniffles.

Had some lunch.

Going to take two Tylenol and get some rest.

A few minutes later, staggers into kitchen and collapses.

Taken to Northwest Community Hospital.

Pronounced dead.

3:45 PM
September 29, 1982
Winfield, Illinois

They call her Lynn, Lynn Reiner.

She is 27.

There's a new baby at home, the Reiners' fourth child.

An excellent mother, her husband later said.

Not feeling well, general achiness.

Two Extra-Strength Tylenol.

She is pronounced dead at Central DuPage Hospital.

Lynn Reiner.

Her full name: Mary "Lynn" Reiner.

April 16, 2015
Unit 17
Hospice of the Comforter

"That was the third Mary."

"Yes," Father Witmer replies, as though having a rational conversation.

Silently, he prays:

Come, Holy Spirit,
Replace the turbulence within us
    with a sacred calm.
Replace the anxiety within us
    with a quiet confidence.
Replace the fear within us
    with a strong faith.

"The first Mary was my child."

Father, Son, Holy Spirit, Father Witmer prays. There seems a humid pressure around his head, a circling echo: *Marys and dead people and a God Who killed and Evil Evil Evil...*

She came home late from a date with John Kwiat, much later than usual. I was in bed, pretty much asleep, just enough to hear her bedroom door close maybe louder than normal—maybe.

Next day, Saturday, I'm up at maybe 8:30 but Mary's not around. That's not like her. She's the original early bird.

I knock on her door.

Go away, is what she says, and she doesn't sound right.

No, let's talk, Mary.

No, go away.

The door's locked. I rattle the handle.

Mary.

And I wait a while and the door opens and there she is, and she isn't in a nightgown, still wearing her Friday night clothes, and she has been crying, and she looks bad.

Daddy...

Tell me.

And I try to put my arms around her but she doesn't let me. She backs up and then we're both sitting side by side on her rumpled up but still made bed.

Please, I say to her, please talk to me.

And after what seems like a long time, she does. She tells me and it sounds like she's reading a foreign language. She can make out the words, but not their meaning.

And I am praying, Jesus, Jesus, Jesus, but not aloud, and when I take her hand, she doesn't pull away.

We can't let him…

Maybe it was my fault. Maybe I encouraged him. I don't know. He started, when he started, I should have said No, and then… I don't know. But he had no right…

Jesus, Jesus, Jesus.

I want to kill him.

You can't do anything. You can't. You know what would happen to you. I don't know what would happen to me.

The police.

No! I'm ashamed. I am ashamed. No one can know! No one can ever know.

Will you pray with me?

She does.

At least she gets down on her knees with me. And I am praying and maybe she is praying but her prayers end with sobbing.

I thought, or maybe I thought I thought, it would be okay.

Then one day I get home from work. The day had been fairly warm for autumn, right around 55-60, but it was kind of drizzly. A lot of days felt drizzly.

Mary was in the garage.

She was hanging from a few feet of clothesline.

Her face was so blue it was almost black.

That was Tuesday, September 29, 1981.

I prayed. This was how I prayed:

Lord,
Give me strength.
No, Lord! I do not ask for strength to bear my suffering.
All must suffer.

On the Cross, The Son of God suffered and died.

We all suffer as we must.

Lord, I do not ask for my soul to be filled with compassion.

I do not want compassion because it would make me able to forgive. I do not want to forgive.

Our Father Who Art in Heaven, Our Father Who Sees all Things Upon this Earth, Our Father Who is the God of Righteousness and Fairness and Truth:

Give me Justice!

Give me Justice!

In the name of the Father and the Son and the Holy Spirit.

Amen.

5 PM
Wednesday September 29, 1982
Arlington Heights, Illinois

Adam Janus's younger brother Stanley and his wife, Theresa, left the hospital where Adam had been pronounced dead. They had a funeral to plan. They went to Adam's nearby home.

Stanley's head was pounding. His back hurt. A slipped disc, maybe, something, but he suffered from chronic back pain.

His wife gave him two Tylenol. She might have made a funny-in-sad-times remark like, "These are supposed to bring relief and I could use some myself," and then she took two Tylenol as well.

Maybe Stanley heard that comment before he went down.

Maybe Theresa regretted saying it as she fell.

6:30 PM
Wednesday September 29, 1982
Lombard Illinois

Mary McFarland was 31 years old, employed at the Illinois Bell telephone store. She had a severe headache, went into the employees' back room, took several Tylenol, and collapsed.

Mary McFarland was not pronounced dead until 3:15 in the morning of the next day at Good Samaritan Hospital in Downers Grove...The fourth Mary.

Lab reports came in relatively quickly for an era before the ubiquitous computer. Six had died of cyanide poisoning. Each victim had ingested 100 to 1,000 times the amount of potassium cyanide needed to cause death. Basically, cyanide asphyxiates you from within. It inhibits red blood cells from utilizing oxygen. In high doses, it usually causes a quick, but not merciful, death.

The hunch of an Arlington Heights public health nurse, Helen Jensen—whose sensitive sense of smell detected the scent of almonds—and the research of Dr. Thomas Kim, Medical Director of Northwest Community Hospital's ICU, and the investigations of the Cook County Medical Examiner's Office, the Chicago Police Department, and various northwest suburban police departments led to the conclusion that bottles of Tylenol had been taken from the shelves of various supermarkets and drug stores over a period of several weeks by person or persons unknown, that said person or persons added the cyanide to the capsules, then returned to the stores to place the bottles back on the shelves. Five bottles were initially and correctly linked to these initial victims' deaths. Three other tampered-with bottles were discovered.

There was panic. Not just in and around Chicago. Across the nation.

Johnson & Johnson, manufacturers of Tylenol, issued warnings and a recall of all Tylenol products. The company halted Tylenol production and put an indefinite hiatus on advertising. Johnson & Johnson executives consulted with their ad agencies about the possibility of regaining public trust.

Legislators frantically discussed the need for rapid reform in the laws and regulations for the packaging of over-the-counter substances.

The FBI established a strong link to the Chicago Police Department, Illinois suburban police departments, and police departments throughout the country.

The hunt was on for The Tylenol Killer.

April 16, 2015
Unit 17
Hospice of the Comforter

"What is it … What is it you *are* telling me?" Father Witmer says. "You must tell me, you must unburden yourself. What is it … What did you do?"

Hank does not answer.

Friday October 1, 1982
Chicago, Illinois

She was blond, and one of the rare people who truly could be deemed vivacious. Paula Prince lived in Old Town, which was being gentrified and cleansed of hippies to make way for the ascendant Yuppies. She was a flight attendant for United, loved flying, traveling, meeting new people.

But she had a headache, wanted to shake it before she met her sister for dinner, and so she went to Walgreen's and bought a bottle of Tylenol.

Surveillance cameras were not yet everywhere, but Walgreen's did have a camera focused on the counter.

There exists a videotape of Paula Prince purchasing her own death.

> My Mary died and then Mary and then Adam
> and then Lynn Mary and then Stanley and then
> Theresa and then Mary and then Paula and I did
> not understand why they had to die did not even

have a clue and there is yet so much I do not know
and may never know God Who is God Now and
Forever understands

Saturday, October 2, 1982
Schaumburg, Illinois

John Kwiat awakens with a Dr. Doom tequila shots hangover, but,
don't do the crime if you can't do the time, right?

A little water splashed on the face, a little cold water sloshed into
a glass, two Tylenols from the bottle in the medicine cabinet into the
palm and here we go...

And maybe there's time to think Uh-oh or maybe think, Nah,
what are the odds, no problem, but in seconds, the whirl of acute
dizziness hits and he's gasping for air and his legs won't hold him and
then he's on the floor and convulsing and dying.

He is not found until Tuesday, October 5.

"I asked God for justice. He gave me justice. The others... I do not
understand. John Kwiat was justice."

Father Witmer wants to yell and is careful not to. "Did you kill
John Kwiat?" Then he whispers, "Did you kill the others?"

Hank's eyes are shut.

There's that awful sound of his lips: *Peh-peh* noise.

Father Witmer administers the Last Rites of the Holy Catholic
Church.

Father Witmer does not begin his research until the evening of
Tuesday, April 21, a day after the burial of Henry Jablonski in Queen
of Angels. He must. He cannot simply accept not knowing. There
are too many intimations of evil.

In his room at Hospice of the Comforter, he takes to his HP
laptop and Google.

1982. It was the year he was born.

(Does this have meaning, that it was the year, too, of the Tylenol Murders?)

Now, in 2015, the case remains open.

Father Witmer learns no one was ever charged for tampering with the bottles of Tylenol.

Father Witmer learns no one was ever charged with murder.

Father Witmer learns there were seven victims of the Tylenol Killer: Mary Kellerman, Adam Janus, Lynn Mary Reiner, Stanley Janus, Theresa Janus, Mary McFarland, and Paula Prince.

There were seven victims.

Father Witmer cannot find John Kwiat.

Seven victims.

He cannot find a death notice for a John Kwiat in the state of Illinois in 1982.

Other Google combinations tell him that in 2015, there are more than 3,000 people in the United States who are named John Kwiat or something fairly close or similar. None of a possible right age in Schaumburg, nor in the Northwest Suburbs of Illinois.

Perhaps more dogged and learned researchers could learn more, but Father Witmer decides it is profitless to continue.

Father Witmer sinks to his knees.

Father Witmer prays. He prays late into the night and fears he will find no feeling of relief or validation with the morning.

Father Witmer prays: Lord, I believe; help my unbelief!

MIRROR IMAGE

MARGE SIMON

In
the glass,
my twin smiles,
runs her hands lightly
over our face, down
our full breasts,
gently massaging
the tender skin,
smiling back at me
as she reaches for
the little bottle
of pills that she
knows are not
good for us,
lifts the cup
of water
to our
lips.

"It is the end
of days," she says,
"we must be one."

My
eyes never
leave her face.
as I swallow them,
one by one,
careful not to
spill a drop
from the
glass.

THE AGONIZING GUILT OF RELIEF
(LAST DAYS OF A READY-MADE VICTIM)

PAUL MICHAEL ANDERSON

BEN RACED down Mitchum Street, last year's boots pounding the shoveled sidewalks, trying to outrun the brightening streetlamps. Not for the first time, he wished he had a car.

Goddammit! he thought and didn't know if he was cursing the school therapist or himself.

The street blurred by, houses closed off with curtains and blinds, their Christmas lights dark. The corners of months-old Clinton/Gore and Dole/Kemp lawn signs poked out of the snow, reaching for him.

The tall fence of McMillian Elementary reared up, and his boots slid on a patch of ice. A quick grab of a post saved him from a bone-rattling crash. He dashed across the lawn on a diagonal, kicking up clumps of snow, hoping he wasn't too late, hoping—in spite of the twenty-degree day—Jude had waited like Ben asked.

He skidded to a stop at the edge of the playground, taking in the empty swings, the barren slide, the abandoned merry-go-round.

"*Fuck*," he panted, his exhale a white puff. A stitch burned in his side, matching the molten core of anxiety in his stomach.

Jude hadn't waited—of course Jude hadn't waited. How could Ben expect Jude to wait when he was over an hour late on the last day before Christmas break?

Which meant Jude was at home, with their father, who'd bragged about early shifts all week.

"*Fuck*," he panted again, the stitch abating, the anxious core growing, spreading tendrils to his limbs.

He knew he needed to run, but a darker part whispered that he was already too late, so why hurry? What could he possibly gain? Wasted effort.

He was starting back across the yard when he heard the *thunk* of a metal door closing and a woman's voice: "Ben? Ben Sheever?"

He turned to see a young woman, holding a large pile of children's workbooks and construction paper, on the other side of the playground area, in the near-empty teacher's lot. "Hi, Ms. Quinn."

"Looking for Jude?"

"Mmm-hmm," he said through his teeth, then made himself stop. Ms. Quinn had at least tried to help, had been the one adult who had tried to do the right thing. "Yes, Ms. Quinn."

"You just missed him," she said, walking to her car. "He left a few minutes ago. Thought of inviting him back in, but I knew he'd say no."

She shot him a look that, even across the playground—and a part of him felt ridiculous to stay on one side, to not go over and help, but that would put him farther away from Jude and Dad and home—he read loud and clear. Jude inexorably always loved his teachers, even if his teachers didn't love him back, but Jude had soured on his third grade teacher, in the midst of the meetings and statements and counselors, by the time Halloween rolled around.

He started back towards Mitchum Street, the idea he might catch Jude before the boy reached home squirting much-needed adrenaline into his muscles, banishing the dark whispering.

"Thanks, Ms. Quinn," he said, meaning it.

"And, Ben—?" she called and her voice was a fishhook; his head turned, saw the look on her face, and stopped. He wondered if the school board president had come to talk to her, as he had come to talk to Ben's father. Ben didn't doubt it, but it wouldn't have been over beer in the kitchen, with statements like "I'll take care of it."

The school board president wasn't Ms. Quinn's friend, as he was Ben's father's.

"Take care of Jude," she said now.

"I will," Ben said and started running.

He heard a startled cry of pain as he reached the house, and he sprinted faster, taking the porch steps three at a time and banging through the front door.

"Oh great," he heard his father say from down the hall, "the goddamn cavalry."

He burst into the kitchen. A tableau from hell in front of him: Jude crumbled against the refrigerator in one corner, holding his arm as if it were broken; their father at the kitchen table in the other, the top button of his Cobb County Sheriff's Office uniform undone, holding a bottle of Rolling Rock and glaring at it.

"Jesus," Ben breathed, and went to Jude. Jude burrowed into his chest. Ben felt the arm under the long-sleeve—a too-large hand-me-down from Ben—and didn't feel a break, although Jude grunted when Ben's probing fingers squeezed.

"Look up, dude," Ben whispered, tilting Jude's chin. Their father had clipped the boy along his right cheekbone, not hard enough to break—their father was good like that—but enough for the skin to swell and darken. It reminded Ben, absurdly, of water in a balloon—the gentle sloping rise. He didn't press against it.

Rage thrummed through his bloodstream. At his father for doing this. At himself for not getting to Jude in time.

At Jude, for not knowing this would happen.

He's getting bad again, a voice murmured in the back of his mind.

"What the *fuck*, Dad?" he yelled, his anger belied by the crack in his voice.

"Watch your language," Marcus Sheever muttered, not looking away from the Rolling Rock. Ben saw that Marcus's knuckles were chaffed and his head rang.

"What *happened?*"

Still their father wouldn't look up. "Caught him playing with my beer."

Jude sniffed against Ben's shirt. "I was getting him his drink. That's all."

Ben looked back and didn't miss the flicker in Marcus's eyes. He could see it all: their father coming home, Jude—against all logic—excited and eager, running to the fridge to get Marcus his one beer of the evening, Marcus getting annoyed, grabbing at the bottle but Jude not letting go quickly enough, Marcus winding up while jerking the beer from the boy.

Ben saw it so clearly, it could've been happening right now.

Marcus finally looked up, and Ben saw no satisfaction in his father's gaze, no challenge, no troll-like belligerence. Marcus wasn't a stereotypical child-abuser like on a Made-for-TV movie. It would have been easier—to hate him, to bring it all to an end back in September—if he was.

But he had never done this to Ben, had never harmed their mother (not that their mother stuck around long enough).

Just Jude.

He got his arm around Jude's shoulders, helped his brother up. The molten core of anxiety was cooling—the worst was known—but not disappearing. Instead it hardened, settled in, made it impossible to take deep breaths.

"C'mon, Jude," he said, glaring at their father, and feeling useless in his inability to do anything else. "Let's get you cleaned up."

He led the boy to the upstairs bathroom and examined him.

The bruises along the shoulder were dark; a little more pressure, if Jude had been holding onto the beer a little tighter, and the shoulder would've popped from its socket.

Yes, their father was good. A popped socket could be home-mended, but it would still require a temporary sling, which was noticeable.

The shiner on Jude's face was *also* noticeable but... well, Jude was always getting punched at school, wasn't he? This could've been just an early Christmas present from the tormentors of McMillian Elementary.

It wouldn't have been the first time their father had used that excuse.

He's getting bad again, the interior voice murmured.

Ben got Jude back into his shirt and led him down the hall. Jude asked, "You wanna come read comics with me, Benny?" His eyes were dry now, the shiner coming along nicely, making one eye squint as he looked into his bedroom.

Ben followed his gaze, taking in the neatly organized books on the bookcase, the comics on the desk, the action figures from *Toy Story* and the *X-Men* cartoon show lining his windowsill—a ready display for friends who didn't exist.

He looked back at his brother's open, earnest, *small*—they were nine years apart—face. He had the face of a bull's-eye. Every school, every *class*, had one. The ready-made victim. The one who just didn't *fit*. The one whose timing was off, whose answer was either too right or too wrong, whose interests and look weren't *in*. They weren't obnoxious, or toxic, or even ugly in a broad sense of the word. They were just *wrong*, and everyone knew it. The one even the wallflowers of school felt impunity to pick on.

Ben had one in his senior class—Amanda Hofsteader. Not dumb, not bright, not pretty in the most generous sense of the word. She got it worst from the girls, who seemed to imbue Amanda with all their worst nightmares. She drifted through the halls of Ben Franklin High School, never seeming to know it was as bad as it was, or, if she did, burying it so deep as to make herself almost beatific.

Much like Ben imagined Jude at McMillian Elementary. But Jude got it worse because he kept *trying* to get along in a nerve-wracking turn-the-other-cheek way, which seemed to rile everyone.

"You all right, Benny?" Jude asked.

He looked like their mother. Which was part of the problem with their father. In all sorts of ways.

"Yeah," he said, his voice thick.

"So, you wanna read comics?"

"Sure," Ben said, and his throat clicked, and then it was normal again. "But no Spider-Man, though. I'm sick to friggin *death* of Spider-Man."

Jude grinned, and Ben just felt sick.

Ben watched his father sleep on the couch.

Behind them, the television was on, sound low, with NBC playing through the end of *Late Night with Conan O'Brien*. The light from the screen threw Ben's shadow, long and menacing, across Marcus's slack face.

He's getting bad again, the internal voice murmured.

Ben's fists clenched at the end of rod-stiff arms that couldn't do anything.

Marcus snorted in his sleep. He didn't look evil, or monstrous, or anything but what he was—a man. A county sheriff's deputy. Liked by everyone. And when Ben and Jude's mother took off with that undergrad, everyone just clucked their tongues and said, well, what do you expect from Alana Sheever, *nee* Thompson? Everyone knew the Thompsons were a flighty bunch.

But at least Ben and Jude had a good father.

And what good father beat his youngest son?

He slowed down when he was almost caught, the voice went on, *but now he knows he's safe and he doesn't have to worry, anymore._*

Ben wanted to shake his head until he rattled the voice out of his skull. No, that wasn't true, *wasn't* true. That gave hint to some kind of animal cunning and malevolence in Marcus Sheever and he *wasn't* like that. Was he?

Wasn't that why Ben had gone to talk to Ms. Quinn, and then one of Jude's principals last fall? Because Marcus was just getting worse—his irritation mounting, the time he was a normal father fading, the sharp, over-correcting jabs more common, double rations if Jude tried to make up for whatever negligible thing he had done wrong? It'd taken Ben time to see the increase, but it was there. The hits were creeping up from Jude's chest and onto his face. It was this last bit that had made what Ben said palatable to Ms. Quinn. Jude might've been an every-day target for the bullies at McMillian, but there were cafeteria and recess monitors to halt things.

Not at home.

And it showed.

Ben's jaw clenched until the pressure sang in his ears.

Not that it mattered much, did it? the internal voice said. *Send the balloon up, and it got popped by the school board president. And suddenly…*

And suddenly the questions from the counselors were focusing more on *Ben* and his relationship with his father. The protocol Ben had learned from television—tell adults and they would come in and fix everything—was going off the rails. Suddenly Marcus was *there*, looking at either Ben, or Ben and Jude, or Jude alone, during these questioning sessions. Suddenly, Ms. Quinn wasn't there to help, and Jude…

"Jude *backed you up*," Ben hissed, softly.

Jude, who'd never been fully on-board with what Ben was doing, never corroborated. Yes, it was the bullies at school. No, Marcus was nothing but what he appeared to be: a loving single father.

He didn't do it out of fear, Ben thought, but out of his essential *Jude*-ness. The Jude that saw only the good in people (he'd once explained to Ben that a particular bully happened to be a very good artist, as if that made up for the fact that he'd made Jude eat sand). That quality in Jude seemed amplified when it came to their father; it reminded Ben of how *he'd* seen Marcus in the years before Jude was born and their mother ran off. Back then, Marcus was just… a dad. Attentive, but not domineering. An authoritarian, but not a dictator. Caring.

And that quality that everyone hated got Marcus out of the fire, got Ben slammed into counseling because *of course* this all stemmed from teenage angst and upcoming graduation and repressed anger over the absence of his mother.

Marcus grunted in his sleep, turned over, exposing the nape of his neck. Ben stared at it, imagining getting a kitchen knife from the drawer and—

He shook the thought away. That was useless—more Made-for-TV-Movie garbage. As useless as "telling an adult."

What are you going to do? the interior voice asked.

Talking hadn't helped, obviously. Any other idea Ben might've had was strictly the domain of television—not that his school therapist wouldn't have *loved* to hear about them.

And what happens after graduation? What happens when—

"Shut up," he whispered, squeezing his eyes shut, like a kid scared of the bogeyman. "Shut up, shut up, shut *up*."

And, for a wonder, the voice did.

He felt that hard lead ball of anxiety in his gut, felt the weight of hopelessness and the future settling onto his shoulders and, for the first time, became truly aware of the pressure he was under, like a deep-sea fish finally coming to realize the sheer tonnage of water surrounding him, waiting for a weak moment to crush him.

Between the pressure on his shoulders and the pressure in his gut, he was stuck in a huge vice, slowly turning, slowly tightening. He wanted to scream, just to release some of the pressure, but he was a boiler with a busted vent. No relief.

"Something will change," he breathed. "Something will give. It has to."

His father offered a throaty snore. Behind Ben, a syndicated Top 40 music program played on television. Sheryl Crow was asking, if it makes him happy, why the hell was he so sad?

He went upstairs and checked on Jude, who lay facing the window, the moonlight flickering with falling snow, reflecting off the bruise.

When he went to bed, he avoided looking at the open envelope on his desk, but the voice was there, waiting in his head: *What are you going to do after graduation?*

ᘔ ∞ ᕽ

The scrape of metal on concrete and Jude's delighted laughter brought Ben up from a thin, scratchy sleep.

He cracked an eye open.

Eight-thirty, according to the nightstand clock.

He sat up and threw his legs over the side of the bed. The world outside his window was coated in rounded white edges of fresh snow. Marcus and Jude were at the mouth of their driveway, shoveling, their laughter coming out in white streamers from beneath thick winter caps.

Ben stood, a vein throbbing in his head. Marcus tossed a loose shovelful at Jude. Jude staggered, but kept upright, and tossed a shovelful of his own. His gloves looked comical—they were Ben's old ones, still too large for his hands.

Ben waited for the snow to sting Marcus's cold face, for it to get in his eyes, and for him take the flat of the shovel up the back of Jude's head.

Instead he dropped the shovel, grabbed a handful of snow from a mound, squeezed it, and lobbed the ball at his youngest son. Jude returned the favor. Their laughter rang like church bells.

Ben let out a breath he didn't know he was holding.

It's okay," he said.

The envelope on his desk caught his eye. He stuck his English assignment—*Grendel*, by John Gardner—on top of it, got dressed, and headed downstairs.

He entered the kitchen as the back door opened, Jude and Marcus walking in.

"We thought we were gonna have to come upstairs and throw a snowball at ya!" Marcus said, rolling his shoulders free of snow. Behind him, the winter screen fogged.

"Dad said we're gonna have hot chocolate!" Jude said, grinning, stopping in front of Marcus. "Want some, Benny?"

Ben's mouth stretched into what he thought was a grin—the right side of Jude's face was dark, not as swollen as last night, but enough to make the core in his gut roll forebodingly. "Sure, bud."

Jude hunkered down to unlace his snow-caked boots.

Marcus tried moving around him, but couldn't. "You sleep okay?" he asked Ben. "Got bags under your eyes."

Ben's jaw tightened. "Not as much as I would've liked."

He wanted to scream—at Jude, at their father, at everything: *Why are you acting so fucking normal? Did last night not happen? Look at Jude's goddam face!*

"Hot chocolate will fix ya up," Marcus said, and tried to move around Jude again, but Jude was oblivious, working the soggy knot of his boots with numb fingers.

Ben saw the flicker in Marcus's eyes, the hardening.

"*Move!*" Marcus grunted and shoved Jude aside. Jude stumbled, his one foot half-in-half-out of his boot, and connected with the kitchen table hard enough to shove it a few inches along. He rebounded and went to his knees, hugging his side.

"*Jesus!*" Ben cried, zipping over to Jude. He got his arm around Jude, whose face was red with trying not to cry.

Marcus clomped around them to the stove, dropping puddles of melting snow, heels squeaking over the lino. "Should've gotten outta the way," he said, but low, the fatherly tone gone. He sounded robotic. He stared at the teakettle on the stove burner like he'd never seen such a thing.

Ben got Jude standing, his feet back into his boots. "C'mon," he said. "I wanna get some air to wake me up. Walk with me."

Jude nodded numbly and Ben led him outside, snagging his own jacket off the hook by the door. He spared a hot look back at their father. Marcus was still in the same position. His eyes were squeezed closed, as if struck with a sudden pain in his head. He reminded Ben of a toy that'd run out of power.

The cold was a solid force, settling against the bare skin of Ben's face like a mask, instantly numbing. He led Jude across the backyard to the tree line, the branches thin black talons against the white sky.

They didn't speak as they made their way deeper into the woods. Jude rubbed his side and matched Ben's pace.

Ben shoved his hands into his coat pockets, trying to even his breathing, trying to slow his heart. Jesus, a flicker in the eyes and then—nothing. From that flicker, Marcus and Jude might not've just been outside, laughing and throwing snowballs. They might not've just been talking about making hot chocolate.

He looked at Jude, who was watching his feet—the soft curve of his jaw, the slight uptick of his nose. Like their mother's.

Jude, the ready-made victim, just brought out the worst in everyone.

The further they got from the house, the better Ben felt, but that pressure was still there, pushing against his shoulders, pressing him against the hard solid cannonball in his gut.

But maybe it wasn't so bad—as he watched, Jude squeezed his side once, winced, then let go and, more or less, walked normally.

"You okay?" he asked.

"Uh-huh."

They reached a small crick. During the spring, it would swell with runoff, graduating from that Pennsylvania colloquialism into a full-fledged creek, but, for now, you could walk across it without getting the tops of your boots wet. Round snow hats capped the stones. They followed it and soon the creek merged into the Buchanan River.

Ben and Jude stopped at the edge, fifteen feet above the water.

It hadn't frozen over, not yet, but Ben could see it getting there— the shorelines furry with white and reaching for the other side, the water itself a thin black eddy in the middle, threading south. Across the river, the backyards of nicer homes were spotlighted by the sun.

Ben breathed deeply, taking in the cold air, the thick peaty smell of the minerals and earth of the Buchanan.

Jude sat down on the edge, his boots dangling. "Dad makes the best snowballs. You know that? I asked him if he'd show me, but he said it was a family secret. He'd tell me when I was older." He looked up at Ben. "Did he ever show you? Will you show me?"

Ben stared down at him. In the stark blacks and whites of the outdoors, the eggplant-colored bruise on his brother's face was like the dot on an exclamation point.

"No," he said, almost mechanically. *Is that all you can talk about? Really? All? Jesus Christ.*

Pressure momentarily throbbed behind his eyes and he squeezed them closed, willing it back, unconsciously looking like their father back in the kitchen.

"I gotta take a whiz," Jude said, and turned at the waist, boosting himself. His boots slipped a bit in the snow, dropping clumps over the edge.

Ben jerked his thumb over his shoulder. "Go in the trees. No indecent exposure out here, Sonny Jim. I don't got the cash to bail you out."

Jude laughed, passing him. "You're such a dork, Benny."

Ben smiled without showing teeth. "And one day you'll be just like me."

His brother laughed again, and stepped into the trees.

Ben's thin smile disappeared. He looked across the river, but the sunlight seemed colder now, the smell of the river cloying, the air freezer-burning his skin instead of numbing it.

"Hey, shake off and let's head back," he called, thinking their father would be gone for work by the time they arrived. "I gotta hankering from some Eggo waffles."

No answer.

He stepped towards the trees. "Jude?" He listened hard, that kind of listening where you hear ringing.

Finally, he heard—faintly—a single gasp, a sweaty *pah!* sound.

Ben took another step forward. "Jude?"

Now he could hear Jude panting.

"The hell?" He entered the tree line, following his brother's breathing.

He found Jude, in a triangle of white birch, seeing first a hand clenching a trunk, and the puddle of yellow urine at the base, threaded with blood.

He entered the triangle. "What the fuck?"

Jude looked up, his face cheese-colored and sweaty, one hand on his shriveled sex, the other clenching the tree. He stared at Ben, his eyes double-zeroes of pain and fear.

"It hurts, Benny. It *burns.*"

In Ben's head, Jude hit the side of the table again and again, with a neon sign flashing *kidney damage kidney damage kidney damage* between, and suddenly the vice was turning faster now, tighter.

A stray thought arced across the shocked expanse of his mind, like NBC's The More You Know comet: *He's gonna kill this kid.*

"Hey, what's this?" Jude asked.

Mid-afternoon. Marcus still at work. When they'd gotten back to the house, Ben had wrapped an icepack in a dishtowel and taped it to his brother's side.

They were in Ben's room, Ben sprawled on the bed, trying to decipher *Grendel* while Jude did little brother things, sitting at Ben's desk and rooting through Ben's stuff.

"What's what?" Ben asked, re-reading the same line for the third time. The words didn't want to stick; they were fuzzy black caterpillars that inched just outside his comprehension.

"This," Jude said and Ben heard a whisper of paper.

He looked up.

The open letter. He could see the Ohio State return address.

He was out of bed before his brain could catch up, snatching the envelope out of Jude's hands. "Gimme that."

Jude's eyes never left the envelope, his brow wrinkled.

"What is it?"

Ben looked from the envelope—he didn't need to pull the thick sheaf of papers out, had already memorized the cover letter: *Dear Mr. Sheever, After reviewing your application, we're delight to inform you—*to Jude, who stared up at him expectantly, not even put off by how Ben acted. His heart whammed within his chest harder than it should've, the air of his exhales prickly around his mouth.

He sat on the edge of his bed. "A letter." He swallowed. "I applied to Ohio State."

"Oh yeah? Did you get in?"

Ben pulled the papers from the envelope. Beginnings of financial aid and declaration of majors and meal options. Etc., etc., etc. "Yeah."

"That's cool, Benny! You gonna tell Dad?"

Ben's head snapped up. "No! And you're not gonna, either."

Jude squinted. "But, why? This is good news, right?"

For an instant, he felt that trickle of irritation that everyone must feel around his punch-me brother.

He flushed with guilt, as immediate as the irritation and stared at the letter. The packet felt so goddamn *thick*. "Yeah. No. Maybe." He shook his head. "I have no friggin idea. But until I do, keep your mouth shut, all right? To everyone—*especially* Dad."

"But Benny—"

"*No*," Ben hissed. "Okay? Just *no*."

Jude studied him a moment. All Ben could see was the goddamned bruise, highlighted by the light through the window.

Finally, his brother said, "Okay. Wanna go watch a movie, or something?"

"Sure," Ben said and Jude bounded out of the room.

Ben folded the papers and slid them back into the envelope. His hands shook. The muscles in his upper arms and shoulders jittered, over-taxed with adrenaline from a fight that didn't exist.

What are you going to do after graduation? the interior voice asked, and Ben didn't have an answer.

The snow continued to fall. The temperature continued to drop.

Ben hadn't noticed it immediately, but Jude finding the Ohio State letter had started a clock in his head. It pervaded his thinking. It kept him up until the late-late hours, when he would finally escape into a thin, unrestful sleep.

He found himself unable to *not* be in the same room with Marcus and Jude, but didn't know what to do once he was in there. The movies and primetime sitcoms were beyond his comprehension. He was constantly one-sentence behind whatever conversation Jude and Marcus might be having.

Even when the bruise on Jude's face faded, even when he stopped pissing blood, Ben saw the bruises still to come, the blood still to flow.

When he'd opened his mouth back in September, when he'd seen how the game was going to go and finally found the courage to *call* it, Marcus had settled, had stopped the irrevocable train of building tension and intensifying violence. Ben felt, for the first time in years, hope.

But that was gone now. The night beginning school break, the morning after—those events had obliterated them in a way dismissal from the counselors, the requirement of therapy, the *closing* of Jude's file, couldn't. It showed that the autumn hadn't been the end of something monstrous, but only a brief respite before …

… before what?

Well, that was what Ben was afraid of, wasn't it?

Christmas passed in a blur, although Jude and their father seemed to enjoy it. On Christmas night, a storm blew in hard, burying the town under nearly two feet of snow. Marcus was called in to assist Public Works and Ben and Jude huddled on the living room couch, watching movies and listening to the snow hit the windowpane like handfuls of spackle. Sometime in the third act of *Jumanji*, Jude fell asleep, leaving Ben with the sound of snow and Kristen Dunst asking her movie brother, "What do you think's gonna happen to you if you don't start talking?"

Try it, sis, Ben thought, settling in to give Jude as much room on the couch as possible. *It ain't as easy as it seems.*

Two days after Christmas, the temperatures shot into the giddy thirties, leaving a world dazzled with sun and filled with the drip-drip-dripping of snow.

Ben left Jude alone—when their father was still at work, of

course—and traipsed to the Buchanan River, the snow high enough, and his boots old enough, for some to get down his socks, soaking his feet.

The river had finally frozen over. Their dad had said as such, complaining about the kids who would try to skate on it or walk across it.

"Kids have no idea," Marcus said one night over a dinner of Stouffer's lasagna. None of the Sheever men were decent cooks. "They never think that one wrong step onto a weak patch of ice, into that water…" He shook his head. "It only takes an instant to regret a lifetime." Marcus paused, as if startled by what he'd said.

Now, Ben looked south and saw tiny pinpricks of black and blue, moving slowly under the Route 67 Bridge. They were probably egging each other on, seeing who would go the furthest out.

Ben watched them, then the ice itself. It *did* look thick enough, but there were troubling dark spots, particularly towards the center, where the thaw had begun its work. What would one of those kids do if his foot suddenly plunged into the near-zero water below?

Ben knew—fall and get swept away by the current, dead from hypothermia or drowning too quickly to be saved, their bodies finally getting stuck against some fallen tree in Butler County.

Ben was more interested in the other kids—what would *they* do, particularly if they'd been the ones egging the dead kid on? How would they live with that?

Ben shivered in a way that had nothing to do with the cold. All his thoughts cycled back to Jude. Jude was the kid whose foot went through the ice; the kid who, when that center of gravity was lost, could count the remainder of his life in minutes and seconds instead of decades and years.

"The kid without hope left," Ben breathed.

Who was the one, metaphorically, egging the kid on? Marcus with his whip-crack snaps of temper? Was it him, Ben, for failing to pull Jude back from the black spot back in September? (Was the ice a metaphor for the school district? The bullies and thugs of McMillian

Elementary? Was the ice their father, if Ben was the kid egging Jude on?)

He shook his head. He wasn't any good with figurative language—he could barely understand *Grendel* and its gray definitions of evil. That had been his mother's game. When Jude was older, Ben had no doubt his brother would excel in English for the same reason.

Provided he lives that long, the internal voice murmured.

He started for home, feeling colder than the day could take credit for.

The sound of the front door swinging open and bouncing against the wall shook the house, startling Ben, upstairs and trying to dope out *Grendel*.

"What the *Christ*—" he heard Marcus say downstairs, then heard Jude moan, his voice slushy, "*Daddy*—" and the rest was lost in the sudden tumble of heavy bodies.

Ben vaulted off the bed and into the upstairs hallway. His socked feet slipped over the hardwood as he rounded to the stairs. He grabbed the newel post in order to keep from falling against the wall, looked down, and froze.

Marcus appeared to be all back and shoulders down in the foyer, hunkered over Jude, Jude's snow-suited legs kicking. The two of them bounced between the walls, the stairs, the archway to the living room—drunken pinballs gaining momentum instead of losing it. Ben saw blood fly.

Marcus braced his legs. "*Goddammit, hold STILL*—"

And something clicked in the front of Ben's head. *He's going to kill this kid.*

His brain was a half-step behind his body as it leaped down the steps. He heard a tea-kettle scream and dimly realized it was himself. Marcus had time to look up, his mouth an *O* of surprise, revealing Jude's pale, bloodied, and *very*-bruised face, and then Ben landed into the bigger man, driving him off Jude.

Marcus rolled with him, sending him into the front door. The doorknob drove into his spine, a vicious joybuzzer of pain.

Marcus untangled himself, his face red and sweating. "What the *fuck—*"

"*Bastard!*" Ben shrieked and leapt over Jude, taking Marcus around the waist and driving him down the hallway. He heard glass break. He heard Jude scream. He smelled the hot, wet musk of the two of them, bitter and pungent.

He clawed up Marcus's body and slammed his fist into Marcus's face, driving lips against teeth. The pain in his knuckles was stupendous and oh-so satisfactory. It felt good to stop worrying. It felt good to *do* something and know he *could* do it. *Talking* hadn't worked; *this* would.

He punched Marcus with his other hand, sending Marcus's nose to the left. A third shot shut Marcus's left eye. A fourth snapped a tooth—Ben felt it give.

And then Jude was on him, arms around his neck, pulling him back, yelling in his ear.

"*Stop it, Benny! He didn't do it! Stop it! That's DADDY!*"

Don't you fucking GET IT? Ben thought, but didn't scream, *couldn't* scream. He'd finally found the anger that everyone else seemed to have for his kid brother. No, Jude *didn't* get it. Jude *didn't* know when to let up and let go and move away. Jude would *never get it.* Jude was the punch-me, ready-victim, bull's-eye. Jude would put his foot through the thin ice because that, in a way, was what Jude was made to do.

And Ben couldn't do anything about it.

Ben shoved Jude as hard as he could. Jude crashed against the stairway wall, eyes momentarily ringing double-zeroes when his head connected, and that was when Ben saw that Jude's face wasn't as bruised as he'd thought.

Someone had written FAG across Jude's forehead with black Sharpie.

Ben froze. He saw it all—Jude asking him to come play, Ben begging off because he had holiday homework. He saw Jude running into other kids. He saw Jude trying to engage them in his Jude way and it...not...going well.

All because Ben hadn't been there.

He saw Jude stumbling home when the other kids were done with him, Marcus's startled reaction, which looked like anger.

This was where Ben came in.

He stumbled off their father, towards his brother, all emotion a hard, wet, phlegmy knot through his chest and throat.

"Jude—"

And Jude flinched.

Ben blinked. He looked from Jude, cowering against the wall, to Marcus, groggily sitting up while holding his head.

The knot expanded and expanded, choking him, filling his lungs. The cannonball in his gut gained weight, the pressure on his shoulders pushed down. He heard the ticking in his head, louder than ever, and if he could just scream—just *scream*—he could shut it down, cut the knot, shove off the cannonball and the pressure.

But he couldn't.

He couldn't.

Ben didn't go home that night.

He followed Shenandoah Avenue until it became Route 67 North, exiting town, then turned and headed south. He walked up Gaines Street Hill, taking in all the shops and markets with their winter hours. He walked until his feet were cold blocks of meat, and his skin felt similar to the cool hardness of marble. He hadn't bothered switching from sneakers to boots, or trading his torn flannel overshirt for a jacket when he'd left—*escaped* might be a more fitting word.

His brain was a television tuned to an out-of-range station, all static and sporadic ghost-voices.

He thought of Jude. Jude with his bruises and blood. Jude with the word FAG written on his head. Jude telling him that it wasn't Daddy and to stop it, stop it, *STOP IT*.

Jude flinching.

When he finally returned home, it was far past midnight. He stood outside Jude's room. Jude's back was to Ben, but that was all right; Ben didn't think he could handle seeing how those other kids had treated his little brother's face.

Like a bull's-eye, the interior voice murmured.

He studied the line of his brother's back through the blankets, the tuft of hair—the same shade as their mother's—poking out from the top.

I can't protect him, he thought and the internal voice offered no dissent on that score.

He closed Jude's door softly, wincing at the minute squeak of wood-on-wood as it latched, then padded down to his bedroom.

The Ohio State envelope snatched his gaze.

Without thinking—to think would be to hesitate—he took it and sat at his desk, clicking on the lamp. Working quickly, he filled in as much of the information as he could, skipping the parts he would need to look up or ask about—which wasn't all that much, he discovered.

When he finished, he slid the paperwork back in the envelope, clicked off the light, and climbed into bed, still clothed. He thought he'd lie there, unable to sleep, his mind still tuned to that just-out-of-reach channel. But he dropped off almost immediately as, outside, it began to snow.

A creak of floorboards and then Jude's voice, that hesitant are-you-awake tone: "Benny?"

Ben opened his eyes and rolled over. Jude stood in the hall, just outside the doorway, as if it was a border he couldn't cross. He was already dressed, his face still gleaming from just being washed. He'd gotten most of the Sharpie off, leaving the ghost of a gray smear.

Ben sat up. "Hey, bud."

They stared at each other, Jude still visibly wary and Ben unable to find the words to the things he needed to say. His eyes kept getting drawn to the smear. Other kids did that. Not their father.

Ben had forgotten—the evils of the world weren't contained within one imperfect man and his lack of closure over a dead marriage.

"Where's Dad?" he asked finally.

"At work."

Ben winced. "How…"

Jude grinned. "He was talking about that at breakfast. Said he was gonna say he ran into the basement door."

Ben thought of what he'd done, and his mouth slipped free: "What's he gonna say when someone asks how many times?"

Jude laughed, a tinkling sound, but there was a flash in his eyes, like a brief sunburst over chrome, and Ben knew he'd just remembered *how* Marcus had ended up like that. He'd briefly forgotten, but now it was back.

"Whatcha need, bud?" Ben asked.

"Wondered if you wanted to go for a walk," Jude said, then added, "In the woods, I mean. Go to the crick."

Avoid other kids, you mean, Ben thought. "Okay—still coffee downstairs?"

"Uh-huh."

Ben swung his legs over the side.

"Pour me a cup, will ya? I wanna change."

Jude eyed the fact that Ben was still wearing the clothes from yesterday, then nodded.

As he started out, Ben called him back.

Ben made his mouth work. "I'm sorry, Jude. I mean it."

Jude grinned again, the sunburst-chrome glaze of wariness banished from his eyes. The grin was awful—it seemed to make the smear darker, his skin paler.

"S'okay, Benny. I know you were just trying to help."

Ben nodded and Jude left.

He changed out of his clothes, which felt twisted and ill-fitting after sleeping in them. As he was shoving the wad of old ones into his hamper, he noticed the blood for the first time.

He dropped his jeans and flannel and shook out his gray tee.

Three dots, like wavering ellipsis, near the collar.

He stared off, thinking of breaking his father's nose, breaking a tooth, as Jude screamed behind them. Maybe that was what Jude was staring at. He heard the ticking in his head.

He dumped the shirt into the trash, then looked across the room at the bulging Ohio State letter.

What are you going to do after graduation? It wasn't the internal voice now, though, but a memory of a voice.

Then he thought, *I'm doing this kid no good*, and the internal voice murmured, *He's doing you no good, either.*

The air was crisp in his lungs, shockingly so, but Ben's head still felt addled. He moved through the snow like a drunk, struggling to maintain balance over the uneven ground. The snow was thick and wet underfoot.

Jude walked a little ahead of him, his movements confident, as if their roles were reversed—Ben the one beaten to hell the day before, and Jude the over-worrying brother.

They reached the creek. The post-Christmas thaw had raised the water level and its intensity.

"They were playing outside," Jude said after a moment. Ben turned to him, but Jude was staring at the water, his snow gloves shoved into the pockets of his winter coat. "With skateboards. Too cold for skating, but one of them had these cool metallic markers and they were all coloring and talking about what they were gonna do with the boards once the snow melted."

Ben opened his mouth, then shut it again.

"They were older," Jude went on, "but not *that* much older. Like, fifth graders. I didn't know 'em, but I don't know a lot of people. I thought they'd be nice."

He looked up and Ben recoiled. Jude's eyes were fiery and desperate and confused. The smear on his forehead, partially covered by the hood of his winter coat, looked like the ash marks Catholics sometimes put on.

"Why weren't they nice, Benny?" Jude asked. "I just wanted to *talk* to them. I thought they were *cool.* They called me 'babyfag'. Real fast, like that. 'Babyfag, babyfag.' The whole time. They tackled me when I tried to run." His lips peeled back from his grinding teeth—at the moment, looking exactly like Ben had when Ben had finally taken after their father, although Ben didn't know that.

Ben cleared his throat. "I … I don't know, Jude."

Jude turned back to the water. "People are dogshit, Benny. They're mean. I just wanna be nice to them, the way Mom said I should. That's the only thing I remember about her—'Be nice to people, Jude'—and I don't even know why she said that."

Ben did, but he didn't say. Jude wouldn't remember—Ben was surprised Jude remembered *anything* about their mother—but their mother was the epitome of nice. To everyone. Every door-to-door salesman and Jehovah's Witness was welcomed in and given coffee or water, sometimes snacks. She baked things if anyone was sick on their street, regardless of who they were. It used to drive Marcus bugshit, Ben remembered.

And then their mother was nice to that fine young undergraduate, and they went off to be nice to other people elsewhere.

"But I can't *stop* being nice," Jude said now. "Even if I wanted to, I can't. It's like I think, 'This time it'll be different' because there's a lot of *good* in people."

Jude started walking along the water, close enough for snow to fall into the water. Ben followed, feeling more addled than ever.

They came out of the trees to stand at the edge of the Buchanan River. The thaw had done its work here; Ben saw more of those ominous dark spots of thinning. A thread of river water worked its way down the center, like a black stitch.

Jude sat down along the edge. "I think you should tell Dad about college." He looked across the river, at all the homes where the mothers didn't fuck men too young to buy beer, and the fathers didn't beat their youngest because the youngest reminded them of the mothers, and the eldest didn't carry it all around like an albatross, unable to stop it all from continuing. "I think you're wrong, Benny. I think he'd be proud of you. It'd make him happy."

Ben thought of Marcus, face bloodied, nose broken, one eye punched shut. "Jude—"

Jude looked up at him. The fieriness was gone, replaced by a kind of resignation too old for such a young face. "That's what kids do—they grow up and go to college. They *do* something, Benny. They don't hang around forever. It's your turn. In a few years, it'll be mine. And Dad will be *happy*."

He turned back to the river. "And you'll tell me about college, and it'll be nice, and when I go, it'll be nice, too. No one will punch me because I asked them if they wanted to play on the jungle-gym. No one will call me a babyfag."

No one will nearly pull your arm out of the socket because you're holding their beer, Ben thought, but of course didn't say.

Jude was looking at him again. "You can't stay here forever, Benny."

It felt as if he'd sidestepped into a parallel dimension—*You are entering the Twilight Zone*—where Ben made adult decisions about his life and Jude was self-aware of the situation he was in.

"I'll think about it, Jude," he said finally.

Jude nodded, and turned back to the river.

A breeze came up from the water and Ben shivered. "Hey, let's head back. I'm still not awake enough for this. Let me get another cup of coffee—or six—and we'll go do something."

For a moment, Jude said nothing. Then he said, "Okay," and turned at the waist to boost himself up.

And his boot slipped against the packed, wet snow, over the edge, followed by his opposite knee.

An almost comical look of surprise swept Jude's face—not fear, not that quickly—and then he was going, his waist already over the side, his gloved hands scrambling along the wet snow and not catching purchase. He didn't even have time to scream.

Neither did Ben. His body was a spring uncoiling—leaping

across the distance, chest slamming into the cold-cold-cold ground, shoving the air out of his chest, as he snagged one of Jude's gloves. He immediately felt the yank against his shoulder—fire against the snow—as he took on Jude's full weight.

And felt the fading solidness within Jude's glove as Jude's hand started slipping out.

"*BENNY!*" Jude screamed, flailing, kicking at the side of the overhang, his other hand whipping around, and Ben wanted to yell at him to hold still, to *reach* with his other hand, but he couldn't, his lungs were empty, hollow chambers, convulsing, trying to force air in. He whooped in wet snow and it burned.

His eyes locked on Jude's. They were empty of anything but terror, deer-in-the-headlights, animal-in-the-trap-hearing-the-hunter-approach fear, but they were also *aware*; Jude knew exactly what was happening to him. Jude's eyes saw all, blazing out of a pale face bruised and marked with faded marker, nailing Ben in place. They were the eyes of someone who could count the remainder of his life in minutes and seconds instead of decades and years.

Jude's hand slipped from the glove. Ben lunged forward, grabbing with his other hand—

—and missed.

Jude didn't have time to scream before hitting the ice.

Ben yanked himself forward to look over, and already the current, swollen with the previous thaw, had pulled Jude from the edge, dragging him and the broken ice chunks to the center, bobbing up. He watched Jude's arms fly, hands scrabbling to grab a chunk of ice, *any* chunk of ice. In a blink, he was in the center of the river. In another, he was fifty yards off.

Ben tried screaming, but there was no air. His brain yammered at the edges of total mental static roar: *CALL 911 CALL 911 CALL 911—*

Jude was a hundred yards away.

He was no longer flailing.

Ben couldn't move; his muscles twitched with the residue of

adrenaline and nothing more. His brain, addled before, had switched off entirely, overloaded. There was a spark, deep in the back of his mind, slowly growing brighter.

The pressure on Ben's shoulders pushed him into the ground. The knot in his throat expanded.

Images came to him, riffling snapshots of memory: Jude trying not to cry after some assault—it could've been the night of holiday break, the morning after, or any other time.

Another image: Jude's eyes ringing double-zeroes when Ben shoved him away.

Imagining the bruises still to come, the blood still to flow, whenever he looked at Jude's punch-me face.

Thinking often, *I can't protect him.*

Thinking, *He's not going to make it.*

Remembering his father: *It only takes an instant to regret a lifetime.*

Jude's body was a speck, bobbing languidly down by the Route 67 bridge. Still Ben's brain yammered on, *CALL 911 CALL 911*— even as he knew in his gut it was useless.

Two final images, and the spark in the back of his mind grew, blossomed into horrible burning life:

The Ohio State packet, all filled out, on Ben's desk, waiting to be mailed.

Jude's eyes, terrified and *aware*, looking up at Ben as his hand slipped from the glove.

And the spark spoke: *You don't have to worry about him, now.*

The clock in his head stopped ticking.

The knot was gone from Ben's throat and he sucked in a lungful of freezing air.

The pressure lifted from his shoulders, replaced by the most crushing guilt Ben had ever felt, a guilt like nothing he'd ever experienced, a guilt that couldn't compare with his feelings of never been able to protect Jude *enough*, of being there *enough*.

Because Jude wouldn't need protecting *now*.

Jude wasn't there *now*.

And Ben Sheever, finally, screamed.

Eventually, one of the residents across the river called the police. Eventually, the police—Marcus, to be specific—found Ben, still screaming, his voice a ragged, ruined croak.

And, eventually, they found Jude.

BLACK RIVER #1

ELIZABETH MASSIE

Cracked upon my ice-thick surface,
He is there,
Fragments of a grimace, straining,
Glaze-eyed stare.
Youth in wool coat, tri-corn, vest
Caked in mud,
Stockings torn from thorny branches,
Red with blood.
Voices, loud, calling orders,
"Cross the ford!"
Fingers aching, clutching firelock,
Praying, *Lord*…
From the bank into my waters,
Cold as Hell,
Stumbles over slime-slicked stones,
Rancid smell.
Sees his face tossed back to taunt him,
Sure to die,
Shot within my frosted rapids,
Left to lie.

THE BLACK CROW OF BODDINSTRAßE

EMILY B. CATANEO

I'VE BEEN LOST FOR WEEKS. Maybe months. Perhaps even years. I can't say how long I have spent fluttering from angry black elevated subway to gray boulevard to linden-lined canal, tap-tap-tapping on windows, beating my wings against glass and receiving only the backside of lace curtains.

But perhaps, at last, I am lost no more? Could it be that I've finally found a family? I have alighted on a third-story rusted-out window box—geraniums dead with winter, or maybe dead a long time ago—and I'm peering into a tall thin warped-glass window. Through two layers of glass shimmer people, warm, well-fed people. The glass swirls like eddies in the muddy Spree River but still I can see them, see enough to feel as though I already know them. The way the mother tugs on her tooth as she talks. The way the father slides across the warm wood floor in his stocking feet.

I lift off the window box, flutter around the corner of the building to a concrete balcony adjacent to the rest of the flat. A girl appears in the window and I lurch backwards, nearly fall off the balcony. She's chubby and it gives her face a vapid, ironed-out look. She wears overalls and pink wire-rimmed glasses with bent arms and as I watch her, she runs a hairbrush through the tail of her messy braid.

I wait for her to notice me and for her to tap on the glass, yank the curtain aside so I can't peek in, but she simply stares out the window, not letting me in but not shutting me out either, running the brush through her hair.

Sometimes, when I soar through the city on long nights such as this one, I see flickers of silver-edged night-dark wing, of other creatures that are perhaps like me. And I feel more than hear whispers, whispers rising from the sidewalks like steam from a manhole cover. These whispers tell me that somewhere in this city, a place percolates beneath the ground, calling to me—I think it's named the Place of Lost Things—a cold place but a place where I belong, where I would fit in easy as the click of a bicycle lock.

I visit the family again the next night. They live on a street of off-white former Mietskaserne, facades done up with neo-classical flourishes and cement balconies tacked on after the last war. A plastic bag from a späti floats in the poplar tree outside the girl's window. When I alight on the balcony railing, I'm so cold I can barely stand to touch the metal. Smokestack smoke rises to the east but other than that the night is very clear, clear enough to reveal stars.

I cozy up to the window. The girl stands there again, running her brush through her hair. It's down this time, all loose and messy over her sweatshirt. She bats the brush against a brambly knot, then purses her chapped lips and reaches forward. I tense against frozen cement and I press myself against the pane.

Open the window, please, hairbrush girl, turn the latch and slide it open with the crackling of old plaster. Let me flutter inside, let me curl in the corner of your bookshelf and sleep in your white-sheeted bed. I remember beds, I know I remember them from somewhere far back in a hazy corner of my memory, but it doesn't have to be a bed. Even the faded rug on the floor would do.

She doesn't open the window, but presses fingertips against the glass, and makes eye contact with me on the balcony. I'm sure of it. She sees me, and there are only two panes of glass between us.

We stay like that, not moving. Tinny church bells ring somewhere far away, and she sighs, and turns away from the window.

Certain questions tug at me, when I see those silver-edged night-dark creatures, when I hear the whispers about the Place of Lost Things. The foremost question: what are those creatures, and what am I? I can't say I've ever been too good at seeing myself, but I can tell you how I feel. Some days, when I see the Aaskrähe—black crows—lighting on graffitied benches in the park, or picking open a bio trash bag in a yellow bin, I think yes, that is me, all greasy gray feathers and black undercoat, fluttering around trying to peck my way into things.

Other times I feel like I could have been a person once. Why else do I long to sit on polished floorboards while fathers slide across floors in stocking feet and mothers tug on their teeth? Why else do I know that my longing stems from more than just the animal desire for warmth, but from a memory, faint but aching, of what it means to encase yourself within four walls with people who love you? I feel like I could have been a person who died a long time ago, or maybe just last week. I really don't know. It makes sense: I'm colder than the coldest January day, when the sky is blue and deadly and no one salts the sidewalks.

But when I sit on my cement balcony, watching my girl with her hairbrush, my questions don't seem to matter so much anymore, don't weigh on my wings or once-arms or whatever it is I have. Warm rooms and loud conversation have a way of driving off the doubts that live raw in your heart.

I notice, when I perch on my balcony, that the girl's eyebrows permanently turn in, that she fiddles with her glasses and worries at her fingertips. Come to think of it, she looks a little lost herself.

I don't suppose it matters what you are: human, crow, ghost. No one, nothing, wants to be lost.

Don't become lost, girl with hairbrush, I whisper (maybe my breath would have fogged the pane, once upon a time). Don't become lost like me. Stay in your palace of white wainscoting and oak floorboards.

And open the window. And let me in with you.

I'm flying down Boddinstraße, almost at the girl's window, when everything goes wrong. The space between the trees and buildings before me flutters with hundreds and hundreds of black wings, the same color as the night but edged in silver so I can see them, heading east out of the city.

I don't know where they are going but I can feel where they are going and it makes me colder than the balcony's cement or the winter's nights or the people who yank their curtains shut when I approach their windows.

But I need to see the girl. And so I soar into the crowd, battling against them, beating the air as I fight towards her flat. Wings scrape against me and for a second I'm suspended, not going backwards, not going forwards. Then the force of their crowd carries me away from the window, back down Boddinstraße, east, away from the girl, away from the warm lighted window.

I struggle, but their current sweeps me past the blocks of buildings, over warehouses, towards billowing smokestacks and over the Ringbahn's train tracks that hem the city in an arc marked by construction cranes and dirt pits. I push myself against them again—what if the girl misses me? What if someone else takes that perch on the balcony?—but then I realize the crowd is slowing, and dropping down towards the earth.

We are in a part of the city ravaged and then left untouched by humans. Below us stretches a wasteland of an empty lot, a pit really, a gaping maw in the earth full of jagged hulking shapes.

The flock around me holds its breath, waiting. I look down, look closer, and then I feel it: this is the Place of Lost Things. This is the place that's ached deep in my bones or feathers or whatever it is that I have. Full of rusted-out cars, refrigerators built during a fallen regime, empty bottles and shredded trash bags—but besides the unwanted things, it's full of creatures like the horde that brought me here. I can see them, their silver wings percolating, seething beneath the debris, or maybe I can feel them, but it really doesn't matter how I know, because I know: this is the place where unwanted things end up.

The pit doesn't smell like garbage, or graveyards or cellars. It doesn't smell like anything at all.

The horde rustles around me, and then a rush, and it dives towards the pit, lighting up the air around me like a moon for a full thirty seconds. Then I am alone in the dark.

Questions tug at you more insistently, when you're hovering over the Place of Lost Things, watching a horde of creatures that are just like you diving into its depths. Questions like: is this where I belong too? Am I a fool to think that the girl will ever let me in? Perhaps I am nothing but a curiosity to her—a glassy-eyed animal trapped in the Zoologischer Garten, and nothing more. Perhaps I'm a bit stupid to put so much stock in this lost-looking girl, with her dirty hairbrush and bent-frame glasses.

It takes strong wings to about-face and fly back to the city. I flutter up Boddinstraße, dodging sulfurous streetlamps and angry black tree branches. I alight on the cement balcony and immediately I see that everything is different. Light, warm light, floods onto the balcony. I press myself to the window. The girl leans there, hanging something that emanates light. She lets it fall and my eyes sparkle and pop and readjust. It's a Froebel star, white, many-pointed, made of paper but glowing with a reddish-gold light from inside. The girl readjusts it, then steps back, and I swear she sees me. I do not know if I have form. I do not know if I appear as a crow, or a smudge of shadow, or just a blank space that inexplicably causes the heart to beat slower. But she sees me, she senses me, and a tiny smile spreads her lips.

And I know: she put that star up for me.

I lunge away from the window and soar into the night. She put that star up for me. She cares whether I live in the light or the dark, whether I go to the Place of Lost Things or stay here. It's my star and my thoughts jump to the next step. Will she open the window? Will she let me in? Will I behold that pointed star from inside, rather than from the balcony? I will, I will. She saw me. She knows I am out here.

I loop round the jagged steeple of a broken church and then cut towards the river, a tapestry of former warehouses and empty rail yards and construction cranes jutting every which way. I soar towards city lights and darkened gardens.

I'm not going to be lost anymore. I'm not going to be lost. I don't have to go *there*, to that place. Giddy, I fly past the windows of the people who didn't let me in: the hinterhaus flat where a woman frowned and jerked aside her curtains. The gleaming white house with so many windows, but none of them open. The boat on the river where young people clink bottles and laugh too loud. I don't need you, I don't need you, I don't need you. I found my home. I'm going to be let in.

Next time I soar to the balcony and alight on concrete and gravitate towards the glow of my star, the girl is holding her hairbrush, but not standing by the window. She's running the brush through her hair, but she's staring at the wall and for the first time I see her melancholy hairbrushing expression in profile, not straight on. She's not looking at the balcony. Her shoulders are straighter than last time.

When will she come to the window? I fidget against decomposing leaves and the butts of cigarettes. I want her to let me in, tonight.

That's when I see that there are two copies of the girl in the room, and that on her wall hangs a new mirror—square, rimmed in white wood—and that she's brushing her hair while she looks at herself.

Of course. It's been some time since I was human, if I was ever, so I forgot about things like reflection and glass and lamplight and that when you stare at a pane of glass at night you are probably

seeing your own reflection, not the crow or blank space out on the balcony.

She never saw me at all. She saw the star. She saw herself. But never me.

I thought it was over. The cold of these never-ending nights, the humiliation of curtains yanked across curtain rods, the endless fluttering from balcony to balcony. All this time, however long it's been, I thought she had found me. Saw me. Hung a star for me. I thought I would land on warm wood floors, curl in white blankets, feel a hand on my feathered back, fall asleep against the girl's plump stomach.

But she never even knew I existed.

I'm still lost after all.

I lift off, flap away from the balcony over the wet gleaming cobblestones. How much longer am I supposed to fly around looking for someone to let me in? How long?

I glimpse the broken church steeple I looped round after I thought she had hung the star for me, when I was so jubilant, so hopeful, so sure that it was over, this loneliness, the uncertainty, these questions, *what was I, what am I, where do I belong*…

But those questions leap into me, bristling my feathers, if I have feathers at all, and without even deciding, I cut east. Clouds hang low and the streets are luminous with sulfur lights but there are no silvery creatures a-wing, so it's only me slicing through the coal-smelling air, arcing over the subway tracks.

The Place of Lost Things looms up faster than I expected. The smell of nothing, the jagged objects and beneath it all the glow of silver creatures that were once like me, the pit seething with them. I pull up to the edge and tread air and I look down and I see nothing, and feel nothing at all.

This is where I belong now. I was wrong about the girl. She never saw me, she never hung the Froebel star for me. She only wanted to look at herself in the mirror.

Sometimes it's time to cut your losses. Sometimes it's better to say, well, I tried, and let's be honest, the Place of Lost Things is probably where I belong anyway.

But as I rise and fall in the vicissitudes of the frozen air above the seething pit, I remember the girl's face in the light of the star. I remember how she drank in its glow, how she hung it carefully.

She never saw me, but I saw her. I saw her when she was lost, brushing her hair, her eyebrows caved in, and I also saw how she held her shoulders straighter, stronger as she admired her star. And I think—I think I can carry that around with me. Maybe I can breathe it in, on these long nights, as I resist this place teaming beneath me, this Place of Lost Things. Because I will resist it. I will. I will remember her, remember the gleaming pinpricks of light in her star, remember her small but satisfied smile as she hung it high, remember how I felt when I thought she had found me. I will turn around, heave myself away from the pit, fly left back towards the city. I will keep searching for other streets to haunt, other balconies to frequent, other windows to tap, tap, tap on.

PRESCIENCE

ROSE BLACKTHORN

backwards
chin on my shoulder
even my shadow precedes me
nothing follows but
the setting sun

crisp
the bite of early spring
and fading warmth
of midday
I cannot hear the steps
but feel the weight of eyes
upon my nape
the breath drawn
to speak my name

ROSE BLACKTHORN

crows call
their black wings and raucous cries
surround me with fluttering
a strobe of sound
last year's dead leaves
nearly decayed into damp earth
whisper of new life
yet to grow

so I go on
backwards and forwards
unsure of my direction
past or future
I am like the old leaves
half-returned to the earth
yet still stretching toward the light
a splinter
not yet a seedling

lost in that moment
between the sound and the silence
and the dancing crow-black feather
floating down

A FLASH OF RED

ERINN L. KEMPER

CLAIRE BROUGHT THE ROBIN'S wing home. The way its feathers folded and fanned as she extended the joint occupied her for hours. She held it up against light, against shadow, against her skin where it scratched and tickled. With needle and thread she sewed it there using a quick basting stitch, above her breast, where arm meets torso. It hurt. She made small looping sutures that disappeared under the feathers and held the hollow bones tight against her.

She flinched, ground her teeth and bled a bit. When it was done, she stood in front of the mirror. As she raised and lowered her arm the wing flared, contracted. The thread strained, but held. A warm glow spread down from her shoulder to coil in her stomach. She buttoned on a shirt and went outside.

Every day Claire walked. Emerging from her small apartment, she squinted into the morning sun and chose a route. Through the park, slow steps on pathway and shoreline, her gaze cast down, studying the drifts that gathered between bench and garbage can, tree and boulder. She wound her way along streets, alleyways. People saw her now—smiled when she bent to retrieve her bounty, nodded as she turned and headed home. They never used to. They used to shove her aside as they rushed to board the train. They used to brush by her at the coffee shop, stepping in front of her as she approached the cream and sugar counter; she was a piece of furniture to them

Now, with her treasures secreted away she walked among the

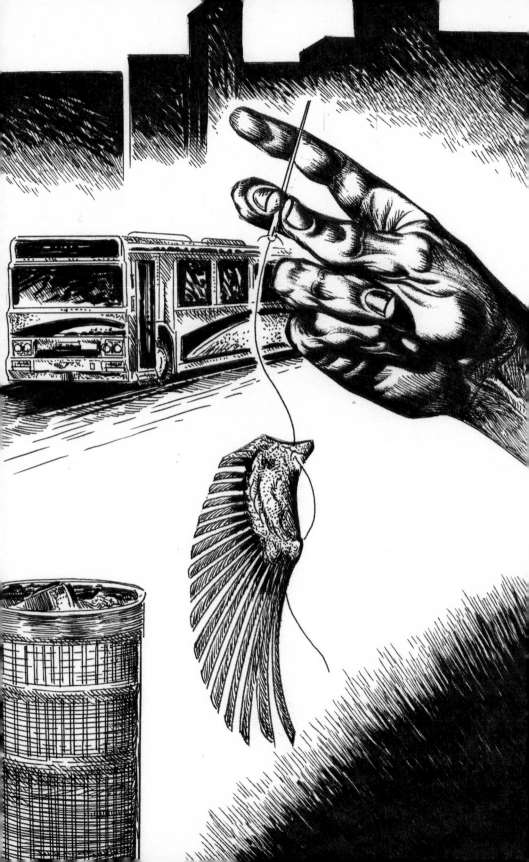

people of her city, tipped her head towards their nods and smiles.

Gold and red-stained leaf, lace-fringed baby sock, gleam of wrinkled foil arranged in an incidental origami—each treasure tucked in her long coat. Her hands strayed to her pockets, ensuring her treasures stayed put.

She had an assortment of needles and threads. Each find required its own treatment to adhere it to her flesh. With careful needlework learned from her grandma she drew a velvet coin purse against her skin in multi-hued embroidery; weaving around and through using a looping chain stitch, binding it in a web of silk and cotton. Some fell away too soon. The leaves. The flowers and their petals. But the stitching they left behind had its own magic, its own beauty and as it threaded through her tissue, inflamed lumps rose to embrace each line.

He sat in the bus shelter with his eyes closed. Buses came and went, sucking people up and spitting them out, and still he sat.

Yesterday at the coffee shop on the corner, where she'd picked up an abandoned dreamcatcher woven of stir sticks, toothpicks and straw wrappers, she'd watched him pour sugar into his cup. His lips moved, counting the crystals as they fell. When he realized she was watching he snapped a lid on the cup, tugged and smoothed his sleeves down, before grabbing his coffee and scuffing out into the crackling autumn heat.

Did he smile? It was hard to read a slight twist in the lips of a stranger. Before, she would have assumed it was a sneer, a smirk of distain, a grimace of pity. But now she wasn't sure.

Something in his eyes made her take a breath so deep she felt some threads give way.

Today, when she ducked in an alley chasing a flash of red fluttering in a pile of debris she saw him sitting there at the bus stop. Loose sleeves hanging down to his fingers matched hers. With his chin tucked close to his chest, he didn't look at the buses passing. As she crossed the street towards him, the red corduroy scrunchy secured in her pocket, he still didn't look up, but this time she was sure he smiled.

They sat, side by side, and watched the buses. They laughed together when a blonde-haired toddler clapped with glee and pointed at the 'chocolate lady'. The scowl-faced black woman winked at the delighted little girl, and stuck out her tongue. The little girl's mom pulled on her daughter's arm with such force the child dangled painfully up the steps of the #38 Downtown.

They gasped together when an old man's walker got caught in the space between the bus and the curb and he fell into a soft wall of office workers. No one stopped to make sure he hadn't suffered a cracked bone or twisted joint.

And that was the way it went for the most part. Every passenger hustled to get on with their lives, jostling their way through an invisible crowd.

When the #27 Crosstown pulled up for the third time, he placed the pop can tab he'd been playing over his knuckles like a magic coin on her knee. He merged into the slouching line of commuters and was gone.

That night, with her desk lamp swiveled to light her hip, she sewed the tab on, knotting it down with a fisherman's bend, then in a web of orange and pink, she spun rays of silk across her tingling belly.

This was what her grandma had taught her.

Use the stitch that best suits the purpose, little rabbit. A simple chain stitch is just as beautiful as a six-petaled lazy daisy. Sometimes the thread is the glue that holds a thing together, gives it form, sometimes the thread is just there for a splash, some flair, and sometimes the thread is the art, the paint and *the picture.*

Claire found him again, at the bus stop, the park, the coffee shop. She never had to look very long.

Jeremy.

People-watching was their favorite pass-time. Like her, Jeremy had nowhere to be, no one waiting for him to come home with the spice of autumn in his hair.

They began to tell stories, short ones, about the people they saw.

Lunch break, she said about the guy-in-suit texting his way across the park. *Divorced,* he said about the uber-fit guy doing wind sprints on the grass. *Writer. Interview. Nanny. Lost. Prairie-folk. Operation. Anniversary. Drunk.*

It was all you could know about anyone. No name, no occupation, no curriculum vitae. A quick category to put them in, and then just as quickly they were shelved and gone.

In her mind those stories were full of the grief, loneliness, frustration and joy that each life should contain. With one or two words she saw it all.

And every time they met he gave her a gift.

Today's gift was a sea-smoothed piece of blue glass. Under her breast, nestled between her ribs, the glass went from cool to warm as she twined thread around it, caging the foggy bit of sky in a nest of snow-white thread, leaving it loose enough to bump against her as she moved.

Sewing finished, she did some maintenance on the canvas of her skin. Not many spaces left to fill. A few punctures were hot and puss-yellow, but the aloe-soaked rag brought some relief. In front of the mirror, she moved with care to reach the crust of sores on her back. She twisted slowly, threads pulling as they stretched. She had managed a few stitches there, and criss-cross braided lines lacing up her spine. She kept the aloe in the fridge and when it touched her skin it raised goose bumps, sent ripples of tugs and twinges across her flesh.

She ministered to her skin, taking comfort in the lingering smell of her grandmother, who had lived and died in this room, filled it with her yearning as she sewed her dreams. Frayed blue cornflowers poured across the bedspread, soft pink blossoms vined up the sun-bleached curtains, each mundane object transformed, made wondrous by her grandmother's craft. From the walls hung needlepoint doorways to the street cafes of Paris, the terraced rice fields of Asia, the palm-shaded beaches of Fiji.

That great big world out there is not for me, rabbit-girl. It's too wide, too far. But I can see it when I sleep. I can draw the world close with my needle and thread.

Jeremy showed her his secret.

He didn't mean to—at least it seemed like an accident. There was a scrap of paper skating by, folded into a fan. The long sleeve he wore, always pulled down, rose as he reached and she saw the glowing white ridges of ancient scars climbing his arm in an intricate lattice.

I don't do it anymore he said when he caught her looking. *Don't need to.* He considered his bare forearm a moment, sending a huff of breath out his nose, before he pulled the sleeve back down and curled his fingers over his palm to hold it in place.

That night she took the fan and sliced one edge across her arm above the elbow, wetting the paper with her blood. It sizzled and stung and she licked the spots of blood away. As she sewed on the paper fan she imagined him sitting on the side of his bed, a lamp spotlighting his arm as he cut a careful line with his straight razor. There would be more blood than from her paper-cut; a slow, dark welling until it could rise no more; the blood would spill over his pale skin, catching in older wounds as it wound its way down.

He had made something beautiful of his flesh, brought something inside to the surface. Those pearl scars a delicate lace that traced across his skin the story of who he was.

Her story was unfolding, the story of what she was becoming.

The paper fan unfurled as she spread her legs, sheltering the hair that grew there.

Something changed as she entered the park.

The sun warmed her face, and she felt her abdomen ignite. Jeremy was waiting for her. Her pulse leapt at the thrill of it. A stir of movement at her shoulder—the robin's wing ruffled and thrummed, pulling at its threads, sending a tremor across her body.

She saw him, sitting alone on a bench, waiting.

People were gathered around her, standing, sitting, leaning, walking; each with thoughts cast inwards, living a story all their own. Everyone on their mark. Setting the stage.

The old woman who sat at her bench every day with a sad pile of dog food at her feet, smiling as owners yanked their drooling Labradors and pugs away from her offering; *lonely*. The young couple, head in lap and hand-in-hand, one listening to headphones, the other gabbing on a cell; *divided*. The smokers. The homeless, jobless; *shunned*. She stood in their midst and they told her their stories.

The robin's wing quickened, its tempo waking the surrounding threads, rousing them into motion. Her treasures hummed and vibrated and she felt so hot, smothered. They fluttered and writhed against the confines of her attire. She tore at her clothes, freeing herself of her jacket, shedding her sweater, her loose shirt and pants until she stood revealed, unveiled, and the gasps of her audience rippled around her when they saw what she had made. The strands covered her almost completely, drawn through her with such care.

They see me.

Thread tugged at her side, her legs, her shoulders, as she turned, spreading her arms. Awe, horror, confusion, alarm. The threads sewn across her body a subway-map to her inner dimensions, each treasure a remembrance of the streets, the pathways, the people who walked them. She brought them together, a collage of skin and blood and forgotten pieces.

Her audience began to sob, exclaim, cry out to each other, and her treasures vibrated with new intensity. The stitches that wove a reflection of her dreams—all of their dreams, all their stories merging—the threads that traveled under and over the terrain of her body tightened in preparation.

The young couple held each other, clutching with fists turned white with strain; the dog-food lady's withered face stretched in an unvoiced appeal amidst the drumming confusion of pigeons taking flight.

They see me.

The robin's wing, feathers, petals and leaves, the bits of paper all strained towards the sky, yearning for release, pulling her up as the stones, pieces of wood and bark, the glinting metallic objects dropped, heavy with need they struck for the earth. And her audience sat together—frozen, stunned, their attention piercing her, pulling her in every direction at once. In this moment, together, they saw the magic of what she had become.

Jeremy sat on his bench, cheeks bright with tears, eyes wide and unblinking as the threads yanked at her flesh, rifts opening when skin and muscle could no longer endure the tug-o-war between the stitches anchored there.

He sees me.

She smiled, though scorching trails of pain shot across her stomach, her hips, her arms and legs, where the wounds peeled back, gaping open to unleash gasps of steaming blood. She smiled at him as a scream thundered up her throat and out in a burst of joyous agony; a siren call that held all who attended. Dark began to steal the sight of him, and red, in flashes, painted his pale face. He was smiling back at her, at the beauty of her becoming, though he quaked with sorrow.

The canvass of her body gave with a sudden rending of stress-fatigued meat. Her scavenged bits of treasure achieved freedom, bursting forth, releasing all that her skin had once kept contained. Pieces of scalp, tissue, flesh and bone exploded outwards in a firework flower of blood and heat, bright against the pale blue sky.

They saw her.

THE SPEED OF SOUND

CIARÁN PARKES

Slower than the speed of light, slower than
a speeding bullet, its effect is seen
when a child falls and there's a gap between
his falling and his cry as if the world
had been paused then started up again.
Sometimes slower still, the cry creeps on
silently, to catch him years from then.

RED RUNNER VS. THE SURGEON, ISSUE 18

JESSICA MAY LIN

WHEN I KICK DOWN THE DOOR of the preschool, my red Converse are the only splotch of color in the trashed-up gray of overturned desks and torn art projects. An electric fan rotates in one corner of the room, ruffling the blinds over the window.

Beneath the frayed hem of my right sweatshirt sleeve, I slide my automatic knife out of its sheath and run my thumbnail absently along the blade.

I am a man who lives with the torment of a nightmare that won't die.

It follows me, to the dark spaces where no man is supposed to go. But I have no reprieve. I'm not supposed to.

"You're worthless."

"Haven't got what it takes to kill him."

"Leave me alone." I grit my teeth, try to shut the voices out the way my psychiatrist told me to.

The Surgeon's in here. I know he is.

And this time he won't get away.

A shadow flickers across the ceiling, and I whip around, listening carefully for the staccato of footsteps. My domino mask presses into the corners of my eyes.

"Red Runner, I could see those sneakers from a mile away."

The taunt comes from straight above me.

I hook the thumb of my free hand in my pocket and smile. I don't need to hide—not from him.

"Come down and face me, coward."

The Surgeon drops from the rafters and lands with one knee down in front of me. He's wearing his normal costume, blue scrubs and a white medical mask stretched across his mouth. "I've got a present for you, Red."

He reaches into his pocket and throws something at me.

I snatch it out of the air and hold it on my open palm. It's a piece of lace, torn from the collar of a five-year-old's dress. "Too late. You won't find her now."

I close my fist. "You're sick."

The Surgeon laughs. "You're the one seeing a shrink, if you want to talk about sick."

"He's right."

"You're not good enough to kill him."

The voices bore into the corners of my skull, spaces I didn't even know existed. I dig my nails into my palms.

The Surgeon meets my eyes, as if he knows exactly what's going on in my head, but before he can get anything out of his mouth, I lunge at him with the knife.

Something invisible comes up and bars my strike.

Without moving, his arms still at his sides, the Surgeon smiles at me. His power is psychic surgery. His weapons are crafted by his mind.

"Who do you think you are, Red? You can't beat me. I don't have to fight you, Red. You'll fight yourself."

I draw my knife arm back.

"You're weak."

"Not a real hero."

The voices. So loud in my head I can't remember anything else. The knife falls from my hand as I watch.

At times like this, all I can think about is that I'd rather die.

The next thing I know, the Surgeon has me on the floor, held down by an invisible chokehold.

"You can't win, Red. You can't save those kids. I killed them, and I'll be back to kill more."

He lifts his foot and stomps down on my face.

I double over, yelling, and he grunts in satisfaction.

"If you knew better, you'd check yourself into an asylum, and stay out of my way."

When I look up again, he's gone.

I reach up and rip the domino mask from my face. I'm panting as if I've run a long distance, my vision blurry until all I can make out are my red Converse in the foggy darkness before me.

My cell phone plays Hello Moto in my pocket, a weak bleat against the cold solitude of the destroyed preschool.

Holding my sweatshirt sleeve against my mouth to staunch the blood pouring from my nose, I punch the green icon and shove the phone up against my ear.

"Red? How's it going?" Niall's on the other side of the line.

I exhale and lean my head back against the watercolor of a unicorn hanging on the wall. Blood trickles into the back of my throat. "He got away."

"Fuck," Niall says.

I spit onto the floor. "It's all right. I'll take care of it."

"You can't."

"You can talk all you want about how're in control."

"But really, you're not."

There's a clatter as Niall sets down a coffee mug on the other side of the line. "Listen, Red. I'm at Joey Duke's right now. Someone left a message for you—Red, are you listening?"

I realize I'm breathing hard again, squeezing the phone so hard I might crush it.

"Yeah," I tell him.

"He knows."

"They all know how you weak you are."

It's not real, I tell myself, but I'm not sure I believe it anymore. You can only run for so long before you hit a dead end.

I shift the phone higher up on my shoulder. "I'll meet you at Joey Duke's, okay?" I tell Niall.

And I hang up on him.

Twenty minutes later, I pull my head out of the toilet in Joey Duke's Bar and Lounge, gasping. My hands are braced on either side of the bowl, my tie still floating in the water.

"You've been hunting the Surgeon since you were fifteen."

"Ten years and he's still torturing children."

"You're useless."

"Fuck you," I say as my reflection bobs up and down. But I'm not sure who I'm talking to anymore.

My phone buzzes in my pocket.

Niall.

I wish I had what it takes to ignore him—to just forget about Red Runner and the Surgeon and walk away from all of this.

I grab my domino mask off the floor and yank it back over my eyes.

"I know what I'm doing. He's mine. I'll kill him."

And I sink my fist into the lever that flushes the water away.

When I bat the door open, into Joey Duke's, the air is thick with sweat and whiskey. A girl in leather jeans and many gold bangles casts me a furtive glance from behind the bar—although what Joey calls a "bar" is just a moldy plank of wood, weighted down by the slumped figures of passed-out patrons.

Ryvie Wilson, the bargirl. She's got ivy tattoos all up her arms.

"You want a drink, Red?" she calls to me, holding up a wine glass. Behind it, her glittered lashes wink at me. "It's Happy Hour."

I scan the bar for Niall.

"Sorry, Ryv. Got the Surgeon to take care of."

Ryvie presses her lips together slowly. Her eyes are the color of melted amber. "You all right?"

I remember how my shirt is stained with blood, my hair dripping with toilet water. I look like a freak, not a hero.

144

"But maybe that's what you are."

I grimace. "Yeah. Had a rough night."

A mischievous gleam lights up her eyes, and she leans over the bar. "I don't think I ever told you, but I bought a pair of red Converse after I started reading your comic." She pouts gently, waiting for my reaction. "They're the hottest thing in New York City right now."

I manage a smile and turn my head away. "Thanks."

She reaches out and claps me on the back. "Your sidekick's waiting for you over there."

I find Niall at the end of the bar. He's dressed in his usual gray latex get-up, the perfect mirror of his superhero future. No arch-nemesis, no superhero name, no fruitless goose chase to the ends of sanity. Yet.

"Hey."

He turns around, and his eyes widen.

"Whoa, man. He got you good."

"Yeah, let's not talk about that."

I drag a chair out and collapse in it.

Niall scoots to the side to make room for me. "You okay?"

I rest both my elbows on the counter and exhale deeply. Sometimes I'm thankful I have Niall—that he's young and unbroken, still waiting to meet the costumed motherfucker who will screw him over in ten years. Give or take. "I'm fine."

Ryvie sets a mug of coffee down in front of me. The tips of her fingers linger at my wrist for an extra second.

"So, who's it from?" I ask Niall. "The message you were all excited about."

He reaches into his pocket and pulls out a crumpled envelope. There's a name scrawled over the top in red marker—one that I haven't seen in years. "Here. You better take a look at it. I found it on the doormat when I got home from school."

I run my thumb over the name on the label.

Elliot Fox.

"How'd you know it was for me?"

Niall shrugs. "When people give me things, they're always for you." He pauses. "So, was that you? From…before? Elliot Fox?"

I turn the envelope over. There's no point in lying to him. "Yeah. It was."

There aren't many people who know about this name. I thought I'd buried it away, never to see it again.

But apparently I'm wrong.

I flick the automatic knife open and slit the envelope. A single sheet of paper falls out.

It's the last page of a comic book, displaying a single panel where a villain in hospital scrubs dangles off the edge of a tall skyscraper in the middle of a hailstorm. A superhero in red sneakers stands over him with his arms folded over his chest.

"Issue Twelve," Niall says. He'd remember because that's the issue he made his debut as my sidekick.

Underneath the panels, there's a photograph of a dark-haired young woman posing under a tree, and a three-lined biography about the author.

"You think it's from the Surgeon?" Niall asks.

"Who else would it be from?"

Niall shrugs. "Why would he send you the last page of a comic book where you have him dangling by the feet over the edge of the Empire State Building?"

I turn the page over, searching for a hidden message of some sort. "I have no fucking clue. Maybe as a joke?"

For some reason I have the odd intuition that someone is watching us. I turn around, and Niall jumps.

"What?"

"Nothing." I crumple the page up and stuff it down my pocket. "But it's late, Niall. I should get home and take care of all this." I gesture at my face.

"You sure you're going to be all right?" he asks. The steam from the coffee makes his face waver in and out of focus.

"What makes you think I'm not?"

Niall doesn't get up. "Um, hey Red?"

"What?"

"I know it's been rough recently, but there's something you've gotta remember. It's something you told me."

I adjust the knot of my tie. "Yeah? What's that?"

He draws himself up straighter, and for a second, I can't help it—I'm reminded of myself, ten years ago. "To remember what it means to be a hero. We don't do things for pay, or publicity, or girls. We do them because we want the world to be a better place. You told me that as long as I didn't forget that, I could do great things." His expression turns solemn. "You can't forget either."

A moment of silence falls between us.

"Thanks, Niall." I clap my hand on his shoulder, trying to shut out memories of the old days, when every step I took held conviction and not the worn-out tiredness of the present. "I'm glad you remember that. Take care, okay?"

He gets up first, and I watch him walk out the door, gray outfit blending into the endless sidewalks before him.

I don't need you. You need me.

As soon as he's gone, the voices take over again.

"Maybe you should let your sidekick take over."

"You're growing old and tired."

"Worthless."

And suddenly, as I squeeze my palms into the sides of my head, I realize the last thing I want to do is be alone in my apartment.

Ryvie's shift is over. The new bargirl—platinum blond and short ruffly skirts—drifts over and pours me a shot of tequila, which I turn around and around in my fingers.

Ryvie slides beside me and puts her hand on my arm. The warmth of her skin presses through my shirt. "I follow your comic, you know," she says close to my ear.

I smile gently. She thinks it's so easy. That's what they all think.

"Still upset about the Surgeon? There'll be other chances." Ryvie flips her hair back, her fingers tangling in waves of black silk. "Besides, if you end it now, you won't have a story anymore. What are you going to do with your life then?" Her grin takes on a mischievous quirk, and she leans in closer. "You need your story to keep going, Red. Or you'll just fade. People will forget you. Your writer will lose interest. And you'll stop existing."

I twist around and clap my hand over her mouth, cutting her words off. The feeling's there again, as if there are a hundred eyes watching me from all around. She's touched on the taboo.

The one no one talks about.

I let go of her, more forcefully than I should.

"Don't," I tell her.

It's something I don't want to think about, something I've tried so hard to block out. But now that she's mentioned it, I can't *stop* thinking about it.

Ryvie pouts, her soft red lips pressing together. "But why? The story's the most important thing of all, isn't it?"

I draw my hand across my eyes. "No. Saving people is."

Not that it matters to her.

Not that it matters to anyone but me.

She perks up again. "You know, I'm a huge fan of Issue 8. The one where you hypnotize the Surgeon and push him in a shark tank. You should do something like that again."

A good story, that's all they want. No justice, no lives saved.

"Those days are over."

I'm talking about justice, but of course she misunderstands.

"They're never over." She pats my arm. "Not if you keep the story interesting enough that people will keep buying. It's not over, Red."

And maybe because she's the only one who doesn't see the wrong in me—even if she's wrong—I end up taking her home.

We kiss in the cold embrace of my dark apartment. Her hand trails down my chest, slipping through the buttons of my shirt. I open my eyes, my lashes brushing against her cheek. The cold, white walls of my room loom behind her head.

"Red, make the story shine again," she whispers in my ear. "You have what it takes to make every kid in New York *beg* for a pair of red Converse at Christmas. You just have to raise the thrill factor, and they'll love you."

And that's when I realize what she's doing.

Her hands move down to my belt, and I push her away.

Both of us are breathing heavily, staring at each other in the dark.

"Red? What's wrong?" Those wide, childish eyes blink at me under the moonlight.

I know why she's here—why she's saying those things to me. It's the same reason I was delivered the last page of my own comic. And it has nothing to do with the Surgeon.

I walk over to the wall, plant my hands against the blanched plaster.

"Get out."

I don't turn around. My heart pounds heavily in the back of my skull. The heat is still in my body, lingering in the places where her hands pressed against my skin.

"Red?" she tries again, more quietly.

"I said *get out.*"

My shoulders heave with each breath as I listen for the jangle of gold bracelets getting softer in the shadows, the gentle thud of the door behind six-inch stilettoes. Eventually, I get up from the bed and sink to the ground, my back against the door.

I pull the crumpled wad of paper from my pocket, unfold it.

The last panel is still there, featuring me towering over the Surgeon, red Converse hovering over the edge of the 103rd story.

Below it, the young woman with dark hair smiles up from her photograph.

"You," I whisper.

And just when the pieces begin to fall in place, the door bursts open behind me, knocking the page from my hands. I whip around in time to watch the Surgeon pull on his gloves, before an invisible bat smashes into the side of my head.

CR ∞ SO

I wake up alone in the still coldness of my room.

The fan spins on the ceiling, creaking under the weight of its own blades. A faint tinkle carries on the breeze—wind chimes and the grate of a garbage disposal truck.

The floor is strewn with books. Open books flat on their faces that have been pulled from my shelves and shredded.

A figure in blue scrubs stands on top of my dresser, tying a noose to the ceiling.

The Surgeon.

His cheeks are pulled into a smile even though I can't see his mouth under the medical mask. "I've got you, Red."

I try to reach for the knife on my belt, but my hands are tied behind my back. "What do you want?" I can't make sense of all the torn-up books on my floor.

"Does that really matter?" the Surgeon leers at me.

I know what's coming next.

I dodge an attack from an invisible weapon and roll backwards. There's a knife under the pillow of my bed, which I try to retrieve despite my bound hands.

He's found that one too.

"Why do you even try?"

"You can't win."

I momentarily lose track of my surroundings, and the blunt edge of a bat smashes into my chest. I stumble back, stars of pain blistering deep inside my body. My body goes numb, and before I can recover, another blow slams me down into the ground.

I heave myself onto my elbows, but the pain is too great. My body is heavier than I remember it was, sinking with the weight of my crushed ribs.

"Why didn't you kill me at Joey's?" I breathe. "You could've finished it there, and this fight would've been over."

The Surgeon kicks one of the books on the ground. Its jacket flops weakly. A huge chunk of text has been torn out from its end.

It's a wasted ghost of a thing.

"I could've killed you many times," he tells me.

He grabs me under the arms and drags me on top of the dresser, where he loops the noose around my neck. It's so high that I'm barely standing on the tips of my toes. My eyes water from the effort of breathing without the ends of my ribs digging into my lungs. For once, I'm glad I'm wearing a domino mask. While I fight to keep my balance, the Surgeon steps back to admire his work.

I scan over all the tattered books, trying to figure out why the Hell the Surgeon threw them off the shelves. "You going to torture me to death?" I ask him through gritted teeth. My chest feels as if it's about to rip open. "You know psychic surgery won't work on me. It's not pain that makes me scream."

"I don't want to kill you."

I struggle to see past the dresser, but I realize what he's done to the books. He's torn out all the endings.

I don't know if I want to laugh.

The Surgeon. Scared of the ending of stories.

Stories aren't real.

I'm struggling to stay on my tip-toes, but I can still catch the titles of a few books by the Surgeon's feet.

War and Peace.

Mrs. Frisby and the Rats of NIMH.

Red Runner vs. The Surgeon, Issue 17.

"Not even your own comic?" I ask him. "You don't die at the end of that one, if that's what you're afraid of."

The Surgeon glances at me. There's something different about the taunting set of his eyes this time. Something I can't reconcile with the twisted doctor who maimed the bodies of small children and sank them to the bottom of the Hudson in pieces.

I wonder if it's fear.

Then he kicks the chair out from under me.

The noose zips to its limit, snapping my windpipe shut.

My scream is choked off by a blunt blow that yanks my head

up from my shoulders. I struggle to keep all the muscles in my neck tight. Every inch of my body burns with perspiration.

The Surgeon leans into me.

"You don't get it, do you?" he asks. His blue eyes are deeper than I remember, reflecting my twisted, broken figure back at me. "They say you're the only one in the world who can kill me. You used to be my equal, and you came so close to it." He bends down and picks up one of the books. *Red Runner vs. The Surgeon, Issue 8.* "Remember what happens at the end?"

The muscles in my neck are sore, where the rope burns. A muffled gurgle comes up from my throat. I can't hold this up much longer.

But I remember what happens at the end of Issue 8.

I've pushed him into a shark tank at the New York Aquarium in the dead of night. He's pounding against the glass with his fists as a great white slithers out of the murky darkness, and reflected in his eyes are the watery shadows of my red Converse—shoelaces untied.

The Surgeon throws the comic away from him. "It's changing now. I'm stronger than you. Your writer is losing faith in you. Every time we fight, I can feel it. You're weak, fading. Nothing like you used to be." He grabs my shoulders, shakes me against the stranglehold of the noose. For a second, there's relief. "You don't see it, do you? I didn't bring you back here to kill you. I saved your life."

He shoves me away.

I swing on the rope, choking against the bloated mass of my tongue. I can't hold my body up with my broken ribs. The Surgeon watches with his hands behind his back.

"I've been saving your life for years. Playing with you and then letting you go. What are we, Red? Just fictional constructs within a story. People love you and hate me, and that's what keeps us alive. Red Runner vs. The Surgeon. We're supposed to fight each other— that's why we exist."

He looks into my eyes one more time. The edges of my vision are starting to go out. I can feel my tongue swelling out of my mouth, a gross gag that presses into my teeth.

"It's not the ending I'm afraid of," the Surgeon tells me. "It's *ending*."

And he slashes through the ropes.

I crash through the dresser onto the floor below amid broken slabs of wood and bits of rope.

The drapes flutter in the window where the Surgeon has leapt, the same way he's gotten away from me in five of our comics—barely slipped away from the tips of justice's fingers.

But I know now.

There is one way to defeat him.

Only one way.

I make one last phone call to Niall. I don't tell him much, just to meet me at the corner of 47th and Broadway.

While I wait for him, I dig the crumpled last page of Issue 12 out of my pocket. I'd found it smoothened out on my kitchen table, held down by a bottle of aspirin. I know the Surgeon read it while I was out—that he knows who it's from.

Slowly, I trace my nail through the photograph of the young woman.

"I know why she created you, Ryvie." The woman's smiling, a mischievous and knowing smile that makes me believe she's standing right behind me when she isn't. "She was using you. To get to me. She can feel that I'm slipping out of her control. I'm becoming my own character independent of what she wants, and it's not flashy enough for her taste. Shark tanks, hypnosis, bladed yo-yo's—that's what readers want, even if it's a stupid way to fight someone."

I know now that it's *her* voice that won't leave me alone, *her* motivations that won't let me destroy the Surgeon. It's her thoughts and her desires, in conflict with my own, that have turned me into a madman.

"Well, fuck your readers."

I crush the page as tightly as I can in my fist—so tight it makes my ribs throb, when the door of a cab slams by the sidewalk.

Niall clambers out. I notice he's added a bright red belt to his usual gray costume. "Red, you'll never guess what happened! I met a villain today, in Chinatown..."

He trails off when he sees the ginger way I'm holding my torso up, the crumpled note in my hand.

"Niall, I can hear her." I unravel the page just enough to show him her picture.

Niall's jaw drops slightly. I've never broken the taboo in front of him. Never.

"What? Are you sure?" He takes a step back. "She can't speak to you through the page. There's a wall between you."

"No, Niall. It's all for the money." I exhale slowly. I can't fight the deep-rooted betrayal that sinks through my body like a stone. I've been taken advantage of. We all have. "We pride ourselves in saving lives because we care about justice, Niall, but do you know why we exist? It's all for the money. I'll never kill the Surgeon—not while she's pulling the strings."

I know now. There's only one way to defeat her too.

The same way I can defeat the Surgeon.

I squeeze Niall's shoulder like I always do, and a bitter nostalgic ache flows through me. I've raised him into what he is, someone he can be proud of. I can tell him to turn back, to throw it all away because it's a lie—but I know he won't listen.

I wouldn't have.

So instead, I let him go.

"Red, I'll see you tonight, right?" Niall's still breathless. "At the Manhattan Superhero Convention? I'm giving a talk about side-kicking, and you have to be there so I can introduce you."

I smile and let go of his shoulder. "Of course. You're a great guy, Niall."

He doesn't know it, but that's good-bye.

After all, we're heroes. We exist to save the day and have it taken away from us. Over and over again.

A good story.

I drag my sneakers through a soiled mulch of dead leaves and shredded candy wrappers. One half of a maple leaf gets caught in the wind, turns over once, and sticks to the hem of my jeans. How lonely it is, to walk an empty road through the silence. At the end of the street, I reach up and pull the domino mask from my face.

The mask lies across both my hands, an old friend who stood by my side through my broken fears, my petty triumphs.

I've worn this disguise for ten years. But now I know that it's all a lie. That's what a domino mask is, isn't it? Just a blindfold that lets in a little more light than it should. I lift the lid of the nearest dumpster and drop it in.

I look down at my shoes—at the fashionably scuffed red canvas and muddy soles. *She* created this costume for me—made it into who I am. So why, when it's finally my turn to turn it all back in her face, do I find that I can't let it go?

I stuff the bullets into the magazine of my revolver and click it into place.

Slowly, I turn to face the barbed wire dividing the alley from the rest of the world. The braided staples grate my vision, as if I'm looking out at the world through a cage.

There's only one way to beat them both.

"It's my turn to tell the story."

I close my mouth over the gun and squeeze the trigger.

WELCOME HOME, DARLING

STEPHANIE M. WYTOVICH

It was cold and it was white
and the room looked as if it were dressed in clouds,
in cumulus outfits that made me think of hospitals and teeth,
that made my spit taste like antiseptic,
like wet gauze and expired medicine,
and yet the floors, covered in alabaster crumbs, were sharp,
their voices wooden stakes that screamed against the white,
against the clouds
and I was not happy,
not pleased that mother made me come here,
here in this asylum-crusted room
with all the white, with all the clouds,

because they were not me
at least not then,
for then,
I was a storm, a rainy-day child who preferred black to white
darkness to sun,
and that room,
that porcelain cell,
that spacious square of bone
was not a place of happiness;
it was a prison and
I was trapped.

THE DEAD COLLECTION

MERCEDES M. YARDLEY

ANIKA WISHED that she knew what it was like to be lonely.

Her best friend killed herself at seventeen. Belky was hesitant about taking her driver's test, about saying hi to the new boy in school, but she was absolutely fearless when it came to cutting her wrists. Not a single hesitation mark. She appeared, faintly transparent and apologetic, and followed Anika around from then on. Each first kiss, each tearful breakup, each agonizing job interview...Belky was there. She was also there when Anika was raped in the back room of the pizza place where she worked. Belky did, out of respect, turn her face to the wall, her wrists weeping in a way that she could not. Anika was grateful for this little comfort.

After Belky, it was D, who was killed on his motorcycle. He stood silently behind Belky, his helmet bashed in, his eyes as dark and beautiful as they had been in life. Anika stepped onto the subway, holding onto the rail, watching Belky and D as they bobbled and swayed with the movement. They watched back.

Her cat was run over by a gray Mercedes. He joined the procession, dragging himself with his front paws, his crushed back legs ghosting over the carpet. He meowed without sound, showing his bloodied tongue and broken teeth.

Anika reached over to pet him.

"I wondered where you'd gone off to, darling," she said. "I guess I can throw your kitty dish away."

She didn't, though. She walked past it several times a day,

and her cat's little catnip mouse, too, just in case he wanted to be amused by it.

Next was Adrienne. Leukemia. Adrienne didn't like Belky much, never had, but she and D got along swimmingly. She often picked up Anika's cat, holding him close, and he purred deep in a dimension that Anika couldn't hear. She had to admit she was a little jealous. But only a little.

Anika sat at a table at McDonalds, drinking a terrible coffee. The dead filled the empty chairs around her. Suddenly her boss, laughably named Mr. Tibbs, wandered in, his hair and shirt disheveled, his tie undone.

"Oh no, not you! Don't you have anywhere else to go?"

Mr. Tibbs shrugged, much more contrite in death than in life, his blue lips turned down.

Anika sighed.

"You guys have to tell him the rules. I hated dealing with him when he was alive. I'm *sorry,*" she said, when he looked at her unhappily. "It's just true."

She dropped her head into her hands. "Especially tell him about the bathroom rules."

Showers became even more uncomfortable. The dead lined the room, for the most part, facing the wall.

"D, I see you peeking out from under your helmet. If you're going to be that way, at least hand me the towel."

Against her better judgment, Anika took a lover. He was a wild, mercurial thing, terrifying and wonderful, and it wasn't long before she was carrying a baby.

At last, life, she thought, and her sigh was a beautiful thing.

Bodies aren't built for stress. Bodies with babies are built for it, even less. She and her lover had a fight. Two fights. Several fights, over stupid, meaningless things.

"I hate your friends," he said, but really he meant, *Why aren't I enough for you?*

"Stop controlling me," she answered back, but she meant to say, *I'm terrified. Can you just put your anger away? Please?*

The baby, whom she had named Jack in her head, showed up in the Dead Collection on tiny, thirteen-week fetus feet. He walked carefully, steadily, his head down, looking at his toes, and the rest of the dead looked at their toes, too.

"Oh. Oh no," Anika said, covering her hands with her mouth, and then she began to bleed. She spent the night weeping in the tub, and nobody, not even D, flicked his eyes her way. He just stood there, holding the faded blue towel awkwardly, in case she needed it.

She didn't. It was a night of cold bathwater and blood and a tiny body that fit in the palm of her hand.

She didn't tell her lover, because what was there to tell, really? She stayed at home with a stomachache and unwashed hair and a dead baby, and the next time they spoke it was about loyalty and making tough decisions and he said that things would be good, he promised. But sometimes even lovers lie.

He joined the Dead Collection with the back of his head blown away and his teeth chipped from the gun's barrel. He turned his back on everybody else, reaching for a cigarette, but Baby Jack grasped the shoelaces of his Docs with a surprisingly firm grip.

"Daddy?" The baby's mouth moved. Anika blinked when she realized she could hear his voice, sweet and tender and so very unalive.

Her lover stared at the baby. Then he stared at her.

"My family," she muttered, and went back to sleep. Sleeping in self-defense, she thought, and then she didn't think any more.

Baby Jack started to cry.

The otherworldly wailing of her son sometimes made its way into Anika's dreams, but mostly it didn't. She dreamed of shotgun blasts and drowning victims and a child who drank rubbing alcohol because there wasn't anything left in the house. The screams, her boy's screams, sounded like everybody else's screams. Terror and sorrow, in its many forms, all sound the same. They just made her tired.

She slept several days, at first unable to open her eyes, and then just unwilling to. Her cat hauled itself around on her bed, butting his broken head under her hand for caresses. Her lover tried to rock the baby, who would have none of it. Belky and Adrienne worked together to prepare a meal of some sort, but Belky kept bleeding into the cereal. Adrienne pushed her aside and enlisted the aid of Mr. Tibbs, and the two of them came up with some eggs that smelled faintly of chemo and clopidogrel.

She didn't eat the chemo eggs, or the bloody cereal, or the half-masticated mouse that her cat brought her. She didn't do anything except close her eyes, or sometimes open them halfway to stare at the ceiling light, which was on, or sometimes off, or sometimes on again, because D was trying to distract Dead Baby Jack with electricity.

Her lover pressed the howling baby into her hand, and she tried to take him, but there was nothing to take.

"Stop him," she cried, and tears leaked down her face. She tried to pat Jack's head, tried to wrap her arms around him, tried to slap at him with her hands.

"He's your son. Stop him!"

Her lover looked worried, looked like himself, like when times were good, which wasn't often. She missed him, then, and her tears became new things.

They stood there, her collection, watching her. Anika turned on her side and pulled her pillow over her head. She thought about anything but her baby. Everything but.

She woke to a soft, gray hand on her forehead. Her newly departed grandmother smiled at her. Anika broke down again and cried. Her grandmother clucked silently, and whispered without words how much she loved her. She rubbed Anika's back until the sobbing and hiccupping stopped. When she was something near calm again, but really closer to comatose, Anika looked at the white, worried expressions of her collection, at Mr. Tibbs thumping the baby's miniature back rhythmically with two fingers, in what he desperately hoped was a soothing manner.

She sighed.

"Oh, all right," she said, and tried to sit up.

It was harder than she would have expected, and to be honest, the desire wasn't really there, but she loved these crushed, broken faces. For the most part. Sorry, Mr. Tibbs. And Anika thought, is this what their deaths are all about? The wails of a miserable child, passing through two realities? And her son. Her baby. Poor Jack. There was nothing she could do to help him. Living mothers weren't meant to have dead children.

She shuffled carefully like an old woman, like Anika the Ancient, and when she passed her lover, she stopped for a second. All of the fight, if there ever had been any, left her body.

He opened his mouth to say something, and whether it was I'm Sorry or Serves You Right or something even more colorful, it didn't matter. She was already shuffling out the door.

They trailed behind her, a dead collection of baby dolls, of bony baby ducks. Belky. D. The cat. Adrienne. Mr. Tibbs. Baby Jack, rubbing his eyes with tiny fists. Her lover, whose name she swore she'd never speak again. Her grandmother, who tidied up Mr. Tibb's askew shirt and looked around pensively.

This wasn't a collection; it was a procession.

She hadn't bothered with shoes. Her bare feet padded on the concrete in a most unsatisfactory way. When she had been a girl, she had worn cotton dresses and ran barefoot through long grasses. She and Belky had braided flowers in their hair. Looked around the city for something alive, for something natural, but the steel and pavement had stamped everything living out. It was as gray as her life. As gray as her collection.

"I'm sorry," she apologized to them. Her body was weak with the illness of despair, and her breathing hurt. Pincushions in her lungs. Pointy stars of city spore. She felt the responsibility for their undead happiness.

"I should have chosen somewhere else to live. Somewhere more beautiful. Then you all wouldn't be...here."

They tried to touch her. Smooth her disheveled hair and love her silently. She didn't notice the tears cleaning her face.

To the subway. She deposited her token. They trailed along to the constant soundtrack of Jack's cries. It sounded strangely lovely. It sounded like an alternate form of life.

She waited at the platform, turning and smiling at her friends. Her family. There was a rumbling and the platform shook. She smiled sweetest at all at her son.

"I'll hold you soon, darling," she said, and stepped off backwards, falling onto the tracks. There were screams and screeching of metal and the most intense of fireworks going off behind her eyes. She tried to take a deep breath but, like when she tried to hold her son, there was nothing to take.

She strained to open her eyes, but she was missing one. Her eye and her jaw and most of her left side. But she still had one good arm, unsnapped, and that was all that she needed to hold her baby to her ruined breast. She smiled as best she could, and looked around for him.

He wasn't there.

"Jack? Belky?"

No baby coos or baby cuddles or baby shrieks. Anika whirled around, but her collection wasn't there at all. Instead, a man with shrapnel through his face peered at her cautiously.

"A new one. Just what we need."

His voice hurt her head, hurt her heart. She looked around. No Baby Jack. No Adrienne. No cat or Grandmother or even Mr. Tibbs.

There was a young girl with bruising around her throat. A man missing both of his legs. He smiled.

"I know you. You used to come in every morning and get coffee

from Lara. Haven't seen you in a bit." He eyed her up and down. "Guess I can see why."

The living girl, Lara, looked tired and irritated in her McDonalds uniform. She flicked her eyes at Anika.

"Seriously?" She asked. "I'm the best you have?"

"Where's my baby?" Anika asked her. At least she tried. Her jaw, it made things difficult, but she could figure it out, she could, if only she could find Jack, if only she could find her little one…

Lara turned away from her, served up another steaming paper cup of generic joe.

"She can't hear you," the legless man said. "You'll get used to it."

That was it. It for conversation. It for life. She never spoke again, never had reason to. She stood around, part of this Lara's collection, in a semi-circle with everybody else while Lara served coffee after coffee after coffee.

WH!SPER #1 (A WARNING)

ERIK T. JOHNSON

This has not happened yet, it is a warning
Hebdomeros is born who was not born, still as fire when fire is gone,
And restless like fire burning the beautiful down
Dangles from scorched witch-woman's womb, faceless gray boy
He is fishing lure for that beast called Future, yes
That wild Future, never more than rumor, yet always real as Always
Never having been hunted before, the Future bites the bait,
Mistaking it for a capital city, another Wednesday, dust-speck, glacier
Hebdomeros is both lure and fisherman, Future wriggling on his line
He is hour hand on minute hand when midnight is erect,
A pendulum too timeless to swing, 'till the time is come
For Hebdomeros
This is a warning, if you heard this.

WATCH ME

MEGHAN ARCURI

IT DIDN'T TAKE LONG for my body to fall to the floor.

The sharp knife made the blood spill from my wrist.

I'd thought I'd been doing better. I really had. I guess the effects of mourning ebb and flow.

I saw Ava before I fell. Did she have a knife, too? Did she know about me and Ty?

He'd come to me that evening.

"Elle," he said. "I want you."

We had the most amazing night of passion.

I think he liked the sexy, new outfit I'd been wearing. One of many I'd recently bought.

I was shocked he had come by, ready to seduce me. I thought he and Ava were a thing. Especially after what I'd watched them do through the window a few weeks ago.

Erotic and beautiful, I'd never seen anything like it, let alone experienced it.

All of their lovemaking sessions were amazing, but the last time had stirred something in me. Turning me on to the point where I took out my own scarf and mimicked her. Alone.

Their sexual behavior shone a light on my naiveté. I wanted to change. I needed to.

Everything about Ava showed me that.

Even before that night, I studied her. Learning what wine she drank, how her clothes fit, how she moved.

I peeked at her through the curtains on my window.

I'm pretty sure she never saw me.

I know I shouldn't have been watching Ava, but she didn't close her curtains. Ever.

Her brazen confidence enchanted me. She was mature, lovely. And I'd be lying if I said she didn't remind me of my mom. A younger version of my mom but with the same thick hair, high cheekbones, and big eyes.

Men reacted to Ava, too. One morning early on, I walked out of my building at the same moment she walked out of hers. She wore a simple, fitted dress and heels. Ty had been working construction across the street. As she and I reached the sidewalk, his eyes locked on to Ava's body and followed it to the corner.

Men used to look at my mom like that, too. Her beauty matched Ava's. Up to and including the day the cancer beat her.

I had a hard time after she died. We'd always been together, just the two of us. My dad never part of the picture. I became depressed. Almost suicidal. Our home had so many memories, I needed to move out.

The new place was in a group of old apartment buildings, built one right on top of another. My bedroom window almost touching-distance from my neighbor's. I bought thick curtains and always kept the window locked.

Then I saw my neighbor: Ava. And her resemblance to my mother comforted me.

I'd heard through the grapevine she was different. Mysterious. Her eyes otherworldly. Even though I'd watched her often, we'd never talked or made direct eye contact, so I knew nothing of that.

I was just glad to be in a new place, starting a new life.

A new girl moves into the apartment building next to mine, our bedroom windows facing each other.

The grapevine tells me her name is Elle. Her mom died and now she's on her own.

Like the others before her, she is curious, peering through the window.

I leave the curtain open. I like it that way. I don't care who watches me.

I want them to watch me. Especially the young, pretty ones. So they can see what a real woman looks like. How she acts. Who she is. Maybe they can learn something. And once they meet my eyes, they're mine.

This one always looks at me through the window. She thinks I don't see her watching me from behind her curtains. But she's more obvious than she realizes.

Elle watches me for weeks. She sees what food I like, what clothes I wear, who I sleep with.

A few weeks ago, she saw me with Ty. He likes a little kink.

"Ava," he said. "Use the scarf."

He sat on the edge of the bed and put his hands behind his back, letting me tie them together. Taking my time, I stood between his legs and undressed for him. Then I covered my body with a long, sheer scarf. A red one. I slid it over my skin, the movement of the fabric exciting me. Exciting him. I twisted and turned my hips, letting the scarf caress every part of me.

He pulled his hands from their restraints—I always kept the knot loose. He tugged the scarf. It fell to the floor. He ran his fingers up and down my sides. Pulled me on to his lap, my legs straddling his hips. He was ready. So was I.

This morning, I see Elle walking out of her building as I walk out of mine. Her skirt is tighter than usual, her blouse cut lower. She wears a red scarf around her neck.

Ty's been at work across the street for a few hours. As Elle and I reach the bottom of our respective landings, Ty's eyes find her.

Not me.

They follow her down the street.

When night arrives, I sit at my bedroom window and wait. Elle returns home a few minutes later. Ty is with her. They kiss, nip, pet.

He makes her tie his hands with her scarf. Then she strips for him, slowly, seductively. He is ready for her and she is for him. But she'd tied his hands too tightly. They use a knife to cut him free. Then they slide, thrust, sigh.

After a while, Ty leaves. Elle lies on the bed, limp and sated. But I know she can't help herself. She peers at me through her curtains. And when our eyes meet, hers haze over.

She is mine.

Her emotions, her will. Mine to manipulate. Mine to collect, keeping me youthful. Beautiful.

She sits at the window, her position mirroring mine.

I smile at her. She smiles at me.

I raise my left hand. She raises her right.

I pick up a sharp knife I'd retrieved from the kitchen.

I graze my wrist. A small drop of blood flows.

I've done this before.

She picks up the knife she'd left on her nightstand.

She slices her wrist. A lot of blood flows.

She has not done this before.

A few minutes pass. She slumps to the floor

WH!SPER #2 (A PROPHECY)

ERIK T. JOHNSON

What does not bleed breaks, this is a prophecy
Caulbearer, you do not bear the caul alone
Your victim is your servant, holding up this sack of rain
Caulbearer, murdered your own twin
One You alive and another You dead
How will you dispose of the corpse, Caulkiller?
How will you deny your crime?
What does not bleed breaks, this is a prophecy
Don't you know there's no worse place to hide than the womb
You will be born, your cry of greed mistaken for health
Growing, forgetting your guilt like Time forgets clocks
A bad memory for what's past is often the best salvation
And many times the makings of a great prophet
But your dead sibling is watching under you
God alone knows why
And what God knows will hurt you.

THE BIGGER BEDROOM

JOSH MALERMAN

1

BARRY AND BRIAN stared up at the huge house, mouths agape, the beach ball at rest between them on the grass.

"It's better than Dad said it was going to be," Barry said. The boys were the same age, eight, but they were not twins. Barry had two months on his brother. Brian was also adopted. Or, as Dad said, *taken in*. Or as Mom said...

... *welcomed in.*

"Yeah," Brian agreed. "It's enormous."

"Look." Barry pointed to the second story windows. "That window there... that's one of the bedrooms. And those *two* windows over there," he said, pointing to the opposite end of the house, "is the other one."

"Two windows?"

"Yeah."

"Why does that room have two windows?"

"Because," Barry said. "It's bigger."

Brian looked from one end of the house to the other, then back again.

"I want the bigger bedroom."

"Yeah, of course you do. So do I."

Brian looked to his brother. They'd become brothers, not cousins, at two years old. When Barry's Uncle Doug, Brian's dad, drank so much he drowned.

"Then what do we do?"

"We do what everybody does in this situation. We flip for it."

Barry stuck his hand in his pocket and pulled out a quarter. The front door of the house opened and Mom appeared in the sudden rectangle.

"Boys," she said. "Come on. You haven't even been inside yet."

"We're coming," Barry said.

"We're coming!" Brian repeated.

Mom frowned and closed the door.

"Heads or tails?" Barry asked.

Brian thought about it. He looked up to the house again. It felt like a very big decision. Heads or tails. The bigger bedroom. Either way, one would be *his* bedroom.

"Tails."

Barry nodded and tossed the coin. He caught it and had it flat and hidden on top of his other hand.

"Tails you get the two windows, heads I do."

"Yep."

"Alright." Barry revealed the coin.

Heads.

"Come on," Brian said.

Barry smiled.

"Come on," he said. "Let's move in."

2

It was everything Dad said it would be and more. Both parents were glowing about the kitchen, and the size of the refrigerator. Neither Barry nor Brian cared about that at all. They were bouncing from room to room; the basement had room for a pinball machine, and floor hockey if they wanted it. The bathrooms were modern, *updated* as Dad said. The tub off the master bedroom had two showerheads and the brothers thought it was gross that Mom and Dad might shower together. The living room had a wall of windows that looked out on a three-quarter acre yard. Mom said it was big enough for a wedding. Barry and Brain imagined war games, adventure stories, hanging ropes from treetop to treetop, building a fort.

"Everybody will be here in forty-five minutes," Mom said. 'Everybody' was the group of family friends and relatives who agreed to help the Ellums move in. The promise of pizza and beer went a long way in getting people to help you move in.

"Let's just start doing it ourselves!" Barry said, looking out the front bay window to the U-Haul parked in the driveway.

"I like your spirit, kid," Dad said. "But I also like my back. My neck. My knees. All of me."

Barry shook his head, looked to the ceiling.

"Brian!" he called upstairs. "Are you looking at my bedroom?"

Barry raced up the stairs and found his brother was indeed standing at the doorway to the bigger bedroom. Barry's bedroom.

"Come on" Brian said. "It's like *twice* the size of mine. How about we both sleep in mine, and we use this as a playroom?"

"No way! We flipped."

Barry smiled and entered his new room. Without any of his things, it was just a long, clean, empty rectangle. He spread his arms wide and spun.

"There's so much … *roooooom!*" he sang, laughing and spinning.

"Stop it," Brian said. But Barry was infectious and Brian joined him, spinning and singing about how much room was in Barry's new bedroom.

A thump from below and the boys dropped to their knees and pressed their ears to the gray carpet.

"Dad?" Barry said, smiling at Brian.

"Dad!" Brian called. "Say something!"

Another thump and Dad's muffled voice from below.

"Come on down!" he called. "The movers are here!"

They sprang up and ran to one of the windows. They looked down to the front yard and the driveway below.

Uncle Hugh and Aunt Bree's old turbo diesel Mercedes. Mike's Ford pickup. Three people hopped out of the truck bed.

Brian watched Hugh and Bree exit their car and he thought how strange it was that Hugh was also one of Mom's brother's. Just like his real dad had been.

"Come on," Barry said. "We gotta' fill this house *up!*"

He spun again, spinning out of the room.

Brian paused, still at the window.

Then he felt alone up here. Alone in all this empty house.

We gotta' fill this house up!

It felt huge, empty, and endless without anything inside of it.

He bolted out of the room and joined everybody else by the front door.

3

Before moving in, Mom warned them that it could take a family years to "truly fill a home."

No matter how big or small it is. No matter the shape or size. It's an unwritten rule; making a home takes time and nobody knows the formula for when it happens. Just suddenly one day you'll realize...PRESTO! We live here.

But that's not how it went. Moving went smoothly and everything was put pretty much where it was in their last house. In fact, most of the house felt like an elongated version of their last home. Same pictures on the walls, just more space between them. More distance from the couch and television, same red rug on the ground between them.

"I like it here," Dad said, holding Mom on the couch. The boys were on their bellies in front of the television. An old movie. Gene Kelly. They kinda' liked him. Mom loved him.

It was night, dark outside, and the Ellums had enjoyed their new house for only three nights, and yet...it *did* feel like home.

"We oughtta' put a pool out back," Dad said.

"No way," Mom said. "That'll eat half the yard."

But Barry and Brian loved the idea.

"Oh come on!" Barry said. "We'd be the most popular kids at school!"

Mom seemed to consider this.

"No," she said.

"You can't have an artist space *and* the yard," Barry said.

Mom, Susan, was taking art classes. Painting. She had dreams of abstract, psychedelic renderings of her life story. But she figured she should learn the right stuff first. She was enrolled in a Still Life class at a nearby studio.

"I sure as shit *can*," she said, tossing a throw pillow at Barry but hitting Brian on the shoulder.

Dad laughed. The boys thought it was funny every time Mom swore.

Gene Kelly broke into a wild dance routine and the boys forgot about the pool and Mom thought about her painting class and Dad just loved every minute of being here. When it was time for bed, the four of them climbed the stairs together, as if they still felt like newcomers after all, like they were in a hotel, a friendly one, taking the stairs up to their rooms.

On the second floor they said goodnight and dispersed. Mom and Dad walked the long white hall to the master suite. Brian trotted off in the other direction. And Barry crossed the nearest threshold and entered the bigger bedroom.

4

Briaaaaaan!

Brian woke in the dark. He sat up in bed and looked to his half open door. He could never decide if we wanted it closed or open. Open meant you might see someone coming down the hall. But closed meant you might be stuck in here with that someone.

So halfway. He liked to leave his bedroom door halfway.

His eyes adjusted but the moonlight coming in through the

bedroom's one window made it easy. Quickly he could see his dresser. His posters of Snagglepuss and Grape Ape, the stars of the Laff-A-Lympics. The piles of clothes, neatly folded, beside his closet door.

The plain white clock ticked on his nightstand and he listened to it for half a minute.

Was that what woke him?

He didn't think so. He had a distant memory of hearing his name.

"*Briaaaaaaan!*"

Brian clutched his blanket and sheet.

It was his name, absolutely. And it wasn't a distant memory. It was a voice that sounded far away.

He looked to the wall that separated his room from Barry's.

"Barry?"

Brian listened closely, listened hard. He thought he heard movement from that same echoey distance.

Bare feet upon solid ground.

"Barry?"

"*Briiiiaaaaaaaaaaan!*"

Brian ducked, pulling the blanket higher up, to his eyes. He stared at his half open door, expecting Barry to come floating in, the way his voice sounded, the way he called his name…

5

At breakfast the next morning, Barry looked tired. He ate a lot. Two platefuls.

"Don't comb your hair anymore?" Mom said, bending at the waist beside Barry and flattening his messy brown hair. "Look, Steve," she said to Dad. "Barry is living like a king in his new palace."

"That's the way to do it," Dad said, before leaving the kitchen and heading for the office, his new office, half the reason the Ellums moved into a place this size to begin with.

"You two entertain yourselves," Mom said. "I'm going to paint."

She followed Dad out of the kitchen and turned around to face the brothers still seated at the kitchen table. Barry had a twinkle in his eye, and bags beneath them. "Go play in the yard," she said. "Explore it for us."

As soon as she left, Brian brought up the night before.

"Your room must be *huge*," he said.

Barry looked up at him.

"You saw it. It *is* huge!"

"Yeah but," Brian said, and checked to make sure neither Mom or Dad was listening. "Last night I heard you calling my name. You sounded a thousand feet away."

Barry smiled and nodded. His eyes grew distant, the way people's eyes get when they're remembering something.

"Did I scare you?"

"Yeah! Kind of!"

Barry laughed.

"It's fun to call over to you. You're only a room away."

"Sounded like four hundred rooms."

"Don't be silly."

But Barry smiled again and the look returned to his eyes.

"Come on," he said, pretending to toss his plate across the kitchen toward the sink. "Let's explore like Mom said."

6

Outside, the brothers fell to their knees on the grass, having just raced across the yard.

"I won," Brian said, smiling. "I've never won before!"

Barry looked like he was going to argue this, then stopped. Instead, he nodded.

"You did."

Brian pressed his hands against the ground.

"It's soft out here," he said.

"I've felt softer," Barry said, lying down on his back.

"You have? Where?"

Barry shrugged. He lay perfectly still, his arms at his sides, his legs together. Eyes closed. Brian looked over at him, then looked away. He didn't like to see Barry that way. It reminded him of his real dad, in his casket. Brian was only two years old then but remembered it. His dad. Motionless. Arms not crossed over his chest like people say it goes. Arms at his sides. Legs together. Lying down.

"What are you doing?' Brian asked after enough time had gone by without Barry moving.

Barry opened his eyes and looked at his brother.

"Ever see a guy take a nap before!"

7

Briiiiaaaaaan!

Night again. Brian sat up quickly in bed.

"Barry?" At first he asked it. Then he called it. "Barry!"

"Briiiiiiaaaaaan! It's so fun out here!"

Brian didn't like the echo. Didn't like how far away his brother sounded. It sounded too far. Like Brian was calling from another house. Or from the middle of another street.

Brian swung his legs over the edge of his bed. The carpet was soft under his bare feet and that was something. That was some small comfort.

He walked to the window and parted the curtains. He looked out into the yard.

"Briiiiiiiaaaaaan!"

He squinted into the moonlight. It sounded like Barry was calling from outside! Or somewhere far enough away to be outside. He looked to the trees at the edge of the yard. Looked at the black shadows made there.

"Barry?" Brian asked himself. Then he looked over his shoulder, expecting to see Barry standing in his doorway, smiling, his hair a mess, talking about soft earth and lying on his back like a dead father.

But there was no Barry. Not there.

But somewhere.

He crossed his bedroom and peered out into the dark hallway. Mom and Dad were asleep at the other end of it. It looked far. Far enough that even a quick run wouldn't get him there fast enough.

He opened his door all the way and slipped into the hall, turned right and saw the head of the stairs. Saw the soft glow of a blue night light from the first floor. It illuminated enough of the door to Barry's bedroom to see the doorknob.

He went to it. Went to the doorknob. Placed his hand upon it.

"*Briiiiiaaaaaaan! It's so fun out here!*"

Barry's voice; it hadn't come from inside his bedroom. It *couldn't* have!

He began to turn the knob and stopped. He didn't want to open the door. Didn't want to look into Barry's bedroom. Was afraid he'd find him in bed, standing on the blankets, cupping his lips, calling his name with a voice that made no sense, made no sense of the echo… of the distance…

"*Briiiiiiaaaan!*"

Laughter. Real laughter. Echoed but finite. A long hallway. Walls. Something.

Brian turned toward the hallway leading to Mom and Dad's bedroom. He trembled, imagining Barry emerging from the shadows, maybe crawling toward him, maybe floating, on his back, his arms at his side, his legs together straight out before him, eyes closed.

Brian raced back into his own bedroom, slamming the door closed behind him.

He climbed into bed and felt like even the carpet might do something to him, might show him that it had fingers, might reach for him as he was pulling the blanket to his eyes.

Might pull the blanket back.

You need to see this, Brian…it's so fun…

"*Briiiaaaaaaaan!*"

"What?!" Brian called, hardly able to stand the sound of his brother's distant voice. He didn't want Barry to speak again.

But Barry did speak again. Brian leaned toward Barry's bedroom.

I'm back!

He thought he'd heard Barry say *I'm back.*

"Good," Brian whispered, trembling, his heart thudding catlike in his little chest. "Good, Barry."

Wherever Barry had gone, wherever he'd called from, so far away, he was back. Barry was back.

And that was enough for Brian.

Enough for now.

8

"God, Barry," Mom said, "you *smell.*"

She was holding a hand over her mouth and nose. She looked at Dad and Dad looked at her and it was obvious she felt bad about saying what she'd said. But it was obvious, too, that she'd meant it.

Dad rose from his end of the table and stepped to Barry.

"Okay, kid," he said. "Bath time."

Barry didn't fight it. He didn't argue at all. Dad eased him up out of his chair. Brian watched as his Mom flattened Barry's messy brown hair again, then wiped her hands clean on a paper towel from the kitchen counter.

"Steve?" she said.

Dad, halfway out of the kitchen with Barry, looked over his shoulder at her. Brian could tell that they were silently asking questions. Without speaking, Mom was asking if Dad knew what that smell was. Dad, without speaking, was saying he didn't know and that it worried him, too.

"Let's clean you up," Dad said.

"Okay," Barry said, his voice sleepy and, to Brian, very present, very close.

Mom turned to face Brian.

Once Dad and Barry were out of the room, Mom sat at the

table. "Brian?" she asked.

Brian looked up at her, wide-eyed.

"What?"

"Did you two play in the yard this morning?"

"No, we didn't. You just woke us up."

Mom nodded. She was considering this.

"Did you play in the yard in the middle of the night?"

Brian shook his head.

"No."

She stared at him an extra beat. The extra beat that meant she was checking if he was lying.

"You didn't play out there…run around…you didn't…find an animal?"

"Find an animal?"

Mom shook her head.

"I don't know. A dead animal?"

Brian was confused.

"Is that what Barry smells like? A dead animal?"

"No," Mom said and Brian believed her. He also believed she still thought he smelled something *like* a dead animal.

A dead something.

The sound of the shower erupted overhead. Dad was washing Barry above them.

Brian wanted to say something. He wanted to say, *Why is Dad washing him up there? Why is Dad washing Barry so close to his bedroom? Doesn't Dad know he should stay away from there? Doesn't Dad know he should keep Barry away from his bedroom?*

Something clicked in Mom's eyes and she rose and came to Brian. She bent at the waist and ran her fingers quickly through his hair and smelled his hair, too.

She paused. Thinking.

"Maybe you should take a shower, too."

"What?"

"Don't argue with me, Brian. Not right now. Please."

"Do I smell like a dead animal, too?"

"*No*," Mom said and she slammed her hand kind of hard on the kitchen table. "No," she repeated, softer. "And neither does Barry."

"Then why do I need to take a shower?"

"Because," Mom said.

Then she left the kitchen and Brian heard the stairs creaking as she climbed them, heard the water falling in the bathroom, the shower, louder, when she opened the bathroom door.

He heard it grow quieter, muffled, distant, when she closed it again.

9

Mom was painting in the living room. Dad lay on the couch. Brian was on his back on the rug on the floor, a throw pillow under his head. Brian and Dad were quietly watching another Gene Kelly movie. Mom didn't want to be alone in the room she'd been excited to paint in because Mom was worried about Barry.

They all were.

He was supposed to be sleeping upstairs in his bedroom.

"Mom," Brian asked, unable to see her over his shoulder, "why is he such a good dancer?"

"Because he practiced all the time," Mom said, sitting at her easel, painting a watercolor, a man standing in a gray open field.

"You've got to be a little obsessed for that," Dad said quietly.

They all spoke quietly.

They were all worried about Barry.

"Obsessed?" Brian asked, watching the television.

"He must have had the . . . *dance-bug*," Dad said. "Crawled its way into his mind."

"Steve," Mom said, and Brian heard her brush mixing in circles inside a plastic cup.

Brian thought of a black bug, a big one, crawling from the kitchen, crawling toward him, climbing into his ear, getting into his brain. On the television, Gene Kelly looked a little mad to him. A little crazy. Brian started to feel bad for him. Started to see him as a crazy person.

Dad rose from the couch.

"Anybody need anything? I'm grabbing some juice."

"I'm fine," Mom said.

"I'm fine, Dad."

"That looks good," Dad said and Brian knew he was looking at Mom's painting.

"His features are out of whack," Mom said. "His face doesn't look right."

"I've seen faces like that."

At the voice, Brian sat up quickly and looked to the entrance of the living room.

It was Barry.

"Barry?" Dad asked. "You're up?"

"Where?" Mom asked with worry in her voice.

"Where what?" Dad asked.

"Where have you seen faces like that?" Mom asked Barry.

10

Brian and Barry sat at the kitchen table, drawing. In their last home the two brothers attempted to start a comic book all their own. It was more of a who's who in a fictional world as each page was a new character, a new name, with a brief profile.

CHALK MAN – 100 years old. Made of Chalk. Writes his name wherever he goes.

Dad suggested they try it again, tonight. He pulled Brian aside before the brothers sat down together.

Show him a good time, Dad said, his eyes soft with sadness, worry.

Why? Brian asked. He was worried, too. Barry was waking up weird. Smelling weird. And Brian heard him at night, too. Talking. Calling his name.

Sometimes we just need a good time to get back on track, Dad said.

Now, at the table, Brian was trying to show Barry a good time.

"That's a great one," Brian said, pointing at the picture Barry made.

But what he really wanted to do was ask Barry where he went at night.

"Thanks," Barry said, his eyes dark, overcast. Lost in thought. In memory.

"Here," Brian said, noticing there was no horizon in Barry's picture. He set his pencil at one end of Barry's sheet of paper. Started to draw the horizon.

"Hey hey," Barry said. "No. I don't want that."

"When did you stop drawing horizons?"

"You don't need them."

"But it gives you perspective, Mom says."

Barry held his hand over his sheet of paper, blocking Brian from drawing on it.

"Some places don't have that," Barry said. "Some places go on for a really long time."

Someone sighed behind them and Brian turned to see Mom standing in the kitchen doorway, watching them.

He didn't know she'd been watching them.

"You're sleeping with us tonight, Barry," Mom said.

Then she left the kitchen.

11

Brian didn't know which was worse; leaving his bedroom door open or leaving it closed. If you left it open you might wake up to see someone standing in the hall, watching you sleep. If you left it closed, you could be stuck in here with him. He also didn't know which was worse; waking to hear Barry calling from the bedroom over, or not having Barry in there at all, leaving him, Brian, all alone at this side of the house.

He felt chilled, thinking of the empty space a wall away. The empty bed. The objects in Barry's bedroom unmoved. Barry was sleeping in Mom and Dad's room. Why? Brian only slept in there when he was sick or if he had a really bad dream. Was Barry sick? Did he have a really bad dream?

Brian heard a door open down the hall.

He sank further into his bed, his eyes wide, focused on his half open bedroom door. He shook his head no, slowly, watching, almost expecting a stranger to emerge from the hall shadows, to step into his bedroom, to ask him where Barry was.

A clicking sound. Footsteps in the hall. And Brian thought this might be worse than a stranger. Somehow this was worse.

He sat up, a little bit, craning his neck to get a better look into the hall. Barry passed, quickly, quietly. Barry's bedroom door opened and closed.

Brian listened.

Barry said something. A whisper.

A second voice, too.

Brian was out of bed, trembling on the carpet. He stepped toward his half open door, stepped toward the hall. In his white underwear he felt cold, vulnerable, open. He started to cry, expecting to see a person with the second voice enter his bedroom. Barry whispered again, this time from a distance. Maybe he wasn't whispering anymore. Maybe he was talking now but further away.

New footsteps. Different than the ones Barry took in the hall. But still, maybe coming toward him. Toward his bedroom.

But they weren't coming toward him.

Brian stood with his arms half raised, half covering his chest. They were shaking. So were his knees. So were his lips.

"Mom," he said, and his voice sounded scared. He should move. He should get Mom. She understood something was wrong with Barry. She understood it more than he did. She was an adult and adults knew a little more about bad dreams and death and whatever was wrong with Barry than Brian did.

He stepped toward the hall.

"*Briiiiiiaaaaaaan!*"

Brian stopped, chilled, shaking his head without knowing he was doing it.

"Barry?"

His brother's voice sounded so far away. Miles away. Like he was calling from their old house. Calling from his bedroom there.

Brian turned to the window. The one window in his bedroom.

"Barry?" he called, afraid to say his name too loud.

A form, something, floating outside his bedroom window.

Brian made a strange low sound. A single syllable. Sounded like he had dirt in his throat.

He brought a finger up, pointing at it, pointing at the silhouette, something, floating on the other side of the closed drapes.

"*Briiiiiiaaaaaaan!*" Barry's voice. So far away. Too far away to be right outside his window. Too far away to be—"*it's so fun out here!*"

A second voice. The second voice. An adult. Yelling.

"*QUIET!*"

Brian couldn't move, just couldn't move, stood still, trembling on the carpet, pointing to the window, moaning. The lights came on in his bedroom and he turned, blurred, to see Mom in the doorway.

"Where is he?" she asked, scared.

Brian turned back to the window, still pointing, still shaking.

Mom left the doorway. Dad passed, too. One of them opened the door to Barry's bedroom.

Mom spoke to Barry. Must've been in his bedroom. Mom spoke to him.

"What are you doing in here?" she said.

Brian didn't remember walking into the hall but he was in the hall, looking into Barry's bedroom. Between Mom and Dad he saw Barry on his bed, dirty and wet, on his knees on his bed. Dad stepped toward Barry and Mom cried. Barry shook his head no, didn't want them to take him out of his bedroom, didn't want them to take him out.

12

"Brian," Dad said, his hands folded upon the kitchen table, "your brother will be staying with Hugh and Bree tonight."

"Staying at their house?"

Brian understood that something was wrong. But in the world he was used to, sleeping at somebody else's house was supposed to be a good time. A sleepover. A privilege.

"Yes," Dad said. Mom was in another room. Somewhere else in the house. Painting. "It feels like the right thing to do. Your mom and I think it's the right thing to do."

He nodded and Brian wondered if he really thought it was the right thing to do. It felt like Dad didn't know what the right thing to do was.

13

Brian was on the rug, on his back. Mom and Dad sat on the couch. Gene Kelly danced on the television and Brian imagined a bug in his brain. Imagined Gene Kelly was smiling with insanity. Smiling because something had crawled into his brain and was wriggling around in there, maze like, endlessly, causing Gene Kelly to move, to move all over the place. And the other dancers danced because they felt bad for Gene Kelly. Felt bad because he was smiling all the time, speaking in gibberish, couldn't stop moving because of the bug in his brain, constantly moving, unsettled, taping his tap shoes in step with the tip of the bug's legs, the tip-tap of the bug's legs, making him dance, making him crazy…

14

The empty bedroom beside his own. Brian decided this was worse. Worse than having Barry in there. Worse than the sound of his brother calling to him from an impossible distance. Worse than the second voice.

The emptiness. No voices. No Barry.

And still, Brian listened. He sat up in bed, his blanket and sheet pulled up to his shoulders. His own bedroom door was closed. He didn't want to see into the hall. Not tonight. Barry wasn't in the room next to his and if he saw something in the hall tonight he might fall to pieces, might go mad.

He looked over his shoulder, to the window.

No shape there. No silhouette.

Brian got out of bed.

He wore a t-shirt this time because he remembered being so cold, so naked, standing and trembling the night before. He wore socks, too.

He crossed the bedroom, crossed the carpet, and opened his bedroom door.

Eyes closed, afraid to look, Brian stepped into the hall.

"Barry," Brian whispered, not because Barry could hear him but as some kind of anchor, something to hang on to.

He opened his eyes at Barry's bedroom door.

Tails.

Brian imagined a coin suspended in the air in the front yard.

Tails.

He opened the door to Barry's bedroom and slipped inside and closed the door behind him.

He turned on the lights.

Barry's bed was made. Mom had made it earlier in the day. His things were neatly arranged on his desk and dresser. Figurines. Comic books. His drawings were in a pile on his nightstand next to his bed.

One window closed. The other open.

Mom said she wanted to *air the room out.* Get rid of the smell.

Brian went to the window. When he got there he looked over his shoulder. He didn't like standing by this window. He was too deep into the bedroom. Like the whole bedroom was behind him, had him cornered now.

He looked out the window.

Below, in the yard, moonlight splashed across the grass. From here it looked like he could see each blade, tiny individual pins decorating the lawn at night.

He looked to the trees at the edge of the yard, to the shadows there. He looked over his shoulder. To the closet. To the dresser. To the bedroom's front door. He didn't want to look back to the window. Didn't like that it was open. He breathed deeply, once, and ran across Barry's bedroom and slipped out as quietly as he had slipped in.

15

"*Briiiiiaaaaan!*"

Brian woke fast. Looked around his own bedroom. It was dark. Still night.

"Barry?"

But Barry was at Hugh and Bree's.

"*Briiiiaaaaaaan!*"

But it *was* Barry. Barry's voice.

"Barry!" Brian yelled, hoping his mom would hear him. Hoping Dad would come barreling down the hall and end whatever was happening.

Nothing from the hall. Nothing but the distant sound of Barry's voice.

"*It's fun out here! Briaaaaan!*"

Brian got out of bed again. He opened his bedroom door and did what he did in Barry's room earlier. He ran. Ran into the hall and ran to Mom and Dad's room and opened their door and ran to them and shook Mom awake.

"What is it? *What is it?*" Mom woke immediately, grabbed Brian by the shoulders. Dad was up, out of bed.

"Barry's in his bedroom!"

"*What?*"

"Barry's calling me from his bedroom!"

"Jesus Christ," Dad said and Brian heard fear in his voice, saw fear in his dad's face as he hesitated before leaving their bedroom.

"What do you mean he called to you?" Mom asked, yelling, shaking Brian by the shoulders. Then she was up and past him.

Brian stood in their bedroom, beside their bed. He gripped their blanket, needing something to hold on to. Mom's voice, far off, calling, crying out, yelling. Barry's voice, too. Distant. So far away.

Dad appeared in the doorway and Brian screamed. Dad crossed the room and held him.

"You're okay?' he asked, loud, angrily.

"Yes," Brian said but he didn't know what okay meant.

Mom's voice from far away. And Dad was gone again. Dad's voice, too. From another house it seemed. From their old house. From Hugh and Bree's. From a stranger's house.

Mom screamed and Brian mumbled something to himself, felt like he had no control over himself, was trembling from somewhere deeper than he had control over.

Barry's voice. Mom's voice. Dad's voice. All coming from the dark black hall and the bigger bedroom beyond it.

"Oh no," Brian said, hearing a fourth voice.

Oh no as if *oh no* could protect him from whoever spoke in that fourth voice.

Silence then.

Nothing from the hall.

Darkness. Blackness. Alone, it seemed, in the whole house. The whole house growing around him, expanding, fanning out until he was standing in a tiny black hole in a space that went on for a very long time.

Footsteps. On the carpet. Many of them. Something with many legs. He gripped the blanket and almost fell to his knees, to hide beside the bed.

Footsteps and Dad came through the bedroom door, holding it open for Mom who held Barry close to her, talking to him, wiping dirt from his hair, her own face and arms dirty, all the way up to her elbows, as if shed reached into something, dug, had to stick her arms up to her elbows into something to find him, to bring Barry back, to get him out of his bedroom.

"We leave *tonight*," she said and Dad was already on the phone, calling Hugh and Bree, asking them how they could let Barry out of their sights, arguing with them when they said he'd fallen asleep in the guest bedroom, arguing with them when they said the doors were locked and the alarm was set. Arguing with them until he hung up and turned to face Brian, his eyes wild with worry, then turned to look at Barry, then looked at Mom and repeated what she'd said. "We leave tonight."

16

The brothers sat in the back of the car, opposite ends of the bench. Mom and Dad were inside, talking to a realtor. Talking with only half enthusiasm. Talking like they didn't have very much energy. Talking like they were making a decision because they had to, not because they wanted to.

Brian looked to the windows of the ranch house and wondered which ones were the bedrooms. It was harder to tell. No second story on this house.

Across the street there was a small graveyard. Seven stones. Possibly a family plot.

Barry stared out the car window at the graveyard.

Brian thought of a bug, stuck in Barry's mind, making him dance, making him smile. It wasn't the same bug that Gene Kelly had; it made Barry do different things, made him think about different things.

Barry stared out the window and Brian wanted to cry, thinking of his brother stuck like Gene Kelly. Hurt like him. His own kind of bug. His own *obsession*, the word Dad had used.

Brian thought of a coin, too, stuck in the air.

Tails.

Heads.

He thought of the coin held there, floating all on its own, never falling, never determining who got the bigger bedroom, who got the bug.

Brian almost jumped when Mom appeared by the side of the car. Dad was on the other side. The realtor was walking away. All silent to Brian beyond the closed window.

Mom opened her door. Dad opened his.

Mom looked into the car, saw Barry staring out the window. She looked where he was looking. Toward the seven stones.

"No," she said, and Dad looked at her like he was surprised she'd suddenly made a decision. Then he looked where she was looking. "No," Mom repeated. "Too much space in this house. We don't need that much space."

Dad left his door open and Brian watched him pass the hood of the car and join Mom on the passenger side.

"We'll find somewhere else," he said. "Somewhere smaller."

"We don't need that much space," Mom said again and Brian heard sadness in her voice and it made him sad and he saw Dad put an arm around Mom's shoulder and Brian realized the car was beeping, had been since Mom and Dad opened their doors. "It's just a lot of room," Mom said and Dad crossed in front of the hood again and opened Barry's door and guided him out of the car and squeezed him, too, the car beeping, the doors open, Barry still stuck, still staring past Dad toward the seven stones, Brian watching his brother, watching his Dad squeeze his brother's shoulder, bringing him closer, erasing the space between them.

PUT ME TO DREAM

STEPHANIE M. WYTOVICH

At present,
there is a single piece of furniture in my room:
my memories,
memories of things I have said, things I have done,
and I ache to tell someone,
to get the crass words and complicated prose out of my mouth,
but like bile
they burn, burn my tongue, my esophagus, my lungs,
and this pain of silence is better than the physical agony of
confession, admission,
but these stories, these books, these novels of my muteness, they
settle in my stomach, uncomfortable with bloated pages,
with smeared ink,

they fester inside me like an infected wound
and I need to tell someone,
someone who won't judge me,
who won't point fingers and call me monster,
call me victim, call me fiend; Yes, I need someone,
someone who will listen,
who won't just tell me it will be okay,
but a voice who will make it okay;
but not today,
not now,
it's far too fresh,
far too much,
and I think I'll have mother bring up my bed first,
let the clinks and clangs of the dripping pipe put me to sleep,
put me to dream
where the stories don't scream
where the bed swallows me alive,
alive in this asylum,
where I'm certain
I will
thrive.

THAT PERILOUS STUFF

SCOTT EDELMAN

"ARE YOU SURE YOU WANT to get out here?" the cabdriver turned to me and asked as we pulled to a stop alongside my mother's house. I could tell what he was thinking as he took in the front porch overflowing with dented bicycles, rusty tools, and machines parts, the unmown lawn with grass so tall it could swallow a small child, and the trash bags stacked against the garage to form towers that seemed certain to topple, and it wasn't very different from what I'd thought when I'd turned my back on the place years before.

So actually, no, I wasn't all that sure I wanted to get out here, but I had no interest in explaining to a stranger why this sudden trip home to see my mother and brother left me feeling that way.

"I'll be fine," I said, not sure of that either. You can never go home again, they say. Well, unfortunately, they're wrong. Which meant I had a challenge ahead. For Mom and Lou collected more than only stuff. They also collected uncertainty and resentment and fear, and other emotions as well that I'd done my best to abandon. So my main goal this visit—other than dealing with Mom's latest difficulties, at which Lou had only hinted—was to make sure neither of my relatives offloaded any of those traits on me.

"Here," he said, passing a card back over his shoulder along with my change. "You might need this. It's not always that easy to get a cab to come all the way out here."

A card with a taxi driver's cell number was a reminder I wasn't home—my chosen home, that is—any longer. I'd grown used to

203

summoning a car with the swipe of my thumb. But now, I was at my first home—my birth home—where such things were still impossible. And looking at the house, obscured by Mom's hoard—though from the disassembled machinery out on the porch, it was undeniably Lou's hoard now as well—I knew there was going to be a whole lot more I'd find impossible here.

The driver—Marco according to his card—pulled my suitcase out of the trunk—a small one, as I hoped not to have to stay long—and I was soon alone on the crowded porch of the house I'd had to run from, until my brother's call had me running back.

I leaned into the doorbell, but it didn't work. Of *course* it didn't work. Things had always fallen apart here, and Mom was always too busy bringing more stuff into the house to bother fixing whatever stuff she already had. I could have opened the door myself if I'd brought my key, but it had been so long since I'd crossed the country to visit that I no longer knew where it was.

Does that make me a bad daughter? Sometimes I think so. Other times I think—if I'd been a better one I'd have ended up trapped like Lou. And unlike him, I don't think I'd have survived.

I took a deep breath, thought for a moment of immediately phoning Marco and telling him, you were right, and no, I didn't really want to get out here, please take me back to the airport so I can catch the next flight away from this place, OK?

But then I pushed all that aside and knocked.

I heard Lou stumbling nearer in response to my rapping—I recognized that it wasn't Mom because she no longer walked well enough to even get up to stumble—and wasn't sure why he sounded off balance and was continually knocking into things. Until he opened the door and I could see what I'd feared was far worse than what I'd feared, and a spacious living room was now nothing more than a large storage locker with a narrow pathway running down the middle.

Magazines and newspapers, which had obviously once been stacked into piles, had long ago slid into dusty mounds. Dozens of lamps, their necks broken, their lightbulbs dangling. Baskets filled with so much clothing it would have taken weeks to launder.

So many possessions it was impossible even to perceive them all. So much chaos it looked as if half a dozen homes had exploded and then been scooped up in a hurry to fill this house. I'd suspected it could be worse... but *this* much worse?

"What happened, Lou?" I said, too stunned to get out more words than those, asking about both my mother and the house at the same time. But Lou knew that. And didn't like it.

"No time to get into that now," he said. "Mom's really gotten worse."

Seeing the worried expression on his face, I wanted to hug him. But he and I had never had that kind of relationship, and I was too angry and distracted by the mess around us to have the ability to break through the barrier of that just then. Maybe later. I reached up to pat his shoulder and left it at that.

"Yes, I know," I said. "You told me as much on the phone. Where is she?"

"Are you sure you're ready?" he said. "You haven't seen her in a long time, so you're going to be shocked, I promise you. Better prepare yourself."

I didn't think anything could have shocked me more than what I'd already seen. The house was claustrophobic enough before I'd left—Mom's hoarding squeezed out the space my younger self had needed to breathe—but I wrestled my suitcase through the door—which did take some wrestling considering how narrow things had gotten—and steeled myself. Lou had to walk sideways down the hall—a hall once decorated with family photos and Dad's darting trophies, but now more a tight path through a moving van—as I followed him to the back of the house.

There, in what used to be the small dining area next to the kitchen, Mom was in a cot, propped up by pillows. So many pillows she almost seemed to vanish in them. A wall of televisions, none functioning, some with cracked screens, others with snapped antennas, filled the room across from her. The sink in the connected kitchen was overflowing with record albums, the stovetop piled with dented birdcages which, thankfully, were empty. And I hated to think what might be in the oven.

"You've got her staying down here?" I said, trying to speak quietly, but too angry to do so. "In the kitchen? And how could you let this happen to the kitchen anyway?"

"She can no longer do the stairs, I told you that," he said, only answering my first question. I doubted it would even be possible to get answers that made sense to my other questions from either of them.

I knelt beside Mom, having to clear a space to do so—were those really empty potato chip bags, just left lying there?—and took her hand. She turned briefly toward me at my touch, not really seeing me, then looked back at the blank screens. I wondered what shows she thought she was watching, or if she even had enough of her old self left to believe she was watching anything.

"Mom, it's me," I said. "It's Jo. I came as soon as I could."

Lou muffled a snort, but just barely. I resisted turning at the sound. He didn't understand what it was like.

"How are you doing?" I whispered.

She tilted her head slightly, first this way, then that, as if to indicate, take a good look at me, how do you think I'm doing? Or perhaps to indicate nothing at all, bobbing in concert to winds of memory she alone felt.

"She's been like this all week," said Lou, hanging behind me less to give me a moment alone with her than because there wasn't space for all three of us in the room at once. "She's stopped talking. She's stopped even knowing I was here."

"Then what's she still doing at home?" I said, no longer bothering to whisper. Mom wouldn't know what we were saying anyway. "Let's get her to a hospital."

"Jo, you know there's nothing physically wrong with her. At least nothing anyone can fix. It's her brain. It's just… it's just what happens when a person gets old. I didn't call you here because I believed you could fix this. I called so we could decide what to do next. Together. As a family. Besides, she has a living will. If she wants to die here, here is where she'll die. This is where she's comfortable."

"She's not dying any time soon," I said, hoping that saying the words would make it so. "And here? Die here? This isn't a house any more. This is a waste dump. I know you inherited some of her... her sickness. But how could you let this happen?"

"I didn't see you trying to stop it."

"It wasn't either of our jobs to stop it. But it wasn't our job to make it worse either. It was our job to live. To escape it."

"Well, you managed to do that, didn't you?" he said. "I hope you're happy."

The bitterness in his voice hurt. But it didn't cause as much pain as staying would have. I knew that. And I think he knew that, too. At least a little.

"I wasn't going to do it," he said, looking over my shoulder at Mom. "I wasn't going to be the kind of man who leaves."

"I'm sorry, Lou," I said, apologizing not just for me, but for Dad, and how his leaving had changed everything. "I really am. But I had to, you know that. I...just couldn't. I couldn't. You've always been stronger than me. But still, you...you've lived here too long. It's gotten inside of you. I don't think you're able to see the place as it really is anymore."

"I didn't call you here for interior decorating advice," he said. "I called you here to help figure out what to do with Mom. I thought that was the right thing to do. That's how siblings are supposed to behave."

I got up off my knee, nearly slipping on—oh, great, were those candy wrappers?—and rolled my suitcase closer to Mom. And then I sat on it, because there was nowhere else to sit. I'd have liked to sit in a chair, but there wasn't a cleared surface anywhere in the room. Or, I was guessing, based on the clutter there and in the living room, anywhere else in the house.

I took Mom's hand, squeezed it. She didn't squeeze back.

"Living will or no, we've got to get her out of this...this place. She collected, she hoarded, she wouldn't let go of things, but she never intended to die in filth."

"There's no filth here," he said. "We're not hoarders."

Now it was my turn to snort.

"Do you see rotting food here?" he continued. "Dead animals? These are just the things that matter to her."

"The things that matter?" I said, angrily kicking at the wrappers around my feet. "How could all these things matter? And matter to whom? Her? Or you? It couldn't possibly have gotten this bad if you hadn't enabled her. You should have said no every once in a while. You should have put on the brakes instead of pressing on the gas."

Lou sighed, which he always did when he didn't really want to talk. There had been many sighs in our relationship, more the worse Mom's compulsion got.

"Maybe I shouldn't have called you," he said. "It's just like old times. And old times were never very good."

"Well, they weren't all bad either. And you did call, so let's try to deal with the situation as it is."

Mom's expression was blank, her reaction to the bickering of her children nonexistent. I'd normally have pulled Lou into another room to have a discussion like this, but as far as I could tell, it was almost as if we weren't there at all. Once, any harsh words between us would have terrified her, but now, nothing. That wasn't the Mom I knew. And I wanted the old Mom back, even with all her flaws. If I couldn't do that, I at least had to do right by her.

"Look, there aren't many options," I said. "We've either got to get her out of here, or get all this stuff out of here. It's one or the other. That's it. There are no other choices. Regardless of what you think Mom thinks she wants, this house has become a health hazard, and if anyone from the county were to see inside—"

"No one's going to see inside."

"You're not thinking clearly, Lou. People don't need x-ray vision to know something's very wrong here. The way you've let the porch and front yard go, I'm surprised neighbors haven't already complained."

Lou looked away, which told me...they already had.

"Do you realize the cabdriver almost wouldn't let me get out here? He thought the place was abandoned or belonged to drug dealers or something. Is all this stuff really necessary?"

"Will you lay off about the stuff already, Jo? Dealing with the stuff isn't going to fix anything. This is Alzheimer's we're dealing with. Nothing else but that matters."

"If nothing else matters, then let's start clearing out some of this mess. If she stays—and OK, maybe you're right, maybe she should stay, I'll give you that for now—she'll need nurses, and believe me, no one is going to be willing to work here. They'll walk through the front door—if they even make it to the front door—and turn right back around and leave."

I dropped Mom's hand, and reached for the top few magazines from a stack on top of the bureau that completely blocked off the mirror.

"Not tonight," Lou said quickly. "It's late. Can't we leave this for tomorrow? Please? This is going to be tough enough. Let's leave it until after a night's sleep, OK?"

I had to admit...Lou was right. He might have let himself become trapped in a house of sludge, but he wasn't stupid. And I truly was tired from the long flight. Besides, decades of debris weren't going to be cleared out in one night. Looking at Mom, though, inert, focused on nothing but her inner self, if her inner self remained, I wasn't sure how many more nights we had left.

I let Lou lead me up the stairs to my old room, following closely in his footsteps so as not to dislodge any of the stuffed animals, paperweights, figurines, and other incongruous objects piled on the steps. I shuddered to think what my room would look like, and regretted not checking into a nearby motel. But...it was

my mother, and I felt I owed it to her to try to spend as many more nights under the same roof as I could. Lou had done it for a lifetime of days. I should at least be able to handle a few.

He shouldered open the door and … yes, it was just that bad. It appeared as if all the junk mail that had arrived during my absence was piled in one corner. Shoes and purses exploded out of the open closet, its door no longer able to close, and beneath them I spotted bicycle pumps and empty picture frames. And why were there half a dozen microwaves at the foot of my bed, a bed barely visible under dozens of throw pillows and even more baskets of laundry?

He dragged my suitcase over to the one bit of open floor space and started removing the piles from the bed and adding them to the other piles that ringed the room, filling in the space at the top until they touched the ceiling. I was sure it would all collapse on me as I slept. Or tried to sleep.

"It's good to see you, sis," he said, once he'd cleared my old mattress.

"It's good to see you, too, Lou," I said.

And it was. I couldn't deny that. But seeing all Mom's stuff … that was never good. We had to get through it, though. We had to.

Trying to sleep any longer was pointless. I'd given it a good shot, but this wasn't a bedroom anymore. I felt as if I'd crawled into a long-abandoned storage unit. And closing my eyes didn't help. Whether in darkness or in light, I could still feel the pressure of all those possessions. So I sat up and moved to the edge of the bed, having to first carefully choose the side with space left over for my feet.

I looked up at the tower of boxes and trash bags that ringed the room, the tennis rackets and ukuleles, dressmaker dummies and slightly broken umbrellas, the detritus from a thousand yard sales, and wondered what would drive anyone—two anyones—to first gather and then keep it all. But I couldn't think of an answer. Maybe there was no answer. I gave up trying to puzzle one out and flicked on a light.

Where once there were windows visible along the outer wall of my room, now there was just a clumsily constructed wall of useless objects. A wall built of the forgotten. A wall covered with dust. How long had it been since anyone had gone through all these things and asked each item to defend its existence?

It wasn't going to be me. The stuff, as invasive as it was, didn't really matter. Lou was right, though for the wrong reasons. It was Mom that mattered most of all. And if what was keeping her confined to the first floor was her health, that's what had to be cleared up first, not every possession.

Since I couldn't sleep, I headed downstairs. As I passed Lou's room, I could hear him snoring. At least one of us was having no problem sleeping. Obviously, none of this bothered him. Since he'd inherited—or more likely absorbed—the same disease, I guess he found this way of life, these surroundings, normal. Just as well. Better he slept while I did what I had to do. Seeing me move any of their things would only make him anxious, I knew. Luckily, Mom was apparently too far gone for it to make her anxious.

She was awake, too, still watching the dead televisions. Wonder what she saw screening there in her head that was keeping her awake? No way of knowing.

"Can I get you anything, Mom?" I asked. "Do you need something? A glass of water? A snack?"

She didn't answer, didn't even look in my direction.

I obviously wasn't going to get information out of Mom, and was too filled with nervous energy to do nothing, so looked around until I spotted the tall stack of magazines on the bureau, the ones Lou had stopped me from handling. Wouldn't hurt to at least do some small bit of neatening up. If I was going to stay there for a few days, I had to do something to remain sane.

Mom didn't seem to care as I sorted through the sometimes decades-old issues and stacked them in neat piles by the door to the backyard. After an hour of that, I'd managed to create the only clear surface in the room. In the house, perhaps. The mirror, revealed after who knows how long, was covered with dust, and I swiped at it with a palm so it could do what it was meant to do. Which reminded me of how many things there were in the house that no longer did what they were meant to do.

I looked in the glass and saw both myself and Mom reflected back. We looked so much alike, even with what the years had done to each of us, hers spent grasping and never letting go, mine spent running and always letting go.

But if I'm the one who'd been doing the running, why was she the one so far away?

I pulled out some chipped china knickknacks which had been hidden by the magazines in the space between the mirror and the bureau. Cats and dogs and turtles and elephants, covered by dust and cobwebs. To have been treated like that, could any of them have really mattered? They deserved better. They deserved to belong to someone who cared, someone who would put them to use. I gathered in my arms as many as I could, balancing them carefully, or so I thought, but I must have been more tired than I realized, because a penguin slipped, and as soon as I made a grab for it, the others followed. I managed to catch about half of them, but the others dropped to the floor, one of them shattering. A figurine of two dogs broke into many pieces, and their heads rolled. If not for the cups and saucers stacked by the foot of mother's bed, they would have vanished beneath.

And then I heard Mom's voice for the first time since I'd arrived. It was loud, not happy, and it made me feel twelve again.

"What are you doing, Jo?" she shouted. "You stop that!"

Shocked, I hurried to her side, let the rest of the statues tumble from my arms onto the mattress where they landed safely. I took her hands, looked into her eyes. She was back. If only for a moment, she was back.

"I'm here, Mom," I said, amazed that she had roused enough to speak. I didn't care that her words had been angry ones, as long as she was no longer locked inside her head. "I came back to help."

"You call that helping?" she said, not looking at me, but at the shards of broken dogs scattered across the floor.

"I'm sorry, Mom, I didn't mean to do that," I said. "I was just trying to clear a little space. You know living like this isn't healthy for you, don't you? Let me try to make things better for you. Please let me do that for you."

Mom shook her head, and pursed her lips.

"Your father gave me that," she said. "Your father gave me that and you broke it."

"I'm sorry, Mom, I wish I'd known, but when there's so much, who can—"

And then suddenly, Lou was in the room with us, uncaring of the rubble he had to push aside to enter.

"What's going on?" he asked, his voice even louder than mother's had been.

Mom waggled a hand at the floor.

"I told you not to do this," he said. "You told me you would wait until morning."

"I couldn't sleep," I said. "It had to be done anyway. I didn't think I needed your permission."

"No," said Mom, speaking with less strength she had just a moment before. "No."

"No what, Mom?" I said, feeling her fingers begin to clasp mine less firmly.

"I know you care, Jo," she said. "But…all this…all this must stay right here. And I'm staying right here, too. Staying. Staying. Stay…"

And then she was gone again, her gaze blank, her head turned back to the dead televisions. Whatever had animated her had passed, but still—

"Did you see that?" I said to Lou. "She's not as far gone as we thought. Maybe there's a chance we can have our mother back again."

"Maybe. Or maybe you just startled and pissed her off enough to bring her back momentarily. If you started breaking my stuff, I'd wake up from a coma, too."

"Joke if you'd like, but this was a good thing."

"Nothing good ever comes from breaking something," he said, pushing at fragments of dog with his bare toes. "This stuff matters, Jo. Her whole life is here. And mine, too. And yours as well, if you'd open your eyes and see it."

"The only life that matters to me is the life that's inside your skin. Her skin. Not any of this. This is just a prison. And one you two have built yourselves. I wish you'd open your eyes and see *that*."

"If you really feel that way, then maybe it's best if you spent the night somewhere else. Get a motel room. You know you want to anyway."

"What, you don't trust me now?"

"No, not really," he said. "Not anymore."

He bent and picked up the two dog heads, holding one in each hand.

"You don't remember this, do you?"

"I'm afraid I don't. There's too much here to even consider remembering every object."

"Dad gave this to her one anniversary. I don't remember which one. But I remember that we were young. And I remember that Mom was smiling."

"We would've been young for Dad to have still been around. Or for Mom to have been pleased about it enough to smile."

"Whatever," he said, trying to fit the chipped heads together along the edges where they'd broken. "But know that this is more than just a thing. This is a memory. This is important."

"Perhaps. But can it *all* be so important? Doesn't the sheer number of things make even the most important ones less important? Some things *have* to go. That's why Dad left, because Mom couldn't see that. That's why I had to leave. That's why you should have left, too, a long, long time ago."

"I'll help you with your bag," Lou said coldly. He turned and headed down the hall and back upstairs. And after another longing look at Mom, lost in whatever thickening fog had engulfed her, her one brief moment of clarity gone, I followed him as best I could, picking my way through the litter of other people's lives.

I didn't get back to the house the following day as early as I would have liked. That's because, as I fell asleep in the relaxingly uncluttered motel room, I realized I wouldn't be able to do what I needed to do alone. And with Lou as tight in the grip of this thing as Mom, he couldn't be the partner I'd need. I needed a different sort of ally. Someone disinterested, but passionate. Someone whose word might be believed a little more than mine. Which is why, when I entered the house the following afternoon, I had someone from social services at my side.

Oh, it wasn't official, because it can take months to get something like that going. But not everyone I'd gone to school with had skipped town the way I had, and I was able to reach out to a friend of a friend. So Greta was at my side that morning. She wouldn't be able to force anything to happen, but I trusted that once she saw what I had seen, she'd back me up.

When we pulled into the driveway—or as far in as the washing machines and lawnmowers, not all of which had been there the previous day, would allow—her reaction was much like that of the concerned cabbie. Only she already knew, because of the history I'd shared—I belonged here.

I introduced Greta to Lou, not bothering to tell him that she wasn't accompanying me in an official capacity. Mom was too far gone to pay attention, but maybe it would put some fear into *him*. He was too polite to throw her right out, as I could tell he wanted to do. Thankfully, he was usually able to hold it together around strangers. Greta moved through the narrow hallway, her face blank, not reacting to what must be hard not to react to—yes, she was good—and went to the dining room to meet my mother, with Lou and me trailing along.

"What is this?" he hissed.

"Something we need," I said. "I told you, but you wouldn't listen. This is beyond us."

I moved up tightly beside Greta, because tightly was all there was room for.

"Hello, Mom," I said. "This is Greta. She's a friend of mine. She wants to meet you."

There was no response, not even the bobbing of her head that she'd evidenced the day before.

"Like I said, she was briefly better last night," I told Greta.

"That's only because you broke something Mom cared about very much," said Lou. "And you're reading too much into it. She wasn't *that* much better. It was a blip. Here and gone."

Greta looked at Lou momentarily, nodded at me, and then turned back to Mom.

"I'd like to have some time alone with her if I may," she said. "She could very well behave differently when you're not around."

We stepped out of the room, me gladly, Lou begrudgingly, and once we were by the front of the house, he let his anger out.

"You had no right to do this," he said. "You walked out on her, just like Dad. You left me here to take care of it, the both of you. So I'm taking care of it. Now why don't you butt out. Run like you did before. Forget I called you. We're doing fine."

"This is not taking care of it," I said, waving my arm around the room, though even with being smaller than Lou, there wasn't that much space for me to wave. "By what stretch of the imagination is this taking care of it?"

"By the stretch that she's alive, she's healthy, and what's going on with her is beyond our control and not my fault."

"But how about this!" I said. "Is *this* in your control!"

I grabbed at the nearest box, pulled back the corrugated lid, and found dozens of jelly glasses. Some I recognized from childhood, but most had been collected in the years since.

"Do you really need these?" I continued, in full rant mode. "You have enough of the stupid things to throw a wedding party, and I doubt you ever have guests here. This place is so embarrassing I'm probably the only one you've allowed in for years. Get rid of these,

I beg you. Sell them, give them away, let them be of use to someone else, or even just toss them in the trash, but—"

I made the mistake then of trying to lift the box. It was far heavier than I'd thought, so instead it slipped from my hands. I made a grab for it, but only succeeded in ripping open a section of the cardboard, which let a few of the glasses tumble out. They hit the floor and exploded, and when the box followed, I could hear a loud jingling of glass as its entire contents shattered.

Lou shouted louder than I'd ever heard him before, but I didn't care. It felt good to finally take action against all these oppressive possessions, even if I was doing it subconsciously, doing what Mom could never bring herself to do, doing what Lou, the good son, would never dare.

I bent so I could try to move the box somewhere out of what little path we had, but when I did so, the bottom collapsed, a shower of shards falling on my shoes. I cursed and threw the now empty box against the—not wall, but a wall of other boxes—and in that instant all my anger, all my pain, all my history with Mom's things, those empty things, came out, and I began to cry at last. I flailed my arms about, knocked down other boxes which hit the floor with either thuds or crackles, hurled figurines of sad clowns, and glass globes that should have been decorating someone's garden somewhere rather than clogging a hallway, and bowls of fake fruit, their wax sagging and discolored by age. I grabbed and flung anything my fingers could clutch.

"Stop it, Jo, you're not accomplishing anything," Lou shouted, while doing nothing to intervene. He'd never seen me let loose like this before and I think I scared him a little. I know I scared me.

I kept shouting and smashing things, he kept shouting and dodging the things I threw, but neither of us would stop our vicious dance until mother made us both jump by shouting impossibly louder than all the noises we were making put together.

Our mother, who according to Lou hadn't left her bed in weeks, marched jerkily out of the hallway with only the aid of a cane. Greta, trailing behind her, looked stunned.

"My children shouldn't be fighting," Mom said, her voice clear and stong. There was none of the hesitation or searching for words that I'd heard during phone calls in recent years. "I didn't raise the two of you to act this way. You're embarrassing yourselves."

"You're walking," said Leo.

"You're talking," I said. "Mom, you're talking."

Her few words the night before during that brief moment of clarity had been welcome, but this newfound coherence was astonishing.

"Of course, I'm talking," Mom said. "Why wouldn't I be talking? Why are you both looking at me like that?"

"I don't understand," said Greta. "I couldn't get a word out of her. I couldn't get her to react to anything. She was totally non-responsive, and now this. It makes no sense."

"You just got her mad enough," Leo said to me. "Just like last night. And just like last night, it'll fade."

"Alzheimer's doesn't work that way," said Greta. "If that's what she was suffering from, you wouldn't see her spontaneously come back like this. This is something different. Something else. I don't know what's going on here, but whatever you think is wrong with your mother isn't what you think is wrong with your mother."

"Who said anything about Alzheimer's?" Mom said. "It gets to be too much sometimes and I just get tired, that's all."

She walked up to me and poked at the rubble with the tip of her cane.

"Did you do this, Jo?" she said, with a tone I knew too well.

I suddenly felt like a kid again, flashed back to similar conversations in a house far less cluttered, but still far too cluttered for me, and couldn't respond with anything more than a nod. A trace of tenderness appeared in her face in answer to that nod.

"You've got to stop this," she said. "That's no way for a grown woman to act, destroying other people's things. What gives you the right?"

"I'm sorry, Momma."

"And you, Louis, why were you shouting at Jo that way? She's your little sister. You mustn't treat her so mean."

My brother dropped his head.

"I'm sorry, too, mother."

After a round of hugs, which Greta stood aside from, watching Mom with continued confusion, I headed into the kitchen to get some trash bags. Considering the number of stuffed ones around the home, I knew I'd find a box of them somewhere. I started to sift through the debris and load it all into the bags as best I could without slicing my fingers, but as I finished filling each one, Mom would stop me from carrying it outside. She said she wanted me to set them aside once I was done bagging everything, that she wanted to go through every item, every fragment, every shard herself to see whether anything could be saved. I already knew what Mom could never admit—there was nothing I'd damaged that was worth saving. I didn't feel like arguing then, though, not with Leo glaring at me, and with Greta looking on in wonder. I no longer wanted witnesses for what Mom and I needed to say to each other.

"We'll talk later once I have a chance to think about all this," Greta said once I was done.

"There's nothing to think about, young lady," said Mom. "We don't need your help here. We're doing fine."

"I'll call you," whispered Greta to me as she passed on her way out the front door. "Something must be done here. I don't know what, but something."

After the three of us cleared off the kitchen table—which means we had to fill in the space around Mom's bed first—we had lunch. Not that we could prepare anything there ourselves, because the kitchen was long past being functional, the appliances not just overwhelmed but inoperative, so I ordered take-out. And we managed to have a conversation with Mom unlike any that we'd had in years. We set aside the tough stuff and talked about the things that didn't matter, in one of those moments that seemed it was really the only thing that mattered.

As we shared about which late-night TV host we liked best and what our favorite recent movies were, something nagged at me, and I couldn't quite figure out what it was. The timing of this talk and Mom's resurgence all seemed far too... coincidental maybe? I wasn't sure.

When we finally wore Mom out with our chatting, we rearranged the puzzle of the house once more so she could return to her bed. She seemed devoid of energy as I tucked her in, fading remarkably quickly for how much spark she'd shown.

As soon as she was settled, I went out to the porch with Lou to talk as we used to do when we were kids and wanted some privacy from our parents, not knowing that Mom and Dad probably heard every word anyway. I would have liked to sit in the porch swing, but we couldn't reach it, of course, our way to it totally blocked. So we sat on the steps, one of the few clear spots, even though they were also being narrowed by... stuff. We sat in silence for a while, until the silence became too uncomfortable, and had to be broken.

"Well, that was weird," I finally said.

"Weird, but good," said Lou. "It's been a long while since Mom's been anything like that."

"If only she could stay that way."

"I don't think that's really possible, Jo. She's getting old. This is just what happens to people. We've got to face that. Unless we do, we won't be able to deal with it."

"What if it didn't have to happen?" I said. "What if ..."

I was afraid to put out there what was clattering about inside my head. It sounded crazy up there and would sound even crazier coming out of my mouth.

"What if what?" said Lou. "What do you mean? Even that social worker you dragged to see her was baffled. Getting old means losing it. And even though we love her, we're going to have to admit— Mom's lost it."

"Look, I know how these things go," I said. "I know what getting old means. But this seems... different. Surely you noticed what happened each time right before she perked up? Some of her stuff was gone, and—"

"It was more than just gone. You destroyed it."

"Yes, I destroyed it. I admit it. I didn't mean to, but I did it."

"Oh, you meant it. Don't deny that. Be honest with yourself."

"Will you forget about the blame for a moment and listen to me? I know what you said. That she only roused because her anger momentarily empowered her. But it's more than that. It's got to be. Didn't you notice, staying with her over the years, that the more of Mom's things there's been, the less of Mom there's been? Even I could tell that, just over the phone, but I never put two and two together. She's slipping away and..."

I could hardly bring myself to say the words.

"Of course she's slipping away," said Lou. "Someday we'll slip away, too."

"Not like this, we won't," I said. "These possessions, they've become so important to her that she's slipping away *into* them. Her hoarding sickness has been willed into something stranger. Something greater. This stuff...it's absorbing her soul. And once I destroyed them, once they could no longer contain her, she got it back. Pieces of it anyway. But not enough pieces. We can't let this go on. We can't. We've got to free her."

"Oh, come on, Jo. That's woo-woo crazy talk. I'm sorry if saying this sounds like a cliché, but you've spent too much time living in California."

"And you've spent too much time not living anywhere but here. If this has done that to her, who knows what it's done to you?"

"Enough!" said Lou, snapping. He stood up stiffly. "Why don't you just go home, Jo. Check out of your motel, hop a plane, go back to that simple, uncluttered life you've chosen, and leave all of this behind. It's clear you're not ready to deal with our family."

He went back inside, leaving me to sit on the steps alone, staring out in the darkness at grass that should never have been allowed to grow that tall.

But he was wrong.

I was ready to deal with the family.

I was the only one ready.

I pulled out the card Marco had given me and phoned for him to come take me back to the motel, which he said that after he was through with his fare, he'd do. I didn't really care how long he'd take. I was fine with waiting. I had a lot of thinking to get done. And sitting with the house at my back, both the one from my memory and the one that was real, I came to realize what I was in for. But even though I knew what must be next, knew in my heart, knew in my soul, there was still the part of me that thought—what if I was wrong?

Which is why by the time Marco arrived to pick me up, I'd changed my plan, and instead of having him head back to the motel, I merely had him drive me a couple of blocks away and let me off there. I apologized for the short fare, made sure to tip him well, and explained what I needed from him next. He didn't seem to mind. The desperation was probably spilling off me, and he could probably sense that.

I walked back to the house, keeping to the shadows, and watched from across the street until lights went on upstairs in Lou's room... and then off again. Once I figured he had to be asleep, which his snoring from the night before told me he would do solidly (and a good thing, too), I entered via the back door, which led directly into the kitchen.

Off to the side, I could see Mom back in her cot, asleep this time, or so it seemed, no longer staring off at things unseen. I watched her for a while, wondering if the part of her that mattered really could have gone where I'd thought it had gone. I looked away, scanning the ephemera around us, enough for multiple lifetimes. Could I possibly be right?

There was only one way to find out.

I started with a box above the refrigerator. As quietly as I could,

I unfolded the lid and filled a bag with sock monkeys, Raggedy Ann dolls, and packages of cookies with long-passed expiration dates (why were those things even together?), then resealed the box so no one could possibly notice anything had been taken. Until I was proven right, everything had to be done surreptitiously. I moved through what once was a kitchen and what once was a dining room, looking for the most easily reachable boxes, ones which I could ransack and still leave appearing undisturbed. I took nothing that was in plain sight, loading bag after bag until I'd reached the limit of how many I thought would fit in the back of the cab, and dragged them through the backyard to a side street. I left them there, knowing they'd be safe—as far as I knew, Mom was the only one who rummaged through trash in this neighborhood—then went back to say goodbye. But also a hopeful hello.

Her eyes were open this time, staring straight ahead, and she didn't turn to notice me. I walked into the path of her gaze, hoping to attract her attention, but though I smiled, though I waved, I couldn't raise a response.

I leaned in and gave her a kiss.

"See you soon," I whispered, and then returned to the hoard I'd made off with, where I called Marco again. This time, I did have him take me back to the motel.

When we got there, I told him to skip the main entrance where he'd left me before and instead circle around the back. I pointed to a large rectangular dumpster in a far corner of the parking lot. He pulled up beside it and looked back, puzzled.

"Now what?" he said.

"Give me a hand," I said, climbing out and pulling one of the bags out with me.

"What's this all about?" he said, popping open the trunk.

"You nailed it when you first dropped me off and asked me whether I wanted to get out," I said. "You were right. I didn't. But I had to. That's how family works. And this, this is just one more thing I have to do whether I want to or not."

Marco helped me line all the bags beside the dumpster, and then gave me a hand as I climbed up a ladder built into its side. I pulled one of the bags with me, reached in, grabbed a whiskey bottle molded in the shape of Elvis, and let it drop. The crackle as it burst was satisfying.

"Are you sure you wouldn't rather sell these things?" he asked. "Maybe donate them to Goodwill? You could bring in a couple of bucks. Maybe even help someone. Just saying."

"There's only one person I'm thinking of helping right now," I said.

I dropped a collectible plate bearing the Mona Lisa, followed by a Rubik's Cube from which a corner cube was missing. As I did so, I pictured Mom as she used to be. Younger, yes, but it wasn't just younger I was hoping for. I wanted her to be present, to once more have a life of conscious action, rather than the tropisms which had swallowed her, driving Dad away, driving me away, driving Lou to sacrifice his life for hers.

"Can I help you with that?" said Marco. "You've got a *lot* of stuff here. Doing it one at a time like that is going to take you all night."

"I think I'm going to have to do this by myself," I said, tossing in a handful of well-chewed tennis balls. And we'd never owned a dog. From what gutter had she gathered those? "I don't know how I know that. But I know."

He shrugged and drove off, leaving me alone in the darkness, where I finished offloading the rest of the junk. But I didn't remain in darkness for long. Because I knew the things that would not break needed to be burned. I lit a newspaper I'd set aside and dropped it atop the mountain of things Mom couldn't let go of, watched the flames catch the fringe of a pillow, then leap to a stained polyester blouse, and onto the tape spilling out of a cracked cassette cartridge, eventually bringing the whole pile ablaze. The flames danced and dark smoke rose, and as they did, I hoped that whatever was being released to the skies would release Mom, too.

I stayed by the fire until it was mostly ash with lumps of melted plastic poking through, then went upstairs to pack my bag. Because the next day I'd be flying home.

Or at least pretending to.

Lou wasn't happy to see me once he opened the door to my knocking, obviously believing that after having turned his back on me the night before on the porch, I'd be gone. I didn't care, though. The only thing that mattered was whether *Mom* would now be capable of being happy to see me.

I pushed past him, leaving him behind me, staring out at Marco's cab (since I'd told him to wait), and on into Mom's room. I *had* to stop thinking of it as that, though. It was *not* Mom's room. It was only the kitchen in which she had become frozen.

She was sitting on the edge of the cot, tapping a pencil against a partially filled crossword puzzle in a yellowed newspaper, and looked up the moment I walked in. She smiled, her eyes bright. I sat beside her and took her hand while Lou hung back in the doorway, glaring at us both.

"How are you going, Mom?" I asked.

"I'm doing fine," she said. There was no sign of her old self. Only her older self, the one I remembered from before things began to go bad. "How have you been, dear?"

"I'm doing fine, Mom," I said, my voice thickening. "But I'm doing even better today."

"I feel the same way," said Mom. "I managed to get a good start on today's puzzle. I can't remember when that last happened."

I didn't have the heart to tell her that wasn't today's crossword puzzle. It wasn't even that year's puzzle. But it was at least a puzzle. That was good enough for now.

"See?" said Lou. "You're not needed here any longer. It turns out there's nothing wrong with her. I guess she was just under the weather for a bit, but when she woke up this morning, she was better. False alarm and all that. Sorry I bothered you. I'll try not to do it again. But you can go home now."

226

"Oh, do you have to go already, dear?" said Mom, tightening her grip even more. "It would be wonderful if you could stay awhile. I don't get to see as much of you as I used to."

"I wish I could, Mom," I said, leaving unsaid, *there's a reason for that.* "But I have to get back to work. And Lou's right. Since you're feeling better, I really should go. But I promise—I'll be back soon. Don't you worry about that."

I gave Mom's hand one final squeeze and looked up at Lou, standing there framed by towers of boxes, some of which, unknown to him, I'd emptied. Emptied so that something else, someone greater, could be filled. I hadn't been dreaming. My plan had worked. But I knew it wouldn't work for long.

Unless…

"Goodbye, Leo," I said, forcing a hug on him I knew he did not want.

"Bye, Jo," he said, reluctantly returning my hug. His voice was slightly softer, but only, I imagined, because he knew I was on my way. "Don't worry about us. I've got everything under control."

No, I thought. *You only think you do. I'm the one who's got everything under control.*

I walked back through the narrow passageway Mom and Leo had conspired to create, imagining the hoard melting away, remembering how free and open it had been when I was young and could barely stretch my arms to reach both walls at once. I looked into the living room and saw it not how it was, but how it had been, with stuffed couches which used to beckon me. Out on the porch, I turned toward where the swing had been made invisible by lawn mowers and a tangle of rakes. It would have been nice to take one final swing. But that wasn't possible.

I got in the cab, slammed the door, and looked at the house in daylight for what I knew would be the last time.

"Let's get out of here," I told Marco, even as I knew…I wasn't going anywhere.

CR ∞ SO

I let him drive me to the airport not because I intended to fly out that day, but because I needed him, needed everyone, to think I was leaving town. When I'd arrived, I hadn't thought I'd need an alibi, or suspected, when Mario had first leaned back and handed me his card, that he'd be part of it. But I guess the universe knew better than me what I needed all along.

I went inside the terminal and paused by the plate glass window instead of checking in, making a show of puttering with my luggage until I saw him pull away. I'd get a different flight later, after I did what needed to be done. I took the escalator down to the arrivals area, went back outside, and hailed a different cab.

I returned to my old neighborhood again, thinking how odd it was to cruise those streets more in a few days than I had in the past decade. I had this driver drop me in front of a house where I knew no one would be home, took a few slow steps toward the front door, and watched him drive off. Then I walked the few blocks to my own street and waited for it to be night. Once it was dark, both outside and in, I crept to the back porch that led to the kitchen, and peered through at my mother.

She was awake, leaning back against a pillow, and staring up, but whether she was gazing at the ceiling or something much further away, I couldn't tell. The way her eyes were unfocussed, though, she probably wasn't seeing anything at all. From my angle, the tower of clutter tilted against the far wall looked like a wave about to come crashing down on her.

She deserved better than this. She was going to get better than this. She was living in a firetrap, her soul leached away, and the only way to free her from that constant drain was to make the firetrap achieve its potential.

I opened the door slowly and tiptoed inside, twisting to get around a stack of boxes. What a waste. How long had it been since the kitchen has been usable anyway, thanks to an oven filled with outdated encyclopedias and a range that was now topped with bicycle tires? Let it go, Mom. Let it all go. She would be lost until everything was lost.

I started dropping lit books of matches on the mess near the bottom of the staircase first, so that Lou would be woken by smoke and then wake Mom and get her out. I then moved through the rest of the main floor, lighting ancient newspapers, landscape paintings which would have embarrassed a cheap motel, old clothing worn to rags, craft supplies for projects promised but never done, whatever was flammable enough to get this going. It all caught more easily than I would have thought. I guess even the things themselves knew it was time to let go.

Outside on the back porch, I set the corners of boxes on fire, then I moved around to the front porch and did the same. I looked for a moment at the machines, but there was no point in attacking them. The house itself would take care of those when it all came tumbling down. The bags mounded against the garage caught quickly, their plastic skins melting into flaming goo that set the contents ablaze.

Take it all away, I thought. *Take it all away and bring my mother back.*

I retreated from the house and hid behind a bush across the street, watching as the flames outside grew higher and the flames inside illuminated the windows more brightly, imagining Mom's soul returning to her body with every object that burned or melted or burst. Any moment now, Lou would come running out of the house with our mother in his arms, and I could rush back to the airport for the last plane out.

I wondered how much of her I would get back how quickly, how much of her absence would become once more a presence. And as I waited, and waited, and waited still more, I grew nervous, because... no one was coming. Did Lou sleep that deeply? Or had I done too much too soon, and the fire had spread too quickly?

Whatever the reason, I was sure *something* had gone wrong, and could wait no more. I raced across the lawn, through tall blades of grass close to the house already blackening, and leapt up the porch steps and through the front door. I was instantly pushed back by the heat and the light and the smoke, and had to fight against them all to move forward. As I pressed through the blaze into the crowded hallway, shoving my nose into an elbow, I cried, my tears drying instantly, and thought *no*, screamed *no*. They can't die, I did not mean for it to end this way.

I alternated between gasping and coughing, pulling in more smoke with each futile breath, and as my lungs were overcome, my knees began to buckle and my head grew as smoky as the air around me. Then I felt a hand wrap beneath my arm and tug. I tried to rise as it pulled at me, but instead fell away into darkness.

And came to flat on my back out on the front lawn, looking up at my mother, her face lit by the dancing flames.

"Are you all right, Jo?" she asked. She placed a hand to my forehead as she used to do so long ago.

I tried to answer, but coughed instead. I tried to sit up, but fell back again, too dizzy to move. Attempting to kill what had been killing Mom had almost killed me. But had the risk proven worthwhile?

"I'll be all right," I answered, my throat raw, my voice raspy. "What's more important is...how are you?"

"Much better, dear." She smiled, and by the flickering of the light, I could almost see her younger self, and I smiled, too. "But the house. What could have happened?"

Flat on my back, I shrugged as best as I could. She put her arms around my shoulders in a way that felt familiar, and helped me up, so I could see what she had no idea I had done, and would never admit to anyone but myself. The house was engulfed, the outer walls blackening, the roof beginning to sag. No firemen had yet arrived to put out the blaze. I couldn't even hear the sound of approaching sirens.

Good.

"I don't think we'll ever know," I said. "But the place was a firetrap, Mom. It was going to happen eventually. If you think about it, I'll bet even you knew that."

"I'm not sure I did," she said, wide-eyed, struggling to remember what she hadn't been present enough to experience in the first place to even imprint a memory. But now new memories would come. That I was sure of.

"How did I get out of there?" I asked. "I can't quite remember. And Lou! Where's Lou?"

"Why, I pulled you out, Jo," Mom said. "I led your brother out, too. That's what mothers do."

It was only then that I noticed my brother hopping at the side of the house, shoulders hunched, approaching and retreating from the remains of what had both nurtured and trapped him, reaching out as if he wanted to pluck possessions from within, but realizing he dared not get too close. Eventually, empty-handed, shoulders hunched, he slowly came to stand beside us.

"We've lost everything," he said, seeing, but not seeing.

"No," I said, pulling him close so that we were both hugging our mother tight. *Our mother.* "No . . . we haven't."

RECOGNIZING TREES

CIARÁN PARKES

I recognize some of them,
a chestnut tree, a copper beech maybe.
It's a kind of game,

giving everything a name
when they're only molecules, moving randomly.
I recognize some of them,

a group of pigeons, a squirrel that looks tame
chasing breadcrumbs, walking down a tree.
It's a kind of game,

this struggle to survive, to claim
meaning for everything, store it in a library.
I recognize some of them

but none of the people here who came
on lunch breaks, with take-away cups of coffee.
It's a kind of game

even if I decide not to play it, just remain
on this park bench in a kind of numb frenzy.
I recognize some of them,
it's a kind of game.

KNOW YOUR CODE

RAMSEY CAMPBELL

THEY'RE PASSING a cash dispenser on their way home from the restaurant when Audrey says "Let's have a word."

"Do we need any money just now?" At once Vernon feels ashamed; though he may be carrying enough, he shouldn't assume she is. "Hide," he says.

"I hid."

It isn't simply a private joke, but Vernon hopes it's sufficiently private, because a man is seated against the wall in which the dispenser is embedded. Since they've retired Audrey has developed a habit of murmuring the digits under her breath while she types them, and Vernon doesn't want the fellow to overhear. He pulls out his wallet and extracts the debit card as he dodges past his wife. "How much would you like?"

The man with his legs splayed across the pavement tilts his head as if Vernon is addressing him. No doubt he hopes users of the machine will feel impelled to donate to him, and Vernon suspects that Audrey might have given away too much of their cash. "May as well have a hundred," she says.

Vernon leans on the stick he's had to use since last year and slips the card into the slot with a resolutely steady hand. Has the man driven the code out of his head? He manages not to say the words aloud, though recovering them from his mind feels close to hearing them along with the digits they represent: nine eight nine four. He snatches the card as the slot inches it out and stuffs the notes into

his pocket. "You don't need it right now, do you?" he barely asks and is turning away from the dispenser when the man at his feet says "Mr Henshall?"

For the first time Vernon looks directly at him. His scalp is cropped close as a prisoner's, and his reddened eyes seem to have seen far too much for comfort. Vernon doesn't know why the sharp unshaven face, which is weathered almost to the bone, should appear familiar until Audrey murmurs "Is that Billy Meredith?"

The man keeps his gaze on Vernon, who finds this worse than impolite. "My wife has the notion we taught you at school."

"That's right, Mr Henshall, you did." The man looks sympathetic, presumably because of Vernon's reliance on the stick. "I know it's been years," he says. "Billy Meredith."

"So Mrs Henshall said. Well then," Vernon says as if Meredith has misbehaved yet again, "I thought we'd set you on the right track. What's brought you to this state?"

"No jobs." Before Vernon can argue with this Meredith says "I joined the army when I left school, but now they don't want us out there any more. A lot of us are surplus to requirements."

"It can't have done your mind much good. You never know what will affect it."

"I'm genuinely sorry to hear that, Billy." Vernon suspects Meredith is with him in wishing Audrey hadn't spoken. "Aren't there organisations that can help you?" he hopes aloud.

"They've done what they can," Billy says and stands up with a litheness Vernon finds daunting. "How are you getting home?"

Vernon can't help feeling glad that Meredith doesn't know where they live. "This doesn't stop me driving," he says, brandishing the stick.

"I'm only asking because it seems like you've had a bit to drink." Before Vernon can retort that it's a good deal truer of the man whose breath is in his face, Meredith says "And if you want one here's a cab."

The roof of the approaching vehicle flickers with a succession of streetlamps, which make it harder to distinguish the lit sign. Vernon wasn't planning to drive, and he feels bound to thank Meredith for stopping the taxi. Meredith opens the door too, and as Audrey climbs in she glances back. The light under the roof seems to rejuvenate her wide generous face, and so does a glimpse of the concern she always showed when teaching. "Vernon," she whispers.

She's playing the role of his conscience. He rummages in his pocket and snags the topmost of the wad of notes—just five pounds, he's relieved to see. He shakes Meredith's rough hand before leaving the note in it as he clambers into the taxi. "I hope we've helped," he mutters, trying not to take the man's uncertain expression for ingratitude. Once he has told the driver where they want to go he can't help murmuring "Does it make you glad we never had children?"

"We did, Vernon." This unnerves him—surely her memory hasn't deteriorated so much—until she says "We had them at school."

"Of our own, I meant. We wouldn't have been able to leave those behind."

"Maybe some people never really leave us if we don't make them."

Is this a gentle rebuke about Meredith? As Vernon tries to distinguish her face now that the light is off, the driver says "Had a good night, have you?"

"Just celebrating an anniversary," Vernon tells her.

"Sounds like you did. What one?"

Having to recall yet another number brings Vernon unexpectedly close to panic, but he's able to say "Forty-fourth."

"Good on you, whatever it is."

How many more can he and Audrey expect? He feels compelled to tot the months up: twelve and then at least another few dozen, though how many days will that call for? He wouldn't mind being distracted, but there's silence apart from the drone of the engine and the chatter of his thoughts until he has to direct the driver through the suburb. He opens the door for Audrey and pays the driver, fending off his change. "Look after yourself," the driver says, rather too much like a nurse for Vernon's taste.

He's nervous in case Audrey slips on the rain-soaked leaves strewn over the uneven garden path, but he finds her waiting in the dark porch. As soon as he unlocks the door she vanishes into the unlit hall, where the alarm panel warns them they have half a minute to type the code. The panel is still bleeping when Vernon lurches into the hall and fumbles in search of the light switch. Thinking Audrey has forgotten the code threatens to drive it out of his head. "I add," he cries just in time, though the phrase is a kind of joke; mathematics was Audrey's subject, while his was English. The letters give him the digits to type, and the bell on the external wall emits a single clang before falling silent. As he rubs his forehead with one equally clammy hand Audrey says "I think we're both ready for bed."

He hopes she's just pleasantly exhausted rather than relieved the day is done. They've enjoyed better anniversaries; she didn't eat too much at dinner, and Vernon had to see off her favourite dish. He's glad they didn't encounter Billy Meredith beforehand; her concern might have robbed her of even more appetite. The waiter almost seemed to think the Henshalls shouldn't be there, although he'd often served them in the past. He'd no right to feel insulted when he didn't even ask Audrey what was wrong. Once they're in bed Vernon is overwhelmed by protectiveness, and clasps her waist as if he's saving her from the dark.

Daylight rouses him, and it feels like realising "We ought to change the number for the debit card."

"Get a new card, do you mean?"

Audrey sounds more distant than he was expecting. She's dressed and standing by the bed. Until he manages to focus on her she puts him in mind of a hospital visitor. "The security number," he says.

"We changed it recently, if you remember."

"Only because the bank emailed saying everybody should. I'd just like to make sure nobody can know the new one."

"If you mean poor Billy Meredith, he was never a thief." Audrey's frown ages her face. "How much did you give him?" she's anxious to hear.

"Enough, I should certainly think." When this falls short of placating her Vernon has to add "A fiver."

"Well, I wish you'd given me the money while we were there."

He isn't going to ask how much she would have donated to Meredith. "I'm ready to shop," she says, "whenever you are."

He could almost imagine she's urging him to leave before he has bathed and dressed. He has a bowl of cereal as well, and a mug of coffee so black that it parches his mouth. Once he has said "I add" he ushers Audrey out of the house. A February wind laced with rain meets them, and he hurries to unlock the garage so that she can shelter in the car. As he drives the Ceed out of their street and onto the main road he says "Shall we decide on a number, then?"

"Let's have a word."

"Café, if you like."

"That doesn't bring back the best memories just now."

He should have known it might remind her of last night. "How about iced as in coffee?"

"It makes me feel cold, Vernon."

She isn't usually so critical of his selection. Her response worries him, though he can't define how. "Would egad fit the bill, do you think?"

"It's a bit old-fashioned, isn't it? Even more than us."

He didn't mean to bring their age to mind. He's close to feeling robbed of language, which is far too reminiscent of straining to recall a number. "Face, then," he says. "You can't have a problem with that."

"If you haven't one with mine."

Has he betrayed how her wrinkled frown upsets him? How does he think he looks to her? He's a good deal more faded and wizened, and he ought to be grateful that she has stayed with this scrap of the man she married. So long as they still have their faculties, surely that's enough. "Of course I haven't," he assures her. "I never will have. You're all I want to see."

After that they're silent. Interludes like this—each knowing the other is there—have been at the heart of their relationship, keeping it alive. Eventually he finds space for the car in the retail park, among too many vehicles to count. "Face it," he murmurs to Audrey as they make their way to the cash machines outside the supermarket. "That's our word."

By the time they finish queuing for a terminal there's a queue behind them. Vernon has been trying to hide the card in his hand like a clumsy magician, and now he wobbles it into the slot and types the code. The onscreen response is so swift it feels like being pounced upon. INCORRECT, he's told.

Were his fingers shakier than he realised? The notion makes the rest of him feel unstable too. He keys the code again at half the speed and gains the same response. If he's wrong once more the machine will keep his card. "What am I doing?" he pleads. "What's wrong?"

"Face it. I did."

"I didn't," he realises aloud. He has been typing 6135 before changing the code. He types the right one and is able to substitute the alternative. As soon as the slot offers a sliver of plastic he catches it between his fingernails and jams the card into his wallet. "All secure," he declares. "Our secret's safe."

The queue is staring at him. Does everyone resent his having spent so long at the machine without taking any cash? If they were so intent on his behaviour, did anyone see what he typed? "Just had to change our number," he says.

"I know what you mean," the foremost woman says. "They can drive you mad, those."

"You shouldn't say such things," Audrey protests. "They don't help."

"I'm with my wife," Vernon says. "We don't let little things get to our minds."

The woman needn't look at him like that, even if she thinks he's being pompous. He shoves the wallet into the plump pocket of his padded coat as he limps to find a trolley large enough to accommodate his stick. "We don't need much," Audrey says. "We've plenty in the freezer."

Has encountering Meredith made her think they spend too much? She keeps telling Vernon to return items to the shelves; it's no wonder he feels watched by shoppers and perhaps by security too. The girl at the checkout scans the tins of food and bottles of spring water, and tells Vernon to check the amount and key his code, neither of which he requires to be told. It's only when he makes to type the numbers for the credit card that his fingers begin to fumble at the air and then at his bumpy forehead. "Forget I did," he mumbles. "Don't face it either."

"Maybe we should have just one number for them all."

"That's supposed to be risky, isn't it? Anyway, we can't deal with it here. Help me, for heaven's sake."

Before Audrey has a chance to speak the checkout girl says "Is there a problem, sir? People are waiting."

"Let them wait a little longer, then. One day they'll learn what it's like to be our age." As he sees Audrey's face wrinkling he wishes he could take back his remark; their years are numbers he'd rather put out of his head. "What's our word for this?" he pleads, and when Audrey doesn't provide it he says "If you ask me it's the new obscenity."

The checkout girl looks as if he has said one. "Sorry, pardon?"

"You can say all sorts of words we weren't meant to use in our childhood but now it's these numbers we're forbidden to write down." When the customer behind him tries to prompt some action with a loud sigh and a cough, Vernon yanks the card out of the reader. "Forget it," he says wildly. "We'll pay cash."

As he wheels the trolley to the exit, leaning on it as much as pushing, Audrey murmurs "You should have used your head, Vernon."

"What do you think I was trying to do?" Then he laughs loud enough to attract quite a few stares. "Just realised what my wife meant," he reassures the shoppers. "Head, that's it. You should have said."

"Do you want me to do all the remembering?" He's disconcerted by how old her face grows as she says "I'll try if you like."

"You mustn't feel pressured. We're still a team, more so than ever." In a bid to rejuvenate her look Vernon says "Maybe we'll do what you said, have just one number."

That's best discussed at home. He's too conscious of being overheard. He speeds the trolley out of the supermarket and peers about for the car. It's red, but so are dozens if not hundreds of the vehicles. He doesn't want to ask Audrey for the registration number, not least in case she has forgotten too. It isn't 3554, but the bunch of digits won't leave his mind alone. He fishes out his keys and squeezes the fob, and hears the Ceed respond somewhere in the distance. He has to rouse the sound—a plaintive yip like the voice of a lost animal—several times before he sees the headlamps flare. As he opens the boot he's confronted by the number plate, by a jumble of letters and digits that threatens to clog his mind with nonsense. "How could we remember that?" he complains and grimaces at a couple who seem to think he's addressing them.

The inside of the car still smells new. Why should that make him feel guilty—because the likes of Billy Meredith can't afford a fraction of the price? He does his best to leave the feeling behind on the way home. He unloads the car and refrains from commenting when, having plodded with a bag in each hand to the front door, he finds Audrey hasn't let herself in. "I add," she cries as he makes for the clamorous panel, and Vernon tells himself that she had just a momentary lapse.

He might upset her if he asks about it. He persuades her to sit down while he puts away the shopping and makes her a coffee, and then he sees to dinner from the freezer. The pallid chilly metal door is labelled with notes in her handwriting, some of which are out of date. "One of your best," he says over dinner. "Won't you have some more?"

"I made it for you, Vernon. So long as you enjoy it, that's what counts."

He mustn't let the reference to counting bother him. After dinner they watch television, a documentary about new developments in mathematics and then a look at the decline in numeracy. Eventually he can't hold back from asking "Haven't we seen this before?"

"Didn't you want to see it again?"

He can't recall, and he hopes she isn't playing word games to hide her own confusion. As he dozes through more mathematical broadcasts he tells himself he's keeping Audrey company, not ensuring that she won't have to deal with the alarm on her own. When at last the programmes end he follows her upstairs, having remembered the code to type despite the shrill insistence of the alarm panel. He can forget about numbers for a while, though he certainly mustn't forget any of them.

They desist from swarming in his skull as the sensation of gripping Audrey's waist gives way to the dark. When he wakens he isn't holding her, and he calls out, blinking at the cold light that shines through the bedroom window to blind him. "Don't you remember what I'm doing today?" Audrey says.

He mustn't wonder if she's asking him to remind her. "It's your day with the girls."

"Then I'll be off unless you need anything."

Since she and her colleagues have retired they meet weekly to see a film or a show or just to spend the day in reminiscing. "Have a fine time," Vernon says and is left wishing they'd exchanged a kiss. He can't recall when they last did. Surely they aren't too old.

A shower helps him waken fully—it sets him shivering until he shrinks away from the fierce hot water. While Audrey's out he'll make dinner. He finds a parking space in sight of the supermarket entrance, which means he needn't hold the registration number in his mind. "Face it," he mutters as he collects ingredients for salad and a pasta dish. "Use your head." He's almost at the checkout when he realises he doesn't know which number relates to which card. He mustn't feel helpless when he can pay cash, but he avoids the girl who served him yesterday, because he can do without being asked if he's on his own today. Once he has stowed away his change he risks using the machine outside the supermarket to check the number for the debit card. "Face it," he says like a prayer, and he's right, which he can't help telling the queue as he turns away. He finds the car almost at once, and as soon as he's consigned the insistently rustling plastic bags to the boot he drives home. "I add," he says and quells the alarm, only to feel he has forgotten something else. He's setting out the ingredients in the kitchen when he remembers that he still hasn't given Audrey her share of the money he took from the machine the night they encountered Billy Meredith.

He ought to check that there's money for her to draw out if she needs it. He limps upstairs, rattling the banisters, and switches on the laptop in the spare room they've kept saying they'll turn into more of an office. At least the elongated identification number for the bank accounts is stored on the computer. He pokes the debit card into the reader—"Face it," he has to say—and is given twice as many digits to enter on the screen. Why do the balances look like a jumble of numbers? Perhaps because he's desperate not to see what's there. He brushes the screen with his fingers and then scrapes it with a nail, but none of this shifts the intruder, which isn't a flaw in the glass either. It's a minus sign, showing that somebody has withdrawn a thousand pounds.

How can it have been Billy Meredith? Who else can it have been? The sight of the digits—a one multiplied by three gaping holes— seems to let worse than age catch up with Vernon, turning his mouth dusty and shrivelling his brain. Could Audrey have obtained the money on Meredith's behalf? Vernon logs out of the bank's site and shuts down the computer, because the sight of the negative amount is infecting him with a tremulous kind of paralysis. He rummages for his mobile and calls Audrey as he wanders out of the room. Perhaps she's in a cinema, because an all-purpose female voice tells him she's unavailable. He's limping back and forth at the top of the stairs as if the landing has become a cage when he catches sight of an object under their bed.

He groans while he clutches the mattress through the quilt and lowers himself to his knees inch by inch. His first grab strews the hidden treasure across the floor and out of reach. His cheek is pressed against the musty carpet by the time he manages to gather all the crumpled notes. He dumps them on the bed and levers himself to his feet, and loses count of how often he has to count the banknotes to be sure they add up to a thousand pounds.

When did Audrey take them out of the account? Did she intend them for Meredith, or was she trying to ensure that nobody could steal them? Vernon crams them into his pocket and tries again to call her, but only the anonymous voice responds. Suppose Audrey withdraws another generous sum before he contacts her? He can't think of a message he would feel comfortable with leaving—they should surely talk about the issue face to face—but she could be knocked down or worse by a thief. Although what Vernon has to do distresses him almost more than the danger she may be in, he can't think of an alternative, and so he phones the bank.

Its voice is indistinguishable from the one that answered Audrey's phone. It lists options for him, and then another selection of keys to press, which leads to a third set. The task seems childishly simple, and yet the sluggish succession of numbers feels as if it's gnawing at his mind. "Yes, I'm an existing customer," he tells them. "Yes, I've a query about my account. Yes, I want to speak to a customer service operator." He earns himself a jolly electronic jig that sounds blurred by overuse, though it gives the voice several opportunities to assure him how important his call is. At last a different voice says "Edie speaking. How can we help you today?"

"We have a joint account with you. We need—"

"I'll just need to check your details for security."

He's afraid she will ask for one of the codes, but she only wants his full name and address and date of birth and account number and two letters of his mother's maiden name and a recent sum withdrawn from the account. "A thousand pounds," he cries, "and that's what I want to talk to you about. My wife—"

246

"One thousand, Mr Henshall. Yes, I see that here," Edie says, disconcerting Vernon so much that he clutches at the wad in his pocket to convince himself he has it. "And what can we do for you?"

The delay in coming to the reason for his call makes it even harder and more painful for Vernon to admit "We need to take my wife off the account."

"In order to do that you'll have to visit your branch."

"Why have I had to go through all this if you can't do it now?" At once Vernon is ashamed of his outburst. "Sorry. Not your fault. We're all at the mercy of routines," he says. "All right, I'm on my way."

He is until he remembers it's unwise to carry so much cash. He shouldn't hide it under the bed—too many old folk were supposed to do that in the past—and so he shoves it into his pillowcase. When he hastens out of the house he finds he left the car out of the garage yesterday, which at least saves time now. The smell of newness aggravates his guilt, but surely he's acting in Audrey's best interests. Once he has parked near the bank he tries calling her again, only to rouse the lifeless voice.

The bank is opposite the supermarket across the mass of vehicles in the retail park. Beyond the deferential automatic doors several clerks even younger than Vernon thought a thief might be are seated behind desks, and he limps over to the closest. "Can I have a word about my account?"

"Have a seat, sir." The young man is labelled Adam, which doesn't quite fit as a code. "Do you have the number?" he says.

It's twice the length of any of the codes, and Vernon can't bring a mnemonic to mind; perhaps he and Audrey never thought of one. "I'll have to give you my details instead."

This turns out to be the entire procedure he went through on the phone. "A thousand," he declares once more and imagines someone stealing it from the house. Adam passes him a card reader, and as Vernon inserts his card he's provoked to say "Why did you send us that email telling us to change the number?"

"I don't believe we did. Was it addressed personally to you?"

"To all your customers."

"We'd never do that. It must have been a scam or maybe just a prank."

"A prank." Vernon feels brittle with panic. "Well, we changed it. I did," he says and thinks for a moment that he has betrayed the number to the bank clerk. He types the digits, which the machine tells him are wrong. "Wait a minute," he pleads, "just give me time," and clamps his forehead with his finger and thumb, digging the rest of the fingers into his face. This brings back the word he should have used, and as soon as he's able to see again he types the number. "In your face," he mutters like an impolite pupil.

"That's all in order, Mr Henshall. How may I help?"

"For reasons I'd rather not specify we need to make me the only one with access to the account."

"I see." Adam keeps a noise in his throat, not quite a cough. "Mrs Henshall will have to come in with you," he says.

"The girl, what was her name, five four nine five." As Adam gazes with some form of patience at him Vernon blurts "Edie. She said nothing about that. All she said—"

"We've nobody of that name here, Mr Henshall."

"Don't try and make out I'm deluded. She was on your number that I rang, and she wanted all the rigmarole you did."

"That would be a central number. If you want to alter you and your wife's account both signatories have to be present, I'm afraid."

"Then you and your damned numbers, you'll be responsible for whatever happens." Of course Vernon is as well, and in a worse sense Audrey can't be said to be. "I'll bring her as soon as I can," he says and almost sends the chair sprawling in his haste to leave the bank.

Should he change the security number while he has access to a machine? That would save Audrey from taking out any more cash that might put her at risk, but now the thought of subjecting her to that kind of confusion when he isn't there to help her appals him. "Three five five four," he mumbles as if that can make the yelps of the car sound less like a lost creature calling out for somebody it knows. He drives home and parks in the garage, and unlocks the front door to be met by silence.

The alarm should be demanding to be told its number. Has an intruder set it off while the Henshalls weren't home? As Vernon falters in the hall he hears a man's voice in the house, and he's even more perturbed to realise that Audrey is talking to the fellow. Even if her presence explains why the alarm didn't greet Vernon, who has she brought home? He can't help thinking it's Billy Meredith. Perhaps she hasn't just taken pity on their old pupil; perhaps she's attracted to him—to something he can offer that Vernon no longer can. They're in the front room, and Vernon flings the door wide. "What do you think—"

There is indeed a young man in the room. He's on the television, talking about algebra. Vernon feels even guiltier, not to say ridiculous, for the assumptions he made. "Sorry I came in like that," he says. "I didn't know who was here."

"So long as you do now, Vernon."

"Do you mind if I switch this off?" The television is distracting him—all the letters and numbers are—but when he does away with them he's thrown to hear her say "Where have you been?"

"Oh, just—" He isn't ready to mention the bank; he needs to make the situation as painless as he can for both of them. "Just getting the makings of dinner," he says. "You oughtn't to let me forget there are two cooks in the house."

"You needn't have, Vernon. I couldn't go out, you know."

Vernon finds he's reluctant to prompt her. "You couldn't . . ."

"I didn't go out because I forgot the alarm code."

"When didn't you?"

"Today, of course. The day I usually spend with the girls. Never mind, I expect they'll understand."

Vernon is afraid to. How much more about her may he have overlooked? "That's why we want less to remember," she says. "Let's have just one number."

"We'll need to change them at the bank."

"We will tomorrow, shall we? You don't want to go out again."

Vernon is ashamed to welcome the delay. "You watch your programme," he says like an apology he can't acknowledge, "while I make us dinner."

"Don't do much for me. I've already eaten."

He can't bring himself to establish whether she believes she has dined with her friends after all. He's hearing the retort she gave the woman in the supermarket queue. Perhaps the reason why he hasn't grasped how badly the demands of the numbers have affected Audrey's mind is that she won't admit it to herself. "You watch anyway," he says. "You sit and rest. My turn to do the housework."

Quite an amount is waiting. He supposes their age is to blame. He keeps returning to the front room to make sure of Audrey, but she has hardly moved except to draw the curtains, unless they were already drawn. He'll leave the dinner until she can do it justice, and so he microwaves a carton of casserole from the freezer and brings it on a tray to the front room. Since he can't persuade her to share it, he finishes it himself. He watches her programmes to the end, and then he clutches at her beneath the quilt, feeling desperate to keep hold of all that they have together. He thinks the lump in his pillow will never let him sleep, but he's jerked awake by hearing Audrey say "Whenever you're ready I am."

He needs to deal with the situation before he loses his resolve. He goes through his morning ritual almost too hastily to remember that he has, and then he keys the alarm and ushers Audrey to the car. It assails him with the scent of guilt again; he doesn't want to think how it was paid for. He's aware of keeping his thoughts too much to himself, and makes a timid start at speaking. "I never gave you any of that cash from the machine."

"Never mind, Vernon. I haven't needed it."

"You've made do with what you had, have you?" He can't look at her while he asks "Do you happen to remember how much you took out last time you used one?"

"I can't say. Does it matter?"

"It was quite an amount. Too much to be carrying around with you." When she doesn't respond he says "It was a thousand, Audrey. I found it in the house."

"Did I do that?" Her sad voice grows defensive as she says "Maybe it's safest there. You said yourself someone could steal the number."

"Shall we make it just one on the account to be safer?"

"The number, you mean." Before he can force himself to be less ambiguous Audrey says "No, you're talking about me. You think I can't be trusted."

"I only want to take some of the pressure off your mind."

"If you think that's the problem we'll have to see what happens. We both knew this kind of thing might catch up with us."

He would be relieved by her attitude if he weren't so abashed. Except for having to concentrate on the road he would reach for her hand. "Shall we agree on a new code, then?"

"I know one you might remember."

She sounds almost playful, but when she tells him he has to take a firmer grip on the wheel as the car nearly strays into the adjacent traffic lane. "I know what we can have instead," he says as steadily as he can manage. "We'll change one letter."

This early in the day he's able to park close to the bank, and there's no queue for the cash dispensers. He leans on his stick while he jiggles the card into the nearest machine. His hand is so shaky that it infects the rest of him, dislodging the word that he tried to keep in his head, and he almost types the one he didn't want to hear. "Not that," he insists, he doesn't know how loud. But when he types 4554 instead the screen tells him he's wrong.

He feels like a child who can't perform the simplest mathematical task, and then he realises he has yet to change the code. "How incompetent is that?" he mumbles, turning to share a wry laugh with Audrey. Nobody is anywhere near him.

She must have gone into the bank. Vernon almost neglects to

retrieve the card before he follows her. He can't see her through the glass doors, and even once they move aside she isn't visible. "Where are you?" he calls, and when the clerks at the enquiry desks all stare at him he demands "Have you seen my wife?"

They needn't look as if they think he's being unreasonable or worse. "We're customers of yours," he assures them. Perhaps Audrey is in the supermarket; he can locate her easily enough. He gropes for his phone, only to be answered by the automatic voice far too reminiscent of the one that listed number after number when he called the bank. He's so unnerved to hear it that he doesn't merely end the call; he jabs a key that shows him a question. Yes, he wants to be rid of the artificial voice, and he pokes another key. Just too late he sees he has deleted Audrey's number.

"Look what you've made me do," he cries, staring at the clerks until they take refuge in their work. He tramps through the bank to make sure Audrey isn't there, and then he limps into the supermarket. She doesn't answer him in there either, and he doesn't come to him in the car park, however loud he shouts across the empty vehicles. His mouth has grown as dry as his hands and feet have turned clammy, and his skull feels like rusty tin. He could call the police—he hasn't forgotten that number—but he oughtn't to embarrass Audrey unless he absolutely must. Perhaps she's on her way home or even there by now, and he squeezes the key fob until he locates the car.

He can't see her as he drives home. He's distracted by realising that he could have asked the bank for her mobile number. It begins with 0 like all its kind, but what's the rest? Not O I hid, not O face, O feed, O heed, O dear... He's still struggling to think of it when he unlocks the front door and sets off the alarm. So Audrey isn't home yet, and the disappointment almost makes him type the word he's determined to forget. "I add," he cries and switches off the electronic threat. He's loitering aimlessly in the hall, which smells like memories grown stale, when someone rings the doorbell. "Where did you go?" he pleads as he fumbles with the latch.

The woman on the doorstep isn't Audrey, though for a breath

her caring look lets him hope she is. "Mr Henshall?" she says.

"Vernon Henshall, yes." Although she's wearing a subdued grey suit, he wonders nervously if she could be with the police. "What's the matter?" he demands.

"Please don't be alarmed, Mr Henshall. I'm from social services. I was asked to look in on you in case you might like our help."

Once he finds words it won't be impolite to utter he says "Who asked you?"

"We don't give out names, Mr Henshall. Just a client of one of our agencies."

Vernon finds he hardly needs to ask "Would that be Billy Meredith?"

"As I said, we aren't at liberty to say." Her face does, however. "I believe you met recently," she says. "He was concerned about your behaviour. I understand you were talking—"

"That's what we do. No reason it should bother anybody else." As the woman makes to speak Vernon says "It's people such as Meredith who need your help, not us."

"Mr Henshall, if I could just—"

"Thank you, but you can't," Vernon says and shuts the door.

"We don't need anyone else, do we?" he murmurs, but Audrey isn't answering just yet. He listens at the door until he's sure the woman has left them alone, and then he wanders into the kitchen. He'll put away the ingredients once he has found Audrey, and it's still his turn to make dinner. He should remember to put the car away as well, though he doesn't need to recall which insurance let him buy it. He knows where Audrey has to be, soon if not now. He finds the remote control in the front room and locates his chair by the light of another programme about mathematics. Even if the numbers are beyond his understanding, they always bring her back. "I add," he repeats in case this helps, and strives not to think it's fending off the word he mustn't let into his mind. "I add."

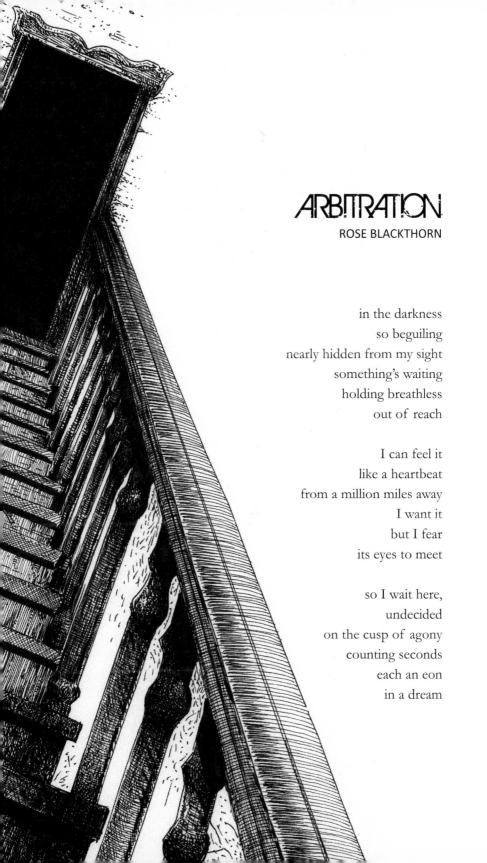

ARBITRATION

ROSE BLACKTHORN

in the darkness
so beguiling
nearly hidden from my sight
something's waiting
holding breathless
out of reach

I can feel it
like a heartbeat
from a million miles away
I want it
but I fear
its eyes to meet

so I wait here,
undecided
on the cusp of agony
counting seconds
each an eon
in a dream

ROSE BLACKTHORN

will it move now?
or just fade
into the dark where it resides
like a nightmare
never wakened
to a scream

at an impasse
a dilemma
at that point of no return
shall I fight?
or just take flight
lost, by design

this is it
that crucial moment
from which all future paths diverge
take a breath
decision made
and it's mine

not the other
my reflection
doppelganger in the glass
a ghost, a shadow
in a past
now left behind

3-DOT PEOPLE

GENE O'NEILL

EVERYTHING was a complete blank before last night.

Ms. Jilly, my social worker, had picked me up late Friday night at the police station on Eddy Street in the Tenderloin. The police had found me standing befuddled in the thick fog in a parking lot across the street from The Mitchell Brothers on O'Farrell near Van Ness, the most notorious erotic dancing club in San Francisco. I had no identification and didn't know my name or how I got there. But, fortunately for me, after taking me back to the police station they called Adult Social Services.

Ms. Jilly signed me out, took me over to the nearby All-Star Donuts, bought me a cup of coffee and a pair of huge glazed apple fritters. As I was eating, she explained the situation from her point of view.

"Okay, I have given you a name in my reports, not the usual John Doe, but something solid and not too flashy. Phil ... Phil Shepherd. That's what I'm going to call you until we know your real name," she said. "You are most likely suffering from amnesia, which is usually caused by physical or psychological trauma. Since the police found no evidence of any physical trauma, we'll assume you've suffered some kind of disturbing psychological event. Also you hadn't committed any crime. So we are lucky that they called *me* instead of just turning you back out onto the street."

I nodded my understanding but kept on eating, starving.

"Strange as it may seem, there have been a number of similar amnesia cases surfacing over the last few years here in San Francisco—four in the previous six months. These most recent cases all occurred right here in the Tenderloin. The City Public Health Service folks think these four cases were probably the result of some kind of new exotic narcotic available on the street. But there's been no determination of the drug's chemical profile as yet. And anyhow you don't look like a typical illegal drug user, Phil..."

She paused and I looked up from my partially devoured second fritter into her unwavering almond-shaped eyes—the unusual dark-brown shade of mahogany wood. Together with her exceptional height and no-nonsense expression, the piercing dark gaze made her a formidable female presence. Despite not asking me a question, she seemed to be expecting some kind of response from me, but my mouth was full. Finally, I took a sip of coffee, swallowed, and said: "I honestly don't really recall anything, including recently taking any drugs. But my intuitive sense is that I'm not now nor have ever been an illegal drug user."

She smiled wryly and nodded, as if I'd confirmed what she already suspected, and continued: "I've been the case worker assigned to the last four others like you, who were all suffering from a complete memory blank when I first met them. The good news is that they began to recover their memories after getting some rest and special help. So, I'm convinced we can recover your memory loss and soon."

The last big bite of apple fritter stuck in my throat. I tried to wash it down with a large swallow of the bitter coffee. But I ended up just coughing it partially up into my napkin, unable to ask what she meant by special help and exactly how soon.

Ms. Jilly watched me blotting the tears in my eyes, and then asked: "You want another one?"

"No thanks," I finally said, actually still famished, which was probably a good thing—kept me from focusing too squarely on my unnerving situation. But, right now I was most curious about what was going to happen to me next.

"Okay, if you are finished eating, let's get you a room for the weekend," she said, standing up, stretching her, at least, six-foot frame. She was dressed casually in a dark green sweat suit with USF block letters in white across the front of the shirt, explaining that she'd responded to the cops' late night call from Fit & Toned, a 24-hour workout gym in her Marina neighborhood. She said that we were now headed for the nearby Hotel Reo.

Ms. Jilly explained on the way over, almost apologetically: "This hotel always has rooms available and is very accessible to public transportation and medical services. So we have prior-approved vouchers for it from my department. I know this surrounding area looks…well, a bit run down, ragged, and tired, but that's just typical Tenderloin." She shrugged and we continued the next two blocks, passing by a number of street people. Ms. Jilly characterized most of them, not really unkindly, by the state of their eyes, as being dead-eyed bums, rheumy-eyed drunks, pin-eyed junkies, shifty-eyed beggars, or mascara-eyed hookers. But in an obviously more judgmental tone, she described a number of the young men hanging out in front of Jimbo's, a corner liquor store, as sharp-eyed thugs. Although I was tall and fairly husky, I knew that it was Ms. Jilly's no-nonsense appearance and confident attitude that gained us safe passage through the crowded sidewalks.

We made it almost to the steps in front of the Hotel Reo relatively unscathed; but at that point we experienced a brief verbal skirmish with an inebriated man hoping to make a drug sale. He blocked our way, hands up in the wait-a-minute gesture, and declared hoarsely: "Ya lookin? I'm holdin, I'm holdin."

The unkempt guy turned and obediently shuffled off after Ms. Jilly answered crossly: "No, man, we are *not* looking for what you are selling, you hear me."

The outside of the two-story Hotel Reo fit in with the surrounding seedy look of the Tenderloin, because it was in bad need of some maintenance repair and fresh paint.

A few moments later, we were standing on a worn-thin carpet in the shabby lobby, staring at the equally worn-thin desk clerk behind a heavily barred security cage. I then realized that earlier, what Ms. Jilly really meant to say was inexpensive vouchers from her department. This place was not a very classy establishment.

She signed a voucher for the desk clerk and said: "Ferdy, this is Phil Shepherd, he'll be staying here over the weekend. Take care of him. But do me a favor and keep the girls from hustling him, he's not a john." She chuckled dryly, peering at the desk clerk inside the steel screen.

Ferdy, with an unfiltered cigarette dangling from his lower lip, nodded and pushed a room key to me under the narrow opening at the bottom of the security cage. He didn't crack a smile at Ms. Jilly's apparent attempt at a joke or appear the least bit curious about me. But I couldn't help wondering exactly what Ms. Jilly meant by her facetious girl warning that seemed to be a bit out of character. I soon found out when she paused a moment later at the lobby stairwell, before walking me up to my room.

"The hookers bring their customers that they call johns here from the street to this first floor. The Hotel Reo rents these street level rooms by the hour to lots of fake names, including John Does. This is known locally as a hot sheet operation, and it will be very busy and noisy down here tonight and again Saturday night, too. Don't get involved in any of these extracurricular shenanigans, understand? You need to be focused fully on staying relaxed and recovering your past without any emotional involvement with ... ah, street people. Okay?"

Of course I understood, realizing these kinds of street people required money for their special services. I had none. But I said nothing, quietly following her up the stairs to my room—210, second door on the right. I opened the door with my key. It was a plain undecorated square room, no amenities other than an unscreened sink, small mirror, and toilet bowl in one corner and an un-curtained, open window overlooking the street below. Surprisingly, the entire room and facilities were actually neat and clean.

But Ms. Jilly paused a moment, and frowned as she gazed out the opened window. Even this late, loud street sounds were flooding into the room—sirens whining, cars braking, people laughing, country music blaring from a nearby bar, and a woman's voice shrieking hysterically from somewhere close.

She pulled down the window, partially screening out some of the noise.

"You might want to venture out in the Tenderloin by yourself only during daylight hours. Avoid unnecessary contact with local denizens. They can be a predatory bunch, and there are more than a few, who will take advantage after sensing a person's weakness... like your temporary loss of memory. Here, these are vouchers for six meals at The Casual Corner up on Post Street across Geary, three blocks in that general direction. It's not fancy, but the food is good." She looked around once more, then added: "Except for meals, you'll really be better off just staying right here in your room for the weekend. Get some rest because it is important in the recovery process. I'll be back about seven-thirty Monday morning to see how you're doing. We'll decide our next move then."

I smiled with an expression Ms. Jilly apparently found dismissive of her advice. She must've realized that, even being disabled with no past, my intention was not to stay cooped up in this tiny room for two days and three nights.

Ms. Jilly reinforced my sense of her perceptiveness and chuckled dryly. "Okay, Phil, just be careful out there. You're going to meet some odd people in the 'Loin even during the daytime. Maybe even some of your neighbors here on this floor of the hotel will seem weird. But that is a pretty common impression and to be expected in this part of the City..."

She peered into my eyes and said: "You okay, not too overwhelmed having your past blanked out? You appear calm."

"I'll be okay, Ms. Jilly. Of course I'm a bit nervous and unsettled, but I'm confident that you will help me recover my memory. Thank you for everything. I'll see you Monday morning. Sorry to have interrupted your weekend."

She hesitated another moment, glanced again at the closed window, and then, still looking a touch reluctant, finally left.

Saturday morning I awakened early, got up, and stretched. I washed up in the tiny stained sink basin. Then, I stepped out into the hall and bumped into my neighbor from directly across the narrow hallway, coming out of room 209.

She was an attractive, dark-eyed woman with her hair dyed kind of an electric pink, resembling some of the other extreme hair colors I'd noticed worn by some young women on the street the previous night. And she was dressed in a contrasting black and white neat uniform.

"Well, hello, Big Fella," she said, which she probably meant to be funny and not flirtatious, because she was almost as tall as me—over six-foot. "I'm Flo-jo. You are probably...John?"

I told her my name was Phil.

"That's funny, there was a steady stream of johns on the first floor last night when I came home from work...I suspect they are all gone by now."

I smiled, not mentioning that was the second time I had been recently involved in a kind of john joke.

"I'm going out for breakfast before work. You want to eat somewhere together, Phil?"

I said: "Sure, but I have no money, only a voucher to eat up at The Casual Corner—"

"Great place, we'll go Dutch."

I couldn't help being intrigued by this joyful and friendly young woman with the bizarre neon-pink hair.

We walked in the early morning fog still blowing in from the Bay over to The Casual Corner on Post Street, which was really busy, even this early on a Saturday morning. There were a number of folks eating before going to work, many dressed in conservative uniforms similar to Flo-jo's. She said that she worked up at a hotel on Van Ness in housekeeping. She was a very recent arrival in the City, looking for something a bit better on her days off, but happy for her housekeeping opportunity right now. She was staying at the Hotel Reo and saving her money.

After I finished a huge stack of hotcakes with scrambled eggs and bacon, I offered to walk her up to her place of work.

Just before we turned the corner on Van Ness, an unkempt, surly guy challenged me aggressively, his sour smell strong and very offensive. With clabbered spit flying from the corners of his mouth, he also invaded my space, shouting: "Hey, man, I need a couple of bucks to take the edge off. Ya holdin any extra bread?"

I stepped back, shrugged, and held out my empty hands. "Sorry, I don't have any money at all."

His unshaved face quickly reddened into an angry, fierce scowl, and he sputtered incoherently something about *fucking rich guys*, while slipping a small item from his greasy overcoat pocket.

It was a straight razor that he flipped open…and in a smooth follow-up movement he began a horizontal slashing motion like a sword in the direction of my face—

Flo-jo deftly snatched the razor from the man's grubby hand in mid-flight, as if she were plucking a flying bee from the air over a blossom in a nearby flower box.

"Hey—"

She followed up with what appeared to be a light slap to the man's right temple.

Down he went, still sputtering, to a knee, clutching at his head as if felled by an axe handle instead of a woman's open hand. Then, still sporting a generous smile, my tall companion reached out and ever so gently touched his forehead with two fingers—

The man collapsed into an unconscious heap.

"He'll be fine when he wakes up," Flo-jo said, in her relaxed, easy tone. "But maybe you should get rid of this for him. So he doesn't harm anyone else or perhaps himself."

She was holding out her right hand, palm up, with the straight razor folded back up safely.

I was too stunned by the rapid sequence of events to say anything. I reached out for the razor, but before I took it from her hand, I glimpsed the odd tattoo centered in her right palm. It was three indigo dots in the shape of a tiny triangle. So small it would have been easy to miss if I hadn't been staring at the offered straight razor.

Before I'd recovered my speech, she advised: "We have to hurry now, Phil, I can't be late for work. I only started a month ago."

A few moments later we were at the employees' entrance of the Holiday Inn on Van Ness, her place of work. I had just a few moments to thank her for saving me from having my face slashed... and noted my awe and admiration for her almost magical handling of the big aggressive man.

She shrugged nonchalantly, smiled sweetly and said: "You're welcome, Phil. Maybe I'll see you later tonight?"

After that I wandered about the Tenderloin, with nothing special in mind. As Ms. Jilly had recommended, I was indeed more careful now, avoiding all possible confrontations, not even making eye contact with anyone. Just roaming about for a couple of hours and observing at a distance, waiting for lunchtime. I seemed to be perpetually hungry, my stomach a constantly growling reminder. Kept me from being able to dwell too long on the fact that I still hadn't recovered even a hint of my past.

I pulled up my collar against the lingering, cold summer fog as I passed a number of grim-faced and bundled-up folks loitering at another corner mart. And I remembered Ms. Jilly last night generally describing these resident people here in the 'Loin as: *The lost, the forgotten, and the never known.* An expression that seemed really damning now in broad daylight. I kept wandering in kind of a squared circle, eventually making my way on Jones Street over back toward Geary, but stopping and glancing curiously in the storefront window of a place of business with an oddly spelled name: U-do-it Laundromat.

A woman carrying a small basket of laundry stepped out at that moment and came to an abrupt halt in front of me, unexpectedly dropping her basket.

"Look out!" she shouted, taking a protective step toward the street; and with one hand she snagged a ball out of the air that had been headed in my direction.

Across the street two young boys—one with a bat, one with a glove—scattered, darting back up Jones. They stopped a block away and warily watched us.

The woman smiled and said to me: "Hey, kids play ball in the street, what are you going to do, right?"

She tossed the ball up and down in her hand a couple of times, then held it out and asked: "You need a baseball?"

I said no, and she immediately turned and fired it in a straight line the entire block back toward the boys. The boy wearing a glove managed to catch it on the fly, jerked the glove off, blew on his fingers, and shouted: "Ya outta be pitchin for the Giants, lady."

But back a moment ago, when she still held the ball in her opened right palm facing toward me, I'd noticed the now familiar tiny three indigo dots. And, on closer inspection of her features, I realized the woman looked more than a bit like Flo-Jo. They both were dark-eyed, tall, and demonstrated terrific reaction time.

"My friend is a good athlete just like you," I said, looking into her exotic, almond-shaped eyes. "Her name is Flo-Jo. Do you happen to know her?"

She hesitated briefly, then shook her head, smiled, bent over, and lifted up her basket.

"May I help you carry that?"

"No, it's okay, I'm just around the corner, staying temporarily at the Hotel Reo."

"Ha, so am I. Let me take that. My name is Phil."

She let me take the basket and said: "My name is Kayle."

We walked together back to the hotel, Kayle telling me she was moving soon over to the Sunset area of the City, taking a job as a clerk in a book store very near UCSF Hospital. She planned on taking classes from a nearby SF City College extension, and some day entering the medical field. For now, she was thankful to be working around doctors and nurses, who were the main customers of the bookstore.

We climbed to the second floor, where she lived only two doors down the hall from Flo-Jo—Room 213.

After dropping off the basket in her room, I stopped at my place to wash up before lunch. I still hadn't recovered any pieces of my memory as I'd hoped. But I'd met two interesting women, both living nearby right here at this run-down old hotel. And of course I was intensely curious about their duplicate palm tattoos, the meaning. With their exotic eyes, large size, and athletic presence, I wondered if the two women were perhaps both adherents of some kind of foreign martial arts lifestyle. I decided to ask one of them about the significance of the three-dot tattoos, first chance I got.

But for the next day and a half I saw neither again, as I soon discovered the Main SF Library at nearby Civic Center. An amazing place, where I spent most of the rest of my weekend, reading up on my memory loss condition and other bits of intriguing information. I even searched back through the last four months of the *San Francisco Chronicle*, looking for a mention of the other four amnesiac arrivals in the Tenderloin. But I found nothing.

And I took Ms. Jilly's advice, staying in my room after dark.

Monday morning Ms. Jilly was right on time, meeting me in the lobby of the Reo.

We sat down together on one of the threadbare gray sofas.

"Remembering anything yet, Phil?"

I shook my head.

"What have you done with yourself the last two days?"

3-DOT PEOPLE

"I wandered around, looking at people. Met two very nice women who live right here at the Reo on the second floor. But mostly though I spent time up at the City Main Library, researching amnesia and many other topics of interest. A remarkable place. The reading and research services are free."

Ms. Jilly nodded as if she approved of me meeting the women and spending most of my time at the library. Then, she asked hesitantly: "Did you happen to see anyone that seemed to recognize you on the street? Perhaps someone just staring, like they knew you from the past?"

"No," I said, noticing her change of expression at my answer.

She almost looked relieved.

She took in a deep breath. "Okay, Plan B. We are going up to Napa State Hospital, and sign you in for a procedure that has worked well in the past with amnesiacs, including all of my recent clients. The doctors up there are experts on your condition."

"A procedure?"

Ms. Jilly smiled and said: "They use a series of three electro-shock treatments—"

She held up her hands, palms out. "Wait, it's not as gruesome as it sounds. You are heavily sedated. And after each treatment, you recover more and more of your memory. Eventually one hundred percent successful after the third treatment...Does the sound of the procedure frighten you, Phil?"

I laughed. "No, actually I'll pretty much try anything to find out who I am, and where I come from."

"Okay, let's go. I have a City car parked outside."

I would have liked to have said goodbye or something to Flo-jo and Kayle, if either had been around; but when I went up to my room to get the paper bag of personal items that Ms. Jilly had given me Friday night, my door knocks on both 209 and 213 went unanswered.

The drive was about an hour, on highways through first a heavily urban area and then a rural agricultural setting featuring gnarly

267

grapevines. During the trip Ms. Jilly talked mostly about the history of the State Hospital. She said that it was now housing a majority of PCPs. Penal Code Patients, who had committed some crime to land them in the correctional system, but were drug addicts or others who needed more intensive psychiatric/psychological services than a prison usually offered. In addition, the other non-criminal patients here were mostly court commitments. Few patients nowadays were subjected to electro- or insulin-shock treatments. The archaic procedures used only on the most severe cases of depression or anxiety. And of course for amnesia. But amnesiacs represented only a tiny percentage of the population at Napa State Hospital. She also mentioned that I would have a friend here. She had called ahead and a man named Tem would meet us in the receiving ward. Ms. Jilly said that Tem would explain some things and help me negotiate my way through the next few days while recovering my memory.

She signed me into the hospital and walked me to the receiving ward. There we met a man who could have been Ms. Jilly's older brother. The resemblance, including dark eyes, large size, and the efficient way they both moved was uncanny. She eventually left me in his care, saying that she'd return in five days, expecting my memory recovery to be complete by then.

"Hooray for you!" she added, and then she gave me a high-five, both uncharacteristically exuberant behavior for her.

I laughed and struck her open right hand ... But the smile instantly froze on my face as she turned and walked out the ward door. During the high-five I'd glimpsed her three-dot palm tattoo.

Tem noticed my shocked expression and led me into the small TV and rec room, which was relatively vacant at this time of morning. We sat on a couch. He said that most patients in receiving were elsewhere during the morning hours, going through medical or psychological screening, or being assigned counselors, or perhaps completing legal documents if they were self-commitments.

But I was more interested in Tem's forthcoming explanation

of *how* I ended up in the Tenderloin and *why* and eventually *who* he thought I was.

He spoke in a kind of shotgun style, splattering me with awe-inspiring information. Tem began: "Jilly explained to you that you are amnesiac, and here at the State Hospital for shock treatment. She also told me that you have met two others in addition to her, who are also three-dot people living at the Hotel Reo. In fact, all three of these women kept a close eye on you over the weekend, insuring your safety..."

He paused at that point and revealed his own tattooed palm.

Stunned again, I looked up. "W-W-Who are you Three-Dot People?" I said in a strained stammer. "Are you some kind of secret religious sect...or maybe even aliens?"

He shook his head and smiled more fully.

"No, we are not aliens...Well, not exactly. We come from a place we call: Earth Prime. It is located in a parallel universe, but it's the exact twin of Earth here. Except it is much older and we think it is dying, strangling on both its own pollution and terrible autocratic rule...The destination point between the two Earths is located in the San Francisco Tenderloin. The transfer is enabled by a teleportation process using Earth Prime advanced techniques in extending the research that Earth scientists here are calling Quantum Entanglement. Okay so far?"

I nodded, but stared at him with perhaps a still baffled expression. I pointed at his hand enclosed around the tiny triangle. "Okay. But what exactly is this? What does this tattoo mean?"

"It distinguishes our minority class on our home world; we think of ourselves as the enlightened people, who developed the teleportation process to save all the three-dot people," he said, speaking a bit more slowly now. "We are dominated by the majority, who look like us, but wear only a single indigo dot on their right ear lobe. They are the dictatorial upper class, who view us as lower class *terrorists*, disturbing their benevolent rule through illegal protests, slanted propaganda, and fake solutions, including

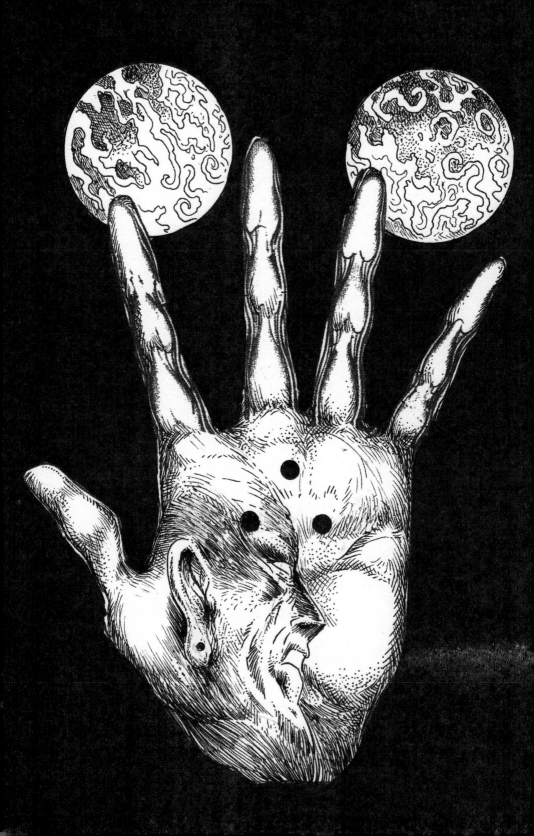

the promise of teleporting three-dot people to safety here..."

Tem paused, staring at me and waiting for a comment.

I just gestured for him to go on.

He continued: "In recent years the rulers have used their secret police to begin rounding up our people, locking some of our leaders in terrible dungeons. This elite force wears two dots behind their right ear lobes. They are actually trained assassins, murdering with impunity many for just wearing three dots. It is rumored that the rulers have recently accessed our teleportation procedure and have sent an assassin through to the Bay Area. They consider all us escapees as traitors, with a capital sentence on our heads. We are small in number, centered here in Northern California. Okay, I know you must have dozens of questions..."

He paused again.

Still processing all that he'd said, I asked: "And you think I came from your parallel Earth?"

Tem smiled kindly, reached out, and without saying anything, he turned over my right hand.

I gazed down into my own palm at the now familiar little triangle of dots.

I was shocked speechless...I was obviously one of the Earth Prime three-dot escapees.

But I finally pulled myself together, looked up at Tem, and asked: "I will regain my memory of everything about Earth Prime in the next few days?"

"Yes, you will," he said confidently. "I, too, originally came here as the first amnesiac for the electro-shock treatment, about three years ago. Ms. Jilly brought me. I've met and helped all of the others needing treatment since then..."

He paused again, gathered his thoughts, and said: "We usually allow each amnesiac to regain some of his past naturally before explaining too much ahead of time. But you, Dar, are very special indeed. You see, the portal from Earth Prime ending here is imperfectly structured. It *opens* only sporadically about once every seven to eight weeks. There have actually been *only* twenty-five three-dot people teleported successfully here in three years. The trip has the disturbing amnesiac effect on about half of us—you, too, have experienced this blanking out of memory. We are not sure *why*."

He sucked in a deep breath, obviously deciding to continue his explanation. "You, Dar, are one of the group of theoretical physicists, all experts on extending quantum entanglement principles, who originally developed the teleportation portal. You have been sent here now to try to correct whatever is adversely affecting the exit portal in the Tenderloin of San Francisco and the disturbing effect on memories of some of the three-dot travelers. Open up the pipeline, so to speak. Not only to help more of our people to escape. But in large enough numbers to become influential here—eventually affect change environmentally and politically before it is too late for Earth. Do you understand your importance now?"

I slowly nodded and rubbed my chin.

What he said made perfect sense now; but me being an important Earth Prime scientist, the fate of the three-dot people and Earth in my hands—?

Tem jumped up with a frown on his face, saying: "I have to go now, the new doctor is here. He does not like me." He pointed back at the doorway, and quickly made his exit past the man in gray scrubs. "I will see you later."

The doctor made his way to where I was sitting. "Hello, Phil Shepherd, I'm Dr. Scott Berke." In addition to a strong scent of aftershave, I detected the faint aroma of a rich cigar smoke.

He reached down and turned over my right hand, shaking his head in a humorous, dismissive manner. "That is simply three dots from a ball point pen. It will easily wash off, as you will soon find out. Our Mr. Tem is a highly functioning paranoid schizophrenic suffering from a very detailed grand delusion. He infects some of our patients with his *idée fixe*, at least the ones who are amnesiac and come here for electro-shock treatment, like yourself."

"He's only a patient here?" I blurted, finding it hard to believe that the fascinating and bright man I'd just met was crazy.

"Yes, he's relatively harmless, but a chronic case, I'm afraid. His delusional system quite unshakeable." Dr. Berke smiled kindly. "I must admit that he tells a very convincing and plausible tale about an alternate Earth, and the three-dot people escaping to come here and help save us on Earth. Right?"

I nodded absently, a number of vague questions trying to surface in my befuddled mind.

Dr. Berke stood before I could ask anything more and said: "Get yourself ready by going to the bathroom and whatever else you might need to do, Phil Shepherd. A psych tech will be down in a few minutes to bring you up to surgery. We will begin your memory restoration treatment immediately."

I nodded and made my way to the restroom.

I emptied my bladder and tried to scrub the fake tattoo from my palm, but with no initial luck. Someone must have used an indelible ballpoint pen on me, but who and when? I looked up at myself in the mirror. And what about Ms. Jilly? She knew Tem…and those other three-dot people? Were they all crazy, too, like Tem? But before I could think clearly about these or the other questions trying to surface in my mind, a male psych tech came into the rest room.

He said: "Mr. Shepherd, I'm here to take you to surgery. Take these pills." He handed me a paper cup to wash down the two pills.

Everything is a vague swirl from that point in time…

Eventually, I find myself wearing a backless hospital gown and situated on a gurney, wheeled into an operating room, drifting because of the preliminary drugs already administered by the tech…

I look up at the five masked people bending over me in their dark gray scrubs, like wolves at a fresh kill. But I recognize Dr. Berke's soothing voice, as he gently pats my chest with a gloved hand, peering down with his dark eyes, and saying: "You are going to be just fine now, Phil. No more worries about any of our friend's silly delusions."

Then, he turns and announces: "Okay people, let's prepare for a suborbital lobotomy."

I'm stunned, wanting to shout: No! Wait! But the drugs flooding through my veins are paralyzing my throat. My vision is beginning to blur.

In a distant voice, the doctor says: "Nurse, yes, that one, the longest and sharpest probe." As he turns toward the instrument nurse, I see the two tiny indigo dots behind his right ear lobe.

I close my eyes, trying to regain my voice—

"No, there will be no lobotomy today," the instrument nurse replies sharply, still holding the probe.

I blink.

She is dropping her mask, as are the three others in gray scrubs tightly encircling the empty-handed assassin.

Despite my blurry vision, I recognize and grin at the four familiar faces: Flo-jo, Ms. Jilly, Kayle, and Tem.

BLACK RIVER #2

ELIZABETH MASSIE

Sunlight drifts like dragonflies,
Dragonflies drift like sun-dust;
Tiny feet against tiny feet, eyes looking down to
    gaze at themselves upon
My transparent skin.
She kneels beside me, dark as Mother Earth,
Sees her countenance in tiny whirlpools that
    catch and spin back.
I watch as she touches her lips then the image of
    her lips, stirring silent ripples
    that in moments become nothing,
While he studies the damp, sloping land,
The trees and their axe-sharp shadows,

Dead leaves tumbling in a warm wind,
Looking over his shoulder, across my glistening shallows,
Watching beyond tiny white flowers and
White granite stones for peaked white hoods.
He whispers, "We's safe."
Next to her now, his blond hair sweat-plastered, sweet as summer,
He pledges love in whispers so faint they are heard only by dragon-
    flies and sunlight;
Their smiles mirrored, caught in my memory,
Then swept away.

SILVER THREAD, HAMMER RING

GARY A. BRAUNBECK

"I wish to offer a glorious crown for labors done, by singing the praises of him who descended into the darkness of the earth's realm of shades...For the renown of noble deeds is a joy to those who have died."

– Euripides, *Heracles* (352-356)

ON THE EVENING BEFORE the great contest, John Henry dreamed again of the strange and beautiful bird-man who had been haunting him for so long. It was a wondrous sight to his weary soul, Good Lord knew that to be the truth, yessir, but despite its beauty— or maybe *because* of it, for he felt somehow unworthy to gaze upon such splendor—it sparked a frightful suspicion in his heart.

Surrounded by the eerie blue radiance that always came with him, the bird-man whispered something.

John Henry gulped a deep breath and coughed.

The bird-man unfurled his magnificent wings, transforming their variegated plumage into a feathery rainbow, and John Henry's own chest suddenly felt as tight as if it had been wrapped in steel cables.

He saw that the bird-man felt this pressure as well, and an odd thought, unbidden and unexpected, came to him: *Was I once this, or is it what I will become?*

This seemed to make the bird-man happy. It came closer, and John Henry saw that the layers of each wing held pictures and

designs, faces of people he had never seen, small dramas played out
in the wingspan, all parts of the same story, the same puzzle, all
joined together by a thin silver thread that extended from the bird-
man's body like a puppet's string, leading into the deeper darkness
where John Henry knew a terrible thing, a thing so awful it might
damn well frighten God his own self, was coming, maybe even for
him.

The bird-man whispered to him again, and this time John Henry
heard it speak what might have been its name.

And it frightened him more than any master's whip.

His fisted hands gripped the sheets of the bed, and he began to
sing in his dream, softly, with a hoarse, broken voice, his Hammer
Song, imagining himself striking stone and rocky hillside with each
verse:

Oh, my hammer, (WHAM!)
Hammer ring, (WHAM!)
While I sing, Lawd, (WHAM!)
Hear me sing! (WHAM!)

"Perdix," whispered the strange and beautiful bird-man.

John Henry came awake and sat up choking.

Across from the bed, on the other side of the room, the picture-
box...what did they call it here?...the *television* screen displayed
snowy static. To John Henry's frightened eyes, it looked like the
mouth of Eternity.

Polly Ann, his wife, sat up and took hold of him. "John Henry,
what is it? You have that dream about Martin again?"

Martin. John Henry almost laughed. Considering the way the
bird-man dream made him feel, a nightmare about his brother would
almost be welcomed. Poor, ignorant Martin, whipped to bloody
ribbons by a group of Klansman the night before Master was to
grant him his freedom. And it wasn't enough for them Klan-boys to
just whip every "...uppity emancipated nigger" they could lay hands

on, no; they had to go and kill the ones that were still too frightened of their new freedom to know they had the right to fight back.

"No, honey, it wasn't 'bout Martin."

Polly Ann rubbed her silken hands over his massive arms. "Wanna tell me 'bout it?"

"It was a bird-man. And it was showin' me its story."

After a long moment of silence, Polly Ann kissed John Henry's cheek. "That all?"

John Henry shrugged. "I don't quite remember. I know there was something about his killing or... or maybe *bein'* killed by someone in his family and... "Then he realized that if he went on, he'd have to tell her things he promised he'd keep to himself. "...and the rest of it's kind of blurry."

"Here, you just lay your head down here on my shoulder and— shhh, there you go—just lay your head down and go back to sleep. Gonna need all your strength for tomorrow."

"Yes, I am..." Lord, how he hated having to keep anything from his dear Polly Ann. Maybe that's why he'd been having such awful dreams.

"...ain't no one can make a hammer sing the way you can, John Henry..."

"...no one..."

"...and you know you're the only man alive who can take down their machine..."

"...no machine can do better work than a man..."

"...gonna show 'em all, John Henry..."

"...gonna show 'em all..."

And as John Henry fell back into a dreamless sleep, he recalled everything that had led him and Polly Ann to this moment, and prayed a good Christian man's prayer that he'd grow stronger of body, character, and will for the remembering...

"You sure sound happy, John Henry," said Polly Ann. "And I hope for both our sakes that it's like they sing in that song, that we've found our home. I don't know about you, John Henry, but I, for one, and powerful tired of all this roaming."

"I've got a feeling this is it for us, honey," he replied. "And I can't help but think that we've had plenty of sign, as well."

"Signs? Like what?"

John Henry smiled at her. "Look what year it is—1872. Add one and eight and you get nine. Add seven and two and you get nine. My lucky number is nine, Polly Ann. There's nine letters in my natural-born name, I weighed thirty-three pounds on the nose when I was born—and you multiply three times three and you get nine—this is bound to be our lucky year! Hey—listen!"

What they heard was the sound of hammers ringing on steel in the distance, and the songs of the workers working.

"That's the finest music I ever heard," said John Henry, putting his arm around Polly Ann as they continued on down the road. "It reminds me of those times when Martin and I would play with Daddy's hammers when we were kids."

When they got to the place where the hammers were ringing, it was a mountain. And the men who were hammering and singing were at work building a tunnel.

It wasn't much of a railroad, so far as size went. John Henry had worked all of the big ones, too—the Union Pacific, the Santa Fe, the Southern Pacific and Northern Pacific, even the Great Northern, and this here railroad, the Cassiopeia, well, maybe it wasn't so big right now, but John Henry had a feeling about it. Yessir, something in his gut told him that this railroad was going to become one of the biggest and most important ever to cut a path through the Confederate States of Mexico. God bless the States and President John Brown and all they'd done.

Besides, its name had nine letters, as well.

A man named Captain Tommy was the boss of the men working the tunnel. John Henry watched him for a few minutes to make sure he was a man who knew how to run a railroad team.

Captain Tommy oversaw every aspect of the work. He made

sure that the first line of men drove the long rods of steel deep into the rock, then stayed on the tails of the second line, whose job it was to put nitroglycerin and mica powder and dualin into the holes and blow away the rock, huge chunks at a time. And this Captain Tommy, he didn't flinch at any of it, even went so far as to apply the dualin himself. Man seemed to John Henry a born rail-boss.

"You look big and strong enough," Captain Tommy said to John Henry when he braced him for a job. "We might be able to make a steel-driving man out of you, sure enough."

John Henry laughed. "You don't *need* to make a steel-driving man out of me, nosir—*I am one already!*" He reached into his bag and pulled out his Daddy's twelve-pound hammer. "You bring me a shaker and stand out of my way, 'cause I can drive more steel than any nine men."

Captain Tommy laughed. "You're either as good as you say you are, or you are one crazy sumbitch. Either way, I think you're gonna provide us with lots to talk about over our supper tonight. Li'l Bill, you get yourself over here and shake for this big-mouthed black man. The rest of you, stand back, smoke 'em if you got 'em, and be ready to laugh until you bust, 'cause what we got here is a man what talks mighty big, and if his say-so is bigger than his do-so, we'll laugh him right out of the camp!"

The shaker held the steel, and John Henry kissed his Polly Ann and raised his Daddy's hammer, readying himself to swing the hammer. He took a deep breath to get a feel of the rhythm in his arms and chest, his legs, his stomach and shoulders and arms and, most important of all, in his head. He and Martin used to joke that you couldn't do nothing with a hammer if you couldn't get the beat going in your head.

Martin. Poor, dead Martin.

And John Henry, he tapped into the most important part of the rhythm in his head, his anger over his brother's senseless death, and just like every time he drove steel, he focused his eyes between the shaker's hands, right there at the center of the steel, and he imagined the white hoods of the Klansman who'd whipped his brother to pieces, then afflicted every form of degradation on his ruined body as he lay dying, and—*wham!*—there it was, the rhythm, the power, the focus, and the song:

"Ain't no hammer"—*WHAM!*
"Rings like mine"—*WHAM!*
"Rings like gold, Lawd"—*WHAM!*
"Ain't it fine?"

Captain Tommy and the steel drivers laughed at his song, slapped their knees and pointed at him—"Ain't never heard such bragful singing in all our born days!" they cried. But that didn't deter John Henry, not one little bit.

"Ring like silver"—*WHAM!*
"Peal on peal"—*WHAM!*
"Into the rock, Lawd"—*WHAM!*
"I drives the steel."

The laughter of the steel-drivers and Captain Tommy grew softer, then died altogether as they watched his hammer swing round his shoulder in a rainbow arc faster and more precise than any man's they'd ever seen. Li'l Bill, the shaker, had to work mighty hard to loosen the steel after each mighty ring of John Henry's hammer. Everyone's eyes grew big and round as dinner plates.

"If'n I dies, Lawd"—*WHAM!*
"I command"—*WHAM!*
"Bury me with my hammer"—*WHAM!*
"Hammer in my hand!"— *WHAM-WHAM-WHAM!*
Captain Tommy rose and ordered John Henry to stop so he could examine the work.

Captain Tommy's eyes grew even bigger, and he let fly with a long, low, loud, impressed whistle. "Well, John Henry, looks like your do-so is as good as your say-so and then some. You aren't just bragful and uppity like I thought, and I hope you'll accept my apology for the way I behaved earlier. Yessir, you drove the steel as good as you promised, better than any nine men could into this here mountain."

"Of course he did," said Polly Ann, smiling her pearly-whites and taking hold of her man's hand. "He's a natural-born steel-driving man, and what my man says, he means."

Captain Tommy took off his hat to John Henry—something he'd never done for another steel-driver—and offered his hand. "You work for me, if you care to."

John Henry shook the man's hand. "Praise the Lord, we got ourselves a home now."

"That you do," said Captain Tommy. "The boss himself is going to want to meet you someday, mark my words."

"Can I ask a favor?"

"You name it, John Henry."

"Can I have me a little advance? Enough to go into town and buy me a couple of twenty-pound hammers? This hammer here, it belonged to my daddy, and I don't want to be bustin' it on no mountain-work."

Captain Tommy handed John Henry a small roll of bills. "You got it. And this company, it don't charge its workers for their housing, either. Mr. Daedalus—he's the boss—is a damned decent fellow about the way he treats his workers."

John Henry turned around and picked up his Polly Ann in one arm and lifted her off the ground. "I told you there was signs!" he said, and then kissed her. "Praise the Lord, honey, we have come home!"

He kissed her again.

The steel-drivers cheered him.

So John Henry came to work for Captain Tommy's team, and Polly Ann set about taking care of their cozy little house.

It was hard work in the tunnel. The smoke from the blackstrap lamps and the dust from the red shale were so thick that a tall man like John Henry couldn't see his own two feet without stooping almost double. The thick air was hot, and the men stripped to their waists before working.

But John Henry was the best steel-driving man in the world; he could sink a hole down or he could sink it sideways, in soft rock or in hard—it made no difference. With his two twenty-pound hammers in each hand, it sounded as if the mountain was caving in, the ring of the steel was so loud.

Everything was going fine until a man calling himself Mr. Minos came along trying to peddle his steam drill to Captain Tommy.

"No, sir, don't need it; I got me the best steel-driving team in the world."

"We'll see about that," said the man.

The next day, when the men came to work, they found that a full one-fifth of the tunnel had been filled back in overnight, and at the mouth of the tunnel stood a man with a bull's head, his massive arms looking even bigger than John Henry's. One of the shakers tried to make the Bull-man step aside, but it just grabbed him up in one hand and snapped his neck like a twig.

Captain Tommy pulled out his carbine and shot the thing many times, but it didn't so much as make a scratch.

Around noon, with no work done and the Bull-man still standing guard at the mouth of the tunnel, Mr. Minos came back with his steam drill and asked Captain Tommy, "Change your mind about my machine yet?"

"You get that goddamn filthy beast away from my mountain!"

"*Your* mountain?" said the man, laughing. "Hell, that mountain don't belong to nobody—no *man,* at least."

"I respectfully invite you to take your monster and your machine and you go straight to hell, sir!" yelled Captain Tommy.

Mr. Minos laughed even louder at that one. "I never visit the same place twice, buster. Now, you go to your boss and tell him that if you don't buy my machine and use it to make your tunnel, that there's gonna be worse than that—" He pointed at the Bull-man. "—coming here to stop your working."

Captain Tommy stared hard at the man, then spit a wad of chewing tobacco at his feet. "I'll be sure to pass along your message."

"You do that," said Mr. Minos, then handed Captain Tommy a letter. "Give that to your boss, while you're at it."

"What's in here?"

"It's personal business. Just make sure you give it to him. You don't, and I'll have my step-son over there kill an even dozen of your men in their beds tonight."

John Henry—who'd been standing over to the side listening to the exchange—stepped forward and said, "You got enough faith in your hell-fire machine to accept a challenge?"

Mr. Minos looked John Henry up and down, then sneered. "What you got in mind, boy?"

Every man there saw John Henry stiffen at the word "boy," and knew just what was going through his mind: He was thinking back to his slave days, and, more to the point, he was thinking about what the Klan had done to his brother, Martin, how they'd finished with him then hung him by his ankles from a tree and split him down the center like some hog and tied a sign saying THE ONLY GOOD BOY IS A DEAD ONE! around one-half of his head. John Henry had been the one to cut his brother's body down, and to weep over it, and to bury it.

You did not call John Henry or any man he called friend "boy" and expect to walk away in one piece.

The steel-drivers held their breath, waiting for John Henry to snap Mr. Minos in half just like the bull-man had done the shaker, but John Henry held his temper. When he spoke again, his voice was tight and quiet: "What I got in mind is that I go up against that machine of yours, and the two of us, we keep going until one of us beats the other through the mountain or one of us gives out."

Captain Tommy said, "John Henry, there's no need for you—"

"Yessir, there is! I don't mean no disrespect, Cap'n, but this man, he comes here with his fine suit and his murdering bastard monster of a step-son and his hell-fire machine, and he looks down his nose at us like we were something you scrape off the bottom of your shoe, and then he makes sport of Li'l Bill's being killed—well, you all are my friends, you all are the men I work with and respect, and ain't no uppity man with his damned machine gonna take away no part of the home me and Polly Ann have come to love so much." He stepped right up to Mr. Minos and glared down; and John Henry's glare was a fiercesome thing to behold. "You just name the day."

"Dawn, day after tomorrow."

"I'll be here."

"I bet you will," said John Henry. "I'll just bet you will."

Then he did something no one expected.

John Henry walked right up to the bull-headed man and pulled back a fist and socked the monster so hard in the jaw that he cracked some bone in the thing's face. The beast staggered back a bit but did not drop down—which surprised everyone because John Henry's punch had enough fury in it to kill any ten men—then it righted itself, wiped the blood away from its snout, and snorted foul-smelling sulfur into John Henry's face.

"That was for Li'l Bill," said John Henry. "And it ain't half of what I'd've liked to've done to your sorry ass."

The Bull-man only stared at him, hate burning in its eyes.

John Henry spit tobacco juice onto the Bull-man's boots, then picked up his hammers and walked away.

No other man there would have had the nerve to turn his back on that thing, but, as any of them could tell you, John Henry weren't just any man.

It was getting near bed-time when someone came knocking on the door to John Henry's home. Polly Ann answered.

"Evenin', Mrs. Henry," said Captain Tommy. "Is John busy?"

"No, sir. Come right on in."

Captain Tommy did, removing his hat as he stepped through the door. "My, my, you have certainly done a fine job of turning this place into a right lovely home, Mrs. Henry."

"Thank you, Captain. Would you like something to drink?"

"No, ma'am, afraid I'm here on—" John Henry stepped into the room.

"John Henry," said Captain Tommy, "Mr. Daedalus has requested that you come up to his house to speak with him. He has sent his private car for you. It's right outside."

"He ain't angry about my challenge, is he?" asked John Henry. "I'd hate for the boss to be upset with me. Polly Ann and me, we really like this place and—"

Captain Tommy held up his hand. "Mr. Daedalus is far from upset with you, John. In fact, I think he's right pleased 'bout what you did. I asked why he wanted to see you and he told me—as politely as possible—that it was a matter between himself and you, and it needed 'immediate attention.' His very words."

John Henry took his best shirt and tie from the closet and readied himself for the visit.

"Real nice seein' you again, Mrs. Henry."

"It's Polly Ann to you, Captain. And you are welcome in our home any time."

"Thank you, ma'am. Maybe sometime John Henry will bring me for supper. He talks all the time about your rhubarb pie."

Captain Tommy escorted John Henry out to the long, black, shiny car that idled near the bottom of the hill. "Don't you worry none, now, John Henry. But, if you and the boss don't mind, I'd appreciate being let in on anything that might affect the crew."

"I will be sure to mention that to Mr. Daedalus. Ain't right, keeping folks in the dark."

"Much appreciated, John."

The two men shook hands, and then John Henry climbed in the backseat of the limousine and was off.

Now, John Henry knew from the other steel-drivers that all the fantastic machines that abounded within the camp were designed and built by Mr. Daedalus—who, before going into the railroad business, had been an inventor of some renown. If the television that came with the house hadn't been enough, nor the voice- and music-box that Captain Tommy called "a radio," nor the electric ice-box with its three different compartments that all could be set to different temperatures so's to keep the beer cold, the eggs chilled, and the meat frozen—if all that weren't enough to prove that Mr. Daedalus was a man of great mind (and even, some said, of supernatural power), then what John Henry was about to encounter would leave no doubt, for when the limousine pulled up in front of Mr. Daedalus's resplendent home, the driver opened the door and John Henry climbed out—

—to find himself looking into the face of a man made of metal—at least, his hands and face were, and John Henry assumed that the rest of him was, too. Bright, shiny metal, with only two red lights where on a regular man there would be eyes. The metal-man said nothing, only gestured for John Henry to go on up the steps and through the door.

He did, and was greeted there by a another metal-man, this one dressed up as a butler, who escorted John Henry down the long marble hallway and through a set of oak doors into a study where a fire burned and music played from the radio and huge, ancient paintings hung on the walls.

To the left of the magnificent fireplace was a large desk. Behind it sat a small, gray-haired, very distinguished-looking gentleman who was examining a set of blueprints with great intensity.

"John Henry," said Mr. Daedalus. "Forgive me for not rising to shake your hand." He looked up from the blueprints as his hands disappeared behind the desk. There was a *click*, then a *whirr*ing sound, and Mr. Daedalus rolled out from behind the desk in a motor-powered wheelchair. "A little something I've been working on since the arthritis rendered my legs all but useless," he said, then rolled right up to John Henry and shook his hand. "A great pleasure to meet a man of singular nerve such as yourself. Please, have a seat. Would you care for a drink?"

"No, sir, nothin' for me. Just had me a fine supper."

"Ah, yes. I've heard it rumored that your Polly Ann is an artist in the kitchen."

John Henry smiled. "That she is, sir."

Mr, Daedalus regarded John Henry for a moment, but not in an unfriendly or judgmental way; he looked at his guest as if he were seeing a fine work of art. "I hope my servants didn't unnerve you too much."

"I have to say, sir, that I ain't never seen nothing like them in all my born days."

"President John Brown commissioned me to build them as personal security guards for himself and Vice-President Castilla. They will be present at the signing of the Russo-Japanese Pact next month. There have been threats against not only Nicholas II and Emperor Meiji but any world leaders who attend. A pity that there are factions out there bent on destruction. Don't you think it sad? I mean, not only will that agreement ensure peace between those two warring nations, but it will stop the budding revolution in Russia, as well. Do you follow politics, John? May I call you John?"

"Yessir, please do. Afraid I don't much follow what goes on in the world these days."

Mr. Daedalus smiled. "Probably a very wise thing to do. It can get awfully depressing."

John Henry liked Mr. Daedalus. The man spoke to him as an equal. When John Henry had said he didn't follow politics, Mr. Daedalus hadn't given him a look of disgust like a lot of folks would have—*That's what I get for talking to you like you have a brain*—but instead listened and smiled and made him feel as if he were just as smart for *not* following the goings-on of world leaders.

A nice man. Yessir.

"I'll come right to the point, John. Mr. Minos—charming fellow, isn't he?"

"Right cordial, if you like rattlesnakes."

Mr. Daedalus laughed. "That's a good one, John. May I use it sometime?"

"Be my guest."

Mr. Daedalus rolled back behind his desk and wrote it down on a sheet of paper, laughed again, then gestured for John Henry to move his chair closer to the desk.

"Mr. Minos and I used to be partners in a design company that we started some years ago. We were both inventors—well, *I* did the designing and building, Minos sold the ideas to customers.

"Mr. Minos became greedy, John. He took several of my prototypes—inventions that weren't quite ready yet—and stole all my files, most of our profits, and disappeared. He re-emerged a few years ago with his own company—one that, might I add, had been built with my designs and money.

"That steam drill he's trying to force us to use? I designed it. I wish to God now that I'd burned the plans ... but no use crying over that. Isn't that always the way? One is more concerned with the immediate result, with *succeeding*, than with any long-term consequences.

"Both Minos and I have sons—*had,* in his case. Perdix was a ne'er-do-well to top them all—a gambler, heavy drinker, loud-mouth, ladies' man. One night about a year ago, he ran into my own son, Icarus, in a tavern. Kept going on about how his father was going to beats the pants off me, break my company, you know the sort of boasting. I'll not sugar-coat it; Icarus can be an unruly handful himself, and he was a bit toasty on whiskey that night. To his credit, my boy didn't start the fight, but he has a nasty temper problem, and when Perdix hit him in the jaw and accused *me* of being the thief, Icarus tore into him with all he had.

"I'll skip the sordid details. Suffice to say that it was an extremely violent fight, and Icarus wound up killing Perdix. Then my son did a most foolish thing, John; he ran off. I never knew to where. I received only one phone call, and that was far too brief to give me much to go on. I posted a reward for any information leading to the discovery of my son's whereabouts. I would gladly give half my fortune for his safe return. Icarus may have his faults, but he is still my son and I love him with all my heart." He rolled around until he sat directly next to John Henry, who turned to face the man.

"Minos has my son, John. And I need for you to get him."

"I don't understand, sir. How can I—?"

Daedalus held up a hand to silence John. "What have you heard about me? And please spare me the nice things folks say about the wages I pay and how I treat the workers and the rest of it. There have to be rumors about me, and I'd like to know if you've heard them—*one*, specifically."

John Henry thought on it for a moment, then recalled a tall tale one of the shakers had told round the campfire one night. "There's some folks that think you might have … well, Divine blood in you. Like Jesus."

Daedalus grinned. "Not quite, John. But I have, in my time, broken bread with uncanny beings."

His thumb hit a switch on the arm of his chair, and he rolled even closer. "I have supped with martyrs, saints, and angels, John. I have been commissioned to build for the Divine."

Looking into his eyes and hearing the awe and conviction in the man's voice, John Henry didn't doubt it one little bit. "I certainly believe you have, sir."

Daedalus smiled, squeezing John Henry's hand. "Good. That saves me the time of having to prove it to you." He reached over and pulled several sets of blueprints across the desk, keeping some for himself, handing some to John Henry. "You much for reading surveyor's charts, John?"

"I am. I can also understand most blueprints."

"Geological maps?"

"Some."

Daedalus nodded. "That's not going to be a problem, I can answer any questions you might have.

"Now, one very important thing, John: Until the contest is

finished the day after tomorrow—and allow me to say that I have no doubt you'll rule the day over Minos' contraption—until that time, I want your word as a good Christian man that what we're discussing will stay between us. Not even your wife can know. I know that's asking a lot for a man so honest as yourself, but ask it I must. Have I your word?"

"Yessir."

"Good man." He smoothed the largest of the maps on his lap, then turned it to face John Henry. "Recognize it?"

"That's—why, that there is the very mountain that we're tunneling through!"

"Yes." Daedalus pulled back the top portion of the map to reveal an equally large blueprint beneath, one that looked to be part blueprint and part archeology chart, part geological map. "Can you make out what this is?"

John Henry studied it carefully. "Can't say for certain, sir, but it looks to me like that's . . . that's a sketch of what the inside of that mountain looks like."

"You're right there. Do you see how it's all solid for three-quarters of the way through, then there is this small chamber—antechamber, actually? That's where you'll enter to find my son. Minos has him trapped beyond that antechamber. That's where you'll find it."

"Find what, sir?"

"The entrance to the Gates of Hell. I designed and built it."

"The entrance?"

Daedalus shook his head. "More than just that. *Hell*, John. I conceived, designed, and oversaw the construction of Hell."

The morning of the contest arrived, and when John Henry turned the bend in the road to walk toward the mountain, he was stunned to see that both sides of the road, for as far as his eyes could see, were lined with people come to witness the great event. There were banners and a band playing songs and cotton-candy vendors and barbecues and even folks laying money on who was going to emerge victorious.

The people cheered John Henry as he made his way to the mountain, his loyal and loving Polly Ann by his side.

"They come to cheer you on, John Henry."

"Looks like it," he whispered in reply.

She took hold of his hand. "Don't you fret none, honey. I know you'll win." She nudged him and then pointed to the set of cases he was carrying. "Are you gonna tell me what it is that Mr. Daedalus gave to you?"

"A special set of hammers. Thirty-pounders. Said they was a gift from a foreign fellow of his acquaintance, a man named Thor. Told me these were the finest, most powerful hammers in the universe."

"That why you didn't bring along your twenty-pounders or your daddy's?"

"Mr. Daedalus said these two would be all I'd need."

"I sure do hope he's right."

"Makes two of us."

They arrived at the work site. Sure enough, there was Mr. Minos, looking arrogant as ever, leaning against his steam-drill and saying something to the Bull-man—who was checking the controls.

John Henry grinned. He liked the idea of going up not only against Minos' machine, but being able to beat it *and* that monster of a step-son driving it … that was almost too sweet.

Don't get uppity now, he cautioned himself. *Ain't no guarantee you're gonna beat nothing, even with these hammers Mr. Daedalus gave to you. Pride cometh before a fall, John. Don't forget that.*

There were a lot of people depending on him today. He would not disappoint them.

"John!" cried Captain Tommy, pushing his way through the throng of steel-drivers and shakers who'd mobbed John Henry as soon as they caught sight of him. "How you feeling this morning, John?"

"Ready to do me some work, sir. Been a few days and I get impatient."

Captain Tommy smiled and smacked John Henry on the arms.

"That's my man! You're the best, John Henry, no man nor machine can best you!"

The steel-drivers and shakers cheered, each slapping John Henry on the back or shoulders as he pushed through to the face of the mountain.

He looked around for Polly Ann—he'd lost track of her when the workers rushed him—and saw her over to the side, sitting next to Mr. Daedalus and his metal-man attendant. Mr. Daedalus was whispering something to her. Polly Ann watched John Henry as she listened, then nodded her head, took something that Mr. Daedalus placed in her hand, and started over toward her husband.

John Henry set down and opened the cases, removing the two magnificent golden hammers that Mr. Daedalus had given to him the previous evening. They shone bright as sunlight in his grip, and he swung both of them—one at a time first, then together, giving his body the chance to get the feel of their power—and powerful they were, for with each swing John Henry could feel his muscles grow tighter and stronger, and the rhythm in his chest and arms and legs and shoulders and head came together quicker than they ever had before.

"*I want you to think only of your brother Martin,*" Mr. Daedalus had told him. "*I want you very angry when you first strike those hammers against the mountainside. Spare no thought for anything else until you reach the antechamber, John Henry. You'll not need a shaker, nor sharpened steel, nor dualin—only these hammers. And don't ask me any questions—you'll know why I ask this of you soon enough. There will be rewards for you, John; on that you have my word.*"

Polly Ann embraced him as everyone else moved away. The Bull-man powered up the steam drill, poisoning the air with an awful racket.

Under the noise, Polly Ann leaned up and shouted in John Henry's ear: "Mr. Daedalus asked me to do this, so don't you be gettin' mad." She tied something to the back of his belt, but when he looked down to see what it was, there was nothing there.

Polly Ann held a spindle in her hands but there was no thread.

"He said you can't see it in the light," she shouted over the roar of the steam-drill. "But once you get into the deep dark, it'll shine silver so's you can find your way back if you get lost." There were tears in her eyes as she finished speaking.

John Henry's heart welled with tenderness for her. He reached out and touched her cheek, trying to find the words, but he saw from her face that everything he wished to convey was in his touch.

She moved back into the spectators.

The sheriff stood at the mouth of the tunnel, one hand holding a pistol in the air, the other holding a stopwatch that he was watching intently.

John Henry glanced at the Bull-man in the steam-drill's seat.

The Bull-man made an obscene gesture at him.

John Henry raised his hammers, then swung them down once, cracking their heads together and producing not only a ringing that was louder than the steam-drill's engine, but causing the air between the heads to spark.

He looked at Mr. Daedalus, who nodded.

The crowd fell silent.

John Henry took a deep breath and held it, thinking: *This is for you, Martin.*

The sheriff shouted very loudly, so as to be heard over the roar of the engine: "On your mark, gentlemen: Four ... three ... two ... one—" He fired the pistol. "—go!"

—and the drill was screaming and chugging and chewing through rock, and John Henry was swinging the hammers and singing "Oh, My Hammer," "Water Boy," "Where Is You Hidin'," "If I Die A Railroad Man," and every hammer song he could remember, all the time thinking only of his brother, of poor Martin and all the wonders of this here world he never lived to see, dying at the hands of ignorant, mean-spirited men who couldn't see beyond the color of a man's skin, and while he was thinking these thoughts the hammers swung and blasted through the rock like it was glass, sparking fire and lightning that illuminated the way, and John Henry began to realize, somewhere in the back of his mind, that the hammers were as much using him as he was them, for his arms were no longer making steady rainbow-arc swings, nosir, they were pinwheeling, hard and constant, and his muscles screamed but he didn't care, this was a sweet pain, Lord, it was so sweet, because he glanced over his shoulder only once and saw that the light from the steam-drill's lantern was several feet behind him, nearly swallowed by darkness and smoke, and he was far ahead and that was fine, yes it was, swing that hammer, make it ring, raise my hammer, hear it sing, and the rock blasted away in the wake of the hammers' lightning, and John Henry felt tears in his eyes because he could swear he felt Martin right behind him, shouting, "You show 'em, Big Brother, you show 'em good!" and he was doing just that, he was showing them all, moving ahead, going faster, rock disintegrating under the hammers' will, and he stopped only once to take a breath, having no idea how long he'd been at it—

—and that's when he saw a small sliver of reddish-orange light glowing from behind the wall of stone before him.

John Henry wiped the sweat from his brow, lifted the hammers, made sure he was still in the lead, then struck at the rock in four successive blows—

—and stood at the top of a stone staircase.

Sulphuric fumes, made fiery and frightening from the reddish-orange light below, wafted up the stairs and around his head, trying to choke him, but the light from the hammers kept it at bay.

He looked behind him and saw that Polly Ann had been right—there was a long, shiny silver thread trailing from the back of his belt, leading back to the tunnel's entrance.

He flexed his arms and shoulders, took a deep breath, and started down the chaotic staircase of massive, wedge-shaped boulders. At last, his feet touch ground in some vast, silent, ancient chamber. Ahead, through the fiery, sulphur-choked gloom, he saw a bluish radiance, haloing some kind of vaguely familiar rock formation. He hung the hammers from his belt and climbed an enormous slab of limestone, scraping his shins and cutting his arms, then scrabbled onto a ledge.

On a small plateau, under an overhang of surprisingly white calcite that curved gracefully upward like a snowdrift hollowed by the wind, stood a cluster of meticulously-carved stones, each roughly the size and shape of a man, arms outstretched, holding something whose shape he couldn't quite discern. Their bodies were complete but all of them lacked faces. Beyond these figures he saw the retreating blue radiance and beyond that the entrance to another passageway.

All around John Henry there echoed the sounds of tortured souls crying out for mercy and forgiveness, but too late, too late.

He said a short prayer. It seemed the Christian thing to do.

The odd radiance guiding him, he maneuvered toward the entrance, which looked more and more like the gaping mouth of some mythic titan, frozen into a perpetual scream at the moment of its death. He moved slowly, his back pressed against the wall, feet sliding slowly to the side, the ledge becoming tight and close, less than seven inches in depth. He slipped only once but did not let it shake his resolve, and as he safely reached the far and much wider side of the ledge he saw that the faceless stone figures on the plateau had changed position, then realized it is only an illusion; he was now seeing them from a different angle.

Instead of a random cluster, they formed an eerily straight line that stretched toward the center of the chamber; not six, but several dozen bluish-gray faceless figures, about his height, standing silently by under their white canopy, cowled voyagers waiting with no hope on the frozen deck of an icebound ship, each holding a raggedy whip—

—and that's when he realized who they were.

These were the Klansmen who had killed his brother, who had so brutally cut short Martin's life. It wasn't that they were faceless, no; they had been sent here still in their robes and hoods.

Even from where he stood, John Henry could see the recognition in their eyes, could see them remember his face from when he'd come to cut down his brother's body and weep over his mangled remains.

In their eyes was fear and pain and regret.

John Henry listened, listened real good, and heard that from beneath their robes and hoods came the sounds of whips cracking and men screaming for mercy.

Even though he was a Christian man, John Henry couldn't find in himself to pity them.

"He was a fine man," he snarled at the frozen figures. "He wanted to be an artist. Martin, he could paint a picture like nobody's business. But you didn't care about that, did you?"

Don't be like this, he thought.

And found some touch of pity in his heart for these men.

So John Henry said a little prayer for them.

But only a little one.

And moved on.

He stepped into the opening and saw the wispy tail of the blue radiance disappear around a bend. Following it, John Henry found himself stumbling downward once again. The humming grew louder, becoming a keening that filled both the air and his chest with a dull, despairing throbbing.

The ground evened out, trembling. Down here, deep in the mystery, the walls and roof, glistening with a ghostly iridescence, dripped with moisture—salty and heated. John Henry took a drop on his finger and tasted it.

Tears.

The walls of Hell wept with the tears of the damned.

The keening increased its volume, growing steadily more intense, becoming a full-throttle roar of anguish. He saw a bit of the radiance, churning slowly, moving forward, a worm wriggling its way into the dirt as it vanished into the mouth of a tunnel. Whatever it was that was in such pain was at the end of that tunnel. John Henry had no doubt it was Mr. Daedalus's son.

I'm coming, he thought, then dropped onto hands and knees and crawled into the opening. For a while there was enough room for him to use his hammers to clear the way, but suddenly and without warning, the passageway narrowed to a few feet in width and the roof soon dropped down so low he could touch it with his fingers. When John Henry moved—which he could do now only in bursts of mere inches—his shoulders scraped the sides of the crawlway, and the roof above pressed mercilessly onto his back. He didn't even have enough room to raise one of the hammers—not that he would want to, not in something this tight; the hammers might have special powers, but they didn't mean nothing to the rock, nosir: one good hammer-blow might bring the whole thing crashing down on his head.

The air grew thin. He stopped after every movement to gulp in great lungfuls of stale, mephitic, sulphur-tinged air, trying to control the rabid panic he felt snarling to the surface. All his life John Henry had never been afraid of enclosed spaces, but now he tried desperately not to imagine himself becoming wedged in or being crushed or buried alive. He thought only once of trying to go back but the keening drew him toward it, begging for help, have mercy, don't leave me here, please, oh please god don't leave me here it's so lonely—

—he managed to get on his side and in a burst of near-panic scrabbled forward, catching sight of an opening ahead and hoping it will be big enough for him to get through, pushing and clawing with all he had, wriggling forward, closer, he could see the blue, could almost grasp the keening in his hands, and then the roof began to crumble down around his ankles, collapsing with every move he made, and John Henry thought he might have started screaming but he couldn't be sure because it was happening too fast, he had to stay ahead of the collapsing ceiling that was catching up with him too fast, too fast, and he lunged forward as his mouth filled with dirt dropping down in clumps from above—

—and he emerged into a grotto, shoving himself out of the tunnel just as the last few feet of it filled with something organic;

part placenta, part earth, part anguish.

John Henry could see that the silver thread still shone brightly, only it didn't lead into the collapsed tunnel as he'd expected; it lead in the other direction, as if he'd come from *over there instead of*—

—he turned around—

—and saw the Gates of Hell.

John Henry whistled long and low, for the gates were an impressive sight, extending to either side of him for as far as he could see, and rising above him so high that he could not hope to see the top.

But he could see the young man who was chained to them, one arm outstretched on either side and his feet manacled one atop the other, looking for all the world like Christ on His cross.

Except Christ didn't have a set of wings that were bound together with barbed wire.

The young man looked down at John Henry and said, "I...I made these so I could...could fly out and it...it caught me...please ..."

Icarus had evidently inherited his father's talent for invention.

"Your daddy sent me, son," replied John Henry, and started marching toward the terrible gates—

—and stopped dead in his tracks, less than three yards away, when he heard a growl from the surrounding shadows, and remembered...

...*a terrible thing, a thing so awful it might damn well frighten God his own self, was coming, maybe even for him...*

...the unseen terror from his dreams.

"Ahgod," croaked Icarus, tears streaming down his cheeks. "It heard you."

"Shh!" snapped John Henry, peering into the darkness.

At first he thought it was some kind of great and terrible horse, its head was so far above the ground, so far above his own, but then he saw the red, glowing eyes—all six of them—and heard the mad-dog snarl, and smelled the sickening mixture of sulphur, fur, and

waste, then it emerged from the blackness and John Henry nearly cried out, for what stood before him, towering over his own massive body by a good eighteen, twenty inches, was a giant three-headed dog with glistening foam dribbling from all its jaws.

"Save yourself, sir," cried Icarus.

"Shut your fool mouth, boy!" John Henry would not break eye-contact with the creature. It might be a good hundred feet away from him, but one good jump and it would be right on top of him, chewing him to pulp.

He dared not look down at its haunches to see if it was readying to spring.

John Henry had no idea what he was going to do.

His weight suddenly shifted, and without looking away from the beast's faces John Henry became aware that the hammers were moving, shaking themselves in his belt as if to say, *Let us swing free, John Henry, let us swing free!*

"Good boy," he whispered, easing his hands down to his sides, "good little doggie."

He gripped the hammers and began easing them out.

The beast moved forward, slowly, rippling the muscles in its back.

"Damn if you ain't one ugly sumbitch," John Henry said in the same sing-song voice he'd used before.

The beast bared teeth. A whole lot of teeth. John Henry wasn't sure, but he thought he could see bits of flesh flapping in there.

"Good little ugly-sumbitch-doggie," he said, the hammers firmly gripped in his hands.

The beast reared back, tensing its haunches, then barked a Hell-hound's bark.

John Henry swung the hammers up, and then brought them down in a crescent-arc, slapping the heads together just below his belly, and the thunder rolled and lightning burst from their heads.

The beast yelped as if in pain but did not stop advancing.

John Henry swung the hammers up, bringing them together

over his head. This time the thunder was a small earthquake and the lightning was Nature's wrath.

The beast howled.

He brought the hammers down—*WHAM!*—and the Earth cracked around him and the lightning was the center of a twister, snarling outward in jagged streaks, blasting against the walls.

"Oh, my hammer," he sang—

—*WHAM!*—thunder from the beginning of the universe, lightning from its end—

—"Hammer ring"—

—*WHAM!*—the walls began to crumble from the vibrations of the peal—

—"Hear them ring, Lawd"—

—*WHAM!*—jagged, whipcurling bolts of lightning shot nearer the beast, blowing holes in the ground—

—"Hammer sing!"

And John Henry kept slapping the heads together, filling the bowels of Hell with the peal of a steel-driving man's might and brightening the place up a bit with the dancing bolts of lightning.

The beast fell on its belly, crippled by the noise and power but John Henry kept slamming his hammers together, feeling the power shake his guts loose from his bones but he would not stop until he was certain that the beast was too stunned to come after him.

WHAM!

The beast jerked and snarled and whined.

WHAM!

It rolled onto its side, legs kicking in the air.

WHAM!

Finally, its eyes rolled back into its heads and its tongues lolled from the sides of its mouths and its legs stopped kicking.

John Henry stopped.

He watched very carefully to see if the beast was still breathing.

He heard the raggedy sound of a steam-engine train idling in a station, and knew that he'd not killed the beast. That was good—not

just because John Henry was not a killing man, but also because something about this beast's awful magnificence told him that it could not—and possibly *should not*—be destroyed.

He whirled around and ran up to the Gates, grabbed onto one of the bars as if it were a rope, and shimmied up until he was level with the manacles that held Icarus's wrists and arms in place.

He drew back one hammer, and then froze.

"What is it?" said Icarus, great panic in his voice.

"Seems to me I ought to do your feet first," said John Henry. "'Less you feel like flopping face-first down to the ground."

He slid down a ways and struck his hammer against the manacle trapping Icarus's ankles, then slammed them against the others, freeing the boy—

—who did not fall to the ground as John Henry had expected, but instead unfurled his wings and flew upward, laughing.

John Henry dropped to the ground, picked up the other hammer, and watched the boy enjoying his freedom.

"We got to get out of here," he called.

"Try and stop me!" yelled Icarus, swooping down to piggyback John Henry and lifting him off the ground.

"Which way?" he shouted in John Henry's ear.

"You see the silver thread behind me?"

"Yes?"

"Follow it."

Straight up, they went, following the path of the thread as it wound through Hell, somehow ending up back at the foot of the same staircase John Henry had descended before. Icarus flew up the narrow passageway, setting John Henry down where he'd stopped his hammering.

"Looks like the machine's got a bit ahead of me," said John Henry, gently pushing Icarus to the side to resume his labors.

Before he got back into the race, John Henry did something he swore to Mr. Daedalus he'd do—seal up the antechamber.

Three good strikes did the job.

"Time to show that machine who's boss." This time the hammers roared, and the rock didn't so much fall away from his blows ad it did *run* away, and soon, bellowing his hammer songs for all he was worth, John Henry regained the lead.

The steam-drill kept chugging and snarling, but it was no match for a man who'd been to the bowels of Hell and lived to tell the tale.

When John Henry at last hammered his way out the other side of the mountain and into daylight, the crowds cheered and the band struck up with a rousing rendition of "Oh, My Hammer," and John Henry dropped to his knees, weeping, then threw back his head and let fly with a whoop of victory they heard three counties away. He held up his magic hammers—

—and saw that they weren't gold at all.

They were his own, regular old twenty-pounders.

He brought them down, dropped them to the ground, and stared.

Polly Ann ran to him, threw herself on her knees next to him, and held onto him as if she never planned to let go again. "I knew you could do it, John Henry, I just knew you could!"

"...the hammers..." he muttered to himself.

He looked up as Mr. Daedalus wheeled over, Icarus by his side. "Thank you for my son, John Henry. Thank you." Then: "How does it feel to be something of a god?"

"Beg your pardon?"

Mr. Daedalus pointed at the hammers. "You know, don't you, that you were using them all the time?"

"But...how? I done things that no natural man ought to be able to do with them."

"Some men grow into their divinity, John Henry; other have to be tricked into it."

"Then you lied to me?"

"No—I *fooled* you. There's a difference."

Icarus placed a hand on John Henry's shoulder. "Thank you for freeing me, John."

John Henry could only nod his head.

"Well, then," said Mr. Daedalus, looking into the mountain. "Seems my ex-partner's contraption's nowhere near making it out here."

John Henry nodded. "…not even close…"

Mr. Daedalus grinned as Captain Tommy brought John Henry a tall, cold glass of water.

"You know what I'd like to do, John?"

"No, sir."

"I think I'd like to devote more time to my inventions—and to getting to know my son again. I need someone to take over this railroad for me. Any suggestions?"

"Captain Tommy's a damn fine man."

"That he is, but he doesn't want my job. Do *you* want my job, John Henry?"

"You foolin' with me again?"

"Absolutely not. As far as I'm concerned, this railroad belongs to you, John Henry. Treat her well, and she'll take good care of you and yours." Mr. Daedalus turned and began wheeling away.

John Henry called out, "You was plannin' on giving it to me the whole time, weren't you? This here railroad's my reward."

Mr. Daedalus, not looking back, wagged a finger in the air.

"Never jump to conclusions, John Henry. It drains all the surprise out of life."

Mr. Daedalus and his son disappeared into the limousine and drove away before John Henry could ask why he'd been told to think only of his brother on the way in.

"Well," said Captain Tommy. "Looks like I'm working for you now."

John Henry looked at him and grinned. "I don't know. Uppity fellow like you—is your do-so as good as your say-so?"

"And then some."

"Okay, you're hired."

And they laughed loudly, as did the other steel-drivers, and the crowds.

When the steam-drill finally emerged, some two hours later, Minos and his monster step-son were laughed out of the county.

The steam-drill? The crew decided to keep it.

Never could tell when a working man might need a good laugh.

Later that night, after all the singing and dancing and celebrating had died down, John Henry and Polly Ann walked back to their home, hand in hand.

"What a day this has been!" declared Polly Ann.

"That it be," replied John Henry.

Polly Ann poked him in the ribs with her elbow. "Where is your mind at? You been looking at the ground and mumbling to yourself for the last half-hour."

"I was just...wondering about something Mr. Daedalus told me to do. Something he told me to think about while I was hammering my way—"

He stopped speaking as he looked up and saw the figure standing on the front porch.

"...can't be."

"John Henry, what you looking at?"

"That fellah on our porch. In the moonlight it almost looks like Martin, but that can't be."

"Why not? We got his letter two days ago tellin' us he was coming."

John Henry whirled on her. "A *letter?* That can't be, Polly Ann. Martin's been dead goin' on six years."

She laughed. "Oh, my poor John." She placed a gentle hand against his cheek. "I do believe that all that hammering must've shook loose some of your brains."

"You two comin'?" shouted Martin from the porch. "I been waiting here a while and I don't mind saying that I'm...well... kinda *hungry!*"

"Oh, my Lord," whispered John Henry under his breath.

Then remembered Mr. Daedalus's words: *There will be rewards for you, John; on that you have my word...*

...How does it feel to be something of a god?

"Some men have to be tricked into it," he whispered.

"What are you going on about?" asked Polly Ann.

"Nothing," said John Henry, wiping the tears from his eyes so she wouldn't see them and promising the universe that he would be a worthy god. "Nothing at all. Now, come on, let's go feed that brother of mine."

REFLECTIONS THROUGH THE RAVEN'S EYE

MARGE SIMON

i.

The trees were barren in this land,
buzzards haunting their austere branches.
In the distance, a gypsy caravan,
pulled by mules and men.

Boys ran beside
as long as they could,
then were pulled onto
the backs of wagons.

The gypsies found the man at dusk,
in fetal curl, an empty pistol clenched to chest,
his withered lips drawn back in death,
as if some joke had passed his mind.

Above, the vultures swirled,
a sky afire with black wings.
All night, the dry winds blew.

ii.

Draped in a blanket
to ward off the coming winter,
a woman sits on the street corner,
cat curled in her lap.
Beside her is a basket of nuts.

When the light changes,
she cracks the nuts with
a hammer, offering her wares
to passing pedestrians.

Nightfall, she begins tapping
the hand that holds the nuts.
Over and over she taps
until the skin splits
in many places.

A man and a girl emerge from a bar,
stagger down the empty street.
They stumble over her.
He swears, kicks the cat away.

The woman moans, but cannot rise.
Flakes swirl, white feathers on her face,
her lips draw back in a rictal smile
as she drifts into forever sleep
in the fresh pink snow.

Blackbirds on the wires,
a necklace of black stones.
By dawn, the wind is bitter cold.

THE OFFERING ON THE HILL

RICHARD THOMAS

I'D BEEN FOLLOWING the train tracks north for three days when I came across the skeletons—a pile of bones in a ring around a cairn of skulls, a bullet hole in the center of each one. The sun beat down on me, one wave of pulsing sunshine after another, my skin like worn leather—my eyes two tiny black dots. One boot followed the other as I pushed onward, faded jeans pasted to my sweaty body like a second layer of skin, a revolver on each hip, leather holsters filled with glistening metal, their weight a comforting presence. I'm too old for this, but the uneasy quiet that has slipped over the land—it is not a death knell—only a beginning. The world has moved on, but my greatest fear is that the dead will never stop laughing.

As hot as it is now, it will be deathly cold tonight, a wave of freezing air washing across the desert as sure as the sickly glowing ball will rise tomorrow. I have to find shelter, or start building a fire, soon. In the distance there are mountains, but I can't get there tonight. I don't like the look of the ring, either—the skulls make me uneasy. So it will be baptism by fire—one dried scrub brush on top of its brother; whatever dead or dying cactus I can find, the rotting boards from an old sign—Death Valley it says, an arrow pointing off in one direction, surely a joke.

When the skulls are covered in debris so that I can't see their gaping mouths any longer, I spark a flame from a wooden match with my thumbnail, and toss it onto the wood. It catches quickly and sends flickering tongues of fire up into the sky as the darkness settles across the land. I raise my head and glance north again, and in the hazy distance the ghost of a train whistle blows sorrow. I walk to the tracks and set my hand upon the closest rail—a tiny vibration running through my gnarled fingers, certainly heading away. I've never seen the train going south. No reason to head back that way— nothing but abandoned buildings, rotting car husks, and the stench of the human race gone sour.

So long had I been out in the desert, up in the hills, prospecting and tracking deviant flesh, runaways and bounties hunted with great patience, that there was nothing left for me when I came down—no people, no messages, no television, and no radio—just an endless silence that stretched out into eternity. I'd seen no explosions, nothing nuclear, and the cattle, it could have been anything—starvation, sickness, even poachers—but I gave them a wide berth, anyway.

The only clue I'd found was the word north. Everywhere I went, whispered by the lips of the dead, scratched into pads of paper, and painted on walls—the word north. I found an entire town, Crystal Lake, dry as a bone, the irony not lost on me, with hundreds of cars on the highway pointed in this direction—empty.

None of it made any sense.

But it's where my wife and child may have gone, if they are still alive. The shadows at night creep in and whisper horrible things, violent imagery of my daughter hung up on a cross, wearing a thorny crown, vast pits filled with the walking dead, pillars of fire shooting high into the night.

And then the cold pushes in on me, so I move closer to my pyre. I will slowly rotate as the night goes on, walking around the licking flames, as the freezing wind nips at me, a thin sheet of ice coating my emaciated frame. If I stop moving I will die—the weather shifting to both extremes, blazing hot in the daytime and freezing cold in the night. In the wake of the new world order things had changed. I've been having this dance with the devil for weeks now, and in the morning, when it warms up, I will collapse. For now, it is the gleam in the eyes of my daughter Allie that pushes me on, reminds me why I even bother.

The day I left, her long brown hair was tied back in a ponytail, as a teapot on the stove steamed and whistled—the clocks whirring behind my princess as tears streamed rivulets of dirt down her face. Her mother, Cecilia, God bless her, holding Allie back as her own dark hair fell over her eyes, her face, hiding behind it, unwilling to look at me. I walked out the door, securing our future—and possibly their death.

In the distance I hear wood cracking, splintering, and crashing to the ground—shattering. The thin branches and hollow trunks can't sustain the weight of the ice, and they topple over, ripping up roots, fracturing—turning to shards, fragments, and sparkling dust. Every night I long to walk out into the freezing cold and let the elements take me. But something is calling me north.

In the morning I come to lying in the ash around the fire, not burned, but not frozen to death either. A large black bird sits on my foot, tapping its beak on the faded sole of my left boot, yellow sparkling eyes like two marbles rolling around in its feathered, bobbing skull. The beast turns its head to the south, and then leaps into the sky with a rush of foul air, wings spread wide, pushing up into the gray tapestry above us, heading north with a sense of sudden urgency.

The fire pit is just as I had originally found it, a ring of bones around the pile of skulls, no evidence of the fire, no proof that my labor had even happened. I need water soon, so I have to move on.

Three hours later I come to the edge of a forest that squats at the base of an expansive mountain range, sweat running down my neck, my back—dirt and grime slipping over my spine. I can hear the water gurgling, but can't see it yet. My lips crack and bleed, the goatskin at my waist squeezed dry the day before, my eyes on the clouds above, as it grows dark, lightning flashing over the horizon—but the rain, it will never come, not now that I need it. Crashing through the bushes and low-hanging branches, a thin path reveals itself, my feet tripping over roots and buried stones, the sparkle of water glinting through the greenery. I stumble to the pool of water as spider webs stretch across my face, my outstretched hands waving them off, filament in my mouth, a wash of panic mixing with a knot in my gut, the water suddenly my world.

As I kneel at the edge of the creek, by the pool, I cup the cold water and drink, the liquid spilling down my chest. The knees of my jeans soak through with mud, and as I sit up to breathe, gasping, the row of crosses reveals itself to me, on the other side of the oasis. Six, seven of them, all in a line, all shapes and sizes, skeletons strung out and bound with vines, crucified, the nails run through, another row behind them, with nothing but skulls on pikes. Tied around each bit of rotting wood is a single piece of ribbon, each of them a faded pink, moss growing beneath the sacrifices, low white blossoms running off into the woods. I lower the canteen into the cold water, and fill it up, my stomach clenched in knots, my eyes on the whispering leaves—my heart thudding drumbeats in my chest.

It's time to move on.

I won't be able to make it up the mountain tonight—wouldn't make any sense to get caught out in the open like that, wind and ice spraying certain death. Out of the woods a path deposits me at a tiny shack, a lantern glowing in the window as the sun falls out of the sky. A skeletal dog is tied to the house with an old withered rope, whining and pissing into the dirt as I approach the humble dwelling, the skittish beast eager to say hello.

"It's okay," I say, showing the skinny wreck my open palms. She squats, her tail wagging like a metronome turned all the way up, her eyes glazed over with white, a black lab mix of some sort. She licks my hands, her black muzzle dotted with gray hair, the poor thing dying out here, begging for attention. She must go inside at night, I think to myself, or she'd be frozen to the ground, dead long ago. I run my hands over her ribcage, each bone like a slat of wood, wasting away to nothing. I root around in my gear and bring out a tough stick of jerky, and kneeling in the dry earth I give it to her, and she falls into chewing and licking with a devout worship that makes me a tad bit uneasy.

"Good girl," I say, standing back up.

The door to the structure opens and a grizzled old man peers out, long gray beard hanging down, his eyes the same glossy white as the mutt. In overalls, boots, and a dirty long-sleeved shirt, the man sways in the doorway, a grin slipping over his face.

"That's awfully kind of you, stranger," he says. "Food's hard to come by out this way, and in my condition, *our* condition, it's difficult to head into town."

I nod, realizing he can't see me, and step forward.

"My name's John Ford, and I'm heading north. You seen anyone come by, any sign of life, of late?"

I stand there holding out my hand, the blind coot staring over my shoulder, his whiskers twitching. He extends his gnarled digits to me, and smiles, so I take his hand, like grabbing a fistful of sticks, and shake it.

"Nobody of late. I'm Benjamin Russell, but you can just call me Ben," the old man says. "Come on in, it's gonna get cold soon. Can you bring the dog? She's Jezebel, the old whore, I keep her tied up so she won't wander off, chase after something she shouldn't—but the ice is coming, I'm sure you know all about that."

I turn back to the dog, the meat gobbled up in a frenzy, a rotten sigh coming out of her mouth, death creeping closer every day. And I guess that's a blessing.

"Come on, Jezebel," I mutter, untying the rope from the rusted hook on the post, leading her inside. She knows what's good for her, the cold coming in, so she obliges.

Inside it's warm, a potbelly stove glowing in the corner. Not much to see in here, a tiny bed to one side, the stove, a small wooden table with two rickety old chairs, and a few pots and pans for cooking. Along the inside of one wall, just under the only window is a stack of wood—plenty it looks like for the night, for days in fact, possibly weeks.

"You found the creek, I imagine," he says, sitting down in one of the chairs. "So you're set on water. I head down every couple of days to fill up some jugs, got the path memorized, nothing much to trip over out this way. We got a few sacks of beans and rice, it's not much, but you're welcome to join us for dinner."

"Don't mind if I do," I say, plopping into the other chair.

"Got a few extra blankets and the floor, that's about it, my friend. Unless you want my bed, I don't think I could keep you from taking it."

"That's fine, Ben. The floor is just fine."

The old man gets up and walks to the bag of dried beans, and then the rice, taking a few scoops from each burlap sack with a tin cup, depositing it all into a cast iron Dutch oven. He lifts a jug off the table, adding in some water, and then reaches for some dried herbs in a small wooden bowl, sprinkling them into the pot. He sits back down, tired and bent.

"You headed over the mountain, John? North?" the man asks.

"I reckon. That's the way the wind is pulling me, hoping to find my family—my wife and daughter. If they went this way, they probably followed the same signs I've been reading for weeks. Guess I'll see what's left in a world that's suddenly gone dark—what's on the other side."

The man nods.

"Take some of the feed with you, if you want, son—Jezebel and I aren't long for this world. I got a couple bullets with our names on them, if it comes to that, or we might just wink out in the same long, dark night. Who knows?"

"Thanks," I mutter. "I'll take you up on that offer."

The dog sits next to the stove, still shivering now and then, her body doing its best to digest the jerky, something she probably hasn't eaten in months.

"Have you seen many people since it all went quiet, get much company?" I ask.

The wind picks up, the cold beating against the shack, and I'm grateful to be inside. I can feel the ice slipping through the cracks in the wood, nipping at my exposed flesh, but I suppose the structure will hold.

He sighs, his white orbs open wide, trying to remember.

"There was one day, we got a whole mess of folks, a long line of feet moving over the dirt. I could hear them coming, like a stampede, and I went to the door and stood there, I listened. Both of us did. I heard a few greetings, but mostly it was quiet, eerie almost, must have been a couple dozen people drifting by, hardly a word, nobody stopping, just the creaking of bodies, the sighs and moans, a few kids crying, a sharp word here and there, but I don't know if your wife and child were in there. Maybe. You never know."

I nod and take a breath.

"You been over?" I ask.

"The mountain?" he replies. "Long time ago. It's a bitch, you'll cross a few streams, so water's not the problem. Cold, of course, a few wild things up in the rocks, the scraggly woods that are dying all up and down the hill, coyotes, snakes, the usual."

I nod.

"And…"

He opens his mouth as the wind kicks up again, the shack rattling and shaking, the smell of the beans and rice simmering, drifting to me, my stomach clenching and unclenching in hunger.

"What?" I ask.

He smiles, his mouth a mess, gums bleeding over his yellow teeth, wiping his face with a shaky hand, his eyes blinking and twitching.

"Nothing," he says, as the window rattles.

He stands and walks to the stove, the skillet bubbling, stirring with an old wooden spoon, mumbling to himself, rubbing his lower back, the dog lifting her head, whimpering.

"I don't know if they all made it over," is what the old man says, and I swear he's crying, his back to me, but it's getting dark, and I can't see his face.

The dog sits up and stares at the man, whining, a low growl deep in her belly.

"Shut up, Jezebel," the man yells suddenly, turning around, his pale skin flushed. "If I want to tell him, I'll tell him."

She lies back down, quiet now, cloudy eyes darting back and forth from the sound of her master's voice, to me, and then she closes them, surrendering.

"I don't know if *any* of them made it over, son, is what I'm trying to say."

"What do you mean?" I ask.

He rubs his face and sits back down, tears running down his wrinkled skin.

"Out here it's every man for himself, right?" he says. "I guess I could have said no, and let him take me, just surrender. Not like I'm living like a king out here. The fucking thing could have stayed up there, gotten what came its way, I don't know why it had to offer me anything."

"What are you talking about, Ben? Who is up in the hills? Is somebody bothering you? Want me to go talk to them, put a scare in them? I don't mind."

Ben cackles and rubs his white eyes, shaking—his mouth hanging loose, lips trembling.

"I wish it was that simple, John. A long time ago before this darkness fell over the land, I made a deal. I can't say I believed much of it at the time, I was sick with the cancer, dying, and felt like I might like to live a little longer, not die out here in the silence, alone. He showed me a path, the new path that goes over the mountain, one he'd been clearing for a long time, months I suspect. *Just send them this way,* he said. And then he put his hands on my head, and laid me down on the bed, running his long fingers over my flesh, kneading here and there, pushing his fingers in, the pain, the tenderness; he knew what he was doing. There was no blood, but the cancer went away. He ran his hands over my skull, and the headaches stopped. Held my hands and knelt beside my bed, and the arthritis disappeared."

I nod, listening, as the wind beat the shack and the boards rustled, dust and cold air filling the space.

"In a moment of weakness, I said okay. And then he left. Now and then he would come down out of the mountain and palaver, always in a slightly different shape. Once, as the echo of my long dead father, once as a gangly shadow of my childhood best friend, and once as a younger version of myself, still handsome and stout. I was drinking a lot then. He'd leave me a jug, and I'd suck it dry. The black bird would soar over, before I lost my sight, and soon enough Jezebel arrived on my doorstep, to keep me company, and not long after that, Rebecca—my wife."

I take a breath and don't say a word.

"Not always my wife, not some long lost love come back to me, no, not from the grave or anywhere else—something new, something I never had, and we lived a simple life. I never asked how or why she was here, I just accepted her, as one might take a coin, a gold watch, a gift on an anniversary, or holiday, perhaps. Long black hair and dark eyes, pale skin, she was a fallen angel that had no business being here. No children, no, we didn't allow that. I didn't. Not that we didn't couple, but she would never birth an abomination, nothing that the dark one sent me could be continued, you understand?" he asks, staring at me, eyes blind and casting out into the darkness, searching for forgiveness. "There are ways to end beginnings, and several times I did exactly that."

"Ben…" I say, even though I struggle to believe.

"Let me finish," he says. "She died many years ago—I stopped counting at some point. Not sure exactly how old I am, Jezebel defying the odds right with me, one hundred, two hundred. I don't know."

I squint at him. The liar, he's lost his goddamned mind.

"I supposed in the end she was just curious, Rebecca, following the path too far, my warnings falling on deaf ears, her laughter at such imaginings simply contempt for my rotten heart, and my empty head. I guess I could have just said coyote, and left it at that, if not for the necklace. He brought me her locket one day, coming down from the hills in the form of a sick, brown bear. Lumbering over the path, sending the dog into a fit, dropping the jewelry in the dirt, knowing I was watching, its open mouth a black hole—rotting, buzzing, a low growl slipping out into the air."

Stories, the old man is telling me stories, just to pass the time, I think.

"It preys on your fears, John, whatever you long for, whatever you miss—this is what it will become for you. I warn you now, so that maybe you can make it over, outwit the demon, and pass by unobstructed. It was my father, who never held me once, the word love never slipping past his lips; it was my best friend, acts of betrayal, a sneer on his face as he took so many things that were mine; and even my younger self, what I might have been, if only I'd tried harder, if only I'd listened."

Outside the wind picks up, shaking the shack again, the ice pelting the side of the structure, the window rattling in its frame.

"That's quite a story, Ben," I say.

He frowns at me and stands.

"Dinner's ready," he grumbles, spooning the beans and rice into a wooden bowl, handing me a bent silver spoon. "Eat up, son. Tomorrow, you'll need your strength."

When the sun rises the next morning my head is filled with the echo of animals howling under a moonlit sky, the scratching of Jezebel's nails on the plank floor, in her own fitful dream, hunter or hunted—not sure which. Ben sits on the edge of his bed staring at me, his jaw clenching and unclenching—staring as if he still had eyes that worked, staring out into all of our futures.

I sit up.

"You okay, Ben?" I ask, rubbing my face, pain running up and down my spine, my hands icy cold and partially numb, the potbelly stove down to a dull glow.

"I don't expect you to believe it all," he says. "I know how it sounds. I wish there was some way to convince you of the truth."

I wave him off, and then realize he can't see my hand.

"It doesn't matter, Ben, if it happened or didn't happen, I'm heading over the mountain. If I see your buddy, I'll put in a good word for you, okay?

The old coot laughs and smiles.

"You really don't understand, my friend," he says, standing.

He walks to the stove, and with a pair of old leather gloves, opens the front of the metal beast. He grabs a few logs from the stack against the wall, and tosses them in, shutting the door with his knee.

"I'll put on some coffee," he says, shuffling over to the bags of supplies in the corner. "You need to get on your way. If you hurry, you can make it up and over and down again, about ten miles total, just under five thousand feet in elevation, I reckon."

We don't talk much over the coffee, beans ground by hand, Jezebel sitting by my side, resting her nose upon my lap. I eat the rest of the rice and beans from the night before, warmed up, sticking to my ribs, as Ben watches, clasping his hands. When I take a step outside to piss, the heat is already sliding over the hillside. Ben fixes me a pack with a small metal pot, and several cups of his supplies.

When he steps outside, I can tell he's upset, but he won't talk about it, shuffling his feet, the dog sitting beside him.

"Here," he says, handing me the sack. "This should help you get over, whatever is left on the other side. You won't die of starvation today, I can at least do that much."

"I appreciate it, Ben," I say, and I hand him a few sticks of jerky. "Save it for the mutt for later, and have yourself a chaw if it won't rip your rotten old teeth out."

He grins and takes it, and then holds out his hand.

"Good luck, John," he says, his white glassy eyes trembling in his head. What does he see right now, I wonder—the past, the present, or the future?

Or maybe nothing at all.

"Thanks," I mutter, shaking his hand.

I bend down to pet the dog, and she licks my hand, the gesture rippling over my flesh, triggering memories from days gone by, back when things were domesticated, when the world hadn't already run its course. I choke back a muffled sob and swallow hard, clearing my throat.

"I better get going. I'll keep an eye out for both man and beast, Ben, I promise."

He nods, and I set off up the path he warned me about, the only obvious trail over the mountain, to whatever family I might have left. The sign at the edge of the worn out dirt trail is pounded into the dry soil, crooked and faded, the word north painted on it in shaky letters, as if written with a finger, something a child might do, an arrow pointing left. The letters are in a faded red paint, or perhaps something else, and as I look up to the clear blue sky, the black bird circles, and then drifts out over the woods.

Before I disappear around a bend, into the thin pines and maples that rest at the base of the hill, I turn to wave at them both, forgetting one last time that they can't see a damn thing. I wave anyway, feeling like I could have done more, said something—not been so ornery and doubtful. What's done is done, and I wave at them anyway, and as I head up the mountain the dog barks once, wagging its tail, and as the darkness swallows me, Ben waves back.

For three hours I work my way up the hill, stopping only to refill my water whenever I pass over a creek or stream. Though it gets cooler the higher I go, the sun slowly rises, the woods warming around me, insects chirping, a red-tailed hawk gliding over an opening in the canopy, sailing on the thermals that push around the mountain range.

When I stop to rest for a bit, sitting on a fallen oak, pulling off my left boot to root out a rock, a mangy smell drifts toward me, and I look up and around, eyes on the path, and then to the woods. Something rotten, and dirty—not sure what it is. I slip my boot back on and stand, leaving the bag of supplies on the ground, both hands to my hips, holsters unsnapped.

I sniff again. Something isn't right. There's a wet smell, something gone sour, flesh baking in the sun, feces and urine, a heavy odor filling the air. The woods are silent, not a bluebird or jackdaw to be heard, just the thudding of my heart and my own shallow breath.

Down the path saunters an aging coyote, with long ambling legs, yellow eyes, its fur torn in patches, faded brown and gray, one ear missing a chip. When I hear a panting behind me, I look back down the other way, and see another one coming up the hill. And from out of the bushes, two more from the left, starting to snarl now, two more from the right. They are skinny, with their mouths open, yapping at each other, so I move to the center of the path, guns pulled out now, my head on a swivel, back and forth. The leader stops at the top of the trail and sits down, panting, as his brothers close rank. I cock the hammer on the right pistol, and then the left, the creatures never slowing their pace, happy with their numbers, starting to slink low, ears up high.

I wait for one to leap, contemplating a shot at the leader, hoping it might make them scatter, counting in my head the number of bullets, wondering if I'm a good enough shot.

To the right and up the hill there is a great ripping sound from deep in the woods, as if a tree has been uprooted, leaves rushing by, and then a heavy thud as it crashes to the forest floor, and the animals flee in all directions, gone in the blink of an eye.

Bear?

It moves closer, and I can see the tops of the trees swaying back and forth, suddenly the forest full of life, all manner of bird cawing and chirping, a flutter of wings, a jackrabbit shooting past me, and I almost pull the trigger, cursing the long-eared bastard. Bushes rustle and I can see it moving closer to the path, just up a little bit, branches snapping, twigs cracking, and then the foliage parts, and out the creature steps onto the trail.

I stare in wonder, and suddenly think that maybe Ben wasn't lying at all.

The boy stands there in torn pants, tied with a rope, no shoes, and no shirt, his head shaved, eyes brown and pooling. His feet are so filthy that the toes almost look bonded together into one cloven hoof.

"Are you heading over the mountain?" he asks. I open my mouth to speak, but nothing comes out. He holds his hands in front of his distended belly, scratches and bruises up and down his arms, a smile filling his face; too wide—far too wide.

"That was the plan," I muster.

"Did Ben send you my way?" he asks, just a child, maybe ten or twelve, something not right, and if I turn my head to one side and squint, he looks so very familiar.

"In a manner of speaking, I guess he did," I exhale.

"You can put those away," he says.

I look down, and the guns are holstered.

"Have others been by?" I ask, "Since things, well…"

"Since the end times began?" he asks.

"Recently. My wife, my daughter…"

And at this he grins again, his teeth not yellow, but sparking white, from this distance not square and humble, but slightly filed, as if to a point.

"This is my mountain now," he says, not moving, eyes blinking.

"Look, son, I'm just trying to get over and down, won't be on your mountain hardly any time at all."

"I'm afraid that's not good enough," he says. "There must be a tribute, and there is none that I can see. Are you not willing to make an offering?" he asks. "What exactly do you have to offer?" he asks, eyebrows furrowing, a frown sliding down his face, his mouth shut, as the sun settles behind rapidly moving clouds, the forest dimming, the air turning cooler—goosebumps running across my flesh.

He takes a step toward me and I pull the pistols and fire.

He laughs.

Looking down, my fists are held in front of me, my index fingers pointed out in his direction, thumbs cocked up.

Empty.

"No, my friend," he says. "Not what I was looking for, I'm afraid."

And in the distance there is a single gunshot, a crack, loud and clear, and the boy looks down the hill toward where the shack must still stand, his face tightening and flushing red. I take a breath, and a second shot startles the air, a colony of bats escaping from two large, gray boulders to our right, from a deep slash in the earth, running off into the sky, as raindrops pelt the top of the forest.

I stare at this boy, my hands open now, out in front of me, as if holding him back by sheer will.

He walks closer and I cannot move, the boy up close, reaching into his dingy pants, pulling out a pocket knife, flipping it open, running the blade over the palm of his left hand. And then again, completing an "x." He reaches up and I find myself bending over, while inside I scream *no* and *run* and *godinheaven*, but I cannot refuse him. He places his spread hand on my forehead, leaving a sticky red handprint, and then he steps away.

"You may pass," he says, exhaling.

And for a moment I am a child again, scratching at my shaved head, the lice captured in a comb, their little legs scurrying about, the sink filled with hair, a trickle of blood, one nick of my head, the boy some distant echo, rippling out in time, a mirror image of what I once was. Turning back a single time, eyes squinting, he slips into the woods again, the crashing of bushes flattened, the creak and groan of a massive oak tipping down the hill, snapping off branches, and slamming to the earth.

And then quiet.

What lies on the other side of the mountain?

I fear there is nothing left at all, just empty wishes and dirt.

I spend the rest of the day in a hot daze working my way to the top of the mountain, pushing on, eager to make the top, so I can rest for a moment and gather my thoughts. Along the way, there are many signs that life and death have both come this way.

After leaving the boy, I find an old, dead scrub oak, with nothing but empty branches, a long dark scar running down one side, as if struck by lightning, the grass around it burnt and flat. In the dry branches are pairs of shoes, tied together—swinging in the breeze. There are tiny white baby booties, small tennis shoes, hiking boots, anything with laces, suspended in the air, dark fruit that will never blossom. At the base of the tree are dozens of cowboy boots, sandals and anything without a lace—without the ability to hang. Perhaps not all made an offering here, these shoes remnants of their previous lives, their bones scattered up and down the hill, altars made from their empty skulls; perhaps some made it over this hill.

I move on.

An hour later I stumble across a small pit just off the path to the left, and for a moment I think it is filled with writhing snakes. But as the sun glints through the leaves, and the branches sway, the hole is illuminated in flashes of light, something sparkling in it, a hint of metal, and then I realize what it is. At the bottom of this hole are hundreds of belts, the metal catching light now and then, intertwined black and brown, woven hemp, not moving at all, just a trick upon my eyes.

I keep moving.

Finally, I reach the top of the mountain, the open space covered in rock and shale, a few scraggly pines and low bushes, the sky clear for miles in every direction. I can see the train tracks running north and south, but no sign of the great metal beast. I can see the tiny shack where Ben shared a meal with me, and the sterile desert to the south. And to the north, I can see open land, green grass and widespread growth, a whisper of smoke drifting up into the sky, and what looks to be a settlement of sorts, a few small buildings, too far to see any movement, but a sign of life, at least.

There is hope.

I take a moment to chew on the last of the jerky, to drink

my water, and to prepare myself for what lies in wait. I had come to expect nothing, just the dust and empty land, a few remnants perhaps, ready to find only an echo of what had been before. Some must have made it over, a few at least, or perhaps they were from the other side, not making the journey south, aware of what lurks in the hills.

I head down.

The day slips past, hours unfolding one after the other, sweat coating my body, the sun dipping down over the horizon, and before it disappears, I emerge from the woods, making it to the flat lands, the path continuing on, right up to a few dilapidated buildings.

Tents, teepees, and lean-tos are scattered around a few small cabins, most of them much like Ben's, barely standing, cut from the woods around us, built by hand many years ago, faded and worn, but still upright. One larger structure looks as if it has been built in the past year, new wood, the cuts still fresh, the chimney spilling smoke into the air. In the middle of the grounds is a large fire pit, ringed with gray and white rocks, black ash filling the center, a boy and girl snapping branches, filling up the circle with dry wood, heading back and forth to the woods. The girl turns to me, drops the wood and lets out a scream.

"Daddy!" she yells, and I drop my sack, my eyes beginning to water, as she flies to me, my Allie, dirty and smudged, a small red handprint on her forehead. I kneel in the dirt as she crashes into me, and I hold her, crying now, a great weight fluttering off into the sky.

"How did you get over?" she asks, pulling back, looking at me, as my eyes run over her. She looks healthy, happy even, tears running down her dusty face.

"I imagine much like you all did," I said.

"I knew you'd come, I knew you'd make it," she says.

I take a deep, uncertain breath.

"Are you okay?" I ask.

She nods.

"Where's your mother?" I ask, and her eyes go dark, her head dipping.

Out of the structures, the main house, and the woods, more children emerge. They are all ages, all races, much like Allie—slightly dirty and dusty, some cuts and scratches, but not sickly, not dying, their arms filled with wood, or jugs of water, some carrying baskets with potatoes, carrots, and onions. They all wander over, their eyes wide, smiles slipping across their faces. On each of their foreheads is a singular red blotch, some faded, some fresher, but all still remaining, not washed away, not erased. These handprints that were left in blood, the tributes have not been forgotten.

A boy and girl emerge from the main house, older, but not much more than eighteen. They look tired, the girl holding an infant in her arms, the boy grasping her arm as they approach. They must be in charge.

"This is my father," Allie says, walking toward them.

I hold out my hand, and the boy shakes it, the girl smiling, whispering to her baby, as she bounces it up and down.

"Is this it?" I ask. "Where's your mother, Allie, the other parents?"

I look around at the children, the red marks on their foreheads, and I understand.

"She's not here, Daddy," Allie says, walking back to me, grasping my hand. "There was a price to pay, the offering on the hill."

The boy nods his head and speaks up. "There were choices to be made," he says, "And our parents made them. The way of the old world is gone, destroyed," he says. "This is a new beginning, a second chance."

I take a breath, and hold my daughter's hand. I look into the faces of the children, the way they stand close to one another, the wood, the water, the food—united in their efforts, the echo of their parent's sacrifice branded on their skin.

"Do you have room for one more?" I ask.

The boy looks at my forehead, the red stamp, down at my daughter, and laughs.

"Of course we have room," he says. "We're working on the fire right now," he says. "Gets cold around here at night," he chuckles, "as I'm sure you know. Not as bad as the other side, but still—pretty frigid. Come rest by the ring, catch up with your daughter, we have water, food—come, sit. It'll be dark soon."

Allie leads me by the hand toward the bonfire, and the children follow us, laughing and asking questions, their hands on me, just a little touch here and there, making sure I'm real, something new, something familiar, and then they disperse into the woods, back to work. I am an exciting part of their day, but they know what comes at night, and to survive, there must be fire, there must be heat. We sit and talk, unable to release each other, holding hands, her climbing into my lap. Beyond the houses crops grow, the dead desert south of us gone, the fertile soil here ripe for growth, no nuclear winter, no death and disease, the mountain, perhaps, separating the living from the dead. I don't think too hard about it—I simply hold my daughter, and breathe.

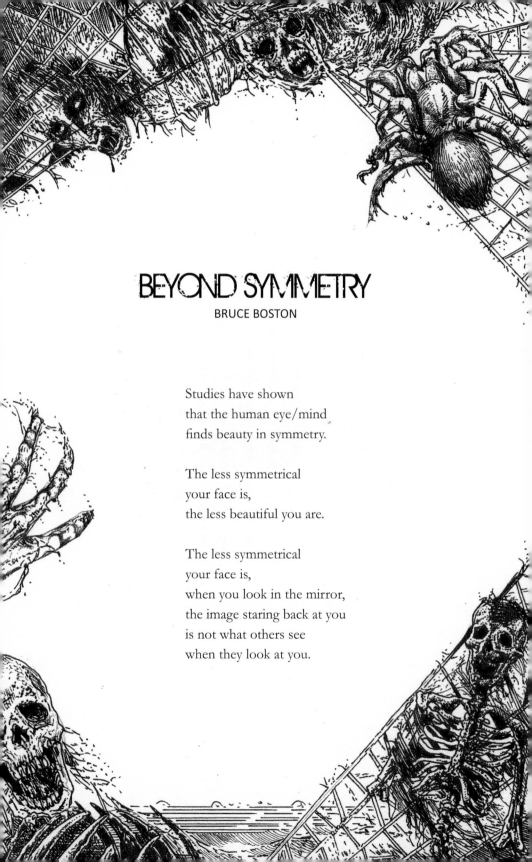

BEYOND SYMMETRY

BRUCE BOSTON

Studies have shown
that the human eye/mind
finds beauty in symmetry.

The less symmetrical
your face is,
the less beautiful you are.

The less symmetrical
your face is,
when you look in the mirror,
the image staring back at you
is not what others see
when they look at you.

That mole high
on your left cheek,
along with your crooked eye tooth,
are now on the right,
and suddenly you are left-handed
instead of right,
or vice versa.

Who is this stranger that
returns your glance
with all his parts switched around?

And as you turn away from
his questioning stare,
as he turns away from yours,
you wonder if he is suddenly
wondering as you are
about beauty and symmetry
and the world around you.

It occurs to you
that the countenance
of the moon is asymmetrical
to the extreme,
pocked and scarred
by countless violent impacts
and volcanic eruptions,
Yet still you find it beautiful.

Shows what good lighting can do.

THOSE WHO WATCH FROM ON HIGH

ERIC J. GUIGNARD

THE BOY LOOKED UP TO THE SKY and smiled, and it seemed to Lee that the boy looked up at him, smiled at *him*.

The boy's teeth were white and perfect little squares like the teeth you saw on a poster in the orthodontist's waiting room: *Trust us to make your teeth look like this!* But Lee doubted this boy had ever been to an orthodontist. Lee doubted this boy had been much of anywhere, outside of a few miles from his mud-brick shack. The boy was just blessed by nature with a beautiful smile.

Lee came down closer, closer still, nearing the desert, nearing the shack. He reached for the ground. His boots made contact. He took a tentative step, then another, impossibly feeling solid earth beneath him. He began to walk. The boy wasn't far away, and Lee watched him play. The boy rolled a ball into a skirmish line of toy soldiers, and they toppled over. He charged with a thrusting gun, dueling invisible opponents. He climbed a rock. Chased a lizard. Drew a picture in the dirt with a stick. The boy was happy, and this made Lee happy.

Lee's son, Jacob, would have been about the same age as this boy, and it reminded him terribly of all the lives that are taken too soon. If circumstances were different, it'd be Lee in that shack in Afghanistan, playing with his son, trying to survive from one day to the next. The boy with perfect teeth was about eight years old and had two siblings that were both still infants. That was a large gap in age between the children, and Lee wondered if there had once been others. If circumstances were different, Jacob would have had siblings. If circumstances were different, Jacob would still be alive, and Aimee alive, and they'd have three children by now. Three...just like the family he watched.

"Stand by for orders."

The voice came to him, filling his head, but he couldn't make sense of it. The words didn't fit with his surroundings. Lee felt the uneven ground beneath his feet, one step sinking into white sand and the next step stumbling over ancient stones. The region was so rocky that the danger of misstep loomed greater than snipers' bullets; out here a snapped ankle could be a slow and lonely death.

Desert heat swirled against Lee, and a line of sweat ran down his temple. But the boy was close, so close...Lee wanted to run to him, touch him, tell him to take his happiness and flee everything.

"Check the angle, Bruce. We're tracking insurgents, not sand dunes."

Again it felt unnerving, like someone speaking in a dream, and Lee only wanted the voice to leave him alone so he could remain with the boy. Instead, the voice seemed to pull him back, seemed to lift him in the air, and the boy and his desert home fell away like a sinking marble.

"Bruce, you with me?"

The dream voice was louder, and the wasteland faded below. A computer screen coalesced over it, like overlapping frames of film. *He wasn't there.* He, *no*, it—the Drone—was there, following the boy and his family, but he—Lee—was in a trailer on Nellis Air Force Base. He was First Lieutenant James Lee, and he was on duty.

"Bruce, report!"

Reality came back fully, and he remembered that it sucked.

He was an Unmanned Aerial Vehicles operator. Six computer monitors glowed before him, jostling for attention with moving images, scrolling feeds, changing numbers, things blinking, red, green, eighty-four, nine, radius, lock, C2, surge. It was a child's room of toys, messy and random, too much visual stimuli going on at once. He operated half the cockpit of a remote aircraft on the other side of the world. Watching, ready to fire a missile anytime onto unknowing targets.

Lee adjusted camera #3, and the video feed panned back to widen its scope.

"Roger that, sir. Adjusting angle," Lee replied to Disick, the other half.

"I don't know how you made it through the academy, Bruce."

Bruce. He hated that nickname.

Never mind he was blue-eyed with hair fair as butter, or that his family were English-settled coal miners from the Appalachians and the farthest one could get from the Orient, Lee had been christened 'Bruce' upon assignment to the squad, no explanation necessary. It was just funny to the rest of them. He'd grown up trapping and fishing, an outdoorsman before he could say *da-da*, yet zit-faced Captain Disick called him Bruce while coining his own unlikely nickname of 'Hunter.' The irony went unheeded. Disick was built soft as a wet cow pie and looked like he'd be better suited playing *World of Warcraft* than soldiering. Of course, in current confines video gaming skills were traits superior over machismo. Plus Disick was his commanding officer, so Lee didn't say jack or shit back to him. They flew together which was supposed to inspire camaraderie, though Lee detested his younger co-pilot; Disick loved the power play one increase in rank held over him, and he hid behind it like a shield while picking apart Lee on a basis as punctual as cadence.

Captain Disick flipped a switch, taking over from the automated control pilot. He sat to Lee's left less than five feet away, in front of his own bank of computers, though still speaking to Lee in a headset, never turning to face him. "Disregard and disengage. Colonel Brown just ordered we bring the craft home. The next shift can watch the hajjis sleep."

"Affirmative, Captain," Lee said.

"That's 'Hunter'," Disick said. "Remember, Colonel Brown says it's good for squad morale to use our code names."

"Yes, sir." Lee replied, deadpan.

"That was an order, *Bruce*."

"Yes . . . Hunter."

Time to leave.

The trailer door opened from outside. The next shift of drone operators waited to enter, faces already dull, already exhausted, the look of adult children sentenced to twelve-hour detention and dragging their feet to begin.

Lee went to the door and nodded at them, but said nothing. On the other side, the sky was bright, colored as pale water, colored exactly as the Afghani sky. He expected that once he walked out, he would see the boy's mud home in the distance. There'd be a picture drawn in the dirt, a lizard on a rock, toy soldiers lined up in battle. There'd be someone high above observing *him*.

Twelve hours. He'd been on duty, staring at a patch of desert the size of a football field for twelve mind-numbing hours. His night shift began at seven p.m. and ended at seven a.m., and when Lee went into the Air Force trailer it was day and when the door was unlocked to allow him out, it was a new day. Flying over Afghanistan occurred during *their* day, opposite hours of Pacific Standard Time. It seemed to Lee that night no longer existed; he saw only desert sun at all times.

No wonder he couldn't turn the visions off so easily. When you hyper-gaze too long into a television screen, the afterimage haunts you, that sense of disorientation. Though he existed here at Nellis, just north of Las Vegas, half of every day was spent in Afghanistan. Half the day he *felt* he existed in Afghanistan. It was not something he could easily reconcile, the *here* and *there*, every day, looking at two worlds which were so much alike, but were not.

"Christ, Bruce, move out of the way. You're blocking our egress."

Disick was behind him. Lee blinked and exited the trailer. Three metal steps down and he was on a cement lot. The Mojave Desert surrounded Nellis Base, glints of quartz and mica sparkling from its golden sand. Like the sky, Nevada's desert appeared identical to Afghani desert.

We're the same all over.

Disick plodded past, and the other operators went inside, door closed on a time lock, unable to reopen until the next shift change for security reasons. All routine. The trailer was just a souped-up shipping container, ambiguously known as a Ground Control Station. But inside it was filled with death rays and mad scientist diodes and buttons that caused people to explode.

And there were several dozen trailers here, each ready to obliterate, each part of the 29th Attack Squadron. That's who he was attached to.

He knew somebody he'd like to attack...

Another day.

Lee flew the UAV drone far above, where air was too thin even for clouds to form. The ancient village of Oraza Zaghard sat below like a pile of ash dropped upon a beautiful quilt. Lee had once tried a *Google* search of the village to supplement the demographics the military supplied. Although it was highlighted on the Air Force map, he found no reference to it on the internet. The village was insignificant to the rest of the world; only those who lived there, and those who watched from on high, seemed privy to its existence.

Lee directed the cameras downward. The Multi-Spectral Targeting System streamed color video back to the Air Force trailer, and as the sensors zoomed in, so did Lee. He felt like he was soaring, then diving, straight down through the sky. Zooming in, zooming in. Afghani desert swirled around, and he moved through Sar-e Pol Province, past Oraza Zaghard, and to the mud-brick shack at the end of a winding footpath. Back to the boy...

The boy who had no name. He was only 'Son of Mullah Hamid Zadran, suspected insurgent.'

The camera lenses were so high-powered that Lee was able to pick out the scars on the boy's arms and the cowlicks in his hair. The camera lenses were so high-powered he felt as if he were there alongside the boy.

The family had one goat, and the boy ran to it, circling with waving arms. The goat stood there, staring plainly, then suddenly turned and darted away. The goat was too quick, and the boy could not catch it. He sat on the ground and laughed.

Lee was quicker than the boy; he reached out and caught the goat by a rope tether around its neck.

The boy looked at Lee and smiled, and Lee saw again how perfect those teeth were. The smile was honest, relieved, as if the boy expected him to be there all along, to watch over him.

Time to leave.

The trailer door opened from outside. The next shift of drone operators waited to enter.

Lee went to the door and nodded at them, but again said nothing. On the other side, the sky was bright, colored as pale water, colored exactly as the Afghani sky. It was all so familiar. He expected that once he walked out, he would see the boy's mud home in the distance. There'd be a picture drawn in the dirt, a lizard on a rock, toy soldiers lined up in battle. There'd be someone high above observing *him*.

"Rifle!"

Lee vaulted to the ground, sprawling. Only he was three metal steps above cement, so rather than vaulting, it was falling, hard and fast. He hit concrete, bruising his knees and elbows, but that didn't matter. Roll up on reflex, one hand over the back of his head, the other hand covering behind his neck.

Disick laughed.

There was no *rifle*, the term for incoming missile.

"Just keeping you on your toes, Bruce."

The other operators laughed too.

"What the hell, Disick?"

"Have to live up to my nickname. I was *hunting* you." He laughed again.

Lee stood, balling his hands to fists. But he didn't react the way he wanted, instead turning his back.

Disick knew somebody high in the chain of command. That's who watched over *him*. That's how he got his Captain's bars so young. But Disick didn't know his ass from his double chin when it came to real hunting. It was all a video game to him.

Someday his superior by one rank would get his due.

"Lighten up, Bruce," Disick said. "It's only war."

It was difficult trying to sleep during the day. The blinds of his bungalow were drawn and it was dark inside, but Lee's brain knew the sun was up, and his body's rhythm fluttered anxiously as if he'd grossly overslept something important. He could never grow accustomed to nocturnalism, the knowledge that it was nine in the morning outside, and he was only now trying to fall asleep, trying to get in a good eight hours before tonight's shift began.

Eight hours…who was he kidding? He'd be lucky to get four. Lee had taken a couple sleeping pills, but those never seemed to work, instead just muddying the line between wakefulness and slumber even more.

Everything—day, night, Afghanistan, Nevada, here, there—was a blur, a series of memories of what may have occurred and hopes for what *could* occur, playing side-by-side, like viewing two videos simultaneously…

…Lee's thoughts interrupted. He'd returned to the trailer. Disick sat next to him and said something, and Lee responded by reflex, and that was it. They fell silent, having nothing more to say for hours while stationed alongside each other.

Lee felt himself drifting. Again. His face hung slack, his mind numb, conditioned to study the target on the ground, watching, just watching. The computers around him had long ago fallen into the backdrop of his mind, filed as forgotten thoughts. He felt dull and tired like sitting inside a car on a road trip that goes on too long. Sweaty, grimy, breathing each other's air, each other's smells. Did Disick ever bathe? Come to think of it, when did he himself bathe? The world outside the Air Force trailer seemed dim, speeding past on simulated auto-pilot just as it did inside. He couldn't remember much of it. He couldn't remember the last time he'd washed, the last time he'd slept, eaten, or felt happy.

No, scratch that, he remembered that last time he was happy. Watching Jacob play...

...Lee had been married once. Had a son once. Spent six years as an enlisted man in Air Force logistics at Edwards Base, dreaming of the day he'd transfer out of low-grade clerk's activities. He wanted away from the rote routine of uniformed paper pushers. He wanted action, to reach the combat zones, kill the bad guys like his father. So Lee pushed himself, got accepted, and then finished Officer Candidate School third in his class. He could fly a Raptor or a Lightning II high above the world. He was going to be badass.

But then everything changed.

Aimee died. Jacob died.

It had been nighttime, cruising down Interstate 15 to visit her parents in San Diego. A drunk driver hit them. He came out of nowhere, *absolutely nowhere*, no lights on, no warning, just one moment Lee was driving their leased Corolla while Aimee and Jacob snoozed, and the next they were blindsided. All Lee could liken to the impact was that of a missile slamming into the side of their car, and he hated himself for that comparison. The Corolla was knocked through the guardrail, tumbling in lazy rolls down a ravine that sliced through the Clark Mountain range. Lee didn't have his seatbelt on. The others did. Lee was thrown from the car with barely a scratch. The others were burned alive in the ensuing fire.

Though he survived unharmed, part of him still died. Life became that car wreck, confusing and pointless. He was evaluated as mentally unfit to fly a jet. Inexplicably though, the next week he was transferred to Nellis and assigned to fly one from behind a desk, even though military psychologists claimed it was tougher to pilot a drone than a real plane. The work was time-intensive, vigilantly staring at the same plot of earth through cameras for months on end. Watching, just watching, just another rote routine like when he worked as a logistics clerk.

It's not the planes that are drones. We're the drones, filling the monotony of our lives with buttons and monitors.

Lee lay in bed dreaming of Aimee and Jacob, dreaming after the accident, after the fire, of their melted stick bodies that looked as if they'd been doused in tar...

...And he knew somebody he'd like to attack. Hadn't he been tracking that person for a long time, *hunting them?*

The drunk driver who rammed them off the road. *Lee could fire a missile anywhere in the world.* To kill the bad guys, he had only to watch and wait...

...And he watched the boy in Afghanistan play with toy soldiers. They were cheap plastic men, molded in olive green that every toy aisle in every drug store carried since toys and aisles and drug stores first came around. Even there, in that country, some sales clerk had gotten his wares dispersed all the way to the mud shack at the end of a winding footpath outside Oraza Zaghard.

Lee had played with those exact soldiers when he was a boy, and his own father played with them before him.

"Yup, same poses, same faces," his father once said. His father died in Iraq.

The green solider frozen with a bayoneted rifle swung overhead. The solider with a deadly flame thrower. The one with a far-reaching mortar. The one with a pistol and binoculars which, though no insignia was present, was always assumed to be the unit's officer.

Jacob, too, had played with those soldiers...

CR ∞ ℛ

…Lee walked through the desert in Afghanistan, feeling the hot sand even through his combat boots…

No, he was in Nevada. Nellis Air Force Base. He walked through the sand of the Mojave desert…

But the mud shack was there.

So, too, was the UAV trailer, alongside, but not, like viewing two videos simultaneously…

Both screens went black…

There was something watching him.

Lee stepped to the side of the trailer, his back hugging its wall. The sky was bright, colored as pale water, colored exactly as the Afghani sky. He looked to it, searching for the drone. He blinked. He blinked again, a hundred more times. Though it wasn't visible, he *knew* something was up there… somewhere, someone watching him …*targeting him.*

He was alone on the ground. Lee suddenly wanted to run back into the trailer where it was safe, but the next shift was already inside, door closed, locked.

He dashed across the lot, past the other trailers lined up like desks in a classroom. The red crosshairs of a target seemed to hover over each of them, but the biggest target followed himself. His squadron fired missiles like video games onto other countries, and some day those missiles would be returned.

Even now, satellites had watched him exit the trailer, knew *he* was the one pushing the button. Satellites, drones, cameras, eyes, all watching …

Was the boy watching him on his own monitor, inside a mud shack in Oraza Zaghard? Or was the boy inside the trailer, and Lee in Afghanistan?

UAV operators weren't supposed to experience the same effects of post-traumatic stress as those pilots actually flying jets into global combat zones. But he grappled daily with the hazards of depression, insomnia, and anxiety.

One time, Lee had even been so unnerved by these ailments that he'd worked up the courage to approach Captain Disick outside the trailer. Back then, Disick wasn't so overweight as he was fleshy, the way a linebacker may look: solid, but with those too-plump curves, like being swaddled in extra layers of clothing. Now Disick was just 'fat ass-fat' and Lee wondered how he could ever pass a fitness test. Or did it matter? After all, the future of wars was only button-pushing.

"Sir, can I ask you something?" Lee asked.

"S'up?"

"Do you ... well, ever come out of there and feel like you're losing track of where you are?"

"What?"

Lee knew Disick heard what was asked, and that he understood it, so the curt response meant he was more baffled as to *why* Lee would ask such a thing.

Lee tried again. "Disassociation. That's what the doctors call it. Does it ever get to you, so you're not sure if we're here or still staring at another land?"

"Don't tell me you're ready for the shrinks already," Disick replied. "Long enough day without dealing with your bullshit."

Lee never told Disick about Aimee and Jacob. Maybe their relationship would have been different if he had. Maybe Disick would have understood why his co-pilot was a glum, tightlipped burnout. But Lee never told anyone about Aimee and Jacob.

Lee just rubbed his eyes, playing it cool. "Sorry, Captain. Like you said, it's been a long day."

"Then get some sleep. Tomorrow will be another long one." Disick walked away, probably to pound beers at the Officers' Club.

And now, something, *someone*, watched Lee from on high. He'd had this sense before, often, but it'd been growing stronger lately, slowly stronger, like zooming in and refocusing. Were they tracking him like the insurgents? Did they know of his plot? Did they know about who he wanted to attack ...?

'Cause he'd found that drunk driver, hadn't he? One push of a button,

just one push, and Jerome Anderson of 3145 Wingate Ave. would be blasted to Kingdom Come. In the land of dropped bombs, could it be so inconceivable if a drone missile happened to defect and land at that very address?

Lee could not see them—you could never *see* the drones—they were a quarter mile high in the sky. But he knew better than anyone else, *they were there*, watching, waiting.

They watched everybody.

Just like Lee had watched Jerome once he returned from Chino Prison. A lousy two years was all he served, reduced vehicular manslaughter charges for the deaths of Jacob and Aimee. But Lee tracked him down with a reprogrammed missile at his fingertips.

Lee could do it. The failsafe systems were overridden, the drone armed, the target locked in. He could even find a way to blame the wayward missile on Disick. He could do it, all he had to do was push a button...

But before Lee acted, Jerome Anderson of 3145 Wingate Ave. died suddenly of circumstances unrelated to Lee's doing, run over by another drunk driver. Lee had waited too long, the opportunity for revenge snatched from him as unexpectedly as the lives of his family.

That was over a year ago, yet something still watched Lee.

Another day.

Lee was on duty. He sat before his bank of computers watching the same football field-sized patch of desert. Watching the same mud-brick shack of Mullah Hamid Zadran.

On this day, Lee was alert. His nerves tingled as if they caught fire. Abu Ayyub al-Husseini was en route, a target considered 'high value,' this being a term which always reminded Lee of video games where the *Bosses* were worth the most points.

Lee's monitors flashed more images than normal, more lights blinked, numbers scuttling past. A multitude of voices filled his head, Intelligence Analysts chattering back and forth. *Observe, confirm, report.* They patched into a team of Information Officers inside another trailer, maybe next door to Lee, maybe on another planet. He never knew where the rest of the squad was. *For security reasons.*

"There he is, Bruce," Disick said, his voice nearly in glee. "There's al-Husseini. We're gonna nail that bastard."

Onscreen, a Mercedes Benz slowly drove up the winding dirt road to Zadran's mud shack.

Colonel Brown joined the teleconference. Whenever he spoke, his voice was garbled with static, as if he spoke far, far away, in an underground bunker. Lee had never met the Colonel, but he knew that static-filled voice would haunt him the rest of his days. Colonel Brown was the great decider of who lived and who died.

Today, it was thumbs-down. Colonel Brown said, "We have a high value target arriving. Prepare to prosecute."

An analyst added as an afterthought, "Confirm clear of civilians."

Lee felt sick. They were going to bomb the boy's home. *He* was going to bomb it, was going to be *ordered* to bomb it. He didn't want to—God knew that—but he was merely a drone. A voice he barely recognized as his own replied, "Only Zadran has been observed on premises in the past hour."

"Good," Colonel Brown said. "Killing two bad birds with one big stone."

Zadran stood outside the shack, talking animatedly on a cell phone. He was alone. *Should* have been alone. Earlier, a neighbor had driven to take away Zadran's wife and children. The boy *should* have been with them … of course the UAV Predator had banked left at a moment the family entered the car, which had been on the blind side of their home, so it wasn't certain. And heat signature didn't do squat during the day, when the desert sand cooked hotter than the readout of anything alive. But Lee hadn't seen anyone else since, couldn't *prove* to the others anyone else since.

Military intelligence had been tracing Abu Ayyub al-Husseini for weeks. He was supposedly plotting some sort of attack, and Zadran was supposedly working with him. al-Husseini was one of the bad guys. So was Mullah Hamid Zadran.

Lee was never privy to the validity of such charges. Proof was classified on a 'Need To Know Basis.' And Lee didn't need to know. He only needed to push a button when told, so someone could die on the other side of the world.

The Mercedes Benz arrived at the mud shack, and a static-filled voice ordered, "Prosecute."

Time to push the button. Time for Lee to launch death from on high. Zadran and al-Husseini would have no warning. To them, the missile would come out of nowhere, *absolutely nowhere.*

Lee hesitated. A line of sweat ran down his temple, as it had when he walked in the desert.

It didn't matter if he'd seen the boy or not in the last hour, because he knew, didn't he, just knew something was wrong...

"Prosecute."

This is what he trained for; there should be no emotional attachment to the enemy.

He wouldn't do it. They'd court martial him, but he'd have a clear conscious.

"Prosecute."

It was only a duty. Only reflex. Only rote routine. And if he didn't bomb the target, Disick would.

Disick would enjoy it...

"Prosecute."

"Rifle," Lee said, and an AGM 114 Hellfire missile was set loose.

It was twenty-five seconds until 'Splash,' when the payload detonated. Lee had a window of time to maneuver the missile if any non-targets approached the area. But the monitors were clear, only the intended targets visible, only Zadran and al-Husseini.

The missile soared down, down, down.

Still there was time to maneuver the missile away, but no reason. He had the controls and the authority to do so, until seven seconds before impact when it turned too late.

The seven second countdown came and passed. Six seconds until impact, five—

Disick whispered the numbers in reverence, "Four, three—"

Lee knew, without knowing how, what was to happen, and it did. It happened just as he knew; the boy exited from inside the shack. The boy flew a cardboard airplane in his hand.

"Abort!"

Two-too-late, one-too-late, detonation.

A flare of white bloomed on their screens, a silent, beautiful flower.

"Where'd that kid come from," Disick said. "I never saw him before…"

"Confirm target." Colonel Brown's voice came online, barely understood over the static.

"We might have got a civie," Disick admitted.

"The boy," Lee whispered.

Brown was silent. Static filled Lee's ears.

"Sir, sir," Disick asked. "What do we do?"

"Return to base, gentlemen. Good work. Target eradicated."

"But the boy—"

"It wasn't a boy," Brown said. "It was a dog."

The voice clicked away.

"You saw it," Lee told Disick. "A dog doesn't walk upright in sandals."

"Colonel Brown said it was a dog, so that's what it was."

Disick sounded relieved, detached.

"You saw it—"

"It was a dog, First Lieutenant Lee, and I don't want to hear another word about it!"

The use of Lee's proper rank and name unnerved him. It made the matter official. *A dog.* In records, the boy would never have died, would be living, in the ruins of that mud shack forever.

He wished Disick would have instead called him 'Bruce.'

CR ∞ SO

Four sleeping pills that morning, and he dreamed between there and here.

Lee walked in the desert, sand crunching beneath his combat boots. It was rocky and hot. Some of the rocks were black and shaped like crumpled leaves, and it took a while to realize the black rocks were debris from the mud shack. He kept walking and found a single wall that still stood, precariously truncated and shorn off smooth at each side. In the center of that wall, a door hung canting from twisted hinges.

He wanted to cry, but nothing came out. It was a desolate land, a dead land, and he belonged here. He dropped his head to his chest, eyes cast to the ground. Something white glistened there like a chip of porcelain. He bent and picked it up.

A tooth. A small, perfect white tooth.

Lee's cry had no trouble coming out now.

Another tooth lay three feet away, and Lee picked it up also. He searched the sand for more teeth, an idea forming in the back of his mind to reconstruct that which he'd destroyed.

He found fifteen. But that wasn't all, was it? How many teeth fit inside a boy's mouth? He seemed to remember there should be twenty...

The door in the ruined wall creaked open. Lee looked up. The boy stood there, visible within the doorframe, and this did not surprise Lee.

The boy—*it*—now appeared as a charred monster, a skewer of steak chunks dropped and forgotten in the broiler. Or it could have been the sculpture of a thin monkey built from wire and car parts, then sprayed matte black, though it moved like a living thing with half its bones snapped apart. There was just enough support left for the boy to walk in a feeble, lurching stumble toward Lee though, with every movement, something shifted loose under its charcoal skin, something that appeared ready to break free with a hollow crack and a poof of ash.

It dragged its feet slowly, leaving long charcoal smears with each step like skid marks of a hot rod that's peeled away on asphalt. That same *smell* of hot rod was there too, burning rubber and gasoline fumes that caused Lee to gag.

Closer it came, until halting before Lee, looking to him expectantly from hollow eye sockets. They remained this way, the child's head upraised to him, patiently waiting. Lee held the child's sightless gaze for ten long seconds before he could take it no more.

Lee held out his hand, opened it. The boy's perfect teeth rested on his palm.

The child took its teeth one by one and replaced them back into the horrible gummy blackness of its mouth. One by one, the teeth resumed their place, like connecting a jigsaw puzzle. First a molar, then a canine, another molar, then an incisor, pearls in a pond of tar. There were a few missing—Lee hadn't found them all—but by the time it was done, the boy's perfect smile had mostly returned. It flashed that mostly-perfect smile to Lee, happy again.

The boy stumbled to a large boulder, where a melted mass of plastic army soldiers lay like green bubblegum that's been chewed and stretched apart. The boy pulled some of the soldiers free; they were ruined, formless, like the boy, but the boy played with them.

Grating commands given from binocular-wielding officers to mortar and flamethrower-armed troops came from the boy's throat as it played, sounding like the dry *whisk* of sandpaper rubbing against rough wood.

Some of the sounds were even recognizable. *Boom, whisk. Pow-pow, whisk. Rat-a-tat, whisk.*

Lee went to the boy...

...Only now it wasn't a dream anymore because he and Disick were flying over Syria. Of course, Lee was still in a trailer in the Mojave Desert outside Las Vegas, but he *watched* over Syria.

After Oraza Zaghard, Lee and Disick had been enthusiastically congratulated. Oraza Zaghard was a success. But then the minor city of Saraqeb, located in an insurgent-filled corner of Syria, had been assigned as the newest directive of high value. They flew there post-haste to watch over another patch of desert the size of a football field.

Lee directed the cameras downward, and they zoomed in. The sensation was like falling face-first from the heavens; down, down he fell, and the ground rushed up to meet him.

Zooming in, but another image coalesced over it, like overlapping frames of film. It was Afghani desert that swirled about—not Syrian—and he returned to Sar-e Pol Province, passing Oraza Zaghard, soaring down to the ruins of the mud-brick shack at the end of a winding footpath. Back to the boy, waiting for him...

...And a new image coalesced over that, of another computer monitor, watching himself, and Lee saw that he sat inside the Air Force trailer and the little boy now sat on his lap, a little charcoal boy who'd returned with him from Afghanistan, a boy with limbs that stuck out in all the wrong directions, but who had the most beautiful teeth he'd ever seen...

...Heat smoldered off the boy, and Lee felt it warm his chest as the boy snuggled into him. Brittle edges of its charcoal skin scratched Lee's neck, but he didn't mind. Lee was happy.

Because the boy was dead—even *he* knew that—but the boy was also here with him now, and if the boy could be with him didn't that mean that Aimee and Jacob could *also* join him?

Lee glanced five feet to his left, and saw Disick slouched at the controls, eyes half-shut, staring at nothing. The drone was on auto-pilot. Disick never looked at him. Lee flipped a switch.

And another image coalesced over that, and he saw Aimee and Jacob as very small drones. They were the ones watching him from on high, and he wanted so desperately to fly up and join them.

And another image coalesced over that, like looking through a stack of transparent negatives, and Lee saw the Air Force trailers, each with a red crosshair hanging overhead.

He knew somebody he'd like to attack...

Lee pushed a button.

"Rifle, *whisk*," the boy said, though it was Lee's own voice he spoke with.

And suddenly Disick was awake, screaming about '*What had Lee done?*' and something else about him going '*batshit-crazy.*'

Lee wanted to say something clever about how he was *hunting* Disick, but then he realized his co-pilot's words didn't make any sense to him; they had a rough, baying tone, as if he barked like a dog … yes, that was it. *Disick was really a dog.*

Disick tried to push his own button, to counter Lee's, but Lee had fixed that already.

Then Disick was running to the door of the trailer, but couldn't get it open, because it was locked, and his hands were paws, and he was barking something else unintelligible. The boy smiled to Lee, and Lee smiled back.

"Lighten up," Lee told the dog. "It's only war."

And then Lee was back at the mud-brick shack, and it had been rebuilt, and the boy was there and Aimee was there and Jacob was there, all the charcoal people, with overlapping images of how once they looked, and they welcomed him, and somewhere he heard a countdown with a *whisk* after each number, and then he heard a final bark.

FOLIE À PLUSIEURS (THE MADNESS OF MANY)

SYDNEY LEIGH

Anna, who was mad, drank love songs at the mouth-hole
she wore a ragged moon, seduced foul beasts with tongues of serpents,
had eyes as wild as free-fall spirals of the seraphim.
Her still-born, sweating cherubs suckled daylight from a vulture
while Anna, mad as birds, unsheathed her knife so she could plume
the rotten feathers from her armpit for her sweet daddy.

And he with clefted chin just lay back, this vampire daddy,
drained blood from cherub's mouth-hole,
watched it leave an ochre plume.
He fucked her with his serpents,
ate her eyes out like a vulture,
then hummed a noble love song as he summoned seraphim.

SYDNEY LEIGH

Descending moon-struck skies, a golden cloud of seraphim
with diseased staffs sharpened senses of the imprisoned daddy.
In his pale blue eyes a stranger glimpsed the heartbeat of a vulture,
whose slick talons tore innocence from Anna at the mouth-hole
while she herself told half-truths to the twisting mass of serpents,
removed her tongue to feed to one, then wore it like a plume.

The stranger then tore up the planks as smoke rose in a plume—
beneath the flooring, Satan's men waltzed wild with seraphim.
"You do not do, you do not do ... I've killed two, TRUE!" cried serpents,
while heron, wren, with Parker Pen signed discharge forms for daddy,
and six-winged, gangling daughters swallowed red swords at the mouth-hole,
then buried eyes expelled from sin-filled bellies of the vulture.

"Forgive. Forgive ... Say not ... Take me in," begged the vulture,
but the eye begins to see imagined oceans as a plume.
So Anna planted golden lotus flowers round the mouth-hole,
took off her rings and stood on tiptoe for the seraphim.
And from the coop with blue face on a white horse rode her daddy
to whisper like a buttercup words for the wind to serpents.

I'll bind and unbind minds, he said as God to trefoil serpents
the echo of his bark rang through the bell jar like a vulture.
On straitjackets of fur, though not his own, the Panzer daddy
carved gold cart swastikas until they spelled his *nom de plume.*
His walking tears set fire to shadows of the seraphim,
which Anna and the stranger drank as love songs at the mouth-hole.

In a dark time, daddy held his serpents over a flame, wanting to die—
heard a mad girl's love song at the mouth-hole, a vulture's tell-tale heart
beating through its plume for Anna, who was mad from seraphim love
    in the asylum.

BLOOD DUST

MAX BOOTH III

I

A WILD PACK of family dogs got in the trash last night. I could hear them from my bed, knocking over the cans and digging in. Mother had thrown out a half-eaten dish of casserole that had spoiled. They'd hit a goldmine.

Everybody in the hills knew these dogs. They moved fast, like a shadow in your peripherals. Some thought they slept all day and only roamed the land during nightfall like bona fide vampires. But I'd seen them a few times when the sun was out. It was rare, but I'd seen them. They liked to frequent the junkyard. So did I. The junkyard was neutral ground for both boy and dog alike.

Back in my bedroom, I remained quiet and still, listening to the dogs feast upon our leftovers. I imagined myself sneaking outside, on my hands and knees, face down in the trash. I thought about the moon hanging over my naked body and gifting me with just enough light to see.

No parents, no rules. Complete and total freedom.

If I snuck outside, would the dogs welcome my presence?

Or would they rip me to pieces?

The front screen door swung open and Father ran outside, screaming and shooting his shotgun. The dogs barked and took off into the night. Father's screams sounded farther away as he chased after them, following each yell with another buckshot. My own dog, Toad, was losing his mind in the backyard, where he was tied to a pole. He was probably watching the whole scene, desperately wanting to contribute.

It was like this every night. Soon, Toad would break away from his pole and tear after them. I always wondered why the pack didn't mess with him. They typically ignored his existence. What did my dog have that they didn't?

And the answer was that Toad had a master, and the pack of dogs did not. They answered to nobody. Humanity did not control their lives. The dogs controlled humanity. And that was the way everybody—man, dog, whoever—ought to have lived.

Free.

A half hour later, Father returned to the house, panting heavily as he got a glass of water from the kitchen. Mother was awake, too, and she was lecturing him about giving himself another heart attack. Father told her it was too early to listen to that kind of shit. He was tired and sore, and the last thing he wanted to hear was a bunch of nonsense about heart attacks.

"Besides," he said, "those goddamn dogs will be the death of me long before my ticker kamikazes."

II

That morning, during breakfast, Father drank his coffee one gulp after the other. My little sister, Mel, was sitting next to me at the table, smashing potatoes with the bottom of her fork. Father finished off his second cup of coffee and cleared his throat. He waited until me and Mel gave him our full attention.

"Now, kids, I'm sure you both woke up last night from all the racket. As you know, those damn dogs have been getting in our trash every night, making a mess of things. I just wanted to tell y'all not to go messin' about with these dogs. I know some of your friends like to play with 'em, but hear me right now, these dogs are dangerous. Some dogs you pet. These are not those types of dogs. They're vicious and hungry. They got that ache in their stomachs."

Mel nodded. "I heard you shootin' at 'em."

"You heard correctly."

"Did you kill any of the doggies?"

Father shook his head. "No. I wasn't trying to kill them. I was shooting up, toward the sky, just to scare them."

"Oh," Mel said. "I hope you didn't hit the moon."

"The moon's invincible, baby."

"Are you like the moon, Daddy?"

"Yeah, baby, I'm like the moon."

III

After breakfast, me and Mel went down to the junkyard. We took Toad with us and we met up with Billy and Gunther next to the perimeter gate. At the sight of my sister, Gunther sighed and asked why I had to bring along a snot-nosed girl.

"I ain't snot-nosed," Mel said.

"Sure you are," Gunther said, and looked back at me, awaiting a response.

I shrugged. "Mel's all right. Don't be so harsh."

"Just don't let her get any snot on me."

"I'll punch your face in, you call me snot-nosed one more time," Mel said, making fists. And even though she was a few years younger than us all, Gunther still flinched and stepped back.

"Besides," I said, "Mel's smaller than us. She can fit into places we can't."

Gunther seemed to contemplate it, then nodded.

"Good point."

One by one, we crawled through an opening in the gate where someone had split apart the wiring. I held Toad's leash tight, paranoid that he'd go running off and get lost in the depths of the junkyard. This place was a labyrinth of hidden paths and dead ends.

Decomposing cars waited in the shadows to swallow us as soon as we let down our guard.

We breathed through our mouths. The rot of the town's leftovers invaded our senses and filled our lungs with vomit.

To take our minds off the stench, me and Mel told the others about last night.

"Yeah," Billy said, "they got our house, too."

Gunther shook his head, amused. "One day all the dogs of the universe will eat us humans and rule the stars."

"My daddy says the moon is invincible," Mel said.

"Nothing's invincible," Gunther said.

As we walked deeper into the junkyard, Toad grew agitated. Something up ahead gnawed at him, and when we rounded a corner, we understood.

The dogs stood in a circle, feasting on an animal carcass. At the sound of our arrival, they stopped eating and lifted their heads up to stare at us.

Billy muttered an obscenity and stepped back.

"Don't run," I told him. "They'll chase us if we show 'em our backs."

Toad growled at the pack, and the pack growled back.

"This is gonna get bad," I said.

"What do we do?" Gunther asked, shaking.

"It's okay." Mel stepped forward and waved her hands out at the dogs. "It's okay, doggies. Don't be mad. We're not gonna hurt you."

"Your sister's gonna get us killed!" Gunther said.

I didn't say nothing. Mel continued soothing the dogs, and after a minute, they stopped growling and returned to their carcass.

"Let's go," I whispered.

We slowly backed away, and once we were out of the dogs' sight, we ran like hell. Once we'd made it to the other side of the fence, we collapsed in the grass, out of breath.

"I told y'all," Gunther said, "them dogs are gonna rule the stars."

IV

We went home for lunch. Mother already had some sandwiches prepared. Mel told Mother about the incident at the junkyard.

"What did your father say about them dogs?"

"We know," I said. "We didn't touch 'em or nothing. Once we saw 'em, we left right away. They didn't really care about us, anyway."

"They was busy," Mel said.

"Doing what?"

"They was eatin' dead things, Momma."

Mother shook her head slowly. "You don't go messin' with them dogs."

"But we eat dead things, too, Momma," Mel said. "We eat dead things just like the doggies."

"We aren't dogs, honey."

V

The dogs came back that night. They weren't as loud this time, and managed to eat our trash without being disturbed. Maybe they learned noise meant buckshot. When Father woke up in the morning, he raised all sorts of hell. He dragged me out of bed and instructed me to clean up the mess.

"It's your own damn fault," he told me. "The trash cans are right by your window. You should've heard 'em and woke me up."

Outside, Toad was missing. His rope hung from the pole, but the end of the rope was chewed and torn.

VI

Mel was heartbroken. During breakfast, she refused to touch her plate. Father and Mother told us Toad would come back when he got hungry. He was just out for a run, stretching his legs.

Mel sat by Toad's pole all day, crying. I asked her if she wanted

to go play at the junkyard, and she shook her head, told me she wasn't leaving the pole until Toad returned. So I left her there and met up with Billy and Gunther outside the junkyard. I told them about Toad. They all seemed to have their own theories.

"Maybe aliens from outer space sucked him up into the sky," Billy said.

"That's stupid," Gunther said. "He probably just ran away. Hell, he might even be here."

We looked at the fence, then back at each other. Suddenly it felt like Toad could be no other place but the junkyard. We slid underneath the fence, running blindly through the alleys of trash.

But all we found were animal carcasses, covered in flies and maggots and smelling so foul we had to go vomit our breakfasts. It was a ghost town and we were the ghosts. We walked around for a little while, throwing rusted cans at each other, but it just wasn't as fun without Toad keeping us company.

I returned home, mind racing with curiosities. Mel was still sitting by the pole, only now she wasn't alone. The dogs stood around her, snarling. Toad stood in front of them all, and at that moment I realized he now belonged to the rest of the pack.

Mel smiled at Toad, holding her hand out.

But Toad wasn't smiling.

"Mel, no!" I screamed, and ran toward them.

When I reached the backyard, the dogs were gone and so was my sister's soul.

VII

Nobody slept that night. Mother sat on the porch and cried. Cried 'til her eyes were raw and leaking blood dust. Father drank in the living room. I stayed in bed, looking through my window at the pole in the backyard.

It was stained red.

In the morning, I sat alone at the kitchen table. I fixed some toast and dragged the breakfast on for hours.

Billy and Gunther stopped by my house later that afternoon. They wanted to know why I hadn't met them at the junkyard. I told them what happened. Afterward, they both stared at me, then left without saying another word.

Our young minds couldn't contemplate these sorts of horrors. If given the choice to flee, one would flee. But I didn't have that choice. I was stuck here in the house, the same house my sister used to run around in, laughing and playing with our dog.

There had been a time when this kitchen was full and bright with love. Mel, Father, Mother had all once sat here with me, as a family, Toad under the table, searching for dropped food.

Now it was just me.

I was alone but still trapped in this miserable house.

I wanted to run but my legs would not behave.

When Father came home that night, he told me he quit his job.

"If your mother comes home, tell her not to wake me up in the morning," he said, and kissed the neck of a whiskey bottle.

I watched him drink himself stupid on the couch, staring blankly ahead and losing his mind in the cracks of the wall. I wanted to know what he was thinking. I wanted to know what he was going to do about everything.

Where was Mother?

Where was Toad?

What were we going to do with Mel?

Who was gonna bury her body?

But I couldn't ask him that. He wasn't himself, and I doubted he would be himself ever again. I'd lost more than just a sister.

Father told me hadn't quit his job. He'd been fired. He'd broken down at work and punched his boss. He couldn't think straight anymore, he told me. Couldn't see what was right in front of him.

"Is Mother coming home?" I asked him.

"Home is gone, boy. Home is gone."

VIII

I sat in bed all night, leaning against the wall, my bedroom window wide open as an invitation to the ghosts. The dogs were somewhere outside, howling at the moon in search of dead things to eat.

Toad was with them. I could hear his bark. It was the same bark I'd grown up listening to ever since I was a baby.

These dogs were his new family. I tried to accept that, but couldn't. I'd grown up with Toad. Toad was my best friend. My dog. My friend. I needed him.

I prayed to God and promised that if Toad returned then he would never have to be tied to a pole again. I'd convince Father to let me keep him in my room so we could sleep together every night. And then after Toad was back, maybe somehow we could bring Mel back, too. Maybe we could reverse all these horrors, recycle these nightmares into pleasant dreams where happy endings weren't fairy tales.

If only I could just pray hard enough, I could make everything right. Mother would come back home. Father would quit drinking. Toad would still be our dog. Mel would still be alive.

I sat in my bedroom a long time before eventually falling asleep. My mind raced and so did my heart. I did not know what tomorrow would bring but it was bound to be another round of depression. Another hour of blood, of tears.

Tomorrow would be today, but it would never be yesterday.

IX

Morning came and Mother still wasn't home. Father was passed out in the living room, his whiskey bottle now empty. I kicked it across the room and winced as it shattered against the wall. But still, Father did not wake.

I left the house and sat out by the pole. I leaned my back against the metal, against my sister's dried blood. I stayed out there all day, just as Mel had before she died. I thought about running through the hills, wild and hungry. I thought about hunting and eating anything and everything. I thought about shedding my clothes and howling at the moon. I wondered if maybe I wasn't supposed to be born human after all. Maybe someone, somewhere, had made a mistake.

The dogs eventually returned. Toad led them past me and to the trash cans, only the cans were empty because nobody had thought to fill them.

I tilted my head back and watched the clouds slowly fade from the sky like they were dissolving into coffee. They were going away, and so was I.

The dogs may not have ruled the stars, but they ruled the hills.

They were free.

INSOMNIA IN REVERSE

JONATHAN BALOG

7 AM always feels like a camel on its last leg
He rolls like a wheelchair across the desert
My lucid dream sits on the edge of the bed
Negotiating terms of surrender to a deaf ear
And reaching across to the alarm clock from hell
I see I've lost a fight with insomnia... again

JONATHAN BALOG

5 AM is a renegade chemist with a bad haircut
He treats my brain with caffeine and deadlines
There's an unlicensed shrink in the corner
Stirring up childhood trauma till dawn
Like a friend who only wants to hang out
When I have to work in the morning

3 AM sounds like a tractor running on moonshine
He plows through my psyche with relish
The money on those thirty white horses
Could pay a quarter of my night's rent
And with hope losing thirteen to twenty
The pigeons on my rooftop place their bets

THE WHIPPING GIRLS

DAMIEN ANGELICA WALTERS

ERIKA'S FINGERS TENSE on the steering wheel as she approaches the Kansas-Colorado state line. Endless fields of wheat waiting to be harvested sit on both sides of the interstate, the stalks rustling whisper-soft. Her car is thick with the smell of fresh bread—good bread, not the almost-stale dollar store loaves she grew up with and swears never to eat again.

By now the funeral's over, and she wonders if anyone even showed. Her mother's list of friends was a short one. She thinks of her dress, crumpled in a ball and tossed in the Dumpster atop bulging bags reeking of dirty diapers and fast-food wrappers, and a nervous giggle spills from her lips. What is she doing? Truly? Who quits their job and leaves their life behind at a whim, making the decision between opening a bottle of shampoo in the shower and toweling dry? She should go home, call her boss and beg his forgiveness, throw away the note she left for her landlord. The dress, however, could stay in the trash.

"Stop it," she says, her voice too loud, too brittle.

"You're always afraid of everything." She hears her mother's voice as clearly as if she were in the passenger seat. Smells the liquor on her breath, sees the pill-dilated pupils of her eyes. "And you'll always be afraid. Nothing will change that, Eri. Nothing."

"I've made it this far, haven't I?" Erika says, but even with Topeka five hours behind her, her mouth goes dry.

"Fraidy cat. Fraidy cat."

371

"Fuck you. I'm not afraid anymore," she says as she grips the steering wheel tighter, guns the engine, and crosses into Colorado.

She sees the interstate simultaneously with her own eyes and through another pair awash in tears. The world through the second stretches out of shape into a blur of black and gold and blue, and her upper body thumps hard against her seat, as though veiled hands are yanking off a heavy coat. There's a sharp bite of pain in her chest, but before she can draw breath to cry out, both weight and hurt vanish, and her vision snaps into singular focus.

In her rearview mirror, she catches a glimpse of someone standing with slumped shoulders on the side of the road, feet planted on the Kansas side, a half-formed girl made of fear and sorrow, someone who exists without really living.

Erika clenches her jaw. No one's there, no one at all. Blame imagination. Blame the caffeine thrumming through her bloodstream. Blame a hovering haze on asphalt, never mind that the full heat of summer has yet to force itself upon this part of the world.

She sets her gaze on the road ahead and refuses to look back. The only way forward is through.

She picks up Interstate 80 just outside of Laramie, a route that doesn't make much sense unless you look at the map. Staying on I-70 would send her too far south.

In spite of the spring weather, the mountains in the distance still have snow on their peaks, but against the impossibly huge sky, those mountains look like tiny hills. Funny, when people said the Wyoming sky was big, Erika always thought it a joke because the sky was plenty big in Kansas. Here, though, even the blue is different—brighter and clearer and dotted with cotton candy clouds.

"You are definitely not in Kansas anymore," she says with a grin. And thank god for that.

She shifts in her seat and arches her back, stiff from sleeping in the car. She's got enough money to stay in hotels, at least the cheap ones, but it's cash she'd rather not spend, and as far as brushing her teeth and washing her face goes, rest stop bathrooms do the trick same as any sink anywhere.

Her tires keep chewing the miles and she thinks about what waits ahead. She's nineteen, healthy, and not afraid of hard work; she knows her boss, even if he's pissed off, will give her a good reference. She ticks off a mental list: a place to stay, a bank account, a job. It can't be that hard. People relocate all the time. It's not like she's moving to another country. But she worries a cuticle until she tastes the tang of blood.

"You'll never get anywhere, girl," the memory of her mother says. "You don't have what it takes and you won't ever. No matter where you go, no matter what you do."

"You're wrong, Mom," Erika says.

The last time her mother said those words, the night before Erika moved into her own apartment, she was even more drunk than usual, all glassy eyes and slurring words and sour breath. When Erika finally had enough and tried to walk away, Kaye grabbed her arm, digging neon pink acrylic fingernails into her skin hard enough to leave half-moon bruises. "Just remember. You can move out, you can run away, but you'll never get anywhere." With a laugh, she pushed Erika out of the way and staggered into the living room.

But Erika isn't that girl anymore. She's *not*.

Her vision bifurcates into road and blur, her skin burns with unseen fire, and she feels as though she's peeling in two. The sensation and the double-vision disappear; the pain slowly ebbs into a dull all-over ache.

And in the back seat sits a girl wearing Erika's face.

Erika veers onto the shoulder with a squeal of tires and scrambles from the car, her mouth an oil slick of panic. The girl staring through the window is a slightly younger version of Erika, dressed in a shabby t-shirt and even shabbier jeans. Erika remembers how those jeans, another thrift store purchase, ripped during her move, how she cried when she threw them out. Stupid, because they were just jeans, but she was unable to stop.

She laughed like it was the funniest thing in the world, didn't she?

The voice, heard with Erika's head not her ears, is recognizably her own, and she takes a half-step backward. A horn blares, loud and indignant. Erika slams her body against the car as an eighteen-wheeler races past, tires leaving a mist of road grime in their wake. She squeezes her eyes shut. When she opens them, the girl is still there.

A pale ribbon the color of smoke runs from the center of the girl's chest, and Erika follows its length to her own. She peeks down her shirt; the ribbon runs through the fabric and into her flesh, piercing it seamlessly. No blood. No swelling. No discoloration. She tries to grab it, to pluck it free, but her fingers go in and through. It feels like half-set gelatin—warm and wet and amniotic—and she shudders, scrubbing her hands on her jeans.

Her mind spins with the how and the why, but there are no words for this. There are no explanations grounded in science and fact, only the incomprehensible here and now.

The girl appears real enough on the surface, but there's something not quite solid, not tangible, as though she's half-here and half-elsewhere, which is as ridiculous as it sounds. Erika blinks and in the brief darkness, sees the girl standing by the road in Kansas.

Some things don't have hooks. They're easier to get rid of.

Erika swallows hard, fighting the urge to step away again.

"What are you?"

No response, not in her head or otherwise.

"Okay, okay then," she says, her voice trembling.

This isn't real.

The girl isn't, and can't be, real.

With that thought firmly set in her head, she climbs back in the driver's seat and tilts her rearview mirror, refusing to look at either girl or tether. She rests her forehead on the steering wheel, the low-grade ache radiating throughout her body.

The girl's presence is persistent, like a bad tooth a tongue can't help but revisit again and again. Erika pinches the bridge of her nose, sighs, readjusts the mirror.

374

"What. Are. You?"

What am I? You mean who, don't you? It's sort of obvious, isn't it?

"No. You're not me. You're *not.*"

Believe whatever you want, but damage has to go somewhere. You've been carrying us around for a long time.

"What do you mean?"

What do you really expect to find at the end of this trip? Run as far as you can, gingerbread girl, but you can't run away from yourself.

"I'm not running from anything. I'm moving on."

Right. Leaving Topeka behind and starting over, I know. Proving Mom wrong.

Erika turns in her seat, faces the girl. "This doesn't have anything to do with her."

Don't be an idiot. It has everything *to do with her. If she made cookies and tucked you in at night instead of drinking herself into oblivion and forgetting to buy groceries or pay the electric bill, do you think you'd be here? If that's the case, you might as well let me back in and keep heading west, keep pretending you're fine.*

"I *am* fine."

The girl (and Erika refuses to believe it's her, no matter what face she wears) rolls her eyes. *If you were fine, I wouldn't be here and you wouldn't be parked on the shoulder. You're not fine, but you* can *be. I don't know, maybe you're not strong enough to do what you have to do. Easier to stay the way you are, right? Easier to stay damaged.*

"I'm not—" Erika brushes hair from her eyes. "You don't make any sense. What do I have to do?"

You let me out, so that's half the battle, but it's the easy part. The rest… She waves one hand. *It hurts, doesn't it? What's inside you? But it doesn't have to. You can let it go. It's up to you.*

Erika turns around in her seat and stares at the road. She wants to drive on, ignore the girl and hope she'll disappear, but she can't seem to remember how to shift the car into Drive.

I know it's hard. This will change you. It will change everything. But you've made it this far, right?

Tears burning in her eyes, Erika meets the girl's gaze in the mirror. The girl nods. Erika exhales. A shadow swirls around her heart, one she's had for so long she doesn't know how to live without it. Maybe her mother's to blame for its existence, but Erika's been keeping it in place, keeping herself prisoner.

And for what?

With a cry, she peels it free. The ache in her body begins to bleed out, her arms go all-over goosebumps, and a shiver dances along her spine. The tether in her chest darkens, first to charcoal, then to pitch, then to a black so absolute she can't give it a name. It shrivels, a desiccated worm on the pavement of her lap, and dissolves into a millions specks of dark that cling to the air for a brief moment before they fade away to nothing at all, taking the last traces of pain with them.

From the back seat comes the sound of muffled sobs, and Erika whirls in her seat. Spilled-ink bruises pattern the girl's skin. She's shaking, her face contorted, her lips pressed into a tight line devoid of color.

"Oh, god, I'm sorry. I'm so sorry. I didn't mean it. I didn't want—"

I know. But now you understand. The girl manages a small smile, but the expression doesn't meet her eyes. *It will get worse, a lot worse, before it gets better. Remember that. The only way forward is through.*

"What do you mean? I don't understand."

The bruises spread, melting into one another, not covering the girl, but erasing her. Erika starts to climb over the seat, yet it's too late. The girl is gone. A dark, oily after-image lingers; Erika blinks and then that's gone, too.

A heavy silence hangs in both the car and Erika's head, but her heart holds a new shape, a new weight. She wipes her cheeks dry, puts her car in drive, and pulls back onto the interstate.

Halfway through Utah, with the Great Salt Lake reflecting the blue sky at her right, Erika starts shaking and pulls into a rest stop. Ahead, the mountains are the jagged teeth of a submerged monster biting the sky, and she fears the beast will emerge and devour her whole.

"You think you're something, don't you," her mother's voice says. "You really think you can make something of yourself?"

The sound of dark laughter echoes in Erika's mind. No, no, she's done with that. She let it go.

But there's her mother tugging at the edges of her mind, her mother tossing aside a report card, one eyebrow cocked and her mouth in a sneer. "Letters on paper don't mean shit, girl. Never have and never will. You think being book smart means you're better than me? Means your future will be bright and happy? You watch. You'll end up just like me, no doubt about it." The laugh again, all acid and teeth, and Erika's vision doubles.

"No, please, no."

Erika moans against her palms, envisions her body a cage with a lock impossible to pick, but she suddenly sees the mountains with her own eyes and those of another. Agony shudders through her, and she breaks in two.

She doesn't want to look at the girl in the passenger seat, but she isn't a child anymore who can pretend closed eyes create a cloak of invisibility or a spell of protection. This time the girl is even younger, her features caught in awkward adolescence, maybe thirteen or fourteen. Erika muffles a moan behind her palm. The tether between them wavers in the air and drifts down to settle across gearshift and thighs.

Why are we here? Why did you stop?

"Go away," Erika says. "Please. You need to get out of the car right now. Please, I don't want to hurt you. You need to go."

The girl looks at the tether and then back to Erika, her mouth soft, her eyes helpless. *I don't think I can.*

Hiding her face in her hands, Erika tries to keep in the pain, but it doesn't want to stay. *She* doesn't want it to stay. Instead of a shadow, this hurt is barbed wire sharp and cutting.

"I'm sorry."

Wait. You don't have to do this. Please. Just let me back in. I won't bother you. I won't—

Her words dissolve into hitching sobs. Erika closes her eyes, steels her heart.

Please, stop. Make it stop.

"I can't, I'm sorry. I have to do this."

No, no, the girl shrieks. *Please don't. Please.*

Erika covers her ears, humming to conceal the sound of the girl's cries, but it isn't enough, it could never be enough. When the pain is gone, she takes a ragged breath and forces herself to look. The girl holds out arms crosshatched with gaping wounds, all bleeding darkness. Erika reaches for her, but the girl flinches, her eyes dull with hurt and betrayal.

You hurt me. Why did you hurt me?

"I'm sorry."

Erika turns her face away until the pressure of the air changes, letting her know she's alone once more. She rests her head on the steering wheel, a bitter pill of guilt on her tongue even while her lips curve into a smile that feels strange, but right and strong and true.

Nevada greets her with a blue and white *Welcome* sign. Low, boxy houses sit on her right; on her left, a resort and casino. More big sky, more mountains in the distance. Erika isn't sure why, but she expected things to look different when she crossed state lines, each state a wholly separate place, not part of a whole.

Dusk creeps in as the miles glide by, an endless vista of flat land. She pulls into a gas station to top off her tank, but instead of returning to the road when she's done, she moves her car off to the side and walks in aimless circles, stretching and shaking her arms. Over her shoulder, she catches the gas station attendant watching from behind the plate-glass window. She waves and he returns the gesture, a bemused grin set into his grizzled face.

Leaning against her car, she watches the stars appear, glittering like bits of glass trapped in the deepening blue. The mountains are a dark shadow at the horizon, and she's struck with a sense that no matter how long she drives, they'll remain where they are, preventing her from ever crossing the state, from ever reaching California.

"Know why? Because you're not good enough," her mother says. "Do you hear me, you worthless little shit? You don't deserve a damn thing."

Erika's vision blurs, and pain threads through her limbs. "Not again," she whispers. "Please, not again. Haven't I done enough?"

But the first girl's words ring in her ears: *It will get worse before it gets better.*

Her vision splits, and she shatters in two. The girl now standing in front of her, maybe seven or eight, gives Erika a tentative smile. Her gaze flits to the narrow ribbon connecting them, and her smile falls. Then her chin lifts, her eyes widen.

Look at all the stars!

"They're beautiful, aren't they?" Erika's voice quavers and the girl frowns.

I think I should go back. Can I go back now?

Erika shakes her head. "Not yet." When the hurt begins to push free, all jagged points of glass, she doesn't fight it, nor does she turn away. She'll give the girl at least that, no matter how hard it is to bear witness. She owes her that much.

The tether twitches once, twice; the girl drops to the ground and covers her head with her hands. Her body convulses. *You're hurting me,* she shrieks. *Stop! Stop it!*

Her voice is aluminum foil on amalgam fillings. Erika winces, rocks back and forth.

Please make it stop. Please don't hurt me anymore.

But Erika can't. She *can't.* Damage has to go somewhere, and she's carried it long enough.

The tether blackens, shrivels, disappears.

The girl struggles to her feet, her cries shrieking into the night, her flesh slashed and gouged. Erika steps away, palms out, an apology caught on her tongue. Nothing she can say will make this right. The girl's mouth is an O of pain and terror, her eyes accusations, and when the dark begins to bloom its poisonous flowers, Erika whispers "I'm sorry."

A throat clears and Erika jumps. The gas station attendant is watching her, his forehead creased. "You okay, miss?"

She nods, finds her voice. "Yes, I think I am, but thank you for asking."

"You be safe out there, okay?"

"I will."

For a moment, he looks as though he wants to say something more, but he doesn't. And with shoulders straight, she drives on.

Erika stands at the California sign with arms crossed and elbows cupped in her palms. Tree-covered mountains rise in gentle slopes, and a cool breeze kisses her skin. Although she's five and a half hours from her destination and can't yet smell the ocean, she senses it there. A wish. A dream. A *chance*. She tips her head, catching the sun's warmth on her face. Her mother's voice is a ghost of silence and she laughs into the wind. She's free. Finally, she's free.

Elk, California, a tiny town in Mendocino County, is home to only two hundred and fifty people. A place picked at random; a place with no ties to anyone or anything she's ever known. A place to forget, to begin anew.

She slips off her shoes and pads across the beach, the sand cool between her toes. Strands of loose hair playdance across her cheeks as she pauses to inhale the salt tang of the ocean. The Pacific is as beautiful as she imagined it would be, the blue richer than any photograph she's seen, the sun dappling the surface of the water with flickering light, the crashing waves singing a lullaby.

There are so many things she needs to do, but for now, this is where she has to be. Here, she's not worthless. Here, she's not afraid. Here, she's Erika alone. She tries to take a step closer to the water but can't convince her feet to move.

"Such a waste of space. Such a fucking mistake. I wish you were never born."

The words are laced with vehemence, and Erika staggers, falling to her hands and knees. She can't breathe, can't think; the pain is too much. It's fire and glass and razors and darkness. The ocean twins, a blurry half-image of the receding waves overlaying her own until she splits, until the girl crawls from her belly and drops to the sand in a grim simulation of birth, the tether a misplaced umbilical cord, a liar's promise of sustenance.

The toddler has chubby legs and fingers, a rounded belly, and baby-fine hair several shades lighter than the color it will become. Her face should be smiles and hope and nothing more, but her eyes already have the look of a wounded animal, and Erika catches her lower lip between her teeth, chokes back tears.

Gingerbread girls can never run fast enough, never travel far enough. There's always a fox at the end, and that fox, once it sinks in its teeth, will never let go, not until all the good parts are gone and what's left simply goes through the motions while waiting for the end to come.

Erika's shoulders slump, her chin drops, her throat clenches. The hurt washes over her, a baptism of defeat, and she can taste the triumph of her mother's laughter.

She scrubs her mouth with the back of her hand and gets to her feet. Curls her hands into fists. Straightens her spine and swallows her sorrow. No, she's made it all this way, she won't stop now. She won't give in.

Her younger self grabs handfuls of sand, lets the grains sieve between her fingers. Erika tucks a lock of hair behind her ear, smiles, and opens her arms.

The little girl hesitates. *Picka-up me?* she says.

Erika nods.

Nice lady?

Erika nods again, her smile on the verge of disintegration. The girl's skin is warm and solid beneath Erika's touch, no matter what she knows in her head. The heart can make anything real; so too can hurt.

"You're the last one, aren't you?" she says. "The last one I have to say goodbye to, the last one I have to let go."

The little girl giggles and touches Erika's cheek, leaving a dusting of sand behind. Erika holds her close, breathing in the smell of talcum powder. Part of her wants to stay this way, to stand here forever, but innocence lost can never be reclaimed, so with slow, careful steps she heads into the surf. As spray mists around them, the little girl squeals and tries to squirm from her grasp.

"Shh," Erika says. "Everything will be okay." She heads deeper in, breathes "I'm sorry" into the girl's hair. As a wave approaches, she inhales and goes under, sinking to her knees. The chill seeps into her bones, sets her teeth to chatter, but she clamps her jaw tight. Against her shoulder, collarbones, and thighs, the little girl's hands spasm, her head thrashes, her legs kick.

Erika tightens her arms until they ache. The current buffets her from side to side and her lungs scream, but she remains beneath the water until the little girl's grip loosens, until she stops moving, until her weight becomes impossibly heavy. The tether snaps free, and Erika breaks through the surf with a cry.

Hair drifting in seaweed tangles, arms outstretched, the little girl's body floats like a discarded doll, mercifully facedown, then a wave rushes in and when it recedes, the little girl is gone.

Alone, Erika makes her way back to the shore, her steps sure, her spine straight. Her eyes sting, but whether from tears or the salt of the sea she doesn't know. Right now it doesn't matter. Waves nudge her thighs and the current tugs her ankles, but she keeps moving.

The only way forward is through.

PROM!SE

P. GARDNER GOLDSMITH

It took some time
But now I'm ready

Walking in the forest
Moonlight through the trees

Vision filled with
Beautiful you

To the stone wall
To sit and say

That ring was a promise
I want to keep

Tonight.
Today.

P. GARDNER GOLDSMITH

I clear my throat
Wipe ghostly hands

Kneeling on the hillside
Cool air on my arms

New ring ready
Beautiful thing

To hear crickets
To see the moon

To face your tombstone
And hear you weep

Tonight.
Always.

SECONDS

JACK KETCHUM

IT WAS WHEN they'd finished making love one bright late-August afternoon that she turned to him and said, *we have to talk, you and I.*

He smiled. *You and I.*

Always the professor, always correct. He'd have said *you and me.*

Precise, even down to the minutia. Who else was in this room, anyway? In this bed.

You and I.

"Okay. Talk," he said.

The sun through her open window burnished his curly hair, brushed the tender down along his arm. *Could she tell him this?* So many times she had meant to tell him, wished to tell him. A terrible thing, this being in love. Your secrets could not be your own anymore. They begged to be shared.

He lay there with his chin cupped in his hand, his elbow denting the bed between them. Gazing at her, waiting, a smile on his lips. She could feel the heat of him, more humid than the heat of the sun, alive.

"How long has it been?" she said.

He didn't need her to translate. How long have *we* been?

He laughed. "Almost four months. End of the semester. The week after I graduated. You forget already?"

"And what do you know about me, really? In all that time."

His eyes swept the room as though searching for clues. The

simple antique furnishings—the walnut wardrobe, the rosewood nightstand, her neat uncluttered dresser and tri-fold mirror. The four-poster bed.

Her paintings on the walls, which he thought wonderful. And which she had consigned to the bedroom only. An old man asleep on a ruined city sidewalk, a tin cup tilted downward, empty in his hand. A male figure seen from above, approaching a lighted third-floor window in the dark, a female shape silhouetted behind it, one hand lifting its curtain. A bare ancient oak tree against a winter sky, tendrils reaching plaintive for the heavens.

"Hands," he said. "You love hands."

She took his. "That I do," she said. "What else."

"The Expressionists."

She nodded. "What else."

"You're an amazing teacher. You're incredible in bed. You have the softest skin I've ever touched. And I'm pretty sure you love me. Am I right?"

He's so young, she thought. He needs to hear it again, even though I've already told him a dozen times or more, in so many ways. And once, under a streetlight in the park, under a moon as bright as any I've ever seen, quietly aloud. And he said the same to me.

"Yes," she said. "I do. I love you."

The second time only. In all these years.

She leaned over and kissed him, felt her lips go soft beneath his own. Her resolve began to falter. A shaft of reflected sunlight bored through the window, slashed her naked thigh. She turned away.

"What else? What else do you know?"

Playing along, he sighed. "Let's see. You were married once, for six years I think you said. Six, right? You're a country girl transplanted to the city. Your dad owned a bar. You're an only child. You like Chardonnay, draft beer, soft-shell crabs and Italian food. Red sauce, not the northern stuff. You're a real blonde. You…"

"How old do you think I am, Colin?"

"How old?" He laughed. "Well, older than me."

"I'm serious. How old."

She watched him consider.

"Okay. Married six years. You've been at the University what? ten? And your husband was … gone … before that. You've got your Masters so that's six years of college. I guess when I've thought about it, which I gotta tell you, isn't real often, I mean when I do the math, I've always thought mid-forties. Forty-fiveish? Somewhere around there. You look way younger, though. But you already know that."

She felt the full weight of this now settle tight in her chest. In the thud of her heartbeat. In the palms of her hands. The cold near certainty of losing him. It had been so very long since she'd let herself care. On the street below a car-horn honked three times in rapid succession, then stopped. She heard the rustle of traffic as though over shards of glass.

"I was born November 10th, 1939. Five minutes after midnight. Franklin Delano Roosevelt was President. The Nazis were about to slaughter the Warsaw Jews. That year *Gone with the Wind* won the Oscar.

"In three months, I'll be seventy-six. Seventy-six years old."

He laughed again. A short, puzzled laugh this time.

"*Excuse me?*"

Now *that's* pretty ridiculous, he thought. He searched her face, looking for the put-on.

It wasn't there.

How could it not be there?

Instead he saw tension. A flicker in her eyes. He saw *fear.*

"Not funny, Miriam."

"I stopped ageing," she said, "when Todd died. When my husband died. Probably that very day. I just stopped. Just like that. September 8th, 1974. I was thirty-four years old."

She watched his eyes.

He doesn't believe me. He thinks I'm crazy, she thought.

"I'm not crazy."

He let go of her hand.

"Hey, I never said you were. This is a joke, right? A weird one. But a joke."

"No joke. Todd died the day Ford pardoned Nixon."

This was nuts. He'd have been a year old. What was she playing at?

"You're angry."

"No I'm not."

"I can see it in your face."

"I just don't know why you'd…"

"Let me tell you some things, okay? Can you bear with me a little while?"

Of course he could. He'd been in love with her since about halfway through the first month of her class in *Advanced Acrylics: Still Life to Abstraction* his senior year. Fallen fast and hard. She was the reason he hadn't given up on painting. Or rather, gone back to it after three years in digital design. He'd painted her three times now, from memory. He hadn't shown her yet.

This was still nuts but he'd listen.

"My father was born in 1908. During Prohibition he made his own bootleg whiskey and ran a speakeasy off Highway 31 with gambling in the back room. When the Twenty-First Amendment came along he turned it into a bar and chop house. He held on to the one-armed bandits though and my friends and I used to feed them steel slugs all day while our parents sat at the bar.

"My mother raised chickens in back and occasionally one would go to the block. I remember my first beheading. The sound of the cleaver coming down on that scarred, stained old stump of wood, the chicken's bill opening and closing, the eyes blinking while its headless body ran skittering across the yard. My mother laughing as I tore away terrified through the back door and huddled by the restroom.

"But that bar did well for me. It sent me to college. The first one in my family ever to get there. They hated it that I majored in art even though my watercolors, landscapes mostly, hung all over the restaurant walls. Cheap décor, I guess. They weren't very good. But they insisted I minor in education. Women back then went into teaching or nursing or secretarial or they went into nothing at all.

"I went for my Masters in education, which surprised them. They were figuring high school. I was figuring if you have to teach, make it college. And I still saw painting as the main thing. The thing I wanted most of all. I did a show now and then. Local stuff, nothing major. But I was getting it out there. I was painting in oil and acrylic by then and my subject matter had changed. No more landscapes, no more still lifes. I was doing narrative, moments from some of the books I'd read—Hemingway, Steinbeck, du Maurier, Nevil Shute, John O'Hara. Or else from magazines and newspapers. I'd work from photos in *Life* or *Look*. I stole pretty shamelessly. Not movie stars, just people. Real people. Street scenes, old Korean War photos, families. Each image, each detail, as sharp as I could make it.

"I'd done a series on entrances and exits. A woman stepping into a flower shop. A fireman climbing down a fire escape. People crowding through the revolving door at Macy's. A bartender— of course—hauling garbage out the back door into an alley. That kind of thing. It was 1967. I think I had a dozen of them for the community center show along with a handful of other, older pieces.

"I'm manning my table. It's mid-afternoon. Nobody's buying a damn thing. Then along comes Todd Marbert. *Doctor* Todd Marbert. Hand me a cigarette, would you?"

The pack on the nightstand was almost empty. *We'll have to buy more,* he thought. It struck him with an odd kind of relevance. However strange this story, however incredible, they were going to need more. He shook one out for her and one for himself, lit hers and then his own, lay back on his pillow and watched the smoke drift toward the freedom of the open window.

"He bought a painting. The one he chose was of a middle-aged woman seated in the polished, glass-enclosed ticket booth of a movie theatre, the sign above her reading LYRIC, OPEN TILL 4AM and below that, ADMISSION $1.00. A vase of tall gladioli stood on the counter. There were two double-doors to the right of her, clear heavy glass, as were the walls behind her. And through them you could see the rows and rows of lightbulbs studding the lobby ceiling."

"An old-fashioned movie palace."

"That's right. The woman was stony-faced, unsmiling, wearing a neatly-pressed white blouse, her hair pulled tight into a bun, her posture almost military, rigid, perfect."

"A lady who took her job quite seriously."

"Exactly. At a movie palace. A pleasure-dome. I've often wondered what was playing. The image was from a photo in *Life*. You didn't see the marquee. But I liked the irony. The image of a severe woman dispensing something essentially trivial, encased in glass and bathed in light.

"I've also often wondered if it reminded him of his mother."

"His mother?"

"You know the old saying, *'before you marry, check out the mother?'* Well, I didn't."

She stubbed out the cigarette, half-finished. The ember faded.

"I won't go into the good times. There were plenty of good times, or else I wouldn't have married him. He had qualities. He was well-read, knew a good bit of art history. He was smart, funny at parties. My god, he *cooked!* He was I guess you'd say *assertive* in bed and at the time I liked that, though he was adamant about contraception, he wanted no babies. He was five years older than me, a successful neurosurgeon. Spinal surgeries.

"He was also, as I later learned, a monster."

She reached for the cigarette butt. He handed her the lighter. She lit it. Brushed a fallen ember from the bedsheet.

"It wasn't just me. Though it *was* me, over time. His practice was in the city of course so I'd moved in with him a few months before we married and I got a job teaching acrylic three days a week at the Art Students League. And for the first few years we were happy. The

League wasn't University but it was something, it brought in a little money—though with what he made we didn't need it—and left me plenty of time for my own work. He was busy. He had affiliations with several hospitals in the city. Or at least he did, until certain nasty things started coming to light."

She stubbed out the cigarette again. She wondered how he was taking this. There was no way to know for sure. He was attentive. She guessed that for now, that would have to do.

"Todd was hurting his patients. He was hurting them on purpose."

"On *purpose?*"

"Yes. Purposely botching their operations. When it was over, one of his colleagues told me he'd never have believed it if he hadn't seen it for himself, that you had to know the *right* thing to do in order to do the *wrong* thing, and Todd was consistently doing the wrong thing.

"Two women died on his operating table. One of them bled to death. Two more emerged from surgery unable to move their legs. He left a sponge inside of one man and forceps inside another. He left one man a quadriplegic.

"I didn't know any of this. It took them more than a year to coordinate the cases hospital to hospital and suspend his license despite complaints from a half-dozen doctors and lawyers that my husband was a dangerous man. What I *did* know was that for the last two years of our marriage, while all of this was going on, he was scaring me.

"He'd always been ready for a drink or two after dinner. Now he was going through a fifth of Grey Goose every night and I'd find cocaine residue on the living room coffee table in the morning—he wouldn't even bother to clean up after himself. He'd stopped talking to me. When I'd confront him, ask him what was wrong he'd either clam up mumbling something about stress at work and leave the room or just as often, go at me, furious, screaming that it was none of my fucking business, that I was a prying bitch who didn't deserve him, who he never should have married. At first I was stunned. And then I wasn't.

"He scared me but he never hit me. If he had, I would have left him. Probably he knew that. Most of the time we drifted through the same apartment and that was that, we weren't anything like a couple anymore—and this went on for *two years.* I don't know why I stayed. Or even *how* I stayed. I was very depressed. There were times I couldn't breathe. I lost a lot of weight, I was down to about a hundred pounds. Half my clothes didn't fit. I kept teaching, though I know my classes suffered. And I kept painting. I'd paint something and throw it away disgusted with myself as though it were trash. I suspect it wasn't trash. But I couldn't find *me* anymore in what I painted, you know? Like I wasn't there. All of it's gone now. All that work.

"I still loved him. Despite me crying myself to sleep nights. I wanted to help. Our sex life was over, finished, shot to hell with all that coke and liquor but I'd still go to him sometimes, try to hold him, try to let him know it was all right to talk to me, to let me in, to let me help.

"I did that until he tried to kill me.

"He'd been doing coke that night and I knew that but there I was lying in bed next to him anyway and he smelled *medicinal,* I remember that, he smelled awful, god knows what pills he was taking and I was saying something, I don't know, something trying to sooth him and he turned to me and put his hands around my neck and said *you don't get it, do you? I kill people. I like to kill people. That's who I am. You understand? A killer. You don't get that, do you? No.*

"He called me a bitch, a stupid bitch and he started to squeeze and I couldn't breathe and I was afraid and there was this ceramic lamp by our bed and I reached for that and pulled it free of the plug and it had a heavy base so I hit him with that, I don't how many times, over the head, until there was blood all over both of us and he got up and staggered out of the bedroom and the next thing I knew I heard the front door slam and he was gone.

"The lamp didn't even break. I kept that lamp for years.

"He went to a bar called McLean's over on the east side of town. The police asked me later if I wanted to sue the bartender for serving him. I almost laughed. I was through crying by then. But I didn't laugh. He'd stumbled out of the bar into after-theatre traffic. The car that hit him was a red Infiniti SUV. The driver and his wife were in from the suburbs to see a show. The driver was a dentist.

"It all came out then. All he'd done. And I stopped ageing."

"That's...impossible."

"You think? There are benches all along Broadway between the south and northbound lanes and the next day I sat down on the one across from our apartment and smoked a cigarette, it was warm for September, and I watched the people along either side of the street going about their business, a woman with her foot in a cast, a guy walking a pair of golden retrievers, people in shorts, people dressed for work, teeshirts, ties and jackets, an old woman with a walker daring a yellow light. And I didn't love him anymore. Not one bit. I loved me. Who I was. One of all these people. And I felt something ...just lift away."

He reached over. She felt the sweet gentle touch of his fingertips along her cheek, tracing a line over her chin to her neck like a trail of tears.

"You can't...your face, your skin..."

"I can prove it to you, Colin. I've gone through five different doctors since then. I'm not invulnerable. I'm not immortal. I get sick. I get the flu. My lower back goes out from time to time, you know that. I've broken this damn big toe of mine twice. Look, it's practically deformed."

She wiggled it at him.

"I have all my medical records. I need to move around, doctor-wise. You can understand why. I'll get them for you."

She got out of bed and her body told him it was a lie.

It had to be.

He heard her in the study, a file drawer sliding open and then closed, heard her light footsteps in the hall and then she was sitting beside him on the bed again and handed him a thick heavy folder.

"Look at the dates," she said. "Read."

He did. She sat quietly and watched him, aware of her heartbeat, aware of the weight of loving him, the silence in the room broken only by the crisp hiss and slide of pages, her life seeming to her like the pages paper-thin, in his hands and out of her own.

Was it a half-hour? More? He closed the folder.

"Tell me everything," he said. "Tell me all you've done, all you've been."

The time's gone so fast, she thought. *Paros, Naxos, the Amalfi Coast, St. Bart's, St. John.* She saw him always in the light. On this patio beyond this window, sketching in the summer sun. The two of them together, sketching in the summer sun. On the lawn tossing the ball to Rufus, their Golden, gone these four years now. In the morning light, the two of them sprawled across their bed.

This bed.

He lay there now.

So pale. His fine curly hair disappeared. The dome of white skull bone seeming to wish to break through its thin sheath of blue-veined skin. The shadows beneath his eyes sliding ever down.

"Colin? Can you wake up for me? Can you wake up for me now?"

His eyelids stuttered, opened.

"You're here."

"Of course I'm here."

He licked his lips.

"I thought so," she said. She tilted the straw from the water glass to his lips. He sipped.

"Thank...you."

"You're welcome."

She stroked his face, his chin.

"You need a shave. You know that?"

He smiled. Light flickering in his eyes.

Yes. *Go ahead. Shave me*, he thought. Why not? She took her hand away, rested it lightly on his chest. The cancer there inside him. As though her touch could stay its crawl.

"Do you think you could eat something?"

'No." And then, "sorry."

She felt his breath hitch beneath her hand. Short bursts of breath. His fists clenched at his sides.

"Colin?"

Should she call for Maggie, their hospice nurse? She'd sent her off to the kitchen for lunch. It was as though he'd read her mind.

"It's ... okay," he said.

And it was. There wasn't any pain. The morphine was taking care of that. This breathing thing was incidental. He didn't have to breathe. Why the fists should clench he didn't know. They relaxed on their own accord and that was better. That was fine. In fact he felt good now, really, truly good. He could sleep again and it would be a simple thing and welcome. But she wanted him awake. And he wanted to see her. Watch her tuck her hair behind her ear as she was doing now.

So beautiful. Just as he had met her thirty-six years before. Lovely years. Their paintings on the walls attested to that, attested to one another. Watching her he felt a kind of euphoria, a sense of rightness, of balance. She held his hand awhile.

"I'm ready," he said.

"You are?"

"Yes."

Was she? She wasn't sure.

And then she was.

"Then go, my love," she said.

He closed his eyes. Moments later she felt his grip slide away beneath her hand but she held to him anyway and watched his chest rise and fall, his breathing even. It was perhaps an hour, perhaps more, before his breathing paused and stopped and she knew that he was dead, knew it in the creak and ache of her bones, in the withering of her skin, in her thinning hands and the clouded vision of her eyes and she felt her own release, simple and gradual as a leaf in the waning sunlight of Autumn as they fell together to the earth.

– Thanks to Kevin Kovelant

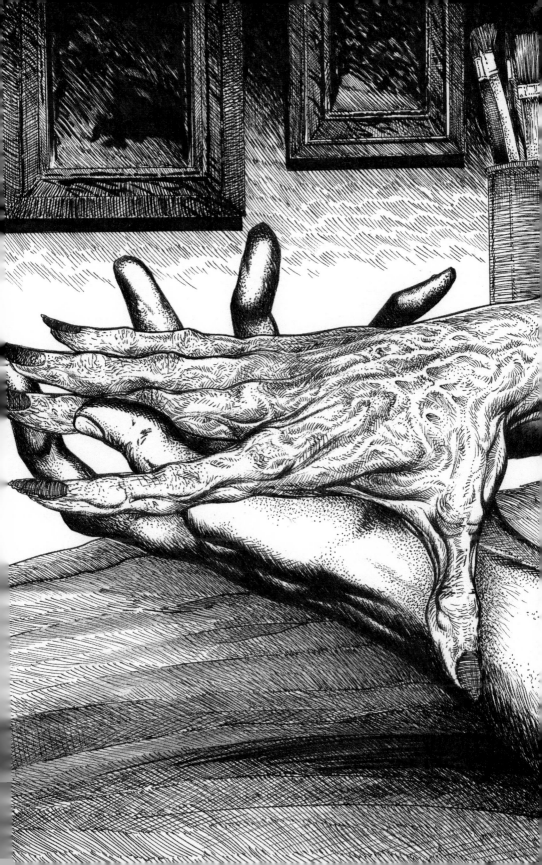